Agatha Christie

Marple

TWELVE NEW STORIES

Naomi Alderman

Leigh Bardugo

Alyssa Cole

Lucy Foley

Elly Griffiths

Natalie Haynes

Jean Kwok

Val McDermid

Karen M. McManus

Dreda Say Mitchell

Kate Mosse

Ruth Ware

HARPER LARGE PRINT

An Imprint of HarperCollinsPublishers

Originally published as *Marple* in the United Kingdom in 2022 by HarperCollins

AGATHA CHRISTIE, MARPLE, the Agatha Christie Signature, and the AC Monogram Logo are registered trademarks of Agatha Christie Limited in the UK and elsewhere. All rights reserved.

HarperCollins books may be purchased for educational, business, or sales promotional use. For information, please e-mail the Special Markets Department at SPsales@harpercollins.com.

FIRST HARPER LARGE PRINT EDITION

ISBN: 978-0-06-326605-6

Library of Congress Cataloging-in-Publication Data is available upon request.

22 23 24 25 26 LSC 10 9 8 7 6 5 4 3 2 1

Contents

Contents

Miss Jane Marple, literature's preeminent amateur detective and one of Agatha Christie's finest creations, first appeared in print in December 1927, in a short story called "The Tuesday Night Club." Christie returned to this intriguing character—with the intention, as she herself put it, "to give old maids a voice"—in 1930's *The Murder at the Vicarage*, which was followed by eleven further Marple novels, and several collections of short stories featuring St. Mary Mead's sharpest mind, with the very last novel, *Sleeping Murder*, appearing posthumously in 1976, the year Christie died.

Christie had noticed that women, especially those in their later years who remained unmarried, were often patronised, overlooked, and underestimated, but the world's bestselling novelist knew well how little escapes such village stalwarts, that underneath demure lace caps could lurk the shrewdest of brains, capable of outsmarting even Scotland Yard's finest. Evil, after all, is just as easily found in the most picturesque corner of England as in the meanest city streets—human nature is human nature, wherever you are. And so one of her most unforgettable characters came into being.

Marple

Evil in Small Places

Lucy Foley

"I wonder, sometimes, if there isn't a concentration of evil in small places."

"What *do* you mean, Jane?" Prudence looked across at her former schoolfriend, who sat in the armchair opposite with a small glass of cherry brandy. In the kind, warm glow of the fire the marks of old age were flatteringly blurred. Jane Marple was so little changed, in the important details, from her girlhood self. The quick, birdlike manner, the bright, inquisitive eyes, the sense of a quiet, perhaps even formidable intelligence.

Just as Miss Marple opened her mouth to answer, a firecracker exploded in the darkness outside, followed by a series of shrieks and howls that might have come from the mouth of hell itself. Someone had begun to beat a drum. The two women could not see out as all the curtains had been drawn by Prudence's maid at four p.m. sharp. Fairweather House—imposing, Georgian—faced on to the main street of Meon Maltravers. And outside in the gloaming, just beyond the windows, a pagan-looking throng was mustering.

As the clamour from outside faded a little, Miss Marple spoke again. "One is aware there is a great deal of wrongdoing in cities and larger towns, of course. The newspapers are desperate to make sure that we do not miss a single grisly detail. But I wonder if there aren't more terrible things happening in England's villages and hamlets than in its metropolises."

Prudence pursed her lips. "Well, it's not true of Meon Maltravers. This is a highly respectable place."

Meon Maltravers was a small town with red-tiled, flint walled buildings built hugger-mugger across the centuries along its sloping, cobbled streets, with soaring views over the South Downs towards the coast. It had certainly had the appearance of a respectable place when Miss Marple had arrived earlier, in the light of day. But now darkness had fallen. And just at this moment came a new round of caterwauling and shrieks from the street.

Miss Marple raised her eyebrows. "Are you sure?"

Prudence waved a hand. "Just some local high jinks.

Perfectly harmless. But you always *did* have a dark imagination, Jane."

"This isn't imagination, dear. I've borne witness to it—" Miss Marple had been about to say "first hand" and speak to some of her experiences over the last few years, but, again, there was another small explosion outside. Perhaps it was no bad thing. Too much talk of evil had a way of discomfiting one's companions, even those with constitutions as strong as Prudence's.

Instead, in the next window of relative calm, Miss Marple said: "People knowing one another's business, that's part of it. It gives rise to all sorts of misunderstandings and resentments. Boredom too: that's another thing. No cinemas or theatres or restaurants to take people out of the humdrum. The terrible acts that are likely committed due to a simple lack of other things to do—"

Prudence frowned and said, in her best head-girl voice (she had in fact been head-girl, all those years ago): "I've been made to feel very welcome here since I lost poor George fifteen years ago—which is no given thing, considering he lived here alone as a bachelor for so many years before Alice and I joined him."

Miss Marple looked to the mantlepiece. "That's from the cruise, isn't it?"

The photograph showed a younger Prudence, along-side Alice, Prudence's daughter from her first marriage, and the late George Fairweather. It had been the last time Miss Marple and Prudence had met: on a tour of the Norwegian Fjords. George Fairweather, considerably Prudence's senior, had been a frail figure of a man, unsteady on his feet, with the mottled complexion of a windfall apple. As for Alice, she remembered a pretty girl dressed in clothes that seemed a little too luxurious for one so young.

"Where is Alice now?" Miss Marple asked.

"Oh, just outside the village. We've always been closer than most mothers and daughters. She married a local landowner, Sir Henry Tyson. They are quite the toast of Meon Maltravers—"

Miss Marple gave a small cough. "And you really are *part* of things here? In my experience, in such places one is often considered a newcomer for several decades before being truly accepted into the fold. Fifteen years is like the blink of an eye."

Prudence drew herself up. "I'm head of the Parish Council, Jane!" she said, as though that settled everything. "And I'm certainly *vieille garde* when compared to our latest newcomer, the new choir mistress. She has been renting Badger's Rest, an Arts and Crafts monstrosity on the outskirts of town, and there is *much* speculation about her."

Miss Marple leaned in. "Of what kind?"

"She's foreign, for one thing. French. Young, or less than forty, anyhow. Near to Alice's age, in fact. And she used to be a rather successful opera singer, but the story is that she had some trouble with her vocal chords and had to leave the stage. Anyhow. She has ruffled a few feathers. An unaccompanied woman, you know how it is. Of course, I don't give in to gossip."

Miss Marple nodded. "Of course."

"But Christopher Palfrey, our resident poet—and a very talented tenor—just published his latest collection, dedicated to 'The Enchantress of Song.' You can only imagine how that went with his wife, Annabelle—who's not what one would have in mind for an 'enchantress' of any kind. She's something of a Socialist, you know— always making a nuisance of herself, opposing some of the most sensible suggestions on the Parish Council, which I find very tiresome. Anyway, she must be spitting feathers over the book, no one has seen her smile for weeks . . . though that isn't entirely unusual."

"I wonder why she'd choose to come and live here?" Miss Marple mused, apparently lost to her own line of thought. "The choir mistress, I mean. An unmarried, foreign woman? To come to such an out-of-the-way place—it seems strange, doesn't it?"

"It's not so out of the way as all that," Prudence said, crisply. "We have a direct train to London, a mainline station. As you have seen yourself."

Miss Marple had wanted to visit the gardens at Honnington Manor—she'd had a rave review from Bunch Harmon about the Japanese maples and their astonishing autumn display at this time of year. It was too far to travel in a day. But Miss Marple had remembered, from their meeting on that cruise, that Prudence lived not far away. She had written to suggest a reunion. The two women hadn't been exactly bosom friends at school, but Miss Marple had always been rather intrigued by her and thought it would make for an interesting visit.

"Anyway," Prudence continued. "You shall meet Celia Beautemps—the choir mistress—tonight. The rehearsal will be at her house; the church roof is being repaired. And hopefully you'll see Alice again: she sings alto too. If she can get away, that is. She and Henry keep some animals—a few sheep and pigs." And then, lest Miss Marple should look down on this enterprise, "Henry is very much a gentleman farmer, of course. But one has to find a way to make all that land pay."

"Tonight?"

"Yes! Choir practice, of course. I *did* mention it, surely? We have so much to rehearse before Advent and it's just around the corner now."

It was not at all what Miss Marple would have preferred. A quiet sit by the fire, some knitting—she was just beginning on an Argyll jumper for her nephew Raymond's Christmas present.

"Besides, I remember you having a lovely soprano, Jane," Prudence said. "Clear as a bell. So if you wanted to join us—"

"It's quite some time since I sang in the school choir, dear. I shall be perfectly happy to watch."

At this moment a gust of wind funnelled down the chimney and a shower of sparks exploded on to the hearthrug. Miss Marple stared deep into the flames as though seeing something in their midst. Prudence caught the direction of her gaze. "It's far too low! I'll ring for the maid immediately!"

"No, no," Miss Marple put up a hand. "I'm warm enough."

But Prudence had turned to ring the bell. A few seconds later the maid had appeared. "New logs! And be quick about it, girl." Miss Marple watched as the flames took hold of the firewood, piled on top of everything below. She would now be far too hot. Here was the problem with staying in other peoples' houses.

Miss Marple didn't do it, as a rule. Nothing was quite as you would have it yourself.

"She's rather a fool, that girl," Prudence sighed, when the maid had retreated. "It's so difficult to find good maids these days."

"I remember you saying the same thing last time I saw you, Prudence."

"I'm sure. George was always rather silly about the servants. He gave the house boy driving lessons, and even though he could be extremely parsimonious at other times, he paid for the former housekeeper's daughter's tuition; thought she was too gifted to spend the rest of her life as a scullery maid. He paid for our butler's holiday to Brighton too. That sort of thing gives them ideas above their station, if you ask me."

Miss Marple couldn't help but be a little amused by this Lady-of-the-Manor act from Prudence, a green-grocer's daughter who had been on a full scholarship at school. Miss Marple also knew that after leaving she had worked for several years in various rather humble positions: a governess, a librarian. She had met her first husband, a pharmacist almost twice her age, while working as his assistant—and had met George as a young widow, while working as his secretary.

"Of course," Prudence said, "I let quite a few of them go when George's heart troubles began and never rehired as it was simply too much to keep on a full staff—Goodness!" she cut herself off mid-sentence, with a glance up at the clock. "We better be going, or we'll be late."

A few moments later they stepped out into the crisp November air, drawing their coats closely about them. Here they were confronted by a stream of masked figures, marching past the front door to the house. They were like something from a medieval painting; demons and fiends come to carry the sinners away. The acrid scent of burning paraffin caught at the back of the throat. Several of them were beating drums. All carried lighted torches and several groups had hoisted aloft life-size, papier-mâché figures with hideously distorted features: oversized heads and bulging eyes, clad in the red robes and caps of Catholic cardinals. There was a strange hum of energy about them. It felt dangerous, even flammable—as though any second the very air might ignite. Miss Marple paused, staring: at once fascinated and repelled.

Prudence beckoned, in her head-girl manner, taking no notice of the throng. "This way."

They had to push their way through the crowd. Several times Miss Marple felt herself jostled—once she could have sworn that a hand reached out to give her a rather hard shove out of the way, and she struggled to regain her footing. It didn't seem to matter a jot to these people that there were two elderly women in their midst. She heard the *whoomp* of the paraffin torches as they swayed above the masked heads, felt the heat of the flames on her cheeks, felt a little frisson of disquiet at being caught among these intent, anonymous figures who moved as one, like a herd or a marauding army.

"I don't understand," Miss Marple said to Prudence, after they had managed to ford the flood of bodies and were standing on the other side of the road. "Guy Fawkes' Night was two weeks ago. They had a bonfire in the fields by St. Mary Mead. Dr. Haydock contributed some Roman Candles and Griselda Clement—the vicar's wife—produced some sort of spiced wine . . . what was it called? Something foreign. *Glühwein,* yes: that was it. Delicious—perhaps a touch too much cinnamon. Of course, I didn't stay for long. Far too cold."

"Ah," said Prudence, "but they do everything rather differently in Meon Maltravers, a little like the Cornish. Tonight's revels commemorate not the death of a band of Catholic rebels but the immolation of seventeen Protestant martyrs at the town cross. It's why they burn the cardinals—the figurines, you know. I suppose you could say it's a sort of revenge, albeit several hundred years later."

"Revenge," said Miss Marple, almost to herself. "Revenge and settling of scores. That's another thing one finds a great deal of in small, out-of-the-way places."

"Well, though the score here is so many centuries old, it's predominantly the youths of the town that are involved. And let me tell you," Prudence said, casting a disapproving eye over the revels, "religion has very little to do with it at all. In fact, it feels rather apt that we should be going to choir practice tonight. We will form a bastion of Christian righteousness in the midst of these pagan goings-on."

They walked down the high street, away from the crowds and noise until they were on the outskirts of town.

"This way," Prudence said. "We'll cut through the woods and it'll take us the quick route to the back of the property." She took out a small torch and switched it on.

Now the street had dwindled to little more than a path between a black thicket of trees. The light from the streetlamps behind them was almost lost but the full moon filtered down in fingers of light between the tangled branches and the beam from Prudence's torch bounced in front of them. It was only about five o'clock or so but it felt much later. It was hard to believe that only a hundred yards or so away were crowded streets and shops, noise and light. Every footstep was audible, every snapped twig. From the undergrowth around them came the secret rustlings of nocturnal animals.

"How much further?" Miss Marple asked, stepping carefully over a tree root that had erupted up in the centre of the path.

"Only a little way along here. We're going via the back entrance, as it's quicker. There's a long driveway, but you reach it from the other end of the high street. You'll see the house lights shortly. Madame Beautemps keeps them on all night, which has caused some controversy with the local bird-watching group; they're convinced she's frightened away all the screech owls. She really has set the cat among the pigeons."

"Or the owls," Miss Marple said.

"No, Jane," Prudence said, "that's not how the saying goes at all—" she stopped short as a terrible, unearthly, animal screeching split the air in two. For a long time afterwards, the echo of it seemed to ricochet among the trees.

"How odd," Prudence said. "There must be a few screech owls about after all. Where was I? Oh, yes. Celia Beautemps has made enemies of most members of our choir too. I told you about the Palfreys before, didn't I? Then there's Colonel Woodage—who sings bass—hates all the French; had a son who lost both legs trying to rescue a band of Gallic deserters in the war, you know. And she's upset Mrs. Prufrock—the former choir mistress for the last three decades—for obvious reasons. We think Reverend Peabody must be in thrall to her, because he ousted poor Mrs. Prufrock from her position with no warning."

"I'd say her quarrel is with the Reverend, then, rather than with her replacement."

"Perhaps. But to add insult to injury, Madame Beautemps has insisted that Mrs. Prufrock shouldn't be singing soprano, because she's no longer able to hit the top notes. And there's Gordon Kipling, master of hounds for the local hunt—also a bass—who is convinced she killed three of his animals: two days after she complained about their barking (he lives just a little way over there, beyond those trees) they ate rat poisoning and perished. And then—"

Suddenly Prudence gave a very uncharacteristic scream. It happened so quickly. They didn't spot the figure until it was almost upon them, as though it had sprung from the darkness itself. Mask-clad, moving towards them at speed from the opposite direction. Prudence was standing plumb in their way. There was a moment's pause, in which the stranger seemed to hesitate, as though deciding whether to step around her.

Then Miss Marple saw a hand shoot out; a second later, Prudence had fallen to the ground, the torch flying from her grip, the light going out with a little "pop." Another few seconds and the figure had disappeared. They were alone again.

"Prudence!" Miss Marple went to her friend and, with some difficulty, helped her to stand. "Are you all right? Are you hurt?"

"I— I don't know," Prudence said, a little shakily. I mean: yes, I think I am—all right, that is. I just . . . just need to catch my breath. He pushed me, Jane! Did you see?"

"Yes, yes. I saw—a frightful thing! Should we go to the police? I noticed we passed the station on the high street—"

"No," Prudence said, bravely. "I don't want any fuss. Nothing's broken. And he'll be long gone by now, into the crowd. They'll never find him. Just take my arm. It's only a little way now." She seemed miraculously unperturbed by the whole affair, but then Prudence had always been made of stern stuff.

Miss Marple stooped to pick up the torch. As she did, she found something beside it, lying in the path: what appeared in the gloom to be a tiny, pale pebble. She picked it up and pocketed it.

Soon they had reached the back of the house. Strains of music floated towards them: Madame Butterfly's famous aria, "Un Bel Di," if Miss Marple was not mistaken. All the lamps—including the outside lights—were on and blazing out into the darkness. A pair of French doors hung open and someone stood there stitched in silhouette against the brightness behind, featureless, still as a statue. As they drew closer, Miss Marple could make her out. A maid, a young girl, her face a mask of horror. She knew at once that it hadn't been a screech owl they had heard.

"Oh, missuses. Missuses . . . something terrible has happened."

"What is it, girl?" Prudence was suddenly all practicality. Miss Marple remembered her words before. *You have to be firm with them. Show them what's what.* "Come on. Out with it."

The girl pointed a trembling finger towards the room behind her.

"I know not to disturb her when she's in the study. And the music was playing so loud on the gramophone—I didn't hear anything. They must have come through the French doors. I— I can't believe it."

A large walnut desk hid half the carpet from view. All they could make out at first was one small foot, clad in a green suede shoe. Then, as they rounded the desk, the rest became visible. The woman's shawl—a theatrical affair in emerald cashmere—was spread all about her where she had fallen. On first glance the shawl appeared to have a burgundy-hued pattern—on a second glance it became clear that this was in fact blood, a great deal of it, which had soaked into it from a vicious slit just above the woman's clavicle. She was evidently very dead indeed.

There was a moment of silence as the three of them stared at the fallen form. In one hand, Miss Marple saw, the dead woman clutched a note. In the other a blank envelope. From here she could read the words, printed in capitals:

I KNOW YOU.
I KNOW WHAT YOU REALLY ARE.
PAY WHAT YOU OWE OR EVERYONE
WILL LEARN THE TRUTH.

Miss Marple couldn't help but notice the hand clutching the envelope. She always noticed hands. Fingernails too. There had been an incident she had been involved in a little while ago and fingernails had come into it. She saw that Celia Beautemps' fingernails were ugly, misshapen affairs, thick and yellowed. She'd seen such a thing before—she simply had to remember where.

The hair was in disarray, half-escaped from its chignon. Miss Marple could make out the mouse-coloured roots beneath a layer of black dye.

"Have you called the police, girl?" Prudence demanded.

The maid wrung her hands. "No, ma'am—I didn't think. I was so shocked . . ."

"Go and do it immediately. We must have them here at once." Prudence glanced up at the clock in the study. "Five thirty. The rest of the choir will be here soon too."

As if in answer, there was a sudden sharp rap on the door. Prudence sent the maid to answer. "I'll ring the police."

For a few moments Miss Marple was left on her own with the body. There was just time, she calculated, to make a quick study of the room, undisturbed, before chaos descended. She took another look at the note— the envelope too. She wandered over to the desk. Another stack of envelopes, these unopened, several stamped with the words FINAL REMINDER. A book of poetry, lying open on a poem entitled "My Lady of Shalott."

She moved to the wall hung with photographs of Celia Beautemps in her prime, performing on various different stages, alongside framed certificates from the Guildhall School of Music. On the mantlepiece sat a small, rather cheap-looking tin urn and next to it a small photograph of a woman wearing what looked like a white cap—though it was difficult to be certain because the image was old and foxed.

Suddenly she became aware that she was no longer alone in the room. The little maid had returned. She saw now that the girl looked not just shocked and upset by what she had found. She looked truly grief-stricken.

"Who could have done this?" she asked, plaintively.

"I don't know, child," Miss Marple told her. "But we will find out."

"She were a good mistress. Not like others I've worked for. She treated me like a person. She bought me special gloves for cleaning and all."

"It sounds as though she was very kind to you."

"She was a kind lady, ma'am. But that's not how they talk about her in Meon Maltravers. All sorts of horrible things they say. She thought someone was spreading lies about. Things to make people turn against her. But she said she'd get even in the end—"

She stopped talking: someone had just burst into the room. It was a youngish man, pale and rather beautiful. He stopped dead at the sight of the body on the floor. Miss Marple suspected this might be the poet, Christopher Palfrey. Hot on his heels came a tall woman with angular, rather fierce looks. This had to be the wife, Annabelle. Just behind them followed a trim, grey-haired gentleman with a thick moustache and military aspect, a faded little woman in the clothes of a previous decade and, finally, a floridly handsome middle-aged man in a smart tweed jacket that was straining slightly at the buttons. All of them seemed to be peering over one another's shoulders with a rather horrid, prurient interest.

The faded woman—presumably the former choir mistress—let out a little cry. It was no doubt meant to signify horror but it sounded oddly like the cries of excitement Miss Marple had heard from the children watching the fireworks in St. Mary Mead.

"Christ Almighty," exclaimed the tweed-clad gentle-man, who Miss Marple guessed to be Gordon Kipling, master of hounds. "Someone's killed the bitch!"

"Steady on, man," said the moustachioed man.

"Very sorry, Colonel," Kipling said, quickly—seeming as appalled by his own outburst as the rest of them. "Damned shocking thing to see, though."

No doubt to his relief, the room's attention was quickly caught by another commotion: a sudden, low groan, more animal than human; a sound of great pain. Christopher Palfrey had fallen to his knees in front of the body. "She's dead," he moaned, words muffled through the hands he held over his mouth. "She's dead and I killed her."

A stunned hush settled over the room. And then: "For God's sake," Annabelle Palfrey said. She stepped towards him and put a claw-like hand on his shoulder, knuckles showing white. "Get up, you bloody fool," she hissed. "Get up this second. Remember your heart. No over-excitement, Dr. Briggs said." She hauled him to his feet. There was a flush high on her cheeks: from the cold, perhaps, or some recent physical exertion—or maybe just anger.

Then she herself knelt over the body, felt for a pulse at both neck and wrist. "Medical training," she threw back to them, by way of explanation. "Drove an ambulance in 1918."

Yet these ministrations might also, Miss Marple thought, be a way to account for any of her fingerprints appearing on the corpse.

"I've called the police," Prudence said, striding into the room. "They should be here any moment—the station's only a couple of minutes' drive away. And come out of here, all of you. It's positively morbid."

A few moments later there was the sound of a car drawing up in the driveway outside and, in a couple of minutes more, two policemen had joined them inside.

The taller man was clearly the more senior of the two. He looked rather like a policeman from a Raymond Chandler novel or an American noir film: the lantern jaw, the overcoat, the hat pulled low over his dark-shadowed eyes. Miss Marple suspected he might have dressed specially to create this impression. The over-all effect was marred slightly by the fact that, when he opened his mouth, he had a broad Sussex accent. "I'm Inspector Eidel," he told the assembled company. "And I'd like to ask you all a few questions."

A little while later, Miss Marple—nearly the last of the company to be interviewed—was led into a small sitting room by the more junior of the two policemen. He indicated an armchair opposite Inspector Eidel.

"Jane Marple," Inspector Eidel stated, then paused—perhaps because Miss Marple was looking beyond him, through the window towards the woods—and said, in a louder voice, "CAN YOU HEAR ME, MADAM?"

Miss Marple gave a little start, then fixed her eyes on him. "Perfectly well, thank you."

"Your friend told me that you had an altercation with a masked man in the woods this evening. Coming in the other direction—from the house, along the path that leads from the back entrance. Correct?"

"Not *quite* correct," Miss Marple answered, brightly.

"Pardon me?"

Miss Marple tilted her head to show that he was, indeed, pardoned. "You see, it wasn't the evening. It was a little past five o'clock—though at this time of year, when it gets dark so quickly, it's so easy to forget, I do understand . . ."

Inspector Eidel cleared his throat rather violently. "Apologies, ma'am, just a figure of speech—"

"But it does seem *so* important to get these things right from the outset, doesn't it? You as a policeman will know this, of course. Words are words but they can be so dangerous, so misleading. So: yes, I was there this afternoon. And we encountered a masked figure. My friend was pushed roughly to the ground—a very shocking thing. Almost, one might say, gratuitously so."

"What do you mean?"

"I'm not sure exactly. Merely that it seemed particularly vicious. To push an old woman to the ground like that when they could simply have stepped around her. As though they were trying to make a point. What that was, of course, I cannot say."

"Well, ma'am," Inspector Eidel said—a little patronisingly, Miss Marple thought—"we *are* talking here of the sort of person who had in all likelihood just murdered a woman. So perhaps it's no great surprise. Unfortunately, whoever it was, they'll be long gone by now into that crowd marching to the town cross. We'll have to—"

"I'm not so sure," Miss Marple interjected. "That's what they would *want* you to think, of course. But if we assume that masked figure was our murderer— and I do agree with you that it is an assumption we can hazard—then, from what Prudence says, many of the people who had a real quarrel with the victim are here in this very house. Don't you see? It would have been a rather clever conceit to costume themselves as one of the revellers. And then it would have been the work of a moment to shrug off the disguise, conceal it in the woods, and return here in their ordinary clothes, ready for the choir practice—as though none of it had happened. So my two pennies' worth, if you would like to hear it, Inspector," Inspector Eidel seemed to understand he didn't have much of a choice in the matter, "would be to search the woods near to where Prudence and I met our masked assailant, search for any signs of them: clothing, for example."

Inspector Eidel turned to the junior who sat perched on the edge of a chaise longue holding his notebook. A wordless exchange passed between them. The junior nodded. "I'll put in a call to Honnington station, see if they can spare some chaps."

Eidel turned back to Miss Marple. "There was a note found in the dead woman's hand."

"I know. I saw it. A rather threatening message."

"You aren't from these parts, are you, Miss Marple?"

"No, I live in St. Mary Mead. Have you heard of it? It's not a very well-known place. A small village, rather charming—"

"So," Eidel cut in, "I suppose, not being from around here, it would be difficult for you to make a guess as to who might have sent it to the victim?"

"Oh, but of course I know the answer to that. No one!"

"Pardon?"

Miss Marple tilted her head again. "The envelope tells us everything, of course."

"The envelope was blank, Miss Marple."

"Precisely! More than blank, it was pristine. It was *unused.* Which I believe tells us that *nobody* sent it. It had not yet found its intended recipient. The victim was the author of the note. She was blackmailing someone. And when she was killed, she had clearly been preparing to send it."

There was a longish silence. Miss Marple could hear

Eidel breathing rather heavily through his mouth. Finally he spoke again.

"One other thing. We have heard from several others that Christopher Palfrey said—"

He looked to the junior, who cleared his throat and spoke, reading from his notebook: "She's dead and I killed her."

Eidel turned to Miss Marple. "Is that—"

"Correct. Indeed. He did say those words."

"Thank you, Miss Marple."

"But I don't think it was a confession at all. These creative types—my nephew Raymond is one, you know—they do have a habit of making everything about themselves and their work."

Eidel frowned. "And how exactly do you make all of this out?"

"Palfrey recently dedicated a collection of poetry to Celia Beautemps. One of the poems was entitled 'My Lady of Shalott.' A nod to Tennyson, I imagine—I am so fond of Tennyson, I do like a poem that actually rhymes . . . perhaps that rather marks me out as the Victorian I am." Miss Marple frowned. "Where was I? Oh yes! In the old tale the Lady of Shalott dies, as you'll know, of course. I think that this is where Palfrey's artistic egoism comes in—he no doubt believes that because he *imagined* Madame Beautemps dead in verse, he somehow visited the Fates upon her. The arrogance of the artistic temperament, you know: my nephew has it too, and I say that as his loving aunt."

"The artistic temperament," Eidel repeated, a little weakly. "The . . . Fates?"

"Besides, Palfrey couldn't have been your masked figure."

"He couldn't?"

"No, because of his heart, of course!"

"His heart?"

"Annabelle Palfrey reminded him of his heart when he got so upset over the body. And I spoke to Colonel Woodage about it while we were waiting to be interviewed: he says Palfrey was exempted from active service because of it. I would be very surprised if he had been able to tear through the woods like that as a result."

There was another long silence.

"Thank you, Miss Marple," Eidel said, finally. "I think we have everything we need now. If you could send in—" he turned to his junior.

"Gordon Kipling," the other clarified.

★★★

Miss Marple joined the group in the dining room. Like the sitting room—and indeed any parts of the house that Miss Marple had glimpsed—it had an uninhabited, provisional look to it. In contrast to the sumptuous furnishings of Fairweather House, for example, there didn't seem to be quite enough furniture for the space, few pictures on the walls and no carpet upon the wooden floorboards. Around the table sat Prudence, the Palfreys, Mrs. Prufrock, Colonel Woodage, Gordon Kipling and the maid.

Christopher Palfrey looked just as agonised as he had when confronted by the scene in the study. He sat white-faced and trembling slightly, slumped over to one side. His wife, her posture ramrod straight, seemed to be supporting him, the only thing preventing him from sliding off his seat and on to the floor.

Miss Marple took the seat beside Prudence and, because no one seemed to be talking, took out her knitting.

"I didn't like the woman," the Colonel said, suddenly, into the silence. "I'll be the first to say it. Cards on the table. And not, before any of you say it, because she was French. In fact, I don't think she was any more French than I am. Something off about that accent. Some dodgy vowels in there. No, I didn't like her because there was something . . . crooked about her, something false."

Miss Marple noticed a little nod from Mrs. Prufrock,

the former choir mistress, in response to this. She was reminded of the words on the note. *I know what you really are.* But if her hunch was correct, and she was sure it was, then Celia Beautemps had been calling someone else out on a deception. Colonel Woodage went on: "I like people to represent themselves honestly. I didn't trust the woman. But I wouldn't wish her dead. I hope they find the scoundrel that did this."

"She killed three of my hounds," Gordon Kipling said. "I'm certain of it. So some might say it's only just desserts—"

He stopped as the door to the dining room swung open.

The junior policeman stood in the doorway.

"We would like to conduct a search of all your effects," he said, a little nervously—as though he were asking a question rather than making a statement. "If you'll submit to it. You don't have to agree, but . . . ah . . . your refusal will be taken into account."

Miss Marple leaned towards Prudence. "That means they've found the disguise, I think. In the woods. But *not* the murder weapon."

"What do you mean, Jane?"

"Oh, I think our murderer—and your assailant—is here somewhere. I think Eidel does too."

One by one they were called into the sitting room

again. Miss Marple passed over her handbag to the policemen and waited as the contents were searched. She knew there was little in there beyond her knitting, her purse and some smelling salts—as a late-Victorian, she took them with her everywhere, since you never knew when such things might come in useful—but it did feel rather lowering, even violating, having these men paw through her personal effects. Afterwards, she waited outside while Prudence underwent the same treatment. Finally, they were free to go. But just as they were leaving through the front door, they heard a sound that seemed half shriek, half howl. "Get your hands off me! How dare you! Unhand me, you fools! This is an outrage!"

"That's Annabelle Palfrey," Prudence said, stopping in the entranceway.

Miss Marple inclined her head. "Yes. I expect they found the knife in her handbag and are making their arrest."

Prudence turned to her. "Jane! Could *that* be what Palfrey meant, when he said he'd killed her? He'd realised his wife had found out about their affair and murdered his lover?"

Miss Marple was about to answer when they were caught in the beam of a pair of headlights, approaching fast. The car slowed and stopped. Prudence's daughter,

Alice, looked out, as pretty as Miss Marple remembered, and the picture of a gentleman farmer's wife in silk scarf and pearls and smart country tweed. Prudence and Miss Marple went to greet her.

"Have I missed the rehearsal?"she asked. "Sorry I'm late, our Persian hurt her paw—" A rather pathetic mewling sounded from a wicker carrier on the passenger seat.

Her gaze took in the parked police cars—several now—and her eyes widened. "What on earth's going on?"

"Madame Beautemps has been found dead," Prudence told her.

"*Dead?*"

"It's a terrible thing," Prudence said, sombrely.

"And the police . . ."Alice asked, "do they have any idea who did it?"

"We believe Annabelle Palfrey has just been arrested. Jane is convinced they must have found the knife in her handbag."

At this moment the woman herself was led from the house, wrists handcuffed behind her and two policemen flanking her. She walked with surprising poise and dignity, even when one of the officers put a hand on her head to steer her into the back seat of the car. The three women watched silently. "Annabelle Palfrey," Alice said, after the police car had left. "Just imagine! But you somehow *can* imagine it, can't you? There's something so . . . ruthless and calculating about her. Something rather masculine." Then she turned to them. "Do hop in. I'll give you both a lift back to Fairweather."

"No, thank you," Miss Marple said. "I'd like to walk back. To clear my head."

"But it's so cold! And besides, there might be a murderer on the loose!" Alice looked at her mother, questioningly, then back to Miss Marple.

"If Jane is walking, I'll go with her," Prudence said.

"I'll be perfectly all right on my own," Miss Marple told her.

Prudence shook her head. "Well, I must insist."

Alice left in the car and the two women made the long walk back along the main drive—considering they'd met a murderer via the other route, they weren't going to risk the dark shortcut through the trees this time. Miss Marple stopped a couple of times to make an inspection of the woods on each side while Prudence stood and waited, a little impatiently. Back at Fairweather House, they shared a light supper and went to bed early. But Miss Marple didn't sleep. She spent the next few hours thinking, until a weak dawn showed itself through the curtains. Then she asked for a restorative pot of tea to be sent to her room.

"Would you take this note to Inspector Eidel at the police station?" she asked the girl, the same one who had tended to the fire the previous day. "Tell him it's urgent."

"It really is shocking," Prudence said at breakfast, buttering a slice of toast and then spooning a small dollop of marmalade on top. "I have never seen eye to eye with Annabelle Palfrey, I'll admit. But I wouldn't have had her pegged as a murderer. You were right, Jane! Evil does happen in small places after all." She took a neat sip of tea.

"It does indeed." Miss Marple carefully buttered her own slice of toast. "Yet I don't believe Annabelle Palfrey had anything to do with that woman's death."

Prudence put down her teacup. "You don't?"

Miss Marple frowned. "Firstly, you see, what I don't understand is why one would go to all the trouble with the disguise, hiding it in the woods, etcetera, only to leave the murder weapon in one's handbag. I suppose it would have been *possible* to conceal a handbag under the cloak. But why not dispose of the knife too? It all seems rather foolish—and not at all in keeping with the woman I met last night. She seems altogether too intelligent for that."

"So what are you saying?"

"I think I am getting ahead of myself. It seems important to start with the victim herself. You see, as soon as I saw those fingernails, I knew that something was amiss."

Prudence's mouth twisted in distaste. "*Fingernails?*"

"I knew I'd seen something like them before. Those ugly, thickened nails, the reddened cuticles. Then I remembered that a maid of mine once suffered from the same condition. I sent her to Dr. Haydock for treatment. Paronychia: common among domestic servants, the kind who spend a lot of time with their fingers in hot soapy water. Left untreated the condition can become chronic, can last for years. It's less common among famous sopranos, I imagine. But what if Celia Beautemps had had another life, before she became a singer? What if she had even, at one stage, worked as a domestic servant? And, perhaps, some kind benefactor had paid for her tuition. There was also the fact that Celia Beautemps went to the Guildhall School of Music and Drama, in London. That in itself seemed strange to me—why would a Frenchwoman not have learned

her craft in her own country? The French are so snob-
bish, so particular about that sort of thing."

Prudence picked up her teacup and took another sip
of tea.

"Shall I go on?" Miss Marple said.

Prudence inclined her head.

"So, you see, I posit that the French persona was
part of the disguise. The Colonel made that comment
about her 'dodgy vowels': still, much easier to disguise
one's working-class origins with a French accent than
with the pretence of an upper-class English one.

"I think Celia Beautemps—if that was indeed her
born name, which I don't believe for a moment it
was—was a domestic servant who learned her craft
with the generosity of a wealthy patron. Didn't you
mention yesterday that your own husband, George,
paid for just such a thing to take place, despite being
rather parsimonious in his other dealings? The former
housekeeper's daughter, you said. And from Meon
Maltravers, of course, with its fast train to London, it
would have been easy for a girl to travel up there in her
free time."

Prudence put the teacup back down. The saucer rattled a little as she did so. "What exactly are you suggesting, Jane?"

"What I am saying is that I believe Celia Beautemps

was a figure from the past. From *your* past, in fact, Prudence. Someone you hoped had disappeared—especially after her mother's death. I think she came back here, after the issue with her vocal chords cut her career short, in the hopes of extorting a living out of you, via blackmail. That note, in her hand? I saw something like it in the fire last night. And you seemed so very eager, all of a sudden, to have the fire built up—to conceal what you hoped I hadn't spotted in the flames."

"This is absurd," Prudence said, in her most ringing head-girl tones. "What reason could anyone have for blackmailing me?"

"Oh," Miss Marple said, "the fact that you'd killed your second husband—and her former employer—I suppose."

Prudence opened her mouth in outrage, but Miss Marple continued.

"Seeing that photograph of the three of you—it reminded me of how frail George had seemed. The blemished, almost bruised-looking skin, the digestive complaints. And the eventual heart failure. All signs of chronic arsenic poisoning."

"But how—"

"Those dyed flowers one used to wear in one's hat: I remember asking the milliner in Much Benham where the lovely green foliage had gone: Scheele's green, the colour was called. She told me about the poor girls in the factories, dyeing the things, getting sicker and sicker. They were slowly being poisoned by the stuff. The patches on the skin, the gastric complaints, the heart trouble—just as it was with George. A one-time pharmacist's wife! You'd know exactly how to do it.

"And you spoke of getting rid of the staff when George got sick. To ease the burden of keeping the household, you said. Or to rid yourself of potential witnesses."

"This is preposterous. And you're saying I had something to do with Celia Beautemps' death too? I was with you when we heard her scream—when the poor wretch was killed. You saw me pushed to the ground by the murderer!"

Miss Marple nodded. "Indeed. And a knife wouldn't be your style, Prudence. Poison is much more your thing. And how clever, to put yourself out of suspicion! To have been attacked by the murderer—it would seem to sever any connection that might be made between the two of you. But it was also a way, I believe, to achieve a transfer of the weapon. You wanted to plant it on Annabelle Palfrey. You told me she crossed you in the Parish Council—oh, I remember you at school, Prudence, and you never liked dissent. It would be a killing of two birds with one stone, as it were. When that masked figure pushed you, I think they were actually passing you the knife. To dispose of when you sat next to Annabelle Palfrey in the dining room, waiting to be questioned. What was it? Something small and neat—I suspect the woman's own paper knife."

"This is utter nonsense—"

But Miss Marple was all ruthlessness now. "And now I come to your accomplice. What was it you said about your daughter? 'We've always been closer than most mothers and daughters.' Alice is tall—a good fit for the masked figure we saw in the woods—who you were careful to describe as a 'man' in your account to the police. She'd also make a good killer—a pig farmer's wife, gentleman farmer or no, would know how to slit a throat."

"Alice arrived after everything had happened, in her car!"

"She arrived in her car, certainly. But I checked the woods on each side of the drive. Plenty of dark, relatively open spots for her to hide in the parked vehicle, once she had rid herself of her costume and crossed through the woods on foot to the driveway, with the headlights off, concealed from sight. It was a risk—the police who found the costume might have stumbled upon her. But it was far enough away—and the costume poorly enough hidden—that it didn't come to that. And then she could glide up the drive with her story about the cat, knowing it wouldn't be properly investigated."

Miss Marple had said it all now.

There was a long silence. A very long silence that seemed to gather shape and weight.

Then Prudence rose from her chair. She was holding the knife she had used for spreading butter on her toast. Miss Marple sat very still. They were alone in the room. And Prudence kept so few staff . . .

Prudence was rounding the corner of the table now, the knife clenched in her hand. A knife might not be her preference, but Miss Marple was beginning to suspect that under duress she might not be so particular. She began to realise, as she rose and took a step backwards and Prudence continued to advance, that she might have done something rather foolish.

The doorbell rang. Then the sound of broad Sussex in the hallway. Prudence froze. Miss Marple let out the breath she had not realised she had been holding. The little maid opened the door to the breakfast room and showed him in.

"Good morning, Mrs. Fairweather." Eidel doffed his hat, revealing the heavily Brylcreemed hair of a noir lead. "I'd like to invite you to the station to answer a few questions, if you don't mind. Your daughter is already in the car. And if you could put that down." He gestured carelessly to the knife.

Prudence drew herself up.

"You have no evidence for any of this," she said.

Miss Marple spoke up now: "The victim herself is evidence. I have no idea what her real name was, though I'm sure it wasn't Celia Beautemps. But Beautemps means 'fair weather' in French. A clue to her origins, to this very building: Fairweather House."

"Wild, unfounded speculation," Prudence said.

"And I have Alice's pearl stud," Miss Marple said. "From where she dropped it in the woods after she 'attacked' you last night."

"You could have found that anywhere!" Prudence said. "Really, Jane, I always knew you were envious of me at school, but this—"

"I took the note," the little maid said, suddenly. "The one in the fire, the one the French woman brung here, yesterday morning." She looked at Prudence. "You're always threatening to turn me out if I"—she mimicked Prudence's ringing tones now—" 'don't buck your ideas up, you silly girl!' So I snatched it out before I put the new logs on, thought I'd keep it, in case it came in useful."

She handed a sooty scrap to Inspector Eidel, who read it and then turned to Prudence. "George Fairweather was your husband, I presume? You know, ma'am"—the next words were spoken with the faintest hint of an American drawl, as though repeating a line from a film—"you can't just go round killing people whenever the notion strikes you."

For once, Prudence Fairweather seemed lost for words.

"And there you have it, Prudence," Miss Marple said, into the silence. "One mistreats or underestimates servants at one's peril. But I would have thought you'd learned that lesson already."

When Prudence had been led away, Miss Marple reflected on the fact that evil hadn't been out there in the street amidst the pagan throng last night. No: it had been right here, inside in the cosy, well-appointed sitting room of this elegant home. Now she had yet another reason to avoid staying in other peoples' houses. The Japanese maples had indeed been glorious, but not altogether worth it in the end.

The Second Murder
at the Vicarage

Val McDermid

To have one murder in one's vicarage is unfortunate; to have a second looks remarkably like carelessness, or worse. It was to no avail that I protested that the dead maid in the kitchen was not *our* maid. The unfortunate fact that she had formerly occupied that role was enough to set the tongues of St. Mary Mead wagging more eagerly than the tails of a pack of hounds catching the scent of a fox.

To make matters worse, my wife had made no secret of our delight at Mary's departure from our employ. Dear Griselda has many fine qualities but the discretion that befits a vicar's wife is not among them. In fairness, however, anyone who had ever dined with us could bear testament to the literally diabolical nature of Mary's cooking.

On one occasion, she put a pan of eggs on the stove to boil and promptly forgot about them. The pan boiled dry, the eggs exploded, filling the house with a dark sulphurous reek. "I imagine this is how the outskirts of hell will smell," our neighbour, Miss Marple, remarked with a twinkle when she arrived later for lunch. It took three coats of paint to restore the kitchen ceiling.

So we felt no sadness when, on hearing that my wife was with child, Mary announced she was leaving us because she couldn't abide children in general and babies in particular. Miss Marple, who has an admirable record in training young women for domestic service, came to our rescue. Flora has all the qualities Mary lacked. She is reliable, capable and devoted to our son David. She is a good plain cook and an even better baker. Griselda further maintains she has a face like a policeman's boot, which she claims will discourage back-door suitors like Bill Archer, who courted Mary until his death only a week ago.

According to Miss Hartnell, the heartiest of our village spinsters, Archer had been hoist by his own petard. That he was a poacher was no secret—but then, there are few secrets in a village like St. Mary Mead, thanks to what Griselda calls "the clowder of old cats," who are swifter with the news than the BBC, though on occasion less accurate.

But I digress. Archer had cooked up a stew of one of Colonel Bantry's pheasants bulked out with wild mushrooms. Although he was an experienced forager, somehow he managed to incorporate sufficient poisonous fungi to have fatal effects. A passing farm labourer was alerted by the anguished barking of Archer's Jack Russell terrier. He peered through the kitchen window and saw Archer lying on the floor amidst a scatter of broken crockery and a smashed beer bottle.

Despite Archer's well-known proclivity for helping himself to other men's produce, the local police did not take his death lightly. Inspector Slack—a misnomer if ever there was one—arrived from Much Benham with his usual flurry of self-importance. He bossed everyone around for the best part of a day, then locked up the cottage and placed a seal on the door.

"A fat lot of use that will be. Any idiot could get inside that ramshackle hovel of Archer's in a matter of minutes," observed my nephew Dennis, whose year as a probationary police constable has rendered him an expert on all matters criminal.

It seemed, however, that even Inspector Slack could find no grounds for suspecting foul play. Only that morning, Miss Marple had stopped me as I passed the bottom of her garden. "Have you heard when Archer's funeral is to be held?" she asked.

"I'm afraid his family can make no plans until the police release his body."

"Had you not heard? The coroner has concluded his death was from natural causes. They removed the seal on his cottage yesterday morning. I believe Mary has already visited. It was her afternoon off." Of course, Miss Marple *would* know the schedule of every domestic servant in the village.

But even Miss Marple could not have predicted that I would walk into my kitchen after our conversation to find the self-same Mary lying on the flagged floor, her head in a pool of blood, a cast-iron omelette pan discarded next to her. Though I feared she was dead, I did crouch beside her and feel for a pulse in her wrist. Not only was there no flutter, her skin was cool to the touch.

I straightened up and made for the phone in the hall. Much to the chagrin of Mrs. Price Ridley, Miss Hartnell and Miss Wetherby, we have no village bobby here in St. Mary Mead. (Just as well, says Dennis, who is already the perpetual target of their complaints.) So I was obliged to ring Much Benham, where Inspector Slack holds sway. I had hoped he might be out on an investigation, but as soon as I said "dead body" I was transferred via a series of clicks and buzzes to the man himself.

"Mr. Clement?" he snapped. "What's this about a dead body in your kitchen?"

I explained what I had discovered. There was a long silence then Slack harrumphed down the line. "I'd have thought one murder in the vicarage would be enough for any man of the cloth." He paused. I had no idea what he expected me to say so I remained silent. Eventually he sighed. "Don't touch anything. We'll be with you shortly." The bang of the phone receiver hitting its rest reverberated unpleasantly through my head.

Slack was as good as his word, arriving with Dennis and another uniformed constable in tow. I was shooed out of the kitchen and into my study, where Slack soon joined me. "PC Hurst tells me the dead woman used to be in service here," he began without preamble.

Before I could reply, there was a tap at the French windows leading into the garden. There stood Miss Marple, carrying her gardening gloves and a pair of secateurs. In spite of Slack's tutting, I opened the door. In the absence of a lawyer, I felt the need of some moral support. "I couldn't help noticing the police arriving," she said, stepping inside. "So indiscreet, those Black Marias."

"No need for discretion when a woman's been beaten to death," Slack said shortly.

Miss Marple's expression reflected surprise but none of the tremulous horror one might expect in an elderly spinster. My neighbour is made of sterner stuff, as I had discovered after Colonel Protheroe's murder in the very room we stood in. "How distressing," she said. "But who has been murdered? I know it can't be dear Griselda or Flora, for I saw them driving off earlier this morning."

"They've taken David to Chipping Marlbury to visit Griselda's parents," I said automatically.

"According to PC Hurst, the victim is Mary Hill," Slack interrupted in his most brusque manner.

Now Miss Marple did look shocked. "Mary? But what was she doing here?"

"That's what I'd like to know." Slack turned to me. "Had she made an appointment to see you?"

I shook my head. "No. She didn't even come to church, not since she handed in her notice. She went to work for Miss Hartnell and I've only ever spoken to her since when she answered the door there."

"Was she a friend of your maid? Flora, is it?"

"Not that I'm aware."

Miss Marple nodded. "Flora is far too sensible a girl to waste her time with Mary. Why Mary should be murdered in your kitchen is indeed a puzzle."

Slack circled the subject for a few minutes, getting no further forward. He asked where I'd been before my discovery and I was able to provide a list of parishioners I'd visited. He made a great performance of noting their names and addresses, which served to make me feel guilty even though I knew myself to be entirely innocent of any assault on Mary.

At last, he left us alone. "I think I should pay a visit of condolence to Miss Hartnell," I said.

"Indeed, vicar. But she may not know about Mary's death yet." Miss Marple stood up. "If you don't mind, I should like to accompany you. Sometimes another woman's presence helps in the breaking of tragic news."

I have always found Miss Marple impossible to refuse. She is never bossy, like Miss Hartnell, nor autocratic, like Mrs. Price Ridley, nor guilt-inducing, like Miss Wetherby. But when she wants something, she has the knack of making it seem inevitable. "I think, vicar, we should leave by the garden and take the back lane," she continued. "The police car on your doorstep will have roused the curiosity of everyone in the village and we should have to satisfy that several times over before we could draw close to our destination."

As we approached Miss Hartnell's garden, I could see that she, like Miss Marple, was using the cover of pruning her roses to keep the vicarage under scrutiny.

No sooner had we come into hailing distance than she popped upright with a speed usually only called into service to terrorise the local youth. "Vicar," she boomed. "I see the constabulary are at your door. Has there been a burglary?"

Miss Marple put a hand on the garden gate. "Might we come in, my dear? I think we could all do with a cup of tea."

Miss Hartnell snorted. "You may have to make it yourself, Jane. Mary seems to have flounced off in one of her sulks. She's been nowhere to be seen since she cleared away the coffee cups after Matilda Merchiston dropped by. You know Matilda, vicar? The romantic novelist? I've no time for that nonsense myself, but the young women seem to swallow all that nonsense wholesale."

"I'm afraid . . ." I stopped, not feeling entirely comfortable delivering my news among the gladioli and the dahlias and the talk of romance.

I often underestimate the steel under the tweeds when it comes to my older female parishioners. "Mary's not sulking, my dear. Mary's been murdered," Miss Marple said, her tone entirely lacking in drama.

Miss Hartnell's jaw dropped, revealing large yellow teeth that would have been more at home in the mouth of Colonel Bantry's favourite hunter. "Mary? Murdered? There must be some mistake, Jane. What motive could anyone have for murdering Mary? It's not as if she's got the brains to be a threat to anyone. Or enough personality to provoke a murderous thought."

It appeared that the concept of never speaking ill of the dead fell into abeyance when the dead were of the servant class. "Nevertheless," Miss Marple continued, "murdered she has been."

"Good lord." Miss Hartnell harrumphed again. "I think this calls for something stronger than tea. A small sherry, anyone?"

Before I could refuse, Miss Hartnell had swept indoors, her neighbour at her heels. She headed for the decanter and glasses that sat on the sideboard, but, as she poured, Miss Marple spoke again. "Might we take a quick look at Mary's room?"

Miss Hartnell frowned. "Isn't that the police's job?"

"Of course. But Inspector Slack won't look at it with a woman's eye. It may be that you and I might notice something he'd overlook." Miss Marple was at her meekest. If Griselda had been present, I knew she'd have been struggling to keep a straight face.

"Brilliant, Jane. You have such a sharp mind. Come, let's take a look."

Miss Hartnell led the way down the hall and through the kitchen to a tiny room I suspect may once have been a pantry. Between the single bed, the single wardrobe and the bedside chest of drawers there was scant room for the two women, so I stayed on the threshold. Miss Marple studied the room, taking in the clumsy watercolour of a woodland glade and the small mirror. She opened the top drawer of the chest and took out a bundle of picture postcards. All but the topmost were held in place by an elastic band.

She turned the bundle over. Even from where I was standing, I could see the cancelled stamp and the ill-educated hand. "From Bill," she said. "Presumably Bill Archer?"

Miss Hartnell stuck her chin out defensively. "I refused to allow Mary to speak to him on the telephone. Instead he sent her postcards confirming their meetings and passing on news."

"You read them?" I asked.

"One could scarcely avoid it." Miss Hartnell was frosty. "And they were delivered to my house, after all."

Miss Marple paid no heed to this exchange. Instead, she was frowning at the loose card. "Most interesting," she murmured, replacing them all in the drawer. There was apparently nothing else of interest in the drawers for she turned next to the wardrobe, going through all the pockets methodically. Apart from a couple of handkerchiefs, her search revealed nothing. "Thank you, my dear," she said, moving inexorably towards the door, causing Miss Hartnell and me to reverse clumsily. "And now for the sherry, if you please."

We returned to the sitting room. I'm not in the habit of drinking before lunch, but the prospect of that meal seemed to have disappeared from the agenda, so I took what was offered gladly. "Who would do such a thing?" Miss Hartnell said at regular intervals, between sips.

She seemed to require no answer, but Miss Marple did inquire as to whether there were any other men who came calling for Mary.

Our hostess snorted in derision. "Hardly, Jane. What Bill Archer saw in her was a mystery to me."

"Bill was hardly a great catch," I dared to point out.

Miss Marple gave me an indulgent look. "You are quite unworldly, vicar."

Before I could argue the point, the doorbell pealed. Miss Hartnell sighed deeply and got to her feet. "I shall have to find another maid now," she complained.

She returned with Inspector Slack bustling at her back. "Vicar! What are you doing here?"

"Conveying the tragic news of Mary's death to her employer," I said.

He glowered at Miss Marple. "And you, Miss Marple? I hope you're not interfering with police business again."

"I came to pass on my condolences," she said sharply. She swallowed the last of her sherry and got to her feet. "And now I will be on my way."

I was torn between waiting to hear whether Slack had made any progress and the desire to discover what had so interested Miss Marple about the loose postcard in Mary's drawer. But I could attempt to draw Miss Marple out at any time, whereas Slack was a very different proposition. So I followed him and Miss Hartnell to Mary's room. I glanced back at Miss Marple, who seemed to be gazing into the middle distance towards the bow window that gave on to the street.

On the threshold of Mary's room, Slack brusquely dismissed us both. "There's no need for you to be interfering with the scene of the crime. Don't you have parishioners to visit, vicar? Or did you manage to squeeze them all in this morning?"

I caught up with Miss Marple on the path to the gate where she had paused to admire the late bloomers in the herbaceous border. Once we were clear of Miss Hartnell's cottage, I ventured to ask what she had found so interesting in Mary's room. She smiled sweetly. "Dear vicar, little escapes you. What struck me was that the stamp on the card had not been franked."

"You mean, it hadn't come through the post?"

"It would appear not. It's my guess that Archer had written it but not posted it before he died and that Mary found it yesterday afternoon when she visited his cottage for the first time since his death."

"What did it say?"

She closed her eyes, as if summoning the image up before her. "Big surprise in the woods today, might be we can turn it to a profit." She blinked and smiled.

"And that's all? No clue as to what he meant?"

"One can speculate. I can think of at least three or four possibilities, can't you? But no, there was nothing more specific than that."

We had almost reached Miss Marple's gate when something dawned on me. "But if that was all it said, why would anyone feel sufficiently threatened by it to kill Mary?"

"That is the question, is it not?" And so saying, she turned in at her gate and left me none the wiser.

Griselda returned shortly before six, accompanied by an exhausted and fractious David. I ruffled his hair affectionately as Flora whisked him off to bath and bed. "How are your parents?" I asked.

"They grow duller and more narrow-minded with age," she sighed. It unnerves me somewhat when Griselda says such things; it's as if she forgets that I am significantly closer in age to her parents than to her. My perennial fear is that she will come to think the same of me.

She caught my moment's apprehension, read my mind and leaned in to kiss my cheek. "Don't be silly, Len. You know it's my mission in life to keep you for ever young." She yawned. "I'm worn out," she complained. "My father excites David so with his model soldiers and then my mother fills him with sweets and lemonade till the poor boy is beside himself. Once he gets to fever pitch, they can't cope and suddenly find something terribly urgent that must be done elsewhere and leave me to deal with the child." She made for the study door.

"Where are you going?" I demanded, more sharply than I'd intended.

Griselda stopped and stared at me. "To the kitchen, to heat up the pie Flora prepared for dinner."

"You can't. You mustn't. You can't go into the kitchen. It's . . . it's out of bounds."

My wife looked at me as if I was mad. "Why ever not? How can we have dinner if the kitchen is out of bounds?"

Before I could reply, Flora's scream answered for me. Griselda raced to the kitchen, where Flora stood wailing, her apron over her face. "The blood, the blood," she hiccupped.

Griselda looked at the puddle of congealed blood on the floor then looked at me. "There's blood all over the floor."

"I know. That's why I was trying to stop you going into the kitchen."

"Len—what on earth has been going on here?"

It took some time to explain what had happened; to persuade Flora not to hand in her notice on the spot; and then to calm David, who was near hysterical at the non-arrival of his bedtime milk and biscuits. The person apparently least affected was Griselda, whose ill-suppressed excitement was only augmented by the return of Dennis from the Much Benham police station at the end of his shift.

"Have you arrested anyone?" Griselda demanded.

Dennis threw himself into an armchair and shook his head. "No. Not likely to either. Slack is beside himself. We've not turned up a single clue or a single witness who saw either Mary or her killer enter or leave the vicarage."

"That's hard to credit," Griselda remarked. "Given the old pussies' network of observation posts."

"It must have happened at that point in the morning where they're all busy making sure their maids polish the lightbulbs," Dennis said.

"More to the point," I said, "it seems impossible to imagine who could have had a motive for murdering Mary."

"Except possibly Miss Hartnell," Griselda said. "But if she wanted never to have to face one of Mary's cremated roasts again, she could simply have given her notice."

"This is not a matter for facetiousness," I scolded. "Mary has been brutally despatched in the very kitchen she once counted home."

Griselda had the grace to look ashamed. "I'm sorry, Len, it's my way of coping."

Before I could accept her apology, Flora showed in Miss Marple. She fluttered on the threshold for a moment then stepped inside. "My dear Griselda, how terrible for you."

"More terrible for Mary," Griselda said. "And for poor Flora who's on her knees trying to scrub the bloodstain off the kitchen floor."

"Of course. And quite disturbing for you, Dennis. Your first murder." She paused and frowned. "At least, I suppose it is your first?"

Dennis straightened in his seat. "It brings home the importance of what we do."

"Indeed." Miss Marple turned back to Griselda and smiled apologetically. "I'm sorry to intrude at a time like this, but I wondered whether you were still planning to go into Much Benham tomorrow? Only, I had rather counted on being able to visit the chemist."

"Good heavens, yes. I don't think Mary would have expected us to go into formal mourning."

Her mission achieved, I showed Miss Marple out through the study. "By the way, what was it that caught your attention through the window at Miss Hartnell's?" I asked as I wrestled with the awkward bolt.

A momentary look of puzzlement was followed by the dawning of comprehension. "Oh, but vicar, it wasn't the window I was looking at." And without further ado, she was gone.

I stared after her, trying to imagine what she had noticed that had escaped both me and Inspector Slack. To one side of the window was a small mahogany bookshelf holding a dozen or so volumes. To the other, a console table with a shallow bowl containing a few calling cards. Surely even Miss Marple could not have managed to decipher any of those at that distance?

As was so often the case with my neighbour, Miss Marple had mystified me again.

Astonishingly, life at the vicarage appeared to have returned to normal by the next morning. Flora served breakfast, David recounted a somewhat confused version of a Rupert Bear story and Griselda complained about having to make jam for the next meeting of the Mothers' Union. I retired to my study to labour over the week's sermon and no police officers interrupted our day.

Over lunch, Griselda entertained me with her outing to Much Benham. "One curious thing," she said. "Miss Marple disappeared into Goodenough's for at least fifteen minutes and came out without a book. That's odd, don't you think? To visit a bookshop and come out empty-handed?"

"They're not always well-stocked. I tried to buy you the new Matilda Merchiston the other week and they didn't have it, even though she's a well-known local author. I was quite taken aback. It's not as if she's a shrinking violet. She always seems to be giving talks to one organisation or another and those pugs of hers must have chewed half the rugs in the shire. Perhaps Goodenough's didn't have what Miss Marple was looking for. Did you ask her?"

"She was very evasive." Griselda helped herself to a second serving of the chicken pie we should have had the previous evening. "Oh, by the way, in all the kerfuffle yesterday, I forgot to tell you I ran into Jeremy Jenner in Chipping Marlbury. He was delivering election leaflets to my parents. You know he's standing in the by-election there next week?"

I could hardly have failed to know. We'd recently had Jenner and his wife to dinner at the vicarage out of obligation and he had spoken of little else. He claimed his experience in business had led the Prime Minister to promise him a cabinet post if elected. "Do your parents think he'll win?"

Griselda pulled a face. "A Gloucester Old Spot with the right party rosette could take that seat."

As Flora came in with the apple crumble, Dennis slipped in behind her. "Greetings, family. I'm supposed to be checking whether there's any sign of Mary having left a note for the vicar, but I thought I might seize the moment and grab some pudding."

"On duty?" I said.

"He's entitled to a lunch break, surely, Len?" Griselda gave Dennis a conspiratorial wink.

I gave in and gestured to his usual chair. He'd started pouring the custard on to his heaped bowl when Flora returned with Miss Marple once more. She apologised profusely for interrupting us at table; Griselda told her she was always welcome, with a slight trace of grit in her voice; and Dennis carried on eating regardless.

"I know it's very rude of me, but when I saw Dennis go in at your gate, I thought I should take advantage of the opportunity to share my discovery."

"A discovery? How exciting," Griselda said. "Is it to do with the murder?"

"It's certainly to do with a murder. I happened to take a walk in Old Hall Woods before lunch and I came upon something I think the police ought to see. And you know, vicar, how hard it can be to capture Inspector Slack's attention." She twinkled at me, reminding me of previous experiences with the inspector. "So I thought I might direct our very own constable to what I'd found. Best to leave it in place, you see?"

Dennis regarded his half-full bowl with regret, wiped his mouth with his napkin and pushed his chair back with a sigh. "No time like the present." With a last look of regret, he led the way out of the room.

"Poor Dennis, missing out on his treat," Griselda said

"He doesn't know it yet, but his standing is about to rise," I told her. "Miss Marple is the last person I'd accuse of wasting police time."

"It was the book that set me on the right track," Miss Marple said, sipping a post-prandial cherry brandy in the vicarage sitting room later that evening. Events had proceeded at a remarkable rate after she'd shown her find to Dennis; two people were already under arrest.

"But you didn't *buy* a book," Griselda said.

"I didn't buy a book because Goodenough's had already sold the only copy they'd had. *Native Fungi of the Home Counties*. I'd spotted it in Miss Hartnell's much-neglected bookcase and it struck me as very odd, since she has never shown any interest in unregimented nature. It looked very new, and I noticed it had Goodenough's sticker on the base of the spine. It made me wonder."

"You wondered about Archer?"

She smiled. "Exactly, vicar. Archer had been living off the land all his life. The idea that he would pick poisonous mushrooms for a stew seemed absurd. But to add them to his stew after the fact would be easy, I thought. His cottage is not in the best repair, and it would take little effort to get inside via one of the windows. The card he wrote to Mary but failed to post clearly indicated a plan to blackmail someone. But to do that effectively, you must be sure your victim lacks the courage—or the desperation—to put a stop to you. And that's where Archer went fatally wrong."

"But who? And why?" Griselda demanded.

Ignoring her, Miss Marple continued. "One would have to be certain of the poison. So the killer had to consult a reliable guide. Once it had served its purpose, his accomplice secreted it in Miss Hartnell's bookcase. If any suspicion had arisen, placing it there would have pointed straight at Mary." Miss Marple pursed her lips. "Such wickedness."

"But who bought the book?" Griselda's voice was noticeably higher in pitch now.

"Jeremy Jenner."

I had no difficulty believing Jenner capable of almost anything in defence of his seat. But Griselda frowned. "He can't have killed Mary. We spoke to him in Chipping Marlbury yesterday morning. He was canvassing for the by-election. He couldn't possibly have been attacking Mary in the vicarage."

"No, dear, Jeremy Jenner is not the kind of man who does his own dirty work. That fell to his partner in crime. And, I venture, his partner in adultery. I imagine Archer came upon them in the woods and thought, as he said in his card to Mary, that there might be some profit in it. I imagine that Jenner and his lover decided murder was preferable to having the sword of Damocles dangling perpetually over their heads and so they hatched their plot. His accomplice poisoned the stew and they thought that was the end of it."

"Who was it?" Griselda demanded.

"And why kill Mary? Surely they were safe with Archer dead?"

Miss Marple shook her head sadly. "Mary was struggling to believe Archer could have made so stupid a mistake, and his message convinced her he'd been killed. She wondered whether she'd be able to convince the police to take her seriously. So she sought advice. From the wrong person. The woman she spoke to tried to persuade her not to go to the police, but Mary still had her doubts." She gave me a kind glance. "I believe she came here to ask your wise counsel, vicar. And that she was followed by her killer."

Griselda was literally on the edge of her seat. "Who was it?"

Miss Marple raised her index finger. "All in good time, Griselda. I believed I had unravelled the plot, but there was still no direct evidence. I wondered whether there might be something apparently insignificant at Archer's cottage that the police had missed. Something that might not seem meaningful to a man."

"Something a woman might leave behind?" I asked.

"Something a woman might not notice she'd left behind. Archer's pantry has a small window that's hidden from view by a *rosa rugosa*. And, on closer inspection, I noticed a strip of fine cotton muslin had snagged on the thorns. I recognised the distinctive fabric at once, for I'd been in Miss Politt's sewing room only a couple of weeks before when its owner happened to pick her dress up. It is, I expect, unique. Not least because it has a strip torn from its very full skirt. I pointed it out to Dennis, and Inspector Slack whirled into action. Now Jeremy Jenner and his mistress are occupying cells in Much Benham police station."

Griselda groaned. "Stop torturing me, Miss Marple. Tell us who murdered Mary."

"Matilda Merchiston."

We both stared open-mouthed at our neighbour. The local celebrity author, doyenne of the romantic novelists, famously devoted to her husband and her pugs—a cold-blooded killer? It was beyond belief. I almost said "There must be some mistake." And then remembered just in time who I was dealing with.

Miss Marple drained her glass and stood up. "This has been a shocking and tragic affair, dear vicar. Let us hope this will be the *final* murder at the vicarage."

Miss Marple Takes Manhattan

Alyssa Cole

Miss Marple wore a serviceable dark blue wool coat paired with a thick cream scarf. Her gloves, kid leather softened by decades of use, were folded neatly in her pocket, and her bare fingers flexed at their knobby knuckles in the frigid air. She was very far from the village of St. Mary Mead; she was, improbably, standing on a traffic island in the centre of Herald Square, Manhattan. A sea of New York's distinctive yellow taxi cabs roared by on either side of her, their exhaust matching the soft grey puffs of air that punctuated her exhalations of delight.

Despite being warned against such a circumstance by her nephew, Raymond West, and his wife, Joan, who had flown her out to the United States with them, she was standing alone.

She was supposed to be in her hotel room at the Martinique New York Hotel; in fact, she could see the window of her room from where she stood. Like most old women, Miss Marple was often *supposed to be* in one place, as if she were a candlestick or a sofa cushion; however, she had the oddest habit of ending up exactly *where she wanted to be* instead.

She assuaged her guilt with the fact that she wasn't alone, really; the idea was preposterous given all of the people bustling around her, just as in the films about this vibrant city. In fact, in addition to the people passing back and forth at every change of the traffic light, and sometimes in between, there was a bearded homeless fellow, and the pigeons he was feeding, sharing the pavement with her. He was good company, as he hadn't bothered her beyond a gruff hello, and a good host to boot, as he clearly saved only the best breadcrumbs for his feathered friends.

In truth, Miss Marple had initially resisted accompanying her nephew to America for the Broadway debut of an adaptation of one of his novels. He already did so much for her, kind boy that he was, and she'd reasoned that New York City was possibly a bit much for an old woman such as herself—one who encountered odd occurrences and mysteries wherever she went. Why, Manhattan was the crime capital of the world, wasn't it? Miss Marple had worried about what might go awry, and how she might be drawn into anything that did, but Raymond and Joan had promised a grand tour of the fancy American department stores, and curiosity had prevailed over practicality.

Yet, since they'd arrived in the city three days ago, Raymond and Joan had seemingly forgotten the most important stops on the proposed itinerary, as their excursions led everywhere but to a household goods department—St. Patrick's Cathedral and the top of the Empire State building were fine indeed, but one couldn't purchase fine linen or an exquisitely crafted tea service at either location. Dinners had been taken at posh restaurants with trendy people who talked *at* her as if she was a drooping old spaniel whose ears must be scratched every now and again to check for signs of life. Worse, Raymond was convinced that she would come to harm if she ventured out by herself, so her choice had been either to tag along on their adventures or to stay in the hotel suite. She had travelled through locales more dangerous than an American shopping district, but she kept her thoughts on that to herself; Raymond only worried because he cared for her after all, and she couldn't begrudge him that.

That morning, when she'd raised the matter of the department store, Raymond had chided her for clinging to the familiar as, to his mind, the bric-a-brac in America was the same as that back home, and just as boring. Then he'd invited her to the Metropolitan Museum of Art, where the Mona Lisa was on loan. Of course, Joan being an artist, they'd already seen the piece several times at its home in the Louvre, but apparently it was different to her own desire to peruse china patterns and tea towels, despite the painting having markedly less functional value.

Miss Marple had politely declined, implying that it might be a good idea that she rest before the play's debut that night. Truth be told, she'd had her fill of the Italian masters when studying in Italy as a young woman, and she didn't consider a museum packed with sweaty people vying for a glance at a glorified postage stamp the height of excitement. After Raymond and Joan had left, she'd perched primly on the velvet-clad chaise longue in the parlour of their suite, musing that the Martinique was nothing at all like the traditional hotels of her youth—it was no Bertram's, for instance. The Renaissance style was gaudy, worse for wear if one had a keen eye for a well-kept home, and, overall, gave her a bit of a headache. She wasn't fond of most things French, apart from their porcelain and their pastries, and this American iteration of Frenchness was even less endearing.

While her eyesight wasn't what it used to be in her hawk-eyed youth, it was still quite good and had been drawn again and again to the room's large window, where the signs for Gimbels and Macy's had beckoned. When she'd looked down at the street below, she'd seen a stream of customers passing from the incivility of winter weather and into the warmth behind the doors of the grand department stores, looking alternately eager to browse or, as they passed out again, delighted with their purchases. The windows of the stores were dressed meticulously, beautiful displays that seemed to show the changing of seasons with a transition from snow-frosted glass into a riot of paper crocuses and daffodils.

Eventually, Miss Marple had placed her knitting aside and announced, "After some reflection, I don't believe I have a dress appropriate for tonight," as if trying to convince the gauche décor around her that anyone cared what an old spinster wore while attending the technical rehearsal of a Broadway show. Then she'd stood gingerly, nodding along to the symphony of joint cracks and pops that come from a life of quiet but continuous adventure. "They don't think leaving the hotel is safe, but the stores are just across the street.

After all, I can't embarrass dear Raymond by showing up looking like some dowdy relic of the past. I should at the very least look like a *present-day* dowd."

With a pleasing course of action thus decided, she'd gathered her coat, gloves and scarf. An hour had now gone by since she'd skulked out, glancing about as if Raymond and Joan might appear and drag her back to the room like a naughty child, and yet she still hadn't gone into any of the shops.

Miss Marple wasn't a woman who impressed easily, as a rule, and she should have found Manhattan a filthy and overcrowded cesspool compared to the simple charms of St. Mary Mead—which was still relatively quaint even with the arrival of the Development People—but impressed she was. There was an energy and vitality to the city that seemed to match the same quality that vibrated in her old bones and always had. And there was so much to *observe*.

A taxi driver lowered his window and shouted at a cyclist who was darting through the intersection against the traffic light, uttering a nasal string of expletives that reddened Miss Marple's cheeks as much as the cold. A well-dressed businessman kindly stuffed a wad of bills into the homeless man's paper coffee cup with a tip of his hat. A couple walked hand in hand across the pedestrian crossing, past the fracas, the woman staring down at a ring on her hand with tears in her eyes and the man looking at her with pride. She thought they very much resembled Mr. and Mrs. Brade, the Montserratian musician couple Raymond had introduced her to, but Raymond had told her she mustn't tell coloured people they resembled one another, for some odd reason. Another incomprehensible modern change.

After absorbing the sights, sounds and smells of the city a moment longer, she finally decided to take leave of the traffic island and make her way inside the store. It was at this moment that she almost made a fatal error that would have proved Raymond's fears well founded—despite having watched the flow of traffic for so long, she looked the wrong way when stepping into the street and didn't see an errant bicyclist barrelling toward her. She was pulled back just in time by the homeless man who'd been feeding the birds—in addition to pigeons, he apparently also looked over old British hens.

"Thank you," she said, and received a rough sound in return.

Having made it safely inside of Gimbels at last, she promptly decided that she didn't need a new dress after all, but since she had taken the trouble to get to the store, she'd have a look around. She rode the wooden escalator up to the household goods section and was met with the beckoning gleam of porcelain and familiar scent of silver polish—a much more agreeable olfactory experience than the perfume the sales girls had sprayed furiously in her direction as she'd entered the department store. It was a good thing her reflexes hadn't entirely quit her, or she'd have smelled like a "sexy, youthful bouquet" when she returned to the hotel, which would have been sure to attract questions from Raymond and Joan.

She made a slow circuit around the displays of Wedgwood and Noritake, admiring some pieces and looking with disdain upon others. The perusal wasn't quite as enjoyable as back in England, not so much because of the quality of merchandise but what was missing—nostalgia. She'd thought she enjoyed department stores by their very nature, but this place had no fond memories of her younger years or familiar markers of home, even if it sold the same brands. It was quite shocking to discover she possessed such a streak of sentimentality—she averted her inward gaze, not wanting to be rude to herself during such an unseemly show of emotion.

A bit disappointed with the excursion she'd built up in her mind having been a bust, she wandered down to the store's discount basement, a new experience for her that had the potential to make the trip worthwhile. Although it was novel, to be certain, she found nothing she'd bother transporting back across the Atlantic. Fifteen minutes later, she was standing half-heartedly stroking some dreadfully shiny tablecloth as she built up the fortitude to go back out into the cold, and was almost relieved when it was snatched from between her fingers.

"Oh, this is *it*!" a fire-haired woman, wearing a lipstick of an even deeper red, said in a voice that gave no indication of knowing it wasn't being used inside of a stable. "This is it, Davey!"

"Are you kiddin' or what? It's a tablecloth, Serena," the man beside her said in a low, frustrated voice. He had a thick moustache and thicker brows that rendered him surprisingly handsome; Miss Marple took an instant dislike to him. She didn't tolerate handsome men, at all. Rarely had she met one that wasn't up to no good, though usually their activities veered toward mischief that didn't require police intervention.

"So what if it is?" the woman held up the tablecloth as if it were a fine tapestry. "I refuse to wear that hideous dress Carl insisted on, just to make a fool of me. If Estelle can pin and drape it, this'll be perfect for the final scene."

"You think she'll defy Mr. High-and-Mighty?" Davey asked.

Serena rolled her eyes. "She'll love it. She told me

he always *accidentally* rubs against her when she's dressing him, and she hates the dress he chose too. He thinks he can bully me out of this production, but I've held on this long, and I'll win in the end. I refuse to step on stage looking like, well—like her!"

Miss Marple looked up into the woman's face after some animal instinct alerted her that she'd been gestured at. The woman had slight pouches of skin beneath her wide brown eyes, and deep laugh lines bracketing her mouth. She was a young thing, not a day over fifty, and Miss Marple thought she was gloriously beautiful. Serena had the air of someone who thought mostly of themselves, but still paid enough attention to her surroundings to notice an old woman who, indeed, might have been mistaken for a pair of drab curtains by less observant passers-by and not given a second thought.

"Wouldn't want that," Miss Marple said with a twinkle, knowing full well what she looked like and not at all bothered by it. "I should say that I doubt any dress could make you look as unremarkable as me. I have decades of experience at it, young lady."

"You're British!" Serena crowed, the skin at the corners of her eyes crinkling in delight, and when she spoke again, her accent had changed from American drama queen to East End urchin. "I'ms an actress, I am. Nothing I loves more than an accent, 'cept a spot o' tea."

The store was near the theatre district, of course, and now Miss Marple could imagine set dressers and stage designers popping in to grab last-minute items or unconventional additions. How splendid.

"You're very good," Miss Marple replied carefully, when she realised Serena was waiting for her assessment. The accent was *not* good, but Miss Marple doubted she herself could pull off a convincing American accent and thus applauded the effort if not the result. She gestured toward the tablecloth. "And you're going to wear this as a theatrical costume? I do think it's very . . . eye catching."

"See?" the fire-haired woman said, shooting a look at Davey before turning back to Miss Marple. "The dress that *creep* made them give me looks like a tablecloth covered in mud—because he wants me to *feel* like a tablecloth covered in mud. He's mad he didn't get a young ingénue as a co-star, one who'd bat her lashes at him and make him feel like something more than a washed-up hack. It'll be a gas to use a *real* tablecloth to show him that he can't shove me out of the spotlight!"

"Oh! Yes. Quite," Miss Marple said. "I do love such ironies."

Serena turned, fanning the cloth dramatically behind her as if it were a fine cape—her physical acting was better than her accent, for in that moment, it *became* a fine cape, flowing majestically. She glanced back at Miss Marple and inclined her head, regally, then turned and walked towards the register of the discount department.

Davey—assistant, lover, or both—trotted behind her, jester to a queen.

"And I suppose I'm gonna pay for this?" he muttered.

Miss Marple smiled. Going to Gimbels hadn't been all for nothing. She'd met someone interesting, and wasn't that what she lived for? The myriad ways you might cross paths with another human? A slight chill went down her spine at that thought; she hoped for the fire-haired woman's sake that they didn't cross paths again. It was during a second meeting with Miss Marple in which other people didn't fare very well.

She ventured out into the cold and back to the hotel, where she found Raymond assailing the doorman for letting a frail, helpless and easily confused old woman wander out into the mean streets of New York City by herself. She wondered who the helpless old woman was for a moment, and then realised it was her.

"Tourists usually come to Manhattan to do just that, sir," the doorman said. "It would be bad for business if I tried to stop every old broad that left the place—it's a hotel, not a prison."

"Well maybe you should add a prison wing!" Raymond retorted. "You Americans are thrilled with the concept, shouldn't be too difficult to implement."

"I'm all right, Raymond," she said, grabbing his arm. He looked down at her with his face as pink and sweaty as when he'd thrown tantrums over not having enough sugar in his tea as a boy. He had always been excitable, her dear nephew.

"There you are, ma'am, safe and sound," the doorman said with a nod, and pulled the door open, ushering them both into the lobby. "Have a good afternoon."

"I thought you were lying in a gutter somewhere!" Raymond exclaimed.

"The sewer system here wouldn't allow for that," she said, then looked back at the doorman. "He's just nervous about tonight," she explained kindly, "we're going to a rehearsal that he's quite anxious about. Don't mind him. And the gutters here are quite the feats of city planning, he meant them no disrespect."

After a tense elevator ride, where Raymond expounded on the many calamities that might have befallen her—including being hit by a bicycle—they reached their suite, where Joan soothed her fretful husband and Miss Marple adjusted her ruffled feathers.

"Well, everything is fine now, isn't it?" Joan asked, handing Raymond a drink to calm his nerves. "We'll rest and then get ready for tonight. They're sending a car to bring us to the rehearsal. I suppose we could walk over to the theatre district, since we're already on Broadway, but these streets are frightfully long—I doubt you and I would make it to Times Square without keeling over first, Aunt Jane."

"If one is going to keel over anywhere, Broadway would be the proper place to do it—it would all be very dramatic," Miss Marple mused, then recalled something. "Are you quite sure about the location of the theatre? I asked that nice young fellow at the door about the address earlier, and he said—"

"The car has already been arranged by one of the actors as a welcome gift for Raymond, Aunt Jane. Please don't worry about a thing; you've been through enough today."

"Why, I haven't been through anything at all," she said, with just a bit of peevish bristle in her tone.

"Let's just rest," Joan said, rubbing her hands reassuringly over Miss Marple's shoulders as she helped her out of her coat. "It's going to be an exciting and exhausting evening. If you think our artist friends are unconventional, these Broadway people are mad—who knows what we'll get into?"

Miss Marple got another one of those brief chills down her spine and hoped it was from the cold, though a woman of her age knew intuition was far more reliable than hope.

"You're quite right," she said. "I do need to rest up. One never knows what the night will bring."

Over the course of his illustrious writing career, Raymond West had come to understand how creative endeavours might fall short of their initially proposed scope. However, as he took in the decrepit theatre he'd been deposited in front of—located on a lower Manhattan street that looked like something out of the pulp novels he so disdained—he couldn't help but feel that this was quite beyond the average idea-to-completion miscalculation.

When Raymond's most popular novel, *Sordid and Unpleasant*, had been licensed for theatrical adaptation "across the pond," he'd taken the news as an affirmation of his under-appreciated genius. That it was being produced by theatre legend G. Gregory Stapleton, who'd snagged the infamous Carl DeVoe as the male lead, had, to his mind, been a harbinger of his long-awaited ascension from "successful English writer" to "international literary giant."

His aunt had often asked in her naive way whether his novels would ever be adapted for the West End, but who needed the Royal Court when his characters were about to surge up Broadway and make a splash on the Great White Way? When he'd regaled her with the news of the production, received via his agent, she'd congratulated him and then hesitated.

"This Stapleton fellow. His name does seem familiar, doesn't it? And it's being adapted and directed by a Ms. Prince, is it? Are you certain this is all on the level? I'm certain I've heard those names before . . ."

"Why should *you* have heard of them, Aunt Jane?" Raymond had asked, amused that a spinster who rarely left her small English village might think herself familiar with movers and shakers of the American theatrical variety. "Maybe you're mixing them up with other people. Perhaps Mr. Stimpleton, the butcher? And Mrs. Price, the new hairdresser over in the Development?"

"I'm probably mistaken, dear. You're right," Miss Marple had said, and taken up her knitting, squinting at her work to avoid dropping a stitch, which happened more often these days.

It was because of things like that—dropping stitches

and walking more slowly and generally being a woman in the winter of her life—that Raymond had convinced her to take leave of St. Mary Mead and travel by plane from London to New York City. He'd wanted to make sure that Aunt Jane lived the remainder of her years to their fullest, but now he wondered if he hadn't actually brought her closer to an untimely demise.

"I believe there's been a misunderstanding," Raymond protested, reflexively tamping down his agitation—it was a skill he'd honed over many years of dealing with writer's blocks, rejections and eviscerating reviews.

His statement was directed at Michael, the driver who'd been sent to fetch them from the hotel to the theatre, but Raymond's gaze was fixed on the marquee sign above him. It was lopsided and rusty, fashioned from scavenged metal and affixed to the front of what had clearly once been a factory, though quite a nice one, to be fair. The street was lined with these looming buildings of cast-iron design—the entire neighbourhood was one that had seemingly gone to rust. The few bulbs around the borders of the marquee were burnt out—some had been shattered, the spiky remnants cradling wisps of filament. The name of the show, *SORDID*, which had been painted in slapdash red, seemed more like a descriptor of their environs than anything else.

"Misunderstanding indeed," Joan said, clutching his arm and looking suspiciously at a man vomiting into the gutter a few feet away from them. While they wore simple but elegant evening wear befitting a meet-and-greet at the theatre, the sallow, retching man wore a paint-spattered apron over denims—sans shirt—and matching paint-spattered boots. A couple walked past them, the woman looking like an inverted-mirror version of Jackie Kennedy, with her high bouffant and a minidress paired with pearls.

"This can't be the right theatre," Joan said. "This isn't even the right neighbourhood. Perhaps it's some kind of joke? American humour can be so crass and perplexing."

Michael, a tall, pale man with the hunched shoulders often seen in the wards of canine humane societies, blinked in their general direction. When he spoke, it was with an accent much like a gangster out of a film, a voice that had seemed quite silly to Raymond upon their introduction but which now seemed somewhat menacing. "I was told to bring you here, to the theatre, and here to the theatre is where I brought you. I did what I was told. I always do what I'm told."

Joan looked at him askance.

"Run the errands, Michael. Clean the floors, Michael. Work the lights, Michael. See about Serena, Michael." The man looked tormented, and Joan shuffled a step away from him.

Raymond was half-listening. Being a writer, he was always ready to fabricate a story that might explain situations both marvellous and unsatisfactory, and so he was doing just that.

"Are you certain?" he ventured, tone ingratiating. New Yorkers had a bit of a feral quality to them, in his experience, and were likely to lash out at the slightest provocation—with sharp wit, scathing reviews, or, judging from the cheap shine of Michael's ill-fitting suit, perhaps something a bit more dangerous. "Perhaps you took a wrong turn, or we've entered some kind of alternate dimension? I do know the American space agency gets up to all sorts of things," he joked.

Michael frowned at him.

Joan gasped at another heave from the man being sick, her elbow jabbing into Raymond's side. "Look, I'm no expert on New York, but this is most certainly *not* Broadway," she said. "You expect me to believe that *this* is the home of *Guys and Dolls* and *My Fair Lady*? More like *Guys and Degenerates* and *My Fair Lush*."

"West Broadway," Miss Marple said, and Raymond jumped, having almost forgotten that his aunt was on his other side. His aunt—elderly and used to a sedate life, not the hustle and bustle of the Big Apple or the vice found in its wormier locales. This was supposed to be a stimulating but safe trip for the old lady, but he'd dragged her into much more dangerous territory than anticipated. A group of rough-looking young people approached from the end of the street in a bright, loud cluster like a swarm of post-modern bees.

"Aunt Jane," said Raymond, taking her by the arm with his free hand, "I'll sort this business out later. We must get you back to the hotel and away from these vagrants. I'm ever so sorry about this."

"Now, now, dear," replied Miss Marple, smiling up at her rattled nephew and resisting his pulling. "There are no vagrants about—well, except for the one."

Raymond glanced at the man who had been vomiting, who was now standing upright, laughing and wiping his arm over the back of his mouth as he fell in with the ruffians. One of them pulled a bandana from his pocket and tossed it to the drunk, who didn't seem quite so drunk any more.

"You mustn't apologise about these kinds of mix-ups," Miss Marple continued. Her gaze went unfocused and the hint of a smile nudged at the wrinkles around her mouth. "It's quite humorous, in a way, how perceptions can change things. It reminds me of when Mr. Smith voted "nay" at the meeting about renovating the vicarage, and Mr. Naysmith voted "yea," yet when the votes were tallied, everyone believed Mr. Naysmith had voted against it."

Joan West leaned forward, past her husband, to look at Miss Marple. "Are you very tired, Aunt Jane? Raymond, let's get her back to the hotel. The jetlag must be muddling her thoughts."

"West Broadway," Miss Marple said again, more firmly, looking around the street lined with old factories that had fallen on hard times and been converted by artists and bohemians. She could see a certain beauty in these brick buildings and their large glass windows; there was a certain continental European appeal to them. Even the burnt-out craters that they'd passed during their drive might have been the result of the Blitz, though an arsonist high on paint fumes was more likely in this neighbourhood.

She wasn't sure why Joan was so upset—while their setting was a bit déclassé, they were clearly in some kind of artists' quarter and Joan herself was an artist. However, their surroundings made her look more kindly on the Development that had sprung up in St. Mary Mead; the people who lived there at least wore shirts when venturing out of doors and hid their drunken sick in the privacy of their home, as was respectable.

"Oh!" Raymond grimaced as his aunt's nonsensical

words found meaning for him. "West Broadway. Not Raymond West *on* Broadway. I'd assumed there was some sort of typo . . ."

"You can't be serious," Joan cried in disbelief. "Raymond, I told you to let me handle the correspondence, but, no, of course you had to—"

Just then, a door creaked open and a middle-aged black woman, wearing a long, loose-fitting patterned dress, stepped through it. Her hair was cut short in a style not very dissimilar from Miss Marple's, though the woman had no need of a permanent to give her curls.

"Mr. West and family?" she asked, in an accent that Miss Marple found delightful—she sounded quite like a take-no-nonsense heroine from an American film. In fact, Miss Marple was immediately aware that this particular American actually *didn't* take any nonsense.

"Might you be the playwright and director, Ms. Prince?" she asked, savouring the momentary surprise that crossed the woman's face.

"Aunt Jane?" Raymond asked tentatively, pulling her aside, as if worried she might say something offensive. "Remember what I told you—"

"No, I'm quite sure it's her. I knew her name sounded familiar—during the Marina Gregg situation I found myself studying magazines about American celebrities, and there were articles about her," Miss Marple continued, then glanced at Raymond and lowered her tone a bit further. "Ms. Prince was being prevented from doing her job, by people who dislike those of her background. You see, my dear, she's a—"

"Aunt Jane!" Raymond exclaimed.

"—a communist," said Miss Marple, looking up at Raymond with worry. "Are you all right? Perhaps it's you who should return to the hotel?"

Raymond ran a hand over his face, hand settling over his mouth as he shook his head. He muttered something, but Miss Marple's hearing was not as good as her eyesight.

"Come on in," Ms. Prince offered. "The rehearsal is about to begin, and I'm so thrilled the writer himself is here to see how we've done. I hope I've been able to capture the unique brilliance of your novel."

Raymond's spirits revived at that, and they all followed her inside.

As they entered the theatre, Miss Marple took the time to appreciate the rustic American architecture— bare brick walls with the occasional metal hook embedded, a remnant from its past existence as a factory. The lights overhead flickered in the high ceilings, and the huge windows let in the dim light from the streetlamps. Rows of seats had been installed on the flat surface of what had once been the shop floor, and a stage with minimalist set dressing had been constructed at the front of the large room.

It had likely not been a munitions factory during the war; from what Miss Marple could tell, perhaps a textile plant. There was a possibility it had produced uniforms, and then garments for everyday use. That was one kind of art, mechanized as it had become, and now the space was being used for another art, one that rejected the notion of assembly-line production.

All remnants of eras past must evolve and adapt, or crumble; even Miss Marple herself. She knew that the younger people around her assumed she had already crumbled, and it did appeal to her, as it would be so much easier than changing. But she was self-aware: Miss Marple understood that she wasn't the crumbling type. She would have to go eventually, as all people do, but she hoped it would be in a blaze of glory, like the burnt-out buildings they'd passed.

"Your aunt is quite right, by the way," Junie Prince said, as she pushed aside a bundle of electrical cords hanging from the wall. "In fact, my political leanings are why your play is being put on here instead of on Broadway. Have you heard of the House Committee on Un-American Activities?"

Raymond stepped over a dubious puddle on the

cement floor, and attempted to lighten the moment. "I have, but in discussions with friends over what could get us called up on charges of being unBritish. Mostly tea-related offences, as one might imagine."

Ms. Prince laughed and then turned to face them as they manoeuvred down the centre aisle. The high-ceilinged warehouse floor wasn't the kind of theatre Miss Marple was used to, but it did remind her of adventures she'd had outside of St. Mary Mead. She remembered how earlier, in the department store, she hadn't enjoyed it because it had been similar but not the same as the stores back home; this theatre reminded her that sometimes there was a thrill in the unknown as well.

"Well, apparently addressing racial inequality in one's work is un-American, so I was hauled before the committee."

Raymond cleared his throat.

"I was quite shocked to read what had happened to you," Miss Marple said, stepping over one of the many lengths of electrical wiring snaking around their feet. "Have you considered coming to England to work? Such a thing would never happen there. We don't have racial inequality, and, if we did, we'd never be so blatant with it. It'd be terribly improper. You'd at least be *quietly* repressed, instead of hauled before cameras and all of that hullabaloo."

Junie Prince gave her a look that managed to convey "I'm quite all right, thank you," and then continued with what she was saying.

"I was found innocent, but after that, the project that was supposed to premiere on Broadway was scrapped, and no one would touch me with a ten-foot pole. My friend Mr. Stapleton was already blacklisted, and he'd purchased this old building after seeing artists were moving into the area. It's been a warehouse and a factory and something not spoken of in front of our elders, but he's now converted it into a theatre where we persona non grata can still ply our craft. We chose your play as our first production because of its powerful meditation on injustice."

Raymond's shoulders dropped back in pride. "Injustice! Meditation! Yes, that's exactly what I was aiming for when writing; it's lovely to meet people who truly understand the deeper meaning of my work."

"Isn't this the book you wrote to spite that reviewer who kept calling your prose bloviated nonsense?" Joan whispered.

Raymond gave her a wounded glance. "Is being unappreciated not injustice?"

"Junie! Junie!" a shrill voice called out from behind the stage's curtain. "He's at it again. Please, can't you make him stop?"

The corners of Ms. Prince's mouth turned down as she glanced at the source of the noise. "What's happened now, Serena?"

From one side of the stage, a woman wearing a drab grey dress stormed out. Her hair was dark brown, or one would have thought so if you didn't note the red whisps poking out from her slightly askew wig. In her hands, she held a shredded bundle of fabric in a pattern that was familiar to Miss Marple.

Miss Marple clutched her hands together. "Oh dear."

"He ruined it! I know it was him!" The actress shook the remnants of what had once been a cheap tablecloth with an eye-catching pattern. "I just wanted this *one thing*, but no, everything has to be done Carl's way. It doesn't matter that we've caved to almost every one of his ridiculous peccadillos, he wants *all* of them catered to."

Junie Prince kept her expression neutral as she repeated, "What's happened now, Serena?"

"You know the dress I showed you? The one that I said was a better reflection of Trudy's character as I embodied her, instead of how *Carl* perceived Trudy?" She jerked a thumb back over her shoulder at the curtain behind her. "He saw me getting it fitted and said I couldn't change things last minute, because his precious little ego wouldn't be able to tolerate it. His acting ability is disturbed by a new dress, but *he's* the stoic headliner and *I'm* the washed-up diva?"

At that instant a clean-shaven grey-haired man walked out on to the stage behind her. He walked calmly, every bit the eye to Serena's storm. His expression was slightly bewildered, his hands in his pockets and slightly hunched shoulders conveying that he hated this conflict and that everyone was having to witness it.

He was handsome in the way of movie stars, with a shining inner charisma that both attracted and repelled, like a lighthouse beacon. Miss Marple gave a polite sniff of disdain.

"Serena, I simply said that it would throw me off to see you in something so different from what you've been wearing in dress rehearsals." He turned to Junie Prince, "And we've already checked the lighting—that'd have to be adjusted again, for some whim of hers. The point of dress rehearsals is for us to get habituated, isn't it?" He paused, very much like a barrister who's just asked a crucial question to a jury, then looked back at Serena. "Yes, I asked that you not make an impulsive and unnecessary change. No, I didn't shred your dress."

"They don't look at all how I envisioned William and Trudy while writing the book," Raymond whispered to Joan. "He's much too short and she's much too—"

"What?" Joan asked archly.

Raymond wiped at his brow nervously and fell silent.

"If it wasn't you, then who was it? The only other person who knew besides you was Estelle, and she wouldn't rip up her own work given how little she's paid." Serena's voice was shrill; it reminded Miss Marple of a very small dog that has quietly growled as it was prodded by every guest at a party, and is then chastised when it finally breaks into a flurry of yipping barks. "Carl wouldn't have known about the change at all if he hadn't barged into the dressing area because he thought my understudy, who might I add is twenty-five years younger than him, was getting changed in there!"

Carl's expression altered the tiniest bit, Miss Marple thought. There was a slight strain at the eyes—perhaps caused by tensing of his jaw—and his gaze sharpened into an ice pick. It was the expression a certain kind of man got when he encountered a woman too coldly proud to be affected by the heat he passed off as charm, but which was more akin to brimstone. It was a look that said, "If you won't melt, I'll shatter you."

"Lying is unbecoming, Serena. A woman your age should try to keep one of the few remaining assets she's got to recommend her."

"Remaining assets? Oh, is that supposed to hurt my feelings?" Serena held a hand to her mouth and, instead of crying, began to slowly and methodically laugh. It was a laugh designed to act like salt on a snail, and even Miss Marple found herself shrinking from it. "You think a crack like that is hurtful, but only because you're old and afraid of getting older. Of being an impotent, withered little man—I hate to break it to you, Carl, honey, but dipping your limp carrot into the dressing of any twenty-something who'll entertain you doesn't stop that."

"You entertained that carrot quite happily when *you* were twenty-something," Carl sneered. "Or are you the only pretty young thing allowed to sleep her way on to the stage?"

Serena sucked in a breath and sent a desperate, plaintive gaze toward Junie Prince, her face suddenly pale as she turned towards the small audience watching the theatrics play out, even though rehearsal hadn't even started. "He's lying. I never did anything like that . . . I—"

"I'll take care of this, Serena. Don't worry." Junie Prince looked unfazed, but her hands had tightened into fists.

"Please do! Or I will." Serena sent Carl a dark look as she flounced past him, and at the last moment, tossed the ribbons of fabric into his face. He grabbed them in a reflexive rage, seething as she walked away from him, and then strode after her.

Junie looked down at Miss Marple. "In case you ever got the idea that being a director is glamorous, we also get babysitting duty when co-stars don't get along. And tantrum duties when one actor seems set on making everything harder than it has to be."

"At least you don't have to change nappies," Miss Marple said. "I had to change Raymond's when he was a wee one, and, I can tell you, it wasn't at all pleasant. I wondered if he didn't have some kind of ailment of the intestine."

Junie Prince broke into a peal of laughter, and at the same time Raymond expostulated "Aunt Jane!" once again. Perhaps the American penchant for loudness was catching, because he'd been shouting her name all day. His face was crimson, and for no reason at all too; when they got back to the hotel, she'd suggest he see a doctor before they boarded the plane back to England.

Ms. Prince hopped up on to the stage, dusting her hands as she followed her two wayward leads.

"Well, they've certainly got the character dynamics down pat," Raymond said, and then gave a sort of nervous chuckle. He looked around the shabby theatre and heaved a deep sigh. "This will make for quite the dinner-party story one day, don't you think? I'm tempted to say we should all just stretch the truth and say it was a smashing success that lit up Broadway, but I invited all my American friends to opening night so—"

Two things then happened at almost the same time—the electricity surged in a sharp stab of light, then went dark, and a chilling scream, straight out of a fifties monster film, filled the entire theatre from floor to rafters. The fading echoes of the terrifying sound still lingered as the lights slowly blinked back on.

"What happened?" Joan cried out.

Miss Marple stayed quiet, determined to go see what could be divined from the unpleasant situation that surely awaited them.

Michael, the driver, came tearing out from behind the curtain, shouting, "Someone's been injured! There's no phone here; I'm going to call the police at the bar down the street!"

Raymond stood frozen for a moment longer, then seemed to come back to himself. He began making his way up the stairs alongside the stage, with Joan and Miss Marple lagging behind him at a slower pace.

Joan's hands shook as she held Miss Marple's arm at the elbow and the wrist, guiding her on to the stage. "What do you think—"

"Murder, dear," Miss Marple pronounced, hating

that bit of herself that was already anticipating figuring out the hows and the whys. It was all a bit morbid but . . . some people knew things, and Miss Marple knew murder. There was no more point in being upset about it than a sparrow being sad that it knew how to build a nest.

They made their way into the chaotic backstage space, a labyrinth partitioned by strips of fabric. All kinds of odd items lay about on the floor, ready to trip one up. The ever-present loops of electrical wire, of course, plus various sorts of tools that might be needed at a moment's notice in set changes. Props too: a walking stick, a tea kettle, and what appeared to be a rubber chicken.

Now they passed between racks of clothing—the dressing room, perhaps—drawing closer to the source of the scream. Miss Marple steeled herself.

"Oh my! The show cannot go on, then," Raymond cried out from somewhere just ahead of them, the words followed by a trilling laugh that she had only ever heard when he'd had a fright.

They passed through the next partition to find Serena standing with her face covered by her hands and Junie Prince sporting an expression of resigned horror. They were flanked on either side by a young black woman holding a pair of sewing shears and a

Puerto Rican woman with full stage make-up—Estelle the set dresser and the unnamed young understudy, Miss Marple supposed.

Carl lay face down on the floor, unmoving.

Junie shook her head.

"This . . . is . . . exactly the last thing this production needs." She looked hard at Serena and, when she spoke again, her question was impressively direct. "Did you kill him? If so, please make it known before the police get here. I've already been falsely accused of a crime once, and I'd rather not have another go at it for murder."

"Attempted murder," Miss Marple corrected. "That man isn't dead."

Indeed, if one looked very closely, Carl DeVoe's back was slowly rising and falling.

"Not yet at least," Raymond said, approaching the body.

None of the people who actually worked with Carl moved toward him.

"Like the Naysmith incident in more ways than one," Miss Marple murmured, though no one paid attention.

"It was an accident!" Serena said. "I came into my dressing room to get away from him! I wanted to calm down and try to get ready for the final rehearsal, but he stormed in after me. He stepped on one of the wires and—"

She mimicked, with what Miss Marple assumed was great accuracy, a man with a quantity of electricity coursing through his body.

"And then you all came running in," she finished.

Miss Marple glanced at Carl's feet—he was clad only in thin house slippers, which were wet. There was a puddle beside him, and a cord that had frayed through. She wasn't entirely certain the puddle had been there before the electrocution or that the cord had frayed naturally; she'd leave the former detail to someone else to verify.

"And why didn't *you* step on the wire?" Junie Prince asked. "And before you get upset, I'm asking because the police will be here soon and they're gonna want to know too."

Serena pulled the wig off in frustration and tossed it across the space. Then she sighed and headed after it, the poise in her steps making it appear that she almost floated.

"How is it that I have to answer for Carl's careless-ness on top of everything else? Will I end up in jail because I'm not some actor with his head so far up his own rear end that he doesn't pay attention to his surroundings?" she bit out over her shoulder, expertly navigating the loose wires and various detritus on the floor as if it was a game of elastics while barely looking down.

"Dancers," Miss Marple ventured, "do seem to have a kind of sixth sense in their feet. I remember a young woman I met after the war; she said that because of her dancer's reflexes she had never once tripped over a pile of rubble while working the tea canteens."

Serena picked up the wig and moved towards Miss Marple, glancing down at the old woman gratefully before hanging the distressed brunette locks on a hook next to various other faux hair pieces.

"I have no idea what most of that means, but yes—I've trained for years to be able to naturally avoid anything that I might trip over while onstage. I do it while dancing forward, dancing backwards, and even while trying to evade a pest of a co-star."

Junie sighed. "I believe you. You would have throttled him, if anything, and not stopped until the light left his eyes. You're thorough, not someone who leaves things up to chance."

Serena smiled at the compliment. "Thank you, Junie. Whatever else happens, it's been lovely working with someone who sees the best in me."

Junie sighed, and turned to the dresser and understudy. "And what about you two? Estelle, those scissors could fray up some wire nice and easy."

Estelle snorted. "Junie, you would have to be out of your mind to think I'd risk my life trying to take out either of these two." She jerked her chin toward Carl's prone body and then Serena.

Serena made a small sound of realisation. "Me?"

Estelle's expression softened. "This is your changing area. If that little trap was meant to take anyone out, it was you."

All eyes turned toward the understudy. The young woman was dark-haired, with freckles smudged across the light brown skin of her cheeks. Miss Marple hoped it wasn't this girl, who probably felt all grown up but whose life was just beginning. It was almost worse than seeing someone die, seeing a young person throw their future away for murder when there was almost always some other solution.

Serena's voice was genuinely hurt for the first time that evening. "Vera . . ."

"It wasn't me," Vera said, her large brown eyes filling with reactive tears. "I love Serena—worship her. You all know that. As for Carl . . . he kept bugging me. Kept telling me if I just . . . did him a favour, he would do one for me. Help my career." A sudden fierceness came into the young woman's eyes. "But I wouldn't do all this if I wanted to hurt him. This whole set-up? When he could just get pushed in front of a subway car with no possibility of being linked to me? What do I look like?"

She shook her head ruefully and Miss Marple smiled. The girl was young, but she had a good head on her shoulders.

"So it was an accident," Raymond said, finally feeling at Carl's neck for a pulse. "There are wires everywhere since this is a converted factory, and that seems enough to prove that it was simple bad luck. Accidents happen in factories, and in theatres, all the time."

Raymond wasn't fazed by the fact that someone had possibly tried to kill the man; he'd met enough men like Carl, and had been told about enough of them by Joan, that he was certain electrocution was a gentle attempt compared to what he might deserve. But having a show cancelled due to accidental electrocution was a great cocktail-party story; having one cancelled due to murder was drama of the lowest kind.

"That's even worse," Junie said. "Who's at fault for an accident? The theatre company. Everything we're trying to build . . . all our hard work . . . it's not fair!"

"Shouldn't the police be here already?" Joan asked. "Michael should be back at the very least."

"With the way he jumps every time Carl snaps his fingers, I'm surprised he didn't carry him to the hospital himself," Estelle said.

"Oh. Oh, I see," said Miss Marple, running her fingers lightly over the front of her coat. "Not quite the same, but very much so. Naysmith."

Raymond looked up at his aunt, dread forming a familiar knot in his belly. "You don't think this was an accident, do you?"

Miss Marple looked around, her expression contemplative and calm. "Oh, I do, but not quite how everyone else is imagining it."

"Is your aunt a medium?" Serena looked at the old woman with renewed interest. "Is that why you were there at Gimbels earlier? You knew handing me that tablecloth—"

"No, no, I do not adhere to any of that sort of thing. Our meeting earlier was simply a delightful prelude to the current unpleasantness." Miss Marple sighed. "But . . . Naysmith. After Mr. Smith was outvoted on the matter of the vicarage, he let everyone believe that Naysmith had voted against it, even though it was he himself who'd voted against it. Some assumed he disliked Mr. Naysmith—not sure why, perhaps they thought it was a simple matter of feeling slighted by his name? But I always thought that Mr. Smith was against the plan for the vicarage and Mr. Naysmith was simply a convenient target."

"I'm not sure what you're talking about," Serena said, lost.

"Me either," added Estelle.

"I . . . think I'm beginning to pick up what you're putting down," Junie Prince said, taking a step closer to Carl DeVoe.

"After the vote failed to go in his favour, Mr. Smith even went so far as to claim Mr. Naysmith was embezzling church funds," Miss Marple continued. "It was all a lie, you see. Mr. Smith, in fact, had been part of a group trying to buy the land the vicarage was to be rebuilt upon in order to construct new houses—I believe some of them went on to be partners in the Development, but that's neither here nor there."

"The development?" Vera asked, and Miss Marple shook her head in apology.

"Oh, never mind that, dear. It took some time to untangle the lies, but Mr. Naysmith was very much discredited in the eyes of others who had respected him, and some people never believed that he'd done nothing wrong. It was all quite unseemly."

"Get up, Carl," Junie said, nudging him gently with her shoe, then not so gently. "Now, or I'll hit you with a real live wire and tell them I was trying to jump start your heart."

Carl didn't move . . . then rolled over slowly, eyes open and sparkling with a mischief that was so inappropriate it bordered on perverse.

Serena let out a shriek that was several decibels lower than her initial one, and Junie crossed her arms over her chest. "George said you were trying to be supportive, but I knew there was something off about you badgering us to be part of this production even though you weren't blacklisted—you're a mole. And one digging away at our foundations."

Carl looked up at Junie, giving her a winning smile. He was back to being charming and engaging. "Aw now, Junie, who'd believe some bunk like that? No one, that's who."

"What on earth do you mean?" Raymond asked, unsure whether to be relieved or upset.

"I mean, he's been undermining this play—we're doing this our way, unsanctioned, and with people who have been blacklisted. Except for Carl." Junie shook her head in frustration. "All that arrogant behaviour, and demanding things that lowered the quality of the production, and trying to drive Serena up the wall, was just to make sure we failed. You set us up."

"Was he going to fake his death?" Vera asked.

Carl shook his head, and when he spoke he was absolutely earnest. "I couldn't fake my death. I'm Carl DeVoe."

Junie sighed. "But tabloids love reporting on intrigue. A theatre run by blacklisted communists is one thing, but a theatre run by blacklisted commies that led to the near death of all-American darling Carl DeVoe would have been *actual* death for our careers."

Miss Marple gave a nod of agreement. "I believe that before Michael ran out so quickly—too quickly to have checked what had occurred—he used the lightboard to create the illusion that Carl had been electrocuted. Then he ran out under the pretence of making a phone call, when he was actually going to get other participants in the charade."

"But how did you figure any of this out, Aunt Jane?" Joan asked. "You've just met these people."

"As I said earlier, there was only one vagrant outside with us tonight." Miss Marple walked over to where the hairpieces hung and pointed at a beard, plucking a grey pigeon feather from it. "I met Serena earlier today, and apparently Michael as well. He was in disguise as a homeless man. I recognised him after we arrived here, but assumed his crime had been panhandling under false pretence, not spying on Serena."

She considered mentioning how he'd saved her, but decided it wasn't relevant to the situation at hand.

"Someone rewarded him handsomely for his spying—quite a lot of money shoved into a beggar's cup and passed off as kindness. Michael reported what he saw to Carl, which was how Carl knew about the dress. It must have sparked this idea of how to anger Serena and also give the show one last push off the rails in one go."

"Are you saying that the adaptation of my play is a casualty of American political intrigue?" Raymond exclaimed, sounding not at all put out by the notion. "*This* will make me the toast of all of literary England!"

"It would if anyone believed you," Carl said, standing up by himself, since no assistance was offered. He grimaced at the dust that had accumulated on his clothes, then looked up at Junie with his ice-pick expression. "I'll be going now. I'm sure the play will flop and be forgotten once it's announced that I'm no longer the lead. It will still die, but with a whimper instead of a bang."

"You can't just leave. Wait until the police get here!" Vera said, as Carl brushed off his trousers.

He laughed. "I haven't done anything illegal, darling. Maybe if you'd waited until after I'd hammed it up at the hospital to figure this all out you could have had me at misuse of public services. But since you didn't . . ."

At that moment Michael rushed back in with two paramedics. All three of the new arrivals looked harried and heroic as they ran in, but their demeanour changed quickly as they took in the scene.

"Jig is up?" Michael asked miserably, and Carl nodded.

With that, Carl, Michael and the faux paramedics all simply left; the anticlimactic nature of it was so startling to Miss Marple that it nearly circled back around to exhilarating.

Serena, Estelle and Vera huddled together, rehashing what had just occurred. Junie Prince left to find Carl's understudy and to contact George Stapleton.

"I'm so glad you convinced me to come with you," Miss Marple said delightedly. "What a marvellous evening."

"Why are you in such high spirits?" Raymond asked.

"Because, dear Raymond, I got to solve a murder with no murder having been committed," Miss Marple said, as if the answer should be evident. "New York really is a city where one's wildest dreams might come true."

The Unravelling

Natalie Haynes

"I don't see how that would explain anything," said Susan Goldingay. "And there's no point in having a haberdasher's if they aren't ever open."

Miss Marple nodded gravely. "Well, yes," she said. "But I'm sure Mrs. Weaver will open up again in the morning."

"Did you see the—" Susan broke off and eyed the tables around them. But the tea-room was bustling on this rainy autumnal day, and no one was eavesdropping. "The brawl?"

"Oh, dear me, no," replied Miss Marple. "I heard about it from Florence. And she heard about it from Williams, when he delivered the post."

"So he saw them?"

"Oh yes," Miss Marple raised her cup and took a

delicate sip. As she returned it to its saucer, she leaned slightly closer. "He saw the whole thing. The farmer and his man arrived in the square just before three o'clock. He was quite sure of it because of the bells and the pigs, you see."

Susan frowned but didn't interrupt. She had been friends with Miss Marple for too long not to know the story was coming, one way or another.

"Syme went into the butcher's and left the new man—Martin, I believe—in charge of the pigs. Williams told Florence that he was waiting for Syme quite calmly. The pigs weren't causing a nuisance at all."

Susan wrinkled her nose. She had always found pigs to be nasty creatures, their sharp teeth like shards of broken crockery.

"And Martin was no trouble until Mr. Weaver came out of the shop and told him to be on his way."

"How odd!" said Susan. "The man could hardly leave without Syme, could he?"

"No, dear," replied Miss Marple. "But when he refused to move on, Mr. Weaver became agitated and began to shout."

Susan raised her eyebrows. "He's usually so quiet!"

"As you know, I don't like to criticise a man who had a difficult war," said Miss Marple. "But Williams was quite sure about what he'd seen. He said this Martin tried to keep calm even while Weaver was shouting. He was darting nervous glances at the butcher's, but Williams couldn't tell if he was afraid Syme would come outside, or afraid that he wouldn't, if you see what I mean."

Susan nodded. "Poor man," she said. "He must have been worried about losing his job."

"Yes," Miss Marple said. "Syme only hired him a week ago, Florence said. So no wonder he was anxious. But I wonder if that explains . . ." Her voice tailed off and she frowned. "I'm really not sure it does, you know."

"What happened then?" asked Susan.

"Williams said that Mr. Weaver raised his fists," said Miss Marple. "And Martin stepped back and tripped on the kerbstone."

"Oh dear!"

"Yes," Miss Marple nodded. "So the poor man was lying on his back among the pigs when Syme reappeared and Mr. Weaver started shouting at him too."

"No!"

"Which was lucky, in a way," Miss Marple continued. "Because it meant Syme could see Martin wasn't at fault, since he blamed Mr. Weaver straightaway."

"I see."

"But then Martin jumped up from the pavement and

began waving his stick in Mr. Weaver's face. Williams said he'd been provoked enough to excuse it, but he'd have certainly lost his job if Syme hadn't been so angry with Mr. Weaver, and if he hadn't also needed help to round up the pigs, which had run all over the square when Martin fell."

"And this was when Sergeant Dover arrived?"

"Precisely."

"I still don't understand about the bells?" said Susan.

"Oh, well, the bells chimed three as three pigs ran past him," said Miss Marple. "That's how Williams could be so sure of the time."

"And what did Dover say?" Susan asked.

"Well, he was all ready to keep Martin in the police station overnight, but Syme persuaded him that the poor man was hardly at fault. So, in the end, Dover let them take the pigs back to the farm and told Mr. Weaver to speak to the police next time he was concerned about livestock in the square."

"Well, that's an end to it," said Susan.

Miss Marple frowned. "Perhaps," she said.

But the Weavers did not open again in the morning. Nor did any of the little shops in the square, leaning higgledy-piggledy against each other. The whole row kept their doors locked while the police searched for the weapon used to kill Martin, whose body—brown eyes clouded and sightless—had been discovered by the milkman just after dawn. At first, they thought the old man must have died from the stress of his argument with Weaver. Then they wondered if he had hit his head on the stone step of the haberdasher's as he fell. There was a small dark stain on the edge of the lowest step, which Dover was sure must be blood.

But when the doctor felt the back of the man's head, he pronounced it uninjured: not even a bump. And, besides, there was no doubt about what had killed him when they turned the body over. The broken shaft of an arrow was still protruding from his chest.

Susan felt no need to wait for the village telegraph to convey the tidings when she could take news of the man's death to Jane herself. To give herself an excuse for calling in the morning, she wrapped some rock cakes in waxed paper, twine sliding to and fro as she tried to tie it in a rush. But, honestly, it was bad enough that she had missed the fight over the pigs the previous day because she had been arranging flowers in church, and so she refused to be cut out of the most extraordinary incident in the village for as long as she could remember. She knew she was due at the vicarage to discuss choir practice, but she was confident that, if God was pleased with her endeavours on His behalf, He would spare her from another church meeting this once so she could have the pleasure of talking murder with Jane. And if He didn't appreciate yesterday's dahlias, she could make amends another day, when less important things were going on.

She hurried up the hill, her stout walking shoes squeaking as she went. But as she rounded the bend, she saw Williams, the postman, sailing downhill on his bicycle. She gritted her teeth with vexation as she returned his cheery wave. Surely the man spent some time delivering letters, and not simply acting as a personal messenger service for Jane? It was—she reflected, as papery leaves crunched beneath her feet—typical of Miss Marple to have found a housemaid who was walking out with the postman. And if the village had no postman, she would doubtless have acquired a gardener who was brother to a delivery boy. News always reached Miss Marple, one way or another.

"Oh!" said Miss Marple, as Susan bustled into the sitting room. "Are those some of your delicious rock cakes, Susan? How kind."

Susan smiled as she handed the parcel to Florence the housemaid, along with her hat and coat.

"You are too bad, Jane. You've already heard it from Williams, haven't you?"

"About the dead man? What an awful thing. A bow and arrow, he said?"

"That's right." Susan was determined to be the authority on something. "I spoke to Sergeant Dover myself before I came up to see you."

"Had the arrow been snapped off?" Miss Marple enquired.

"Yes!" said Susan. "Dover thought it had broken under him when he fell, but they couldn't find the rest of it anywhere."

"I see," said Miss Marple. "That does make things more complicated."

"It's quite mad. Who would shoot a man and then come and try to take the arrow back?"

Miss Marple nodded slowly. "Who indeed?" she murmured.

The answer—as far as Sergeant Dover was concerned—was obvious. The pigman had only arrived in the area a few days earlier and no one knew where he had come from. Syme said he had knocked at the door and offered to work for food and a dry barn to sleep in. The farmer was short-handed and, although he was usually suspicious of strangers, his dog had shown an uncharacteristic fondness for this man, Martin. When he arrived, the animal had pelted across the farmyard, barking loudly. But as soon as the animal approached the stranger, the man had reached down to scratch the dog's ears and it had wagged its tail as though they were old friends. Syme considered his dog's judgement sound as a rule, so gave Martin the benefit of the doubt. But he was not a man to make idle conversation, so he knew little more about the stranger than anyone else.

Sergeant Dover began and ended his investigation in the haberdasher's. He was apologetic in his manner and mild in his questioning: the Weavers were a popular couple in the village. As Miss Marple had put it the previous day, they had endured a difficult war. Mr. Weaver had signed up, patriotically but reluctantly, as he was rather too old and his eyesight was poor. And Mrs. Weaver had run the shop on her own for years, never complaining that she had no help, or that she was trying to bring up her son Eric on her own, or that so many items they used to sell—wool winders, sewing machines—were impossible to source these days. She was practical and kind: as Susan noted, she would always hold wool for her customers so they could buy a jumper's worth at a skein a week when their wages came in. Miss Marple agreed this was the mark of an excellent shopkeeper.

Mr. Weaver, meanwhile, had found himself in the

navy. At first, the village heard plenty of his exploits: he had fought in one battle after another, always managing to avoid serious injury, although, alarmingly, he was reported dead more than once. But as the years dragged on, things went quiet. No one liked to ask Mrs. Weaver too much, because bad news travelled more quickly than good, and no news was often the cruellest kind of all. More than one person speculated that Weaver was working with the French Resistance, others had him in North Africa. There were reports of almost everyone else in the village who'd gone off to war, yet never news of him.

Once the war was won, the men drifted back to the village. Not all of them, of course: many were lost and some were damaged beyond return. But, one by one, they were all accounted for, with one exception. Weaver had disappeared. And so things remained—Mrs. Weaver running the shop, no one remarking that her husband was still missing—for several more years. And then, one day, he came home.

That—Susan reflected, as she collected five new skeins of wool for Miss Marple and carried them up the hill—had been the last time something dramatic had happened in the village. Normally the place was so sleepy and pleasant. But when Mr. Weaver returned, Mrs. Weaver had cried out in shock and delight.

"Do you remember, Jane?" Susan asked, as Miss Marple compared the dye lots of each skein, nodding as they all matched.

"Remember what, dear?" she said. Her spectacles were perched on her nose as she consulted her pattern. She had knitted this baby's blanket pattern many times before, but she still liked to refresh her memory on the number of stitches each repeating motif required.

"When Mrs. Weaver saw her husband again after all that time?"

"Of course I do," said Miss Marple. "One could hardly forget such a scene."

Susan smiled. "She was so happy, do you recall? She dropped a great basket of cloth and screamed for joy."

"Oh, do you think so?" Miss Marple picked up her knitting pins and checked the gauge.

"You said you remembered! A great squawk of delight, it was."

Miss Marple looked up and frowned. "I do remember he was exhausted, poor man. It looked as though he'd been travelling for months."

"Years," Susan agreed. "And it must have been so strange for him to be alone after so long living and fighting alongside his men. He looked lost."

"Indeed he did," said Miss Marple.

"I suppose he must have been to so many places." Susan prided herself on her imagination.

The villagers had welcomed back their long-lost neighbour with kindness and some curiosity. But only children were blunt enough to ask Weaver where he had been for so long, and they received no answer beyond a clip round the ear from the nearest adult. Weaver's pale eyes told their own truth: wherever he had been, it was not for sharing. And if the haberdasher's was somehow quieter with two people working there than it had been when it was just Mrs. Weaver, the villagers still felt lucky to have it.

But as they muttered to one another over the coming days, what was Sergeant Dover to do? The ruckus in the square had been witnessed by several bystanders and they all agreed: Mr. Weaver had been the aggressor. And since no one else admitted to any connection with Martin—beyond Syme's cursory exchanges—Dover had little choice but to speak to the haberdasher.

The questioning took place behind closed doors, with no one present but the sergeant, his constable, Weaver and Mrs. Weaver. Yet the details of this interview—such as there were—flew around the village without delay.

"Was Martin known to you before this week?" asked the sergeant. His round face was reddening and he glanced down at the constable's notebook to avoid making eye contact with anyone. The constable had written "WEAVER" in block capitals, before drawing a double line underneath it.

Weaver shook his head.

"Why were you so angry with him?"

Weaver shrugged. "I would like an answer, sir," said the sergeant, unhappily. He was more accustomed to resolving neighbourly disputes and helping to find missing cats. Murder was not something he had ever expected to deal with. He waited, hoping the haberdasher would yield first.

"I was angry about the mess, I suppose," said Weaver. He sounded so weary that neither policeman could imagine him shouting. But Dover had heard the fracas himself. He had seen its immediate aftermath, and he wasn't going to be put off.

"It was just a few pigs, sir."

"He shouldn't have left them right outside the shop," snapped Weaver. "It puts off our customers. Who wants to walk through a farmyard to get to the door?"

"Has this been a frequent problem?" Dover raised his eyebrows. Syme brought his pigs into town two or three times a year at most.

"That's not the point," the man replied. Sweat was beading on his brow. "If my customers wanted to work on a pig farm, they would."

"So you told him to move along?" asked the sergeant. "And he refused?"

"Yes," said Weaver. "And he was insolent about it."

"How so?"

"He said he wanted to see my wife."

"Your wife, sir? What for?"

"I don't know," he replied. "I didn't ask him why he wanted to speak to her. I told him not to be so damned impertinent."

"I see. And did your wife know what he might have wanted from her?"

The haberdasher's eyes bulged. "Why don't you ask her? Penny! Penny!"

Mrs. Weaver appeared in the doorway so quickly that the sergeant knew she had been listening behind the door.

"Forgive me, madam," Dover said. He thought it best to pretend Mrs. Weaver hadn't heard every word spoken so far. "We wondered if you might have any idea why the dead man wanted to speak to you?"

Mrs. Weaver was a handsome woman with long, dark hair plaited and pinned tight. Her bright blue eyes glinted with suspicion, though Dover half-remembered her as a young girl and he fancied those eyes had once glinted with laughter. When Weaver had left for the war, their son had only been a babe in arms. And what was he now? Twenty? Twenty-one? Old enough to be working as a junior master at the local school anyway. So perhaps it wasn't suspicion he saw in her expression, but the weariness of age.

"I?" Her voice was richly melodic. "Why would I know, sergeant?"

Dover found himself stumbling over his words. "I—we—I hoped you might have recognised him."

"No," she said. "I don't believe I did."

"Had he been here before?" the policeman asked, hopelessly. To his surprise, a flicker of emotion appeared and disappeared on her face. "No," she said.

But this time he knew she was lying.

Miss Marple raised an eyebrow an eighth of an inch and the waitress rushed to their table. Susan—who had been trying to catch her eye for five minutes—tried not to sound irritated as she ordered afternoon tea for the pair of them. Miss Marple wrapped her shawl a little closer around her shoulders: the door kept opening as customers came and went.

"I've never seen it so busy!" Susan said, turning in

her seat to get a better view. "We were lucky to find a table. And I don't recognise half these people."

Miss Marple nodded. "I wonder if the inquest has attracted the attention of the newspapers," she said.

Susan's eyes widened. "Murder tourists!" she hissed. "Is that what they are?"

"I think they might be," Miss Marple replied. "Yes, certainly a possibility."

"Will they leave when the inquest is over, Jane? I don't think I like it."

"They may do," Miss Marple replied. "Yes, once the sergeant has made his arrest, they may leave."

"Arrest? Who is he going to arrest?"

"Mr. Weaver, of course," said Miss Marple.

"Oh no!" Susan put her hand to her chest so emphatically that her pearls jumped. "He couldn't have."

"Couldn't have what, dear?"

"Murdered the pigman," Susan whispered. She didn't want other people to think that she was a murder tourist too.

"No, he didn't murder anyone," said Miss Marple. "You can see the poor man couldn't harm a fly. He shudders when a dog barks."

"But you said—"

"I said he would be arrested. But he certainly didn't

do it. The man was killed—rather theatrically—with a bow and arrow."

"I know," said Susan.

"Mr. Weaver has the shakes, dear. He came back from the war like that."

"Does he?"

"Yes. That's why Mrs. Weaver has to do the weighing and cut the cloth."

"But the dead man wasn't stabbed. Or hit with scales."

Miss Marple did not sigh, but she exhaled with commitment. "He couldn't have held an arrow still, dear. Let alone aimed it."

"Then he mustn't be arrested!"

"I'm afraid the sergeant will be expected to arrest someone," Miss Marple replied.

And as so often, she was right.

The morning light was soft and grey and Susan collected Miss Marple in her car, so her friend wouldn't have to walk to church on the slippery pavement. The cake sale planning committee was abuzz with rumours, as Sergeant Dover and Constable Jebb had taken Mr. Weaver away. The two men must have known each other in the war, it was thought, and Martin had come back to settle a long-held grievance. Or Mrs. Weaver was involved in some way. Certainly, Martin didn't seem like the kind of man she would know, but there was no telling, was there? If she hadn't known him, why did he want to speak to her? And why was Weaver so angry, unless he knew something the rest of them did not?

Miss Marple listened attentively to each question and suggestion but said nothing. Since she had been driven to the meeting, she had brought her knitting. The blanket had grown a little, Susan noted, but surely not as much as it should have.

"Did you run out of wool, dear?" she asked.

Miss Marple smiled as she counted the stitches along the knitting pin. "No, I dropped a stitch," she said. "And I didn't notice for rows and rows, so I had to unravel inches of work."

"How annoying," Susan sympathised. She had never really understood the appeal of knitting. "Yes, of course," she added, this addressed to the chairwoman of the committee. Mrs. Wilson wanted Susan's rock cakes for the sale and no one would be able to say that she had let the church roof fall into disrepair for want of her baking a batch or two.

"Did it take a long time?" she asked Miss Marple, now Mrs. Wilson's sharp gaze had turned in another direction.

"The knitting? Yes, dear. But not the unravelling. It takes longer to pick the stitches back up and—" Miss Marple broke off. "Oh," she said. "I suppose that could be it, couldn't it?"

"What, Jane?" Susan had known her friend for many years, and she recognised the signs of Miss Marple realising something important: her eyes almost glazed as though she were mesmerised.

"But it doesn't tell us who killed him, of course," said Miss Marple. "Although perhaps it narrows the field."

"Jane!" Susan was trying to be discreet, since they were in a room filled with people who knew the Weavers, so she whispered urgently but as quietly as she could. She nonetheless drew a hard stare from Mrs. Wilson.

"Are you volunteering, Susan? Marvellous, thank you."

Susan nodded weakly, wondering what she had just agreed to do. From the grateful expressions on the faces of the other committee members, she had no doubt she would regret it.

Once Mrs. Wilson had declared the meeting finished, Susan and Miss Marple walked slowly out into the square. The rainclouds had melted away and skeletons of damp leaves lay imprinted on the church path.

"I'm not sure what I promised to do," Susan murmured, as the two of them eased away from the other committee members.

"Teas at the school play, I'm afraid," said Miss Marple.

"Oh no." Susan rolled her eyes. "Is it soon?"

"Tonight, I believe." Miss Marple twinkled at her. "I could help you, if you like."

The two women arrived at the school hall at four o'clock precisely. A rather battered box of cups and saucers was perched on the edge of a trestle table, and the urn was already warm to the touch. Miss Marple laid out the saucers in neat rows, while Susan mixed orange squash in a large jug and poured it out into paper cups. By the time the audience started arriving, they were ready to serve tea and biscuits to all who wanted them.

A handsome young man—barely older than the children, it looked to Susan, but carrying himself with an air of authority and wearing an academic gown to boot—appeared from behind the stage curtains and frowned as he scanned the school hall. It was not perhaps quite as full as he was hoping. Susan waved at him before she realised who it was.

"Jane!" she said. "It's Eric! I mean, young Weaver."

"Oh, yes," said Miss Marple, as the young man waved back rather self-consciously and began walking towards them. "He teaches here, does he not?"

"What can we ask him?" Susan muttered, as Eric drew nearer.

"Nothing at all," said Miss Marple firmly. She held out a cup of tea and Eric seized it.

"Thank you so much," he said. He had light brown hair and chestnut eyes, a small shaving cut healing on his left cheek. Susan thought how lucky it was that he favoured his mother, with her strong jaw and straight nose. The same features made mother and son handsome in different ways.

"Were you looking for someone?" asked Miss Marple.

"My mother," the young man explained. "She was hoping to attend tonight's performance."

"I'm sure she knows how much work you've put in to rehearse a whole play," Miss Marple said.

His face broke into a smile. "She has witnessed it first-hand! She's watched me wrangling with the script and the rehearsal schedule for weeks."

"I'm sure she'll be here soon," Susan said.

The children were all filing in now: how tidy they looked, Susan thought. Their navy blazers had the school crest on the pocket, and they walked in pairs to their seats.

"Your pupils are very well behaved," she said.

He nodded. "They've really taken to drama. As soon as I realised the only way to get boys interested in a play was if it was full of violence, they became really keen."

"Oh," said Susan, rather faintly. "What is the play?"

"Aeschylus," he said. "Wives murdering husbands. Never fails." He wandered off, still looking for his mother.

"How very modern, Jane," Susan said.

"In a way," she replied.

Mrs. Weaver appeared just before the lights dimmed, walking straight past their table without pausing. If her face was rather drawn from worry, she nonetheless wanted to support her son.

At the end of the play—having understood no more than one word in five and wondering if anyone was left alive—Susan nudged Miss Marple. Mrs. Weaver was seen hurrying out of the hall before the smattering of applause was over. Susan tried waving to catch her attention, but without success: Mrs. Weaver did not lift her pale gaze from the floor.

"I suppose she doesn't want to talk to anyone," said Susan, as she ferried cups and saucers from beneath the wooden seats and Miss Marple stacked them neatly on the table.

"No," said Miss Marple. "I imagine she has been trying to avoid questions from all sides."

"Do you think the police have interrogated her?" Susan was shocked.

"The police, and her son, of course."

"Why would her son be interrogating her?"

"Because he's afraid she's done something quite awful," said Miss Marple.

"Not murder?" whispered Susan.

"No, I don't think so." Miss Marple stacked the last of the saucers on top of one another. "Something he will find rather harder to forgive, perhaps. But she may be able to keep her secret, if she is lucky. Although, of course, she hasn't been terribly lucky before now, has she?"

But the following morning, it seemed as though the Weavers' luck had changed at last. Mr. Weaver was released from custody, after witnesses had come forward to say they had seen him walking by the mill pond at the hour in question. Even if he had been able to fire an arrow—as Miss Marple had observed he could not—he certainly couldn't have fired one from half a mile away. Why hadn't the witnesses come forward sooner, everyone asked one another, and who were they? The police were not prepared to answer idle gossip and speculation, so the village came to its own conclusions, which happened (in this instance) to be accurate. Weaver had been spied by a couple having an illicit meeting that neither wanted to become public. Nonetheless, they were unwilling to see an innocent man hang for their indiscretion, so they separately made statements to Sergeant Dover.

"The oddest thing about it, Jane, was that I saw Mr. Weaver when he came back to the shop from the police station," said Susan, as the two of them sat in Miss Marple's sitting room. Susan's hands were a foot apart as she held the skein of wool for Miss Marple to wind. "And he didn't look happy at all."

"Oh, that is interesting." Miss Marple wound the wool so quickly that it seemed to leap from Susan's outstretched hands. "How did he look?"

Susan thought for a moment. "Weighed down," she said. "If you'd seen him and not known, you'd have guessed he was walking into prison, not away from it."

Miss Marple didn't slow down. "Then it is just as I thought," she said. "He let himself be arrested because he was protecting someone."

"His wife?" Susan let her hands drop a little, but the wool snagged and jerked them back up again.

Miss Marple looked at the wool, and looked at the baby's blanket that she had carefully unravelled a second time to eliminate another mistake she had made by trying to knit without enough light. So trying, to drop a stitch right near the beginning, impossible to pick it up without tugging the fabric too tight on either side. She had backed the work as carefully as she could, so that she didn't have to begin the whole thing again.

"I do wonder if that is it," she said.

"What?" asked Susan.

"I think we've all been looking at weaving when we should have been thinking about unweaving. Even me, who should know better," Miss Marple replied, absently.

"Unweaving?" said Susan. "Is that even a word?"

"There is one easy way to confirm it, of course." The ball of wool in Miss Marple's hands grew as the skein in Susan's hands shrank.

"Confirm what? How?" asked Susan.

"Did you see Martin?" asked Jane.

"Yes, I walked past him and Syme on my way to church that day, before the argument with Mr. Weaver."

"Were you close enough to notice the colour of his eyes?"

"Yes," said Susan. She screwed up her own in an effort to remember what she had seen. "Brown," she said. "I think they were brown."

"And Mrs. Weaver has blue eyes," said Miss Marple. "I noticed them at the school the other day."

"Yes, that's right," said Susan. "She wears that lovely crimson dress and it brings out the auburn in her hair."

"I see," said Miss Marple. "Well, that changes everything then, doesn't it?"

"Does it?"

"Yes, dear. I've been so foolish. I've been looking at them the wrong way round."

"At who? Honestly, Jane, I do pay attention to everything you say, but sometimes you might as well be speaking in another language."

"I am sorry, Susan, I don't mean to irritate you. But I really have been looking at this puzzle from the wrong perspective. And if I'm right, Mrs. Weaver will be arrested before the end of today."

"No!" said Susan.

"We need to speak to Sergeant Dover," Miss Marple continued. "Or he'll make a terrible mistake, and I don't know what might happen after that. Although I suppose it's too late now to save him."

"Save her," said Susan.

Miss Marple finished winding the ball and dropped

it into her workbox. "I beg your pardon, dear?" she said.

"Save Mrs. Weaver," Susan repeated.

"Oh," said Miss Marple. "I'm not sure she would want to be saved. I think she plans to do exactly what Mr. Weaver tried to do."

"I don't know how you think I can help you," said Sergeant Dover. He had been the village policeman for many years now, and he was fond of the majority of its residents, even the ones who seemed to take up most of his time. He did wonder if things had become rather more difficult when Miss Marple moved into her cottage at the top of the hill. She was, he admitted, a model citizen: helping out at the church, the school, supporting the local shops and so on. And yet, somehow, her presence made him feel less of a model citizen himself. Which was ridiculous, since he was the police sergeant. But something about the old lady in her neat tweeds and carefully positioned hat, hands resting lightly on the wooden handles of her bag, made him feel as though he was eight years old again and had been caught stealing sweets.

"Mrs. Weaver," said Susan. "She's made a terrible mistake."

"I rather think you're underestimating the seriousness of murder, Mrs. Goldingay," said the sergeant.

"She hasn't committed murder, sergeant." Susan was beginning to find him rather irritating. "That's what we've been trying to tell you."

"She has confessed to murder." Sergeant Dover placed his elbows on his desk and clasped his hands. "As a general rule, that means someone has committed murder."

"Ah, but, you see, she has committed a sort of murder," said Miss Marple. "But not the kind she could be arrested for."

The policeman sighed and turned his attention fully to the white-haired old lady, who seemed so patient and never gave in. "What kind of murder would that be, then, Miss Marple?"

"Well, it's rather difficult to give it a name, isn't it?" said Miss Marple. "I suppose she helped to murder her husband, in a way. But only because she believed he was already dead."

"Her husband is very much alive, Miss Marple," Sergeant Dover sighed. "He was in my cells until two days ago."

"No, Sergeant, I'm afraid you're mistaken. He was found dead in the street with an arrow in his chest," Miss Marple replied.

"Miss Marple," said the policeman, "I think you must be confused. Mr. Weaver is at home in their flat above the haberdashery shop. Mrs. Weaver has confessed to murdering the stranger, Martin."

"Well, of course she has," said Miss Marple. "But she didn't kill Martin, and he wasn't a stranger."

"I'm tempted to call them both to the police station to explain things to you slowly," he said.

"Oh, but I don't think they would want to," said Miss Marple. "Their lives together have been built on a lie, so I doubt the truth would come easily to them now."

"I have a dead body that has been identified as Mr. Martin," said the policeman. "And a murderer who has made her confession."

"What reason did she give for killing him?" asked Susan.

"She didn't have to give a reason," said the policeman. "She admitted to it. She admitted to shooting him. She even confessed to breaking off the arrow."

"But she didn't give a reason, of course," said Miss Marple.

The policeman narrowed his eyes. "She did not," he said.

"A decent lawyer will see her leave the court a free woman," said Susan. "Which she should, because she's not guilty."

Sergeant Dover thought for a moment, and relented. "We're visiting Mr. Weaver this afternoon," he said. "To collect some necessities for Mrs. Weaver. If you choose to visit the haberdashery at four o'clock, you can put your questions to them yourselves."

"I think half past four would be preferable," said Miss Marple. "If you want the murderer to attend as well."

The policeman began to laugh. "Does he have something else to do first?" he asked.

"Yes," said Miss Marple. "And he won't be able to leave until four o'clock."

The church bell chimed twice for the half hour as Miss Marple and Susan climbed the steps to the haberdashery shop. Inside, they found Mr. and Mrs. Weaver, standing awkwardly behind the counter as Sergeant Dover and Constable Jebb looked on. Mrs. Weaver's hair was tied back simply, and she looked younger than she had in years.

"Good afternoon," said Susan, brightly. "We wondered if you might answer a few questions?"

"I don't know what you want," said Mrs. Weaver. "Or what you hope to achieve."

"I think the truth might be useful, don't you?" said Miss Marple.

"Why do you think I'm not telling the truth?" she replied.

"Because we don't think you're a murderer," said Susan. "And Jane knows who did it."

Mrs. Weaver looked rather pale, and held on to the ladder she used to reach the higher shelves. "I killed him," she said. "I'll plead guilty."

Miss Marple shook her head sadly. "That won't save him," she said. "He won't let you take the blame for what he did. You know that he'll be here any moment to confess."

Tears sprang from Mrs. Weaver's eyes, and her husband moved to comfort her.

"Who's confessing now?" asked Constable Jebb. The sergeant shook his head.

And then the door behind them swung open, and Eric Weaver burst into the shop.

"But how did you know, Jane?" asked Susan, as they sat together in the tea rooms, restoring their equanimity with sandwiches and scones.

"Well, because he couldn't be Mr. Weaver's son, of course," said Miss Marple. "I mean, the new Mr. Weaver. I suppose we'll never know what his real name is."

"How do you mean?" Susan poured tea into both cups, frowning at its colour as she did so.

"Eric Weaver has brown eyes," Miss Marple explained. "Mr. Weaver—the new Mr. Weaver—has blue eyes."

"Do you mean Mrs. Weaver . . . ?" Susan looked appalled and couldn't finish the question.

"I mean the Mr. Weaver who came back from the war wasn't the same man as the one who went away to fight in it," said Miss Marple, firmly. "I imagine they were comrades. Mr. Weaver has confessed as much to Sergeant Dover. He saw the first Mr. Weaver injured and then captured. In North Africa, I believe, near the end of the war. It never occurred to him the man might have survived. Meanwhile, Mrs. Weaver received notice that her husband was missing in action and obviously feared the worst."

"So the man who came back to the village as Mr. Weaver wasn't him at all?" Susan asked. "But she must have known!"

"Perhaps," said Miss Marple. "But we expect men to change during a war, don't we?"

"You said it yourself, Jane: his eyes were a different colour!"

"Yes. But if you were Mrs. Weaver, running a business, bringing up a boy on your own for all those years, do you think you would have asked that question?" Miss Marple's eyes glittered. "Or might you have simply accepted that a man was standing before you, claiming to be your husband and offering to share the work?"

Susan looked uncertain. "I suppose I can just about imagine that," she said.

"The man who had left her wasn't ever coming back," said Miss Marple. "Or so she thought."

"And so Mr. Martin, Syme's new farmhand, was the original Mr. Weaver?" Susan asked. "But where had he been all this time?"

Miss Marple shook her head. "I don't suppose anyone will ever know that," she said. "Whatever he went through must have been truly terrible, for him to come back changed beyond recognition."

"Yes," said Susan. "Although the new Mr. Weaver recognised him, didn't he? That's why they had the fight in the square."

"I think so," said Miss Marple. "Recognised him or at least recognised something about him. Perhaps his conscience did the rest."

"And Eric Weaver recognised him too?" Susan asked.

"I wonder," Miss Marple said. "He was just a baby when his father went away. And I don't think he ever questioned that it was his father who had returned. Would he even remember what his real father looked like?"

"But if he didn't, then why did he . . . ?"

"I think he saw the fight and drew his own conclusions," said Miss Marple. "Eric is an educated man, and he would know a blue-eyed father and mother would be very unlikely to have a brown-eyed son. I think he believed his mother had had an affair with a stranger and that the stranger had returned—after many years—to throw his family into chaos. That's why he shot him."

Susan placed her hands over her mouth. "No," she whispered. "He killed his own father without knowing? That's too awful."

"Mrs. Weaver took the arrow, of course, when he panicked and told her what he'd done. She was worried there would be fingerprints on it and didn't know what else to do. Mr. Weaver agreed to be arrested, and they hoped to have the case dismissed through lack of evidence. But when the witnesses came forward to say he couldn't possibly have committed the crime, they had to come up with another plan, and quickly."

"Which was Mrs. Weaver taking the blame?"

"Exactly."

"But Eric wouldn't have let his mother hang, surely?"

"No," said Miss Marple. "I don't believe he could have. They were hoping the case would fail in court."

"I almost wish we hadn't interfered, Jane."

Miss Marple nodded. "I understand, dear. But a man cannot kill his father and go unpunished. Not when that father has done nothing wrong except to be unfortunate."

"How did you work it all out?" asked Susan.

"It was the unravelling," said Miss Marple. "It reminded me of Penelope undoing her funeral shroud every night for years, because she believed her husband would come back to her."

"Does anything ever surprise you?" Susan smiled.

Miss Marple shook her head. "Not yet," she said.

Miss Marple's Christmas

Ruth Ware

"So, *dear* Aunt Jane . . ." Raymond West's voice came over the telephone wire with more than his usual dose of cajoling charm. "What do you think? A real old fashioned St. Mary Mead Christmas?"

Miss Marple suppressed a wistful little sigh. What she was thinking was that no modern Christmas could possibly live up to the Christmases of her youth, and certainly not one spent crammed into her little cottage with Raymond and his wife. Christmas, in Miss Marple's childhood, had been an affair of blazing log fires, stockings full of sweets, nuts and trinkets, crackling chestnuts, and a Christmas dinner to rival that of Henry VIII's court, with sirloin, ham and turkey, potatoes both roast and boiled, and not one but two helpings of Christmas pudding.

The rambling country house had been full of children her own age, as well as a plethora of aunts, uncles and assorted relations all now sadly departed, and they had played the kind of games modern parents frowned upon as far too dangerous. Snapdragon had been her own favourite, which had involved snatching burning raisins from a flaming dish of brandy—great fun and accompanied by many shrieks and scalded fingers, she remembered, and very difficult it was for the poor maids to remove the burns from the nursery rug.

Christmas with Raymond and Joan would no doubt be very pleasant, and would probably involve a good deal of listening to music on the wireless, playing bridge with the Bantrys, and a great many cocktails, but a real old fashioned Christmas it very much would not be.

"Of course we can go to an hotel if it's any trouble," Raymond added. "I hear the Savoy does a very creditable Christmas spread. But Joan's rather against the idea—and I thought perhaps you'd like the company?"

"Oh, I shouldn't dream of letting you do such a thing," Miss Marple said, a little shocked at the suggestion. "Hotels are all very well in their way, Raymond dear, but Joan is quite right—*not* for Christmas. And think of the expense. No, I should be delighted to have you and Joan to stay while your plumbing is put right. But I must warn you, it will be very quiet."

"Peace and quiet is just what the doctor ordered," Raymond said cheerfully. "I've got my novel to finish, and Joan—well, Joan's been a bit pulled down recently, so a dose of the old St. Mary Mead pond water will be just the ticket for her. Walks in the country, plenty of fresh air—that sort of thing. If you're quite sure, we'll see you on the 22nd."

"I shall look forward to it," Miss Marple said, truthfully.

"So that makes seven now," Mrs. Bantry said to her husband, putting down the telephone receiver and counting on her fingers. "No, six. No—I was right the first time. It *is* seven. Nine, including you and me."

"What's that? Seven? Seven what?" Colonel Bantry's voice emerged from behind the morning paper.

"Seven guests, for Christmas dinner. I shall have to tell Cook to order a larger turkey. Or do you think two small ones would be safer in case the range is playing up again?"

"Seven?" Her husband folded the paper and stared

at her, nonplussed. "What d'you mean, Dolly? You've invited seven people for Christmas? What possessed you?"

"Arthur, how many more times? We've discussed this. You invited those friends of yours the Dashwoods to stay when you went grouse shooting with Major Dashwood, don't you remember?"

"Hardly friends," the Colonel said, a little grumpily. His wife continued as if he hadn't spoken.

"And then *they* asked if they could bring their nephew, Ronald. And I invited Jane Marple, and now *her* nephew and his wife are staying with her over Christmas because of their drains, or perhaps it's their electricity, I can't quite remember, so I've had to invite them too."

"Oh dash it, Dolly. Not that West chap, the one who writes those frightful books?"

"Yes, and you're to be *polite* to him, Arthur. I don't see how you'd know whether they were frightful or not, you never read novels anyway."

"Well, I still don't see how that makes seven. That's only six."

"Sir Henry Clithering."

"Oh." Colonel Bantry was mollified. He liked Sir Henry—the former commissioner of Scotland Yard was a man after his own heart; traditional, fond of his after-dinner pipe, and not too talkative. "Oh yes, I'd forgotten that. Well, he's all right, but do we really have to put up with all the rest of 'em in the house?"

"They won't be *in* the house, Arthur, not all of them anyway. Raymond and Mrs. West will be staying at Miss Marple's cottage—they're only coming here for Christmas Day. And the Dashwoods are nobody's fault but your own. *I* didn't invite them."

"Well, the rum thing is," Colonel Bantry said ruminatively, "I don't quite know what possessed me. I certainly didn't *mean* to invite them, if you know what I mean. But Major Dashwood was so dashed friendly, and somehow the subject came up and I found I'd extended the old hand of hospitality, don't you know."

"No, I *don't* know, Arthur, I wasn't there. All I know is that you telephoned in a great panic saying had we room for two more at Christmas, and here we are. And now," Mrs. Bantry stood, smoothing down her skirt, "I had better go and break the news to Cook. I only hope we're in time to speak to Footit about putting in an order for another turkey."

"I can't tell you what a treat this is, Mrs. Bantry," Joan West said again. She stirred her cocktail and gazed admiringly around the drawing room at Gossington Hall, from the blazing fire in the hearth to the massed holly and ivy trailing across the mantlepiece. "A real old-fashioned Christmas. And such a lovely tree."

"Collins has outdone himself this year," Mrs. Bantry said. She put her sewing basket aside and looked with satisfaction at the tall Norwegian Spruce standing in the corner of the drawing room. "He's our gardener, you know—although these days he's more of a director of operations. We've had to hire a new under-gardener, Bertie Finch, as poor Collins can't manage the heavy digging any more. Bertie's a little—" She stopped, caught Miss Marple's eye, and coughed, then said, "Well, in any case beggars can't be choosers and I must say we've had no complaints with his work. And it is *so* difficult to get staff these days, and we do have a *lot* of garden."

Joan followed her gaze out of the drawing-room window, across the admittedly expansive lawns. "Oh! It's snowing again! How perfect."

White flakes had begun to fall on to the thick blanket of unbroken snow already covering the sculpted yew trees and hessianed rose trees of the terrace.

"A white Christmas," Raymond said with a wry smile. "Quite the picture postcard cliché."

"Yes, dear, most picturesque," Miss Marple agreed placidly. She was sitting in a tall armchair beside the fire, very much the Victorian old lady with her lace cap and gloves, and she was knitting something snowy and white that frothed over her lap. "Although very inconvenient for the car drivers, or so I have always heard."

"Blasted inconvenient for everyone," Major Dashwood put in. "Heard on the wireless that the train line from London is blocked. Seems like we were bally lucky to get through before the snow started."

"I do hope we won't be trapped, Carlton," the lady opposite said, her blue eyes widening. Mrs. Dashwood was a pretty, rather vacant-looking woman in her early thirties, with a face that was both mobile and yet strangely devoid of emotion. Her eyes, now, were open as wide as they could go, rather in the manner of a china doll, but the expression in them seemed to Joan like a sort of pantomime alarm.

"Don't you worry, Esmé, m'dear," her husband assured her, patting her arm. "We've no reason to hurry back to London, and Arthur and Dolly won't throw you out into the snow, ha ha!"

"What's that?" Colonel Bantry said, looking up from where he was cleaning out his pipe into the fire.

"Throw you out into the snow? I should think not, no question of such a thing."

"Arthur!" Mrs. Bantry's voice cut into the conversation from the centre of the room, where she was standing under a huge bunch of mistletoe suspended from the chandelier. "I have been standing under this mistletoe for quite ten minutes waiting for you to notice me."

"Well, we can't have that!" Major Dashwood said, putting down his whisky and soda and heaving himself to his feet with a show of gallantry. "May I, Mrs. B?"

Mrs. Bantry presented a powdered cheek—rather reluctantly, it seemed to Miss Marple—and Major Dashwood planted a whiskery kiss upon it and then bowed.

"Too late, Bantry, what what!" the Major said with a chuckle, returning to his seat.

"My turn, Raymond," Joan said. She set down her glass by the big scarlet poinsettia and moved to stand under the arrangement. Her husband smiled and stood up to join her.

"Of course, it's all very pagan," he remarked, as he kissed his wife's cheek. "It's a good thing the vicar isn't here—I'm not sure what he'd think of these survivalist vestiges of the old gods. Your pretty little Christmas customs," he waved a finger at the room, encompassing the Bantrys, Dashwoods and his aunt, "are very far from Christian, in fact they're something of a druidical wolf in sheep's clothing. The Norse Gods would have recognised all this holly and ivy for what it was—symbols of fertility, plant worship and renewal. Kissing under the mistletoe is the modern, watered-down remnant of what were once some very earthy customs indeed."

"Ha, steady on now, old chap!" Major Dashwood said with his short barking laugh. "Let's not shock the women and children, what?"

"I don't think your nephew is listening, Major Dashwood," Joan said, with a nod to the far side of the room where Ronald sat droopingly over a book. "He seems far too interested in his book. And speaking for myself, I'm an artist, and I assure you it takes a great deal more than a few Norse Gods to shock *me*."

"Oh, but you're married, Mrs. West," Mrs. Dashwood put in, with a significant glance at Miss Marple. "And that makes a difference, doesn't it? I doubt dear Miss Marple is used to talk of—what was it? Norse fertility rituals?"

"Oh, well," Miss Marple murmured, picking up a stitch. "I wouldn't say—I mean, in a village one is not nearly so protected as outsiders perhaps assume.

Fertility . . . birth . . . I can assure you these are hardly matters unknown in St. Mary Mead. Only the other day, Mrs. Clyde's girl, Dora—but there . . . I mustn't gossip."

"I rather like the old traditions," Sir Henry Clithering said from his seat by the fire, with a smile. "When I was a boy, the tradition in our village was to break off a berry every time one kissed a girl, and when all the berries were gone, so were all the kisses. What do you think, Miss Marple? Shall we?"

He rose and stood beneath the mistletoe, hand outstretched.

Twinkling, the old lady laid aside her knitting and moved to the centre of the room, presenting her pink cheek for Sir Henry's kiss. Sir Henry, for his part, reached up to pluck a berry, but then withdrew quickly, sucking his finger.

"Ouch! I'd forgotten how prickly greenery can be. Well, dash it, the berries will have to stay. But I'll claim the kiss."

He bent and kissed the old lady's cheek, and Miss Marple gave him a rather mischievous smile.

"Not my first kiss beneath the mistletoe, Sir Henry. It always reminds me of hat pins, you know."

"Hat pins?" said Sir Henry, rather bewildered.

"I'm afraid you've lost me with the association there, Miss Marple."

"Oh yes, indeed. Young men used to loiter beneath it at Christmas parties, and if a girl came past that they liked, they would claim a kiss, and *sometimes* they were rather insistent. But my dear mother always used to advise all the young ladies to keep a hat pin in one's bodice. There's nothing like a hat pin to provide a little discouragement to an unwanted suitor. Railway carriages too."

"Railway carriages?" Colonel Bantry sounded disconcerted. Across the room Raymond shot his wife a look of slight concern. Really, his aunt was becoming more than a little scatty these days.

"Oh yes," put in Mrs. Bantry from her seat at the other side of the room, "*I* remember that quite well. The train would go into a tunnel, and all the lights would go out. And the young men would seize the chance to kiss the girl sitting opposite them, complete strangers sometimes. And if it was a long tunnel, of course, they would sit down before the train exited and then, when the lights came on, you would be glaring at a row of young men, quite unable to tell which of them it had been. But if you kept a hatpin to hand, you could jab them with it, and *that* soon sent them scurrying back to their seat."

"Dear me, Dolly," said her husband, looking quite astonished. "I had no idea you were so very fierce."

"Well, Arthur, only if one didn't *like* the young man."

Just then the gong rang out. The drooping young man in the corner raised his head from his book.

"I say, is that dinner ready? I'm starving."

"It's the dressing gong," Mrs. Bantry said briskly. "Not that I shall bother." She picked up her mending again, and smoothed down her rather serviceable dark brown lace dress. Mrs. Dashwood, however, rose and left the room murmuring something about powdering her nose.

"I say, Clithering," Major Dashwood stood and stretched. "Fancy a spot of billiards before lunch?"

"I don't play, I'm afraid," Sir Henry said. "But perhaps Bantry would indulge you in a game and I'll come and keep score?"

"I'll join you for a cigarette," Raymond West said, and the four men departed for the billiards room, leaving Joan, Miss Marple and Mrs. Bantry alone with the listless Ronald.

"I wish he'd put down that book," Mrs. Bantry muttered to the two women, sticking her needle into her mending with a restrained ferocity. "It's so extremely rude, reading in company. I would have my novel confiscated if I'd behaved like that as a child. Oh blast. I've run out of pins."

"Yes, dear, but it's an awkward age," Miss Marple whispered. Then, more loudly, she said, addressing the boy, "Do tell me about yourself, Ronald. You are staying with your aunt and uncle?"

"Yes," the young man said. He looked, Miss Marple thought, a little old to be a student, although it was hard to tell with young people these days. His mannerisms, however, were more that of an awkward schoolboy. Now he flushed an unattractive beet purple and fell silent.

With the air of someone valiantly wringing conversation out of a stone, Mrs. Bantry remarked, "Your book seems to be very engrossing. What is it?"

"Detective stories. *Hangman's Holiday.*"

"What a ghastly-sounding title," Mrs. Bantry said, but Miss Marple shook her head.

"Oh no, dear. Miss Sayers, you know. Lord Peter Wimsey is her detective, a very glamorous young man. I read that one myself last year from the circulating library at Much Benham. Her plots are *so* very clever, and full of literary quotations, although I must confess I don't always understand the Latin. Raymond is very kind about translating for me, but I fear he disapproves of crime fiction."

"Raymond would," Mrs. Bantry said, a little tartly.

"I think it's simply that Raymond is more interested in the *psychology* of the crime than the allocation of blame," Joan put in. "So many crime writers concentrate on *who* did it at the expense of *why*. What Freudian inadequacies lie at the root of these criminal urges?"

"I'm sure you're right, Joan dear," Miss Marple said, her needles clicking placidly. "But you know, although people are very wicked, I am not sure if there are quite so many *sexual neuroses* involved as Raymond seems to believe. So frequently I find the motives are much more mundane. Money, for example, comes up sadly often."

At the mention of the word *sexual*, the young man flushed an even darker shade of beetroot, muttered something about washing his hands, and left the room.

"Who *are* the Dashwoods, Dolly?" Miss Marple asked, as the sound of Ronald's footsteps died away up the corridor. Mrs. Bantry put down her mending, and poked the fire with rather evident ill-temper.

"Oh, really such *awful* people. I have no idea what Arthur was thinking. It's quite unlike him—he's the most unsociable person usually. Well, I mean not with people like *you*, and Sir Henry. People that he likes, I mean. But with people he doesn't really know, he's normally positively antisocial. And then he goes and invites the Dashwoods! *He's* Coleton or Carlton or something—a retired major, and a brother of Lord Archibald Dashwood. Or maybe a cousin. I can't quite remember, they're such a big family. And she's—well, I think she used to be some kind of actress. Her name is Esmé, if you please. And as for their nephew, he's been absolutely tiresome ever since he arrived. Wouldn't even come to church this morning. On Christmas Day, for goodness sake! I thought Arthur was going to threaten him with a horsewhip."

"He's probably bored," Joan said, thoughtlessly, and then flushed, perceiving her faux pas. "I mean, for us it's different, of course! But you know, at that age . . ."

"Of course he's bored," Mrs. Bantry snapped. "Any boy his age would be bored, cooped up in the country with a lot of middle-aged people. But that's hardly my fault, or Arthur's. From what I understand, he's been packed off with his aunt and uncle as some kind of punishment for being sent down from Oxford. Gambling or something. Result, they don't want him here, and he certainly doesn't want to *be* here. And the trouble with young people today is that they don't hesitate to show that. No consideration for Arthur or me. Just sits around with his arms folded giving monosyllabic answers to questions. I'm afraid I've put him next to Raymond at dinner. I thought he might be able to get something out of the boy."

"Oh Dolly, do you think that was wise?" Miss Marple asked. "Raymond is a dear boy, but he can be—forgive me, Joan dear—but, well, just a touch cynical at times. And children that age are so very susceptible to influence."

Joan laughed.

"Well, I'm beyond caring," Mrs. Bantry said with finality. "I've put up with him for long enough, and so has Arthur. As far as I'm concerned, Raymond is welcome to him and perhaps he can turn him into a character in one of his novels. He likes unpleasant people, doesn't he?"

"Dear Raymond—" began Miss Marple, but her remark was cut short by a piercing shriek from upstairs.

"What was that?" Joan said, frowning.

"Oh, probably that awful Dashwood woman's seen a mouse," Mrs. Bantry said. "I told Lorrimer only the other day we needed to set some traps on the upper landing."

"Oh, Carlton!" The cry came again, this time unmistakeably the voice of Mrs. Dashwood. "Carlton, come quick! They're *gone!*"

The three women turned to each other, and then, with one accord, rose and moved out into the hallway, where Mrs. Dashwood was standing at the foot of the staircase, holding a green morocco case and remonstrating with her husband.

"Carlton, they're *gone.*"

"Gone? What d'mean *gone,* Esmé? What's gone?"

"My pearls! I put them in here last night, but then I thought it would be nice to wear them for Christmas dinner. And now——" A sob rose in her voice. "Now they're *gone.*"

"Arthur!" Mrs. Bantry said, her voice filled with alarm as she turned to her husband. "Arthur, what is going on? Have we been burgled?"

"Burgled? Impossible," Colonel Bantry expostulated. "Don't believe a word of it."

"My dear Mrs. Dashwood," Sir Henry Clithering's manner was soothing. "Please don't distress yourself. I'm sure there's a perfectly reasonable explanation. Perhaps the pearls have fallen out into a drawer, or you didn't put them away as you thought?"

"If you're calling my wife a liar—" Major Dashwood said stiffly. Sir Henry looked taken aback.

"Not for a moment, Major. But it seems to me far more probable that this is all an unfortunate misunderstanding. Mrs. Bantry," he turned to his hostess, "will you summon the housemaid and I'm sure we can have this sorted out."

"Yes, yes, of course," Mrs. Bantry replied distractedly. "Perhaps—oh dear. Why don't you all go back to the drawing room and I'll ring for Mary."

The little group filed away and Mrs. Bantry turned despairingly to her friend.

"You see, Jane? Didn't I tell you the Dashwoods were insufferable. And right before Christmas dinner too. Cook will be *so* upset and it's so difficult to keep sirloin *warm*, you know."

Some ten minutes later, Lorrimer, the butler, accompanied by a red-eyed but composed Mary, the housemaid, were standing in the corner of the drawing room, Lorrimer drawn up to every inch of his impressive height and radiating an aura of stiff correctness.

"I have spoken to Mary and she is quite certain,

ma'am, that she never touched the green case, nor saw any pearls when she was putting the room to rights this morning. However, if you will give me leave, perhaps a search of Mrs. Dashwood's room would be in order?"

"I tell you, the necklace isn't *there*," wailed Mrs. Dashwood, from her reclining position on the chaise longue in the corner. She was holding a glass of brandy and looked quite distraught. "I've searched and searched. Do you think I didn't search? I'm not a complete fool, you know!"

"Of course they have to check, Esmé," her husband said gruffly. "Only thing to be done. The question is, who's to do it?"

"I think," Sir Henry put in, gently, "that we should entrust the search to Lorrimer and Mary, but that it would be as well for one of the Bantrys and one of the Dashwoods to be present."

"Excellent idea," said Colonel Bantry. His expression was grim. "Shall we, Dashwood? And I'd like you to come too, Clithering. Third party. Disinterested and all that."

Sir Henry nodded, and the three men stood up and followed Lorrimer and the housemaid up the stairs.

"Well, I *say*," Raymond West drawled, as silence fell

on the drawing room. "This is a turn up for the books. I can see the morning papers: 'Christmas Jewel Heist in Sleepy St. Mary Mead!'"

"Heist!" moaned Mrs. Dashwood from the corner of the sofa. "Oh, don't even say such a thing! The pearls belonged to Carlton's mother, you know—they're priceless, quite priceless. At least three thousand pounds. Probably five! If they're gone—well, I simply don't know how I'll bear it."

Raymond let out a little whistle and shook his head.

"Insured?"

"Heavens, how should I know! Carlton takes care of all that—but even if they are, these companies always find some way of wriggling out of paying up!"

"Oh dear, oh dear," Miss Marple put aside her knitting with an expression of concern. "I know quite well what you mean, Mrs. Dashwood. Mr. Blair, that clever young solicitor in Much Benham, had his motorcycle stolen three times in two years, and the last time the insurance company declined to pay out, you know. He made quite a fuss about it. But then it turned out that his friend had borrowed it and parked it in the wrong garage, so it was all to the good in the end, as I do understand the insurers are very strict about fraudulent claims and, indeed, he might have found himself in a very difficult situation had the claim actually gone through. In fact, some people thought the friend—but there. I mustn't gossip."

Mrs. Dashwood turned a tear-stained face to Miss Marple.

"Why on earth are you going on about motorcycles? I haven't lost a motorcycle! And I highly doubt my pearls are going to turn up in somebody's garage."

"No, no, indeed," Miss Marple murmured apologetically. "I'm so sorry, I'm afraid my mind was wandering. You're quite right, Mrs. Dashwood. Most distressing."

"Come now, let's not write the pearls off just yet," Joan said, comfortingly. "There's every chance they've just slipped into a drawer."

But when Sir Henry Clithering returned to the drawing room some twenty minutes later, it was with a grave face, and he shook his head slightly in reply to Raymond West's interrogatively raised eyebrow.

Mrs. Bantry stood at the sight of him, with the air of someone who has reached the end of their tether.

"I must go and speak to Cook, she'll be simply beside herself. Jane, will you come?"

Miss Marple nodded and, setting aside the fleecy white wool, she followed her old friend down the hallway. She did not say anything for the first few minutes, but as they turned the corner to the library she ventured to speak.

"Surely, Dolly dear, the kitchen is in the opposite direction?"

"I know that perfectly well," Mrs. Bantry said frankly, opening the library door and sinking into a leather armchair with a martyred expression. "I simply had to get out of that drawing room. I couldn't listen to that blasted woman sighing and groaning for another minute. Oh Jane, it's too bad. And on Christmas Day! Arthur was looking forward to his sirloin *so* much—and there's simply nothing worse than dry turkey."

"I suppose she *was* wearing the pearls last night?" Miss Marple asked. "I mean to say—it's not possible that they were left at home or mislaid on the journey down here?"

"Yes, she was wearing the things," Mrs. Bantry said crossly. "In fact, she never stopped going on about them. Made quite a to-do about the value. Arthur said afterwards it very nearly put him off his soup. Rather vulgar, I call it. It's hardly surprising they've been pinched if she goes about boasting how much they cost. It's probably that sulky nephew of hers. Or his. Whichever he is."

"So you *do* think they've been stolen?" Miss Marple enquired. Mrs. Bantry threw up her hands.

"Heaven knows! But if they don't turn up, I don't see what other explanation there is. I utterly refuse to believe Mary has anything to do with it, though! Or any of the staff, in fact. They've been with us for years. But if they aren't found, there will always be that nasty, nagging suspicion. Oh Jane, I could strangle the woman, I really could."

"Strangle who?" said a deep voice from the doorway, and Mrs. Bantry turned with a guilty jump, laying a hand on her breast.

"Arthur! How could you give me such a fright? I quite thought you were one of the Dashwoods. How are things? Any sign of the necklace?"

"Not a bit of it," her husband replied lugubriously. "Mary and Lorrimer have been through the Dashwoods' room with a fine-tooth comb, and now they're starting on the servants' rooms. It's dashed difficult, Dolly, I don't mind telling you. I came down to telephone for Constable Palk in the village. Nothing else to be done at this point."

"Oh Arthur, must we? If we get the police involved . . ."

"Nothing else for it, m'dear." Colonel Bantry's expression was grimly resigned. "Mrs. Dashwood is quite adamant they've been taken, and probably sometime this morning, either while everyone was at church, or while we were all having drinks. She put them away in her jewel case last night before she went to bed, and she's quite certain no one could have come into her room overnight. And she breakfasted in her room too, which gives a window of about ten o'clock onwards. Clithering is questioning Collins as to whether he saw anyone sneaking about the grounds, but I think it's a long shot."

"Oh dear," Mrs. Bantry said distractedly. "Then I suppose there's no alternative to ringing up Palk. But the turkey will be dry as a bone by the time *he's* finished."

Alas, Mrs. Bantry's worst fears came about. It was almost three o'clock by the time Police Constable Palk struggled through the snow to Gossington Hall, and later still when he finished interviewing the Bantrys' servants and turned his attention to the guests. Rather than the sumptuous Christmas repast they had been expecting, the little group in the drawing room dined on cold roast beef sandwiches and hot tea. Very good in their own way, as Raymond pointed out, but *not* quite the same as a full spread of sirloin and turkey, with wine, pudding, cheese, and port to follow.

Mrs. Dashwood had retired to bed with a sick headache after her own interview with Palk, and Colonel Bantry was to be seen pacing the snowy terrace with his pipe clenched between his teeth and a face like thunder, when Palk entered the drawing room and said, "Miss Marple, if I may?"

Miss Marple nodded composedly, folded her knitting, and followed the constable down the corridor to Colonel Bantry's study, where the interviews were taking place.

Sir Henry Clithering was seated in an armchair in the corner, and raised one eyebrow, rather amused, as the old lady entered and sat, very upright, in the straight-backed chair in the centre of the room.

"Detective Inspector Slack wasn't able to make it through the snow," he explained, as Miss Marple arranged her knitting composedly across her lap and folded her hands. "The road from Much Benham is completely blocked. So Palk here invited me to sit in on the interviews. I presume you don't mind, Miss Marple?"

"Oh dear me, no. No indeed. Two heads are better than one, as my dear mother always used to say."

"Or even three?" Sir Henry said, with a little smile. "Do today's events remind you of anything, Miss Marple?"

"Oh dear." Miss Marple became at once a little flustered. "Well, yes and no. But it's so difficult to be *sure*, you know, and I don't quite like to *say* anything. I suppose they found a window open?"

Sir Henry's other eyebrow rose at that, but he gave a nod.

"As a matter of fact, yes. The one in the little boot room by the back door. But what made you say that?"

"Well, of course there would *have* to be a window open—to give an opportunity. I suppose it was forced?"

"Yes," Sir Henry said dryly. "And not very expertly. Looks like some kind of trowel was used. Together with the snow, which effectively rules out any outside intervention, I'm very much afraid this looks like some kind of inside job—but searching for the pearls in a house of this size is proving to be something akin to looking for a needle in a haystack—to say nothing of the grounds."

"Oh dear, yes, I know *quite* what you mean. And the grounds, so very difficult. There were no visitors at all?"

Sir Henry shook his head.

"None. Lorrimer was quite clear on that. And we would have seen the tracks, you know, coming back from church. No, much as I would like to believe in an outside agent, I'm afraid there's no help on that score."

"Oh dear, that poor young man. It is so *very* difficult to shake off a past. And that can lead one to make, well, *foolish* decisions."

"Poor young man?" said Sir Henry, frowning.

"Can I ask where you were between the hours of ten a.m. and half past noon, Miss Marple?" put in Constable Palk, evidently doggedly determined to stick to his brief of obtaining a statement from everyone present. "I'm sorry to ask, but it's purely routine, as I'm sure you understand."

"Oh, but of course," Miss Marple said earnestly. "I do *quite* understand. And I can tell you quite well, I was in church, along with the Bantrys, Joan, Raymond and the Dashwoods. At least, the two older Dashwoods. The nephew, I think, was *not* there."

"No, he stayed here," Sir Henry said. "And I don't mind telling you, Miss Marple, we're looking into his background. He was sent down from Oxford for running up some quite considerable gambling debts."

It was at that moment that the door to the study opened and Mrs. Bantry came in.

"If you'll excuse me, ma'am," Palk began, stiffly, but Mrs. Bantry cut him off.

"Oh, don't give me that, Palk. How could you

upset Collins? I don't know what you said to him, but he's very much put out, and Bertie Finch, the under-gardener, is threatening to give notice. It's too bad, it really is."

"My dear Mrs. Bantry," Sir Henry said, "Constable Palk is only doing his job. If Finch has nothing to hide, then he has nothing to fear."

"Poppycock!" Mrs. Bantry said, turning on him angrily. "You know as well as I do how gossip gets around in a place like this. Collins says that Palk as good as accused Finch of forcing the boot-room window with a trowel. He says he found chips of paint on one in the potting shed."

"I have reason to believe that young man may not be all he says he is," Constable Palk said, with a touch of pomposity. "You might do better to take up references next time, Mrs. Bantry."

"I know quite well who he is!" Mrs. Bantry snapped. "He's the nephew of the baker in Market Basing and he went to prison for petty theft for two months. That's why we were able to get him for a post no one else wanted, and a very good under-gardener he has been!"

"A very good under-gardener, but a rather foolish young man," murmured Sir Henry Clithering, tapping his empty pipe on the table and looking thoughtfully at Miss Marple. "Isn't that right, Miss Marple?"

"Oh dear, oh dear," Miss Marple said with a worried sigh. "So *much* foolishness in the world, and so very difficult for a young man trying to make his way. Dolly, if you will forgive me, I need to speak to Constable Palk and Sir Henry Clithering for just a moment. And then I will join you in the drawing room. I think we all need a spot of hot tea."

"You'd better all stay the night, Jane," Mrs. Bantry said resignedly, over the promised tea. "It's much too dark out, and Arthur says the road to the village is quite blocked."

"Oh, thank you, Dolly. I am sorry to put you out, but I do think it would be for the best. Dear Raymond was talking about walking, but I don't think he's quite used to our country lanes, and as for Joan—"

"As for Joan?" said an inquiring voice from behind them, and Miss Marple turned to see her nephew and his wife standing behind them. Joan laughed. "I'm sorry, Aunt Jane, I didn't mean to eavesdrop, but I couldn't help overhearing my name. Are we quite snowed in then?"

"I'm afraid so," Mrs. Bantry said. "Even Palk hasn't

172 • RUTH WARE

been able to get back—he's bedding down in the empty room above the scullery. I've asked Mary to make up the blue room for you and your husband, Mrs. West. Jane, I've put you in the room over the porch. I dare say you'll all be horridly uncomfortable, but it can't be helped—Mary's usually so efficient, but she's been quite put out by all of this business, and the second housemaid, Dorcas, has gone to bed with hysterics. Hysterics, I ask you! When I was a girl, housemaids didn't have hysterics."

"Yes, indeed, Dolly," said Miss Marple gently, "but, you know, Bertie Finch is her young man, so it's understandable she would be very much upset by the whole affair."

"She's not the only one." A gruff voice came from over Miss Marple's shoulder, and the little group turned to see Colonel Bantry standing behind them, with a very grim expression on his face. "Absolutely damnable business."

"Oh Arthur, they haven't arrested him, have they?"

"Taken for questioning, but I think it's only a matter of time until he's charged. Looks pretty bad for the boy. The pearls are nowhere to be found, but Palk found a piece of the clasp in the flowerbed outside the boot-room window. And the worst of it is that

Dashwood has been on to his insurance company and it looks like the blasted things weren't insured properly—the policy ran out last month."

"Oh Arthur, no!" Mrs. Bantry's face was a picture of horror as she put down her teacup. "So what does that mean?"

"Mean? Means I'll have to pay for the blo—I mean the blasted things. Can hardly refuse to, considering it seems to have been one of *my* servants who took the pearls. I'm going to have a word with Barlett and Mundy when they reopen, see if we can claim on our policy perhaps, but I'm not hopeful, Dolly, not hopeful at all."

"How much were they worth?" Mrs. Bantry asked.

"Between three and five thousand pounds," Colonel Bantry replied, in a voice of deep disgust. Raymond West gave a whistle.

"Nor I," Colonel Bantry said gloomily.

"Oh dear." Miss Marple's expression was one of deep distress. "Oh dear, that poor young man. So *very* foolish. And so difficult to know what to do for the best."

"What on earth d'you mean, Miss Marple?" Colonel Bantry said, his voice gruff. "Nothing to be done apart from take his medicine."

It was five minutes past two in the morning, and gentle snores were coming from the bedrooms all along the east corridor when a stealthy footstep might have been heard on the staircase at Gossington Hall. Softly, very softly, someone was coming down the long flight of stairs in stockinged feet, and padding quietly along the corridor to the drawing room, where a low fire still burned in the grate, sending the shadow of the tiptoeing figure lurching across the hearth rug to the corners of the room.

Softer still, the figure picked up one of the upright chairs from beside the fire and placed it gently in the centre of the room, beneath the huge bouquet of mistletoe that hung from the chandelier. With a slight grunt, the figure climbed up on to the chair, and reached up—only for a voice to speak from the deep shadows beside the fireplace.

"Oh, do be careful, Mrs. Dashwood. Those pins are really very sharp."

The woman standing on the chair gave a little scream and staggered to the ground, peering into the shadows with her hand over her heart.

"Oh! Miss—Miss Marple, isn't it? You gave me a simply frightful shock. What in heaven's name are you doing here? And why on earth are you talking about pins?"

"The pins in the mistletoe," said the old lady earnestly. "I should be very careful if I were you. Sir Henry pricked his finger quite nastily."

"I have no idea what you're talking about," Mrs. Dashwood said, rather flustered. "I—I had asked that poor under-gardener for some mistletoe—we live in London, you know, and it's rather difficult to find, so I thought I'd try to start some of our own on the apple tree in our garden. Only then, with everything that happened—and I didn't like to bother the Bantrys, considering everything—so I thought I'd just slip down and help myself."

"I don't think that's quite true," said Miss Marple gently. "I think, you know, you have come for the pearls. It's why I waited. I couldn't be *sure* who would come for them."

The woman standing in the centre of the room said nothing, but her face and demeanour changed with a suddenness that was almost bewildering. Her hand dropped from her heart to her side, and the foolish, rather vacant expression had vanished, replaced by a kind of hard cunning. She looked at Miss Marple rather appraisingly, as if sizing up the old lady's strength and constitution.

"I shouldn't, you know," said Miss Marple, with equanimity. "I am a good deal tougher than I look, and

I chose this chair because it was *very* close to the servants' bell. I have my finger on it now."

"And who's to say *I* didn't ring it after you wandered down in the night and had a bad turn?" said the woman standing in front of her, her voice hard and cold.

"I am," said a voice from behind her. The woman whipped round, and the lights came on. Constable Palk was standing in the doorway, his expression very grim. "Put that pin cushion down, Mrs. Dashwood. You're under arrest."

"So their name wasn't Dashwood at all?" said Colonel Bantry, rather astonished, over eggs and bacon the next morning. Miss Marple shook her head.

"No. But it's so very easy to take a name like Dashwood, someone with a large sprawling family, and claim to be a distant relation."

"But I don't understand," Mrs. Bantry said plaintively. "The pearls were real. They had a certificate of authenticity and everything."

"Oh yes, *quite* real, that was why it was quite imperative that she got them back."

"And what put you on to the Dashwoods?" said Sir Henry, mystified.

"Well, dear Sir Henry, it was really you," Miss Marple

said, with a twinkle. "Or rather your remark about the prickly greenery. Because, you know, mistletoe doesn't *have* prickles. And that made me wonder."

"But the pearls hadn't even gone missing then," Raymond West said.

"No, indeed. And that was all part of their plan. They displayed the pearls as prominently as possible at dinner the night before, and then the next day they disappeared off to church, leaving that poor foolish boy in charge of what I believe thieves call *the handover*. I don't know what they told him. I dare say the police will get to the bottom of it. But of course he was very badly off, having run up considerable gambling debts and young men will do *very* foolish things for money."

"Ah, the handover," Raymond West said. "And here we come to Bertie Finch, I presume?"

"No, dear. Not Bertie. The problem was, the snow made everything so very difficult. I don't know *when* Ronald discovered that the accomplice wasn't coming—the news of the road closures were on the wireless—but he must have had a very nasty moment when he realised the plan had failed and he could not get the pearls out of the house. Of course the sensible thing would have been to simply call the whole thing off, and somehow intercept his aunt before she could raise a hue and cry. But I think he panicked. And put together with the book he was reading . . ."

"So the original plan was to hand the pearls over to an accomplice?" Mrs. Bantry asked. "And make it look like a break in?"

"Yes. *That* was why the nephew had to remain at home. Then, on return from church, Mrs. Dashwood would raise the alarm and insist on a very thorough search of their belongings, so as to make it *quite* clear that the pearls were not in the possession of the Dashwoods. I think, you know, Sir Henry, you will find that they have done this before. But there is a very great difference between staging a robbery in a place like London, with many people coming and going at all hours, and St. Mary Mead, where every visitor is remarked upon."

"Well, I have to hand it to him," Raymond West said, magnanimously. "He may have panicked, but that was a pretty clever idea about the mistletoe. I wonder how he came up with it?"

"Well, my dear," Miss Marple said, colouring a little. "I don't know whether it really *was* his idea, you know."

"Not his idea?" Raymond looked puzzled. "Whose idea was it then?"

"Dorothy L. Sayers," Miss Marple said simply.

There was a moment's puzzled pause and then Mrs. Bantry spoke.

"The author? That's what the boy was reading, wasn't it?"

"High-society crime," Raymond said. "But I don't see—"

Miss Marple flushed again.

"I know, dear Raymond, that you do not really approve of detective stories. But I must admit to having rather a weakness for them. Lord Peter Wimsey is so *very* dashing, and Miss Sayers' plots are really extremely ingenious. There is a story in *Hangman's Holiday* where a thief hides some unstrung pearls in a bunch of mistletoe and I think when poor Ronald realised he was not going to be able to dispose of the necklace as planned, the inspiration proved irresistible. He snipped the string, took the pins from your pin cushion, Dolly—you remember, you found you had run out—and hastily fastened the pearls into the arrangement. It was a risk—but not such a big one as all that. The servants were all either at church, or occupied with preparing the Christmas dinner. I would imagine he burned the string in the drawing room fire, and that left only the clasp to dispose of—which he dropped out of the boot-room window.

"What I do not know is whether he meant to incriminate poor Bertie Finch. I rather think not—it was simply bad luck that the snow prevented an outsider from being blamed, and of course Ronald was *rather* foolish to use a trowel from the potting shed to force the window. That meant the evidence pointed to Bertie in a very unfortunate way."

"Well, bravo, Aunt Jane," Raymond said, with the air of one magnanimously accepting a point scored against him. "That's one up to you and your lending library. Never again will I cast aspersions on your reading taste! But I must take issue with your theory that they'd done it before—I don't see how that could be. They could hardly keep claiming on their insurance for the pearls. The insurance company wouldn't put up with it for a moment."

"I don't think there ever was an insurance company, dear. *That* was just to make it clear to the Bantrys that if they did not take responsibility for the theft, the Dashwoods would be out of pocket. No, I think they were a rather clever pair. Major Dashwood—although, you know, I am not quite convinced that he is a real major—travelled the country looking for likely, I believe the term is *marks*, for their little game. Upright, honourable types like Colonel Bantry, who could be relied upon to pay up when their own servants were thrown under suspicion."

"Dash it, I *said* the fellow forced himself upon me," muttered Colonel Bantry, rather chagrined. "Couldn't even remember inviting him for Christmas, and then suddenly there we were, lumbered with them."

"Quite right on all counts, Miss Marple," Sir Henry put in, buttering his toast. "I spoke with Detective Inspector Slack in Much Benham this morning. Our so-called Major Dashwood wasn't a major at all—plain Mr. Philip Rider from Friern Barnet, with two outstanding warrants to his name, if you please. He lost his head completely when they took him in. Confessed everything. *She,* on the other hand, was a very cool operator and, I rather think, the brains behind the operation. Quite the contrast from the fluffy-headed type she made herself out to be. The inspector still hadn't got to the bottom of her real identity when I last spoke to him, but I've no doubt he will. They'd run the scheme very successfully in London, Manchester and Leeds, but the last time there were some difficult questions asked about the Major's whereabouts during the window of time when the pearls disappeared. Poor Ronald—his name really *is* Ronald, by the way—must have seemed like a gift from heaven in that respect—someone they could saddle with the risk of the handover, while they were unimpeachably attending church with alibis up to the hilt."

"What *I* want to know," Mrs. Bantry said with some acerbity, "is whether they'll be able to charge them with anything. Is stealing one's own pearls actually a crime? Especially when *they* weren't the ones who made the insurance claims?"

"Well, that is the question," Sir Henry Clithering said, thoughtfully, stroking his moustaches. "But Inspector Slack's a clever chap, and I rather think he may be able to get them on misrepresentation or obtaining goods by deception or something. Mark my words, he'll make sure they're locked up one way or another. And, at the very least, they'll have said goodbye to those pearls—apparently the insurance companies are already fighting over who owns them."

"And good riddance!" Mrs. Bantry said, with satisfaction, sawing at her bacon in a manner suggestive of unspent vindictiveness. "By the way, Mr. West, did your wife hear the breakfast gong? I'm afraid we keep country hours, and the breakfast things are usually cleared by nine o'clock."

"Oh," Raymond said vaguely. "We're not really morning people, you know, and I think perhaps she had one or two too many cocktails last night. She's having coffee in her room. I dare say she'll be down later."

"Ah, the artistic life," said Sir Henry with a twinkle.

———

A few hours later, Inch's taxi was sitting outside the front door of Gossington Hall while Miss Marple fluttered around, packing her knitting, writing out the recipe she had promised Cook, and bidding goodbye to the Bantrys and Sir Henry. As the taxi drew away down the newly shovelled drive, Sir Henry looked after it indulgently.

"You would never think that that lace cap hid one of the finest crime-solving brains in all of Christendom, would you? Mind like a bacon slicer, and there she is fussing about Dundee cake. I doubt we would have caught them, you know, if Miss Marple hadn't tipped Palk to the pearls being hidden in the mistletoe. The Dashwoods would have retrieved them, changed their name, and been off to the next victim, and none of us any the wiser."

"You see, Arthur," said Mrs. Bantry, with a touch of triumph in her voice. "It was a lucky day for you when I invited Jane Marple to Christmas dinner. A lucky day for you," she repeated, with satisfaction.

"Oof!" Joan said with a sigh, sinking back into the armchair in Miss Marple's little cottage. "I feel absolutely beat! I've no idea why."

"Don't you, my dear?" Miss Marple said, giving her a rather curious look.

"I suppose it takes it out of you," Raymond said. "Crime and skulduggery, I mean! Really, Aunt Jane, that was a frightfully lucky guess you made about the mistletoe. The Bantrys would have been in the soup without that."

"Yes, dear, very fortunate. Not to mention poor Bertie Finch." The old lady settled herself in the armchair on the other side of the fire, and shook out her knitting. "Now, if you'll excuse me, I must sort this out. I'm very much afraid I dropped a stitch earlier at the Bantrys, and my eyes are sadly not what they were. Dolly and I were gossiping—*most* reprehensible, but, really, it's only human nature—and I was not concentrating properly."

"What *are* you knitting, Aunt Jane?" Joan asked, looking curiously at the snowy white pile trailing across the old lady's lap. "You've been clicking away all the time we've been here. Is it a shawl?"

"A shawl? Not quite, my dear," Miss Marple said, her cheeks going a little pink. "No, not a shawl, but, indeed, I don't quite like . . ."

"What on earth?" Raymond said, looking astonished. "Don't go all Victorian on us, Aunt Jane, and tell us you're knitting underclothes or something? Though I don't believe that even in St. Mary Mead people wear knitted bloomers."

"Not underclothes, dear, no." She shook out the snowy white square across her lap. "It's, well . . ." She shot a sharp, penetrating look at her nephew's wife. "Well, it's a baby's blanket. But I didn't quite like . . ."

"A baby's blanket?" Raymond said, and suddenly it was his own cheeks that were flushed, as he looked from his aunt to his wife, for the first time almost, in Miss Marple's long experience of her nephew, lost for words.

There was a long pause, and then Joan burst out laughing and threw up her hands.

"I declare, Aunt Jane, you must be a witch. However did you guess?"

"Well, my dear, when one lives in a village like St. Mary Mead, one becomes well acquainted with human nature in that regard. And Raymond did say you had been rather pulled down recently, so I confess I wondered before you came down here, and, of course, once I was looking out for the signs . . ."

"And I thought I was being so clever pouring my Gin and It into the pot plants and stifling my yawns. I couldn't very well tell anyone that cocktails make me feel quite sick these days."

"Yes, dear, and, if I may suggest, in future it would be better *not* to choose a poinsettia. They are rather sensitive to over-watering. And then, of course, when

Raymond said that you were late to breakfast because of too many cocktails, I'm afraid I knew that to be an untruth."

"Well, we're rumbled," Raymond said with a laugh. "Joan and I had wanted to keep it to ourselves for a few weeks more, but I suppose the whole of St. Mary Mead knows by now?"

"Oh no, dear," Miss Marple said, looking a little shocked. She folded the knitting neatly in her lap. "No, I shouldn't dream of breathing a word until you and Joan are ready to announce her—" she gave a little deprecating cough, "her *condition*, you know. No, my dear," she turned to Joan with a smile. "Your secret is *quite* safe with me."

The Open Mind

Naomi Alderman

At the far end of the Fellows' Retiring Room, as the pre-dinner sherries were passed around, Professor Cuthbert Cayling, the Master of St. Bede's College, Oxford, was holding forth, as he so often did.

"Of course, this college would have collapsed after the Restoration had it not been for the intervention of the family of which I have the honour of belonging to a cadet branch . . ."

Miss Marple watched him with interest. She had seen Professor Cayling, expert on constitutional history and politics, on the small black-and-white television set in her parlour. He was a frequent guest on the type of angry discussion programme that she often felt tended a little more towards entertainment than enlightenment. She had had the impression before that he rather enjoyed the sound of his own voice, and everything that she'd seen so far this evening tended to bear that out.

Professor Cayling's voice boomed from the depths of his enormous beard. "Edward Bedlington, the fifth duke, felt a connection to the college owing to the family seat being fairly near Jarrow, you see: the location of the Venerable Bede's abbey." The bored-looking young woman he was addressing suddenly went wide-eyed.

"Look, the poor girl's trying to keep herself awake," Sir Aaron Kahn muttered, in an aside to Miss Marple. "Who is she? Elspeth Something. Works for the BBC, I think. Bloody Cuthbert does this every chance he can get. Just show him a pretty girl and he's off."

"Yes," said Miss Marple, "it does look as if he's trying to impress her. I wonder whether he's succeeding."

Sir Aaron laughed under his breath.

Professor Cayling was now explaining the arcane rules according to which, even though he descended from the Bedlington-Bomarsands via the female line, he was still given access to the family estate at Seaham Ryhope. Elspeth Something of the BBC was feigning interest, nodding and smiling. She wants something from him, thought Miss Marple, I wonder what it is.

It was Founder's Day at St. Bede's College, in the freezing early January of 1970, and Sir Aaron Kahn—retired judge and an honorary fellow at the college—had invited Miss Marple to be his guest at high table. They were celebrating the successful end of a particularly difficult case—the Quaverley choir murders—which had had the police baffled. The solution was only uncovered when Miss Marple, who'd happened to be visiting her dear friend Ruth, a stalwart of said choir, had pointed out the crucial importance of the reversed oil painting. Sir Aaron, having jumped at the chance to be partners in detection, had suggested they could toast the end of that investigation at St. Bede's. The Founder's Dinners were legendarily sumptuous.

"Just don't mind Cuthbert Cayling," Sir Aaron had said, "he's a brilliant scholar and a very ambitious man, only . . . his manners."

Sir Aaron had been right. He had very kindly motored Miss Marple up in his own racing-green MG Roadster, and as he and Miss Marple had pulled up in the college-allotted parking space half an hour earlier, Professor Cayling had been waiting for them.

His first words to Sir Aaron had been: "Pretty little car. Well, I suppose you can spare the shekels, old man."

Sir Aaron introduced Jane Marple—"the genius who puts the bench to shame"—with all politeness, but Miss Marple saw that the casual anti-Jewish insult rankled, and noted an expression she'd never seen before on her friend's face—a flash of pure dislike. Even hatred.

Although the buildings were a glorious mix of High Medieval and Gothic, the event so far was a touch less grand than Miss Marple had anticipated. The leather of the high wing-backed chairs was cracked, the sherry was good but rather frugally poured, and the staff seemed to her less well-trained than her own maids. But, of course, she reminded herself, standards now were not what they once were, and one must permit the permissive society to live by its own lights.

"Budget cuts," said Sir Aaron, noticing Miss Marple's surprise. "It's all 'Open University' now and 'flinging the doors open.' Modernisation and 'serving the great unused reservoir of human talent and potential' are *not* well-represented by the dons of this college supping on honeydew and the milk of paradise, according to Mr. Wilson."

"I notice Harold Wilson doesn't intend to return his Oxford degree and take an Open one instead," laughed Dr. Agnetha Strom, mirthlessly. "Hypocrisy is everywhere." Her English was very mildly accented with traces of unplaceable Northern European. "Not least over there," she indicated Professor Cayling with her pointed chin. "Look at him cosying up with that BBC producer. He thinks he'll be the next Kenneth Clark. A ten-part lecture series on democracy through the ages. Pay lip service to the masses but don't give up your own luxuries. Typical."

Sir Aaron chuckled warmly, "Miss Marple, Agnetha hasn't forgiven Cuthbert for taking her place on one of those late-night arts discussion programmes."

"He knew less than nothing about Schopenhauer," Agnetha hissed.

"But he was fit and well for the discussion with Huw Wheldon and you were . . . indisposed. It's not Cuthbert's fault that one appearance has turned him into an academic celebrity."

"I wouldn't put it past him to have slipped some senna into my soup," said Dr. Strom darkly.

"Oh," said Miss Marple, "oh dear."

On this unappetising note, the butler appeared at the door of the Fellows' Retiring Room and declared in a loud voice, "My lords, ladies and gentlemen, dinner is served!"

St. Bede's College's fifteenth-century dining hall was renowned as one of the most beautiful in Oxford.

Tiled in black-and-white chequerboard, lit by hundreds of fragrant beeswax candles in sconces, and furnished in five-century-old dark polished wood, it was all Miss Marple had hoped for. She couldn't prevent herself from murmuring "Oh my" under her breath as she and the other guests were ushered to their tables. The linen was white as a snow-covered hill, the silver gleamed like a lake in moonlight. Each place-setting was written in swooping calligraphy—as she found her place, Miss Marple noted with relief that Sir Aaron was to her right hand and, with surprise, that "Miss Elspeth Hearken" was to her left. Opposite Miss Marple, a dour, long-faced, rather thin and pale man was swooping toward the seat labelled "Dr. Eammon McManaway."

Dr. McManaway immediately introduced himself, as grim as if they were attending a funeral not a celebration feast: "Eammon. Ancient Languages. What are you? New Medievalist at St. Cross? I hear they're having a bad time there with rats at present. Have you rats? In your rooms?"

"Oh," said Miss Marple, scarcely able to know how to respond to this, "No, no, I don't have . . . rats."

"You will," said Eammon darkly, "that's what I hear. On the subject of rats, look at that."

He pointed towards the top of the table, where Professor Cuthbert Cayling was engaged in a dispute with a shortish red-faced man with luxuriant brown-gold hair.

"You know who that is, don't you? Medievalist, like you. Simon Skipper. You've read his monograph on Mathilda. Seminal. Bursar of the college. Thinks he should have been Master at the last election. Takes any opportunity to undermine Cuthbert. What's he on about now?"

Miss Marple strained her ears but only caught a few snippets of the conversation. Certainly both men seemed extremely angry. The staff were trying to indicate that it was time to sit down for the meal, but neither man took much notice. The undergraduates, who were already seated, were mostly busy with their own boisterous conversation, but a few had started to notice that something was going on at high table.

Without warning, the golden-headed Simon tipped over the Master's half-empty crystal glass of wine, staining the white linen red as blood. He stormed away from high table, his face a dark cloud.

"Bloody hell," said Eammon, "it's never gone that far before."

Professor Cuthbert Cayling looked about, bemused,

as the staff covered the stain with fresh linen and set him a new place. Once this was done, Cuthbert ceremoniously and rather pompously tapped his fresh glass nine times precisely, and waited until there was total silence in the hall, until each undergraduate had stopped whispering to his neighbour or shuffling on his chair. He stood ponderously and declaimed the words "Benedictus Benedicat," before sitting back in his chair with great solemnity. That, it appeared, was that for speeches.

Elspeth Hearken, the producer from the BBC, had taken in the drama unfolding at high table with raw curiosity. She was a modern young woman, with long brown hair and a deep fringe, wearing a black-and-white polka-dot long-sleeved dress in the fashionably short style that showed most of her dimpled, slightly mottled legs. These fashionable styles didn't quite *suit* everyone, Miss Marple thought, and Elspeth Hearken seemed rather a victim of the current trend, as she self-consciously pulled the hem of her dress to try to get it a little lower when she sat.

"I should have worn tweed, like you," said Elspeth, half apologetically, "only I didn't want to seem to be trying too hard to fit in. Tell me, do you know what's going on at the head of the table?"

"Professor Cuthbert Cayling never makes a friend

if he can make an enemy," Eammon McManaway answered her. "He beat Simon Skipper in the election to be Master. You'd think that victory would make a man magnanimous. But, since then, Cuthbert has gone out of his way to humiliate Simon at every opportunity. Last week at college council, he asked him to bring the tea and biscuits. As if he were a scout! And he's trying to get Skipper out of his rooms—he has rather a nice set on staircase five that Cuthbert wants to use as a second office."

"On these tiny differences, academic life is built," said Sir Aaron, pleasantly.

"*Is* it tiny?" asked Elspeth. There was something forceful in her manner that Miss Marple had to respect even if she couldn't quite like it. An ambition. "I do think one must keep an open mind about everything. Hasn't the college received a large bequest? One which the Master can decide what to do with, as long as he has approval of council? Don't you think Professor Cayling might be trying to force Simon Skipper to leave the council—or make it so unpleasant for him here that he leaves college? Isn't it possible that's what's going on?"

"Oho," said Eammon, "we should watch what we say, with a journalist in our midst."

Elspeth continued: "Well, isn't it? Can't you acknowledge that possibility?"

She seemed scarcely able to let the matter lie, but, propitiously, the man on her left asked her about her own academic interests. They set about discussing them with fervour.

The first course, partridge stuffed with prunes on a bed of wild mushrooms—was placed before them all. Miss Marple suddenly felt rather tired. It happened more and more these days that, at a large event such as this, a wave of exhaustion would sweep over her. She found herself longing for her quiet parlour in St. Mary Mead. These young people, she said to herself, have no interest in you any longer, Jane, nor any need for you. To them, you are a Victorian relic; ancient history, just like the manuscripts they study. Snippets of conversation swirled around her: Sir Aaron's stories of his time on the bench, the academic discourse of these terribly intelligent people.

"Do you know, he had been using that baker's shop as a front for his drug-dealing business?" said Sir Aaron conversationally to the young don sitting next to him, "The chicken pies were stuffed with it."

"In a way, one can't help admiring Chatterton for his daring. All those forgeries, took everyone in," said Elspeth, to the man to her left.

"I've heard people say that, but, honestly, what

would most of us *do* with a computing machine at home?" said Eammon McManaway. "I can't even work my Goblin Teasmade. I keep putting the wrong liquid in the wrong place."

From two places down the table, the oddly accented tones of Dr. Agnetha Strom could be heard: "Of course there are ways for him to use it for himself. Every trust needs a generously-paid president, didn't you know?"

Miss Marple's mind snagged on something she'd just heard. She couldn't think which part it was, only that someone had just said something very unexpected. Something that suggested . . . what was it? She thought of Jim the butcher's boy in St. Mary Mead, who'd bet he could jump the mill race. Something . . .

She jumped in her seat as a hand gripped her left shoulder. The thought was gone.

Professor Cuthbert Cayling squeezed Miss Marple's arm with a painful over-familiarity.

"You don't mind, do you?" he peered at the place-setting card, "Jane, my darling. Only Elspeth and I were rather in the middle of a conversation earlier." He chuckled. "I asked Simon Skipper in the friendliest possible way whether he'd mind changing places with you, Elspeth, and he got in a frightful bate."

"Oh," said Elspeth, "but I'm halfway through my meal."

"Don't worry about that. The college staff will deal with it. I was rather interested by what you were saying about a new *political* lecture programme on BBC2."

"She's fine where she is," said Eammon.

Professor Cayling's eyes were pure fury.

"She can decide for herself," he said, "can't you, my dear?"

Elspeth looked around nervously.

"You don't have to go," Eammon said softly, "he can't make you."

And yet, with an appearance half of modesty and half of what seemed to Miss Marple something like fear, two points of high colour on her cheeks, Elspeth Hearken stood up, her short dress barely covering her bottom, and walked up the table to take her place at Professor Cayling's side.

There was a strange silence around Miss Marple. The main course had been served: racks of venison with roast parsnips, blackberries, and a chestnut stuffing. Eammon dug into his meat viciously. Agnetha Strom moved along a few places from her seat to take Elspeth's place. She and Eammon exchanged a dark glance. Even Sir Aaron seemed subdued.

"Forgive me," said Miss Marple, "but I do wonder whether Professor Cuthbert is quite *safe* with young women."

Eammon gave a hollow laugh.

At the far end of the table, Professor Cayling was whispering something into Elspeth Hearken's ear. She looked nervous. She seemed about to refuse, tucking her chin into her chest and making a little frightened shake of the head, but Professor Cayling's arm was around her shoulder, squeezing with that vice-like grip.

"Safe?" said Eammon. "It's going to be that Harrison girl all over again."

"Harrison girl?" prompted Miss Marple mildly.

Even from this end of the table, everyone could tell what Professor Cayling was saying to Elspeth. What a pretty girl she was, and surely she didn't wear a dress that length not thinking that people would look?

Agnetha Strom said, "I told Elspeth about her earlier. She was rather a good friend of mine. Cuthbert touched her up. Everyone said she ought to keep quiet about it. But she made a fuss, went to the University. Of course, Cuthbert said she'd been as keen as he was and just regretted it afterwards. He said, she said. And she *had* been caught in bed with a boyfriend after curfew a year earlier, so it all looked rather bad for her. She was passed over for a Junior Fellowship after that."

Professor Cayling's squeezing hand went lower down Elspeth's arm, the back of his hand almost grazing her breast. He tapped the pocket of his jacket and whispered something in Elspeth's ear.

"Quaaludes," said Eammon, "he gets them from a doctor on Harley Street, to help him relax. He gave them to Harrison. Look," he said to Agnetha, "I know she was your friend, but you haven't heard the half of it. I had the room next to hers. I was the one who heard her crying in the night. I used to sit and talk to her when she was too frightened to sleep."

Miss Marple watched Professor Cayling and Elspeth Hearken. He handed her a small white pill and she dropped it into her wine glass. He did the same with his own glass. They each swirled their glasses and drank them down.

"But Cuthbert has no control over Elspeth, does he?" said Sir Aaron with mild alarm. "She's not a postgraduate. She works for the BBC. She's a free agent and can do as she pleases."

"You say that," said Eammon. "I believe she applied

for a PhD here a year or two ago. Some theory she has about Oliver Cromwell and Lady Sarah Bedlington, Charles II's mistress. Got turned down. A lot of people would like to live this rather sybaritic lifestyle." He paused and glanced up the table again. "Look, I have to say something."

A formal dinner is a difficult place to interrupt a seduction, but Eammon McManaway made a bold attempt. Under cover of speaking to one of the butlers about a rickety chair, he edged closer to the head of the table where Professor Cayling's hand was massaging the small of Elspeth Hearken's back, straying closer to her bottom. Eammon picked up the carafe of wine and offered to pour both of them an extra glass, just to be friendly. Then he suggested that Cayling had taken up quite enough of Elspeth's time and perhaps she might return to her original place. Elspeth shook her head, mutely. Cuthbert Cayling laughed uproariously. Squeezing Elspeth tightly, he said, loud enough for everyone at the table to hear, "Now, before the toasts and the pudding, my dear, perhaps you'd like to freshen up in my rooms."

Elspeth, large eyes gleaming, followed Cuthbert Cayling out through the back of the dining hall.

"Perhaps she actually fancies the old goat?" said Agnetha, watching them depart.

"No one fancies Cuthbert Cayling." said Eammon, returning to his place, "She's too frightened to say no."

"Are we sure something untoward is going on?" asked Sir Aaron, "Perhaps she really does need a moment to freshen up? It is awfully hot in here."

Miss Marple was overcome with a creeping sense of trepidation. Something untoward was certainly happening. Something terrible had been happening at this table all evening. If only she hadn't taken two glasses of sherry before the meal, she would know what it was. She had the sense that they were all chess pieces at this dinner, moving over this chequerboard floor in a pattern already ordained by someone. But who?

It was no more than thirty minutes later that Cuthbert and Elspeth returned to the table. Both of them, to Miss Marple's eye, had clearly taken some sort of drug. She had learned the signs of the new drugs from her friends in the police force over the past decade, and also learned that she was expected by many to disapprove. Drug-taking that had once been considered rather demeaning and low-class in 1959 was now, in 1970, seen even among intelligent people as a sign of an adventurous spirit and a nose for fun. But Miss Marple remembered a time before there were any laws at all about the taking of drugs. She recalled that, during the Great War, one could buy "A Welcome Present for Friends at the Front" at Harrods—cocaine, morphine and all the accoutrements. Young people always thought they'd invented everything.

Elspeth and Cuthbert both looked to Miss Marple to have taken rather a lot of whatever it was. Quaaludes, Eammon McManaway had said. And they had missed their main course. The staff were patently eager to start clearing and serving pudding, but there was the formality of "the address" to get through. Elspeth swayed and stumbled as she took her seat, looking drowsy and confused.

Professor Cayling didn't look much better. Despite this, he stood up again, his face glowing, his eyes very bright, and began the formal address that marked Founder's Day, declaiming the Latin words with which the college's original benefactor had asked to be remembered. But something was wrong. The words were increasingly slurred. He lost his place repeatedly, and muttered "Forgive me" several times. His eyes closed and opened again. And he slipped slowly forward, landing face-first in the remains of the roast venison, sending wine glasses spinning to smash on the floor.

At once, Sir Aaron leapt up. He had had a little medical training during his time in the army, so hauled Professor Cayling bodily out of the venison, felt for his pulse, and looked in his mouth.

"Call a doctor!" cried Sir Aaron. "For God's sake, call a doctor!"

Cuthbert Cayling was still drawing slow, choked, bubbling breaths.

Elspeth Hearken, beside him, fell slowly sideways from her chair. On the floor, her face mashed into the crumbs and fragments of dinner on the polished wood boards, she began to shake and fit, jerkily.

The last voice Miss Marple remembered hearing in that terrible moment was Eammon McManaway's, shouting, "What the hell are you all standing there for?! Call a bloody doctor!"

Miss Marple and Sir Aaron sat together the next morning at breakfast in the spacious dining room of the Randolph Hotel, overlooking the Georgian grace of Beaumont Street and the Martyrs' Memorial. Sir Aaron had thought it unwise to attempt to motor home, nor had either of them wanted to take up their respective guest rooms at the college. Much of the college, in fact, was currently being combed by police for any evidence relating to the taking of illegal drugs and the subsequent death. All the attendees at the dinner had been warned to stay in Oxford for the next few days, until enquiries could be concluded.

Sir Aaron said: "Elspeth Hearken, at least, is out of danger."

"Yes," said Miss Marple, "that is a great relief."

Elspeth Hearken and Professor Cuthbert Cayling had both been taken by ambulance to the Radcliffe Infirmary. Elspeth, younger than Cuthbert by more than thirty-five years, had had—according to the report Sir Aaron had managed to have sight of that morning—a bad night. But after having her stomach pumped, she was now resting easily and was expected to spend only another night or two in hospital before being sent home.

But the late morning copy of *The Times* spread on the table between Miss Marple and Sir Aaron carried a full-page obituary of Professor Cuthbert Cayling. His education at Eton and Balliol, his ancestry in the Bedlington-Bomarsand family, whose vault would be opened for the funeral, his PhD work at Harvard. The obituary listed his considerable achievements in political history, his popular book on democracy published in 1965, his talents as Master of the college, his two wives and two divorces. His face—younger by a couple of decades but still engulfed in his luxuriant beard—stared out from the page, his gaze piercing.

"Tell me," said Sir Aaron, "honestly, how does it smell to you?"

Miss Marple's eyes took on an intelligent gleam.

"Well, I must say," she said, "one must keep an open mind, but there are one or two matters that trouble me."

"All right," said Sir Aaron, "let me guess before you tell me everything. It is a *little* odd that Cuthbert, whose quaaludes they were," Sir Aaron said the word with some distaste, "and who had taken them many times before, managed to take so many on this one occasion that he overdosed and died. And, moreover, that he put Elspeth Hearken in danger."

"Yes," said Miss Marple, "that is one problem. One would have thought that he would know precisely how much to take. It does seem unlikely that that could have killed him. And one notices," she glanced out of the window, still seeming to be shy of her own perspicacity, although Sir Aaron was well aware of it, "one can't help but notice how very easy it would have been for someone to tamper with the drinks."

"I did think of Simon Skipper tipping over that wine glass. He might have been trying pour away a poison he'd already dosed Cuthbert with."

"Yes, quite. And tipping *over* the glass might have been intended to make everyone think he couldn't possibly have given the Master anything—whereas, of course, it would mean that all traces would be immediately removed and the linen laundered by the staff. And then Professor Cayling *did* have quite a number of enemies around the table. He really had quite a talent for making enemies. He made a grotesque anti-Semitic remark to you when we arrived, for example."

"You can't think that *I* killed him."

"Oh, no, no. It would have been rather extraordinary for you to invite *me* to witness you committing a murder. I just mean to say that he was an easy man to dislike. His stance on the college bequest was unpopular. Agnetha Strom believes he deliberately undermined her. Dr. Eammon McManaway can't bear him. Did you happen to notice that Dr. McManaway also picked up the wine carafe at dinner? It would have been easy enough for him to slip pills or powders into it."

"Or the Master's wine or his meal could have been doctored by someone who distracted any of the college staff. The Chief Constable here is a friend of mine. I must tell him to make sure all the serving staff are interviewed thoroughly with that question in mind."

"Yes," said Miss Marple, "that's very wise, of course, very wise. I can't help feeling, though, that there are undercurrents here that I haven't quite understood."

A polite cough interrupted their conversation. A waiter in Randolph livery stood by their table, holding an envelope.

"Just delivered for you, Sir Aaron."

Sir Aaron tipped the waiter and waited for him to leave before tearing open the envelope.

"Analysis of the stomach contents. I asked to see a copy as soon as possible. Now we'll know what Cuthbert and Elspeth were poisoned with."

As he read the document, his curious and intelligent face took on a puzzled expression. He passed the report to Miss Marple in silence. She read it carefully, twice through.

The hospital report stated unequivocally that there had been no additional drugs in Cuthbert Cayling's system; wine and the quaaludes prescribed by his private doctor in Harley Street were the only intoxicating substances.

"Oh," said Miss Marple, "Well then. That makes it all very clear. Very clear indeed." She helped herself to the final crumpet on the rack in front of her, "The only difficulty will be proving it."

Three weeks later, Miss Jane Marple and Sir Aaron Kahn took their seats in the great family chapel on the Bedlington-Bomarsand estate on the Seaham coast a few miles south-east of Jarrow. The marble vaulted ceilings were ribbed and fanned—it was a bit like looking up at the sky through the branches of a great tree, Miss Marple thought. The wooden benches were well-cushioned with hand-embroidered pads and the congregation was made up of famous faces from the academic world, the world of the media, the aristocracy and even two minor members of the royal family. There, too, were many of the people Miss Marple had met and seen three weeks earlier at St. Bede's College: Agnetha Strom in an austere black ankle-length dress, Eammon McManaway in a rumpled suit, Elspeth Hearken still looking a little pale and unwell in black lace, the angry Simon Skipper wearing an extraordinarily moth-eaten black jumper and slacks, defiantly casual. Several of the college staff and servants were there as well.

"I very much suspect, Sir Aaron," murmured Miss Marple, "that the murderer—and I do think a murder *was* committed, whatever the police say—won't be able to stay away from this, don't you agree? This moment, I believe, is the reason for everything."

The choir's voices were raised in the "Dies Irae," the haunting music filling the huge echoing space, resounding from walls, floor, ceiling, seeming at times to come directly from the carved angels above them or from the glowing stained-glass image of Mary Magdalen above the altar. The Magdalen was the patron saint of the Bedlington-Bomarsand family, someone had explained, in a rather knowing nod to the family's having originally been raised to high estate because the first duchess had been one of Charles II's many mistresses. The family's marble busts lined the wall; and, to honour their founding matriarch, the line of Bedlington-Bomarsand descended through the female as well as the male line. Thus, Professor Cuthbert Cayling, to his immense pride, was considered a Bedlington-Bomarsand too by the wider family, because his mother had been a daughter of the duke, even though she had married a Mr. Cayling, a humble industrialist with a fat wallet.

"The women of the family have always been rather formidable, I'm told," said Sir Aaron, "going right back to the first duchess. Look at her there. One can't help imagining the intellect behind those fine eyes and that enormous nose, can't one?"

"Yes," said Miss Marple, "there's a certain kind of mind that is drawn to imagining the past. Even imagining friends among the dead. That kind of person can begin to feel they have more in common with the past than the present."

Professor Cayling's Aunt Constance, the dowager duchess, was a woman in her mid-nineties. She retained an upright and unyielding bearing, and walked with great dignity from her seat at the front of the chapel before taking a great iron key from her beaded bag. Slowly, she walked to the leather-studded, iron-banded great oak door to the left of the altar, inserted the key in the lock and turned it. The door opened slowly, and a chill wind blew from the vault, making the candles sputter in their sconces. There was something grand and glorious about it. The great vault of Bedlington-Bomarsand was open.

"The family vault," said Sir Aaron, "by family tradition it will stand open for seven days and seven nights while Cuthbert lies at the altar, before his coffin is placed in the tomb with his ancestors and the vault is sealed again."

"Ah, yes," said Miss Marple, "I rather thought it must be something like that. I suppose it's been a great many years since it was last opened?"

Sir Aaron frowned at her, "Yes, extraordinary, isn't it? Twenty-two years, I think, since the last Bedlington-Bomarsand died."

"That would make perfect sense," Miss Marple said.

The music rose once more, the choristers of the Seaham Ryhope school melding their voices with the cello, the oboe and the bassoon, the notes plashing on the eardrum like the falling of soft rain.

"I do hope it isn't too cold, that crypt," said Miss Marple.

"The corpses scarcely mind," said Sir Aaron.

"No," said Miss Marple, "but we shall."

Past midnight that night, Miss Jane Marple and Sir Aaron Kahn sat in the dark. It was, in fact, exceedingly cold. Sir Aaron had loaned Miss Marple his own fur-collared driving coat, and he sat there in the lighter Macintosh he kept in his car, shivering.

"Do you think we shall have to wait long?" he asked.

"No," muttered Miss Marple, "I believe the person we're expecting thinks they have waited quite long enough. You've seen the painting *The Death of Chatterton*? I saw it at a summer exhibition some years ago and was very struck by it. The brilliant young poet and forger, flaming curls of red hair, lying amid his papers, which would win him lasting fame even after his death. Only seventeen when he died, in 1770. An extraordinary evocation. Well, you do see, Sir Aaron: an admirer of Thomas Chatterton is someone who thinks that the world ought to take notice of the genius of the very young. That any need to wait for approval or affirmation is too much to bear. An admirer of Thomas Chatterton is impatient."

"Chatterton, the poet?" said Sir Aaron, "What does Chatterton have to do with it?"

"Well, you see, it was the mention of Chatterton at dinner that put me in mind of Jim the butcher's boy. How he couldn't wait for Betsy to notice him of her own accord. Had to jump the mill race to prove himself— and, of course, he tumbled in. Impatience, that's the link. Afterwards, Jim accused one of the farmhands of having greased the rocks, but . . ."

"Sorry, I still don't quite see . . ."

"Shh!" said Miss Marple.

For someone was descending the steps into the family vault. A light and careful tread. And there was a beam of torchlight sweeping over the vault where the coffins sat in their marble niches. Sir Aaron and Miss Marple were well-concealed in a side chamber and the torchlight passed by without touching them. From their viewpoint in the chamber, they saw a figure in a hooded coat bend over one coffin in particular— the ancient oak coffin in the central niche. The figure

pulled a long object from their coat and began to methodically wrench the coffin open.

Sir Aaron gasped in disgust, but quickly muffled the
sound. He patted Miss Marple's shoulder, as if to say
"Surely, now we act," but Miss Marple indicated that
they should both remain silent with a tiny shake of her
head.

The figure at the coffin had it open now. There was
a smell—not entirely unpleasant—of old musty rooms,
of faint decay. The figure was bending over the body,
the coat concealing what it was they were about. They
turned from the coffin, their posture confident, almost
exultant.

"Now," murmured Miss Marple.

Sir Aaron turned on the beam of his torch. The
figure was a young woman.

"Stop right there," he said, in the commanding voice
that had won such acclaim in his years as a KC.

The figure turned to run, but from the chapel
above six police officers were already descending the
steps. In defeat, the grave robber turned her face at
last fully to Miss Marple and Sir Aaron. She pointed a
trembling finger at the coffin where a packet of letters
was clasped between the fingers of the mouldering
skeleton.

"Look, I've found them. I've really found them. You

can say what you like about what I've done, but I've found them," said Elspeth Hearken.

"What exactly were the letters, after all that?" said Miss Marple, "That's the one part of the thing that I didn't know. Something about Cromwell?"

"Good grief, how did you know that?" Sir Aaron looked baffled, as did the local police inspector and the current duke. All of them were seated around a roaring fire in the library at Seaham Ryhope. Tea, whisky and thickly buttered crumpets had been provided to take the chill of the crypt from their bones. Miss Marple was ensconced in front of the fire, a heavy rug over her knees, and Sir Aaron rather suspected she was enjoying her momentary position as the centre of attention.

"Oh, don't you remember that remark of Dr. Mc-Manaway's at dinner? That Elspeth Hearken had been turned down for a PhD and that she had a theory about Oliver Cromwell and Lady Sarah Bedlington, Charles II's mistress?"

"Good lord. Yes. Well. She *did* have a theory. And, as you say, she had a very single-minded and impatient way of pursuing it. The letters are extremely interesting, in fact. I've been allowed a brief chance to look them over—and, of course, I'm no expert in the period—but they are letters between Lady Sarah and Charles II that suggest that Oliver Cromwell was actually in favour of the restoration of the monarchy. That he had secretly worked to undermine his own protectorship and not to provide a successor, so that the rightful king could be restored to the throne after his death. They're certainly going to provide plenty of evidence for academics to chew over."

"Yes, I expect they will," remarked Miss Marple a little tartly, "I quite see that that is the sort of theory that might have caught the attention of a woman like Elspeth Hearken. She's rather earnest, almost painfully sincere in a certain way. Trying to dress like a modern girl, but she'd have been happier in an earlier age. She must have latched on to that theory as a sign of a secret continuity in the world; that even people who were trying to change things might secretly be in favour of the status quo, perhaps? I think she chewed over it, thought about it constantly, in fact. Yes, I can quite see that, having been rebuffed for her PhD on the subject, she might have become so obsessed that she'd kill to prove her point."

"Are you suggesting she plotted to murder Cuthbert Cayling purely so that the crypt would be opened and she could get to these letters?"

"Plotted? No. No, I merely think she saw her chance.

She may not even have known Professor Cayling was part of the Bedlington family until he mentioned it at dinner. And, of course, she hadn't brought a murder weapon with her, let alone a poison. No. He told her of his links to the subject of her obsession, and she realised that, if he died, the family vault would be opened and she could show her theory was correct. She'd heard enough of the gossip about him at the college to know he would have any number of enemies who'd be suspected of the crime before her. And then *he* offered *her* drugs. Well! The chance was too good to miss, I suspect. Impatience, you see. It must have seemed that she would never be caught."

"But how on earth did she get so much of the drug into Cuthbert?"

Miss Marple raised an eyebrow.

"Come now, Sir Aaron, how does a pretty young girl get a foolish older man to do anything? She dared him, I expect. She took some. She said she'd taken them before and she preferred the effect if one took five or six. Perhaps she concealed some in her cheek and spat them out later. He was already drunk. Who would possibly suspect the man's own drugs as a murder weapon?"

"Except you," said the duke, "you're quite an astonishing woman. It's going to be dashed hard to show it was murder even so, I'd think. I must say, though," he sat back, hands folded over his stomach, "while I shall miss curmudgeonly old cousin Cuth, I am rather delighted by the light she's thrown on the history of m'own family. Imagine being secretly involved in a plot orchestrated by Cromwell to bring the king back to the throne!"

He poured himself another generous measure of whisky and offered the decanter around.

"Oh, I'm so sorry, your grace," said Miss Marple, "No, no, I have not explained. The letters aren't real. They're forgeries."

Around the room a short stuttering breath emanated from three men simultaneously.

"Yes," said Jane Marple mildly, "this is exactly the sort of strange theory people *do* get obsessed with. Everything was intended. There was a great conspiracy. There are secret powers moving behind the scenes. No, no. Jim the butcher's boy all over. No one had greased the rocks. Things happen. There is no great secret that everyone knows but you. They happen because they happen. That's why she spoke so highly of Chatterton; he was a famous forger, you see. She was thinking through what she could do, even there at the dinner. Telling herself that if Chatterton could do it, she could do it. If she could somehow get this one man out of the way, and then forge the letters she needed, she could prove her own theory true. I suppose," mused Miss Marple, "that she intended to break the coffin open by night and leave it to be discovered the next day. It wouldn't matter to her that *she* discover the letters, only that someone should and she should be proved right."

"I don't quite follow," said Sir Aaron.

"She didn't *discover* the letters in the coffin. She forged them, like Chatterton. And she planted them there."

"Bless my soul," said the duke.

In the following week, the letters were examined by an expert from the British Museum, who pronounced them very clever forgeries indeed. Written on old paper cut from the backs of books from the period, they would have been virtually undetectable. Elspeth Hearken would have been vindicated; her PhD work would have been accepted by any college in Oxford. Miss Marple felt rather sorry for her, in a way—she remembered Jim the butcher's boy pulling himself bedraggled from the mill race—but as Sir Aaron reminded her, this was a woman who had deliberately killed a man by an overdose, so one needn't feel too sorry for her.

Beside everything else, Simon Skipper, the new Master, had invited Miss Marple back to dine at college.

"The college fellows rather want to befriend you, I think. Moving with the times," said Sir Aaron, "the new open and egalitarian society."

Miss Marple smiled and said she would consider it.

The Jade Empress

Jean Kwok

Miss Marple was mildly surprised to find herself waltzing. She had always admired it as an elegant dance, but given little thought to doing it herself. However, after several weeks aboard the cruise ship *Jade Empress* on its way to Hong Kong, where she was to meet her nephew, the successful novelist Raymond West, she found herself succumbing to the enthusiastic cajoling of the ship's ballroom-dancing instructor.

"If you can walk, you can waltz," the attractive young woman had said, holding her head with its smooth dark chignon high. Like many of the staff on board, she was Chinese.

What Miss Marple liked about the waltz was that a person was allowed to remain dignified, unlike those

Latin dances where one was expected to contort one-self into a pretzel. Her elderly dance partner, Mr. Pang, who had a cabin in her corridor, was also a reasonable height. Most young people these days seemed to shoot up to ridiculous lengths that seemed quite inconvenient for fitting through doorways and the like. Mr. Pang was, in fact, short and stocky, and Miss Marple was relieved to feel no resultant pain from the rheumatism in her neck as she gazed at him.

"The Jade Empress is the Queen Mother of the West, did you know that?" said Mr. Pang, huffing a bit from the exertion. "They say she holds the elixir of life. One swallow and you could live for ever and never grow old. That would be something for the likes of us, eh? When a man gets on in years, he wants to—"

It was fortunate that Mr. Pang only knew a few dance steps, Miss Marple thought, or it would be even more difficult to follow his rambling stories than it already was. Since the two of them had neither the knowledge nor desire to waltz around the upper deck as some other, more adventurous and foolhardy dance couples did, they revolved gently in the corner, like a carousel, only intermittently punctuated by an under-arm turn, which Miss Marple executed quite grace-fully.

She allowed her mind to wander. It was a lovely

afternoon on the top deck. She enjoyed the clear and mild spring weather, as well as the deep blue ocean around them. They'd just left Singapore—such a long way from her own village of St. Mary Mead!—and would be at sea for a few more days before arriving at their ultimate destination. Raymond was truly so kind. He was to be there for a year, producing a play set in China while also serving as some sort of cultural ambassador, waving the flag for Britain, and he'd insisted that Miss Marple join him for a month. He stressed it would be good for her health and mental faculties, as if she were becoming *senile*. But her dear nephew had taken care of everything, and so Miss Marple found herself with little to do but admire the waters of the South China Sea while listening to the lilting strains of "The Blue Danube."

"I haven't seen my son since he was a child," Mr. Pang continued, oblivious to Miss Marple's inattention. "I didn't want to leave him and his mother, you understand, but I had no choice."

"Of course not," murmured Miss Marple, trying to piece the story together. "Why exactly did you leave Hong Kong again?"

"To make a new life for us. Moved to Liverpool, took me years before I could scrape together enough to bring them over, and, by then, his mother had passed away and my son didn't want to come any more. Said he was happy in Hong Kong. In just a few days, I'll be reunited with him again after all these decades." Mr. Pang's eyelid was drooping a bit and Miss Marple politely ignored a tear that he quickly wiped away with a shrug of his shoulder.

"Is that your daughter who is travelling with you?" Miss Marple had noticed a large, rather shambling young woman, in addition to an older lady with a glass eye, who seemed to be some sort of caregiver to Mr. Pang.

"Yes, from my second wife, who sadly also passed away last year." Mr. Pang abruptly jerked his left arm up in the signal for an underarm turn and Miss Marple swept underneath it. "She loved to garden—"

When Miss Marple returned to the appropriate dance position, Mr. Pang was saying, "—peony, treasure of my heart. The sight delights me every day."

Miss Marple said, "A lovely flower."

"As important to the Chinese," said Mr. Pang, "as the English rose—"

They were interrupted by the firm tones of the ballroom dance teacher as she called, "ONE two three, ONE two three . . ." Over Mr. Pang's shoulder, Miss Marple caught a glimpse of the instructor sweeping back and forth with a solid-looking young man who was intently staring at his feet. His neck was so red and blotchy from embarrassment that the dark colour resembled some sort of rash or birthmark. The teacher reminded him, "Eyes up," but was ignored.

"Ah, there come your daughter and friend," Miss Marple said, looking beyond the hapless man to Mr. Pang's rapidly approaching companions.

Mr. Pang glanced in the direction she indicated and froze. He stared fixedly over her shoulder. He seemed to have difficulty breathing for a moment, as his face turned a deep purple.

"Mr. Pang," Miss Marple said, slightly alarmed. "Are you quite all right?"

She followed his gaze and found only the old man's companions, and a married couple in their mid-thirties whom she had met earlier—Victor and Ellen Richards. They were both lean and intense. Victor had an aquiline nose and deeply sunken eyes while Ellen's long face, framed by a curtain of light brown hair, had a morose quality. It seemed they owned a successful pharmaceutical company together, which, Miss Marple had understood from Victor, manufactured all sorts of important drugs, without which society would be quite crippled.

"Yes," Mr. Pang wheezed, after a pause. "Just a bit too much waltzing, I believe."

Seated at her little table at the corner of the ballroom after dinner, Miss Marple peered around with interest. Soft lamps glowed at each table while the sparkling chandeliers bathed the imposing room in golden light. The men were distinguished in their black tie and the women were mainly in colourful evening gowns. Miss Marple herself was tastefully clad in a grey lace dress. Her fellow guests were of all races, ages and sizes, ranging from a few families with small children to elderly couples with silver hair. Many were demonstrating the steps they had learned at the dance lesson that afternoon as the ship's orchestra played a slow melody. Others chatted or drank hot beverages or cocktails at the round tables scattered around the perimeter of the room, as Miss Marple herself was doing.

Ellen Richards, looking somewhat tree-like in a long green dress covered with a leaf pattern, paused by Miss Marple's table. "May I join you?"

"Of course," said Miss Marple. She took a sip of the excellent coffee, then set down her cup. "Where is your husband?"

"Victor had a bit of a headache, so he's retired early."

Ellen waved at the waiter and a fresh pot was brought. "I don't see your dance partner."

"Mr. Pang? Indeed, I was looking for him myself. He seemed a bit unwell earlier, so I hope he's all right."

Ellen sniffed. "It's no wonder with that companion of his. Aunt Faith, they call her. Well, you'd need to have faith in her strange ways to tolerate her, I suppose."

"Do you mean the older lady?"

Ellen nodded and bent closer. Despite Ellen's serious demeanour, Miss Marple had discovered that she dearly loved to gossip. "I believe she's become quite friendly with the crew. She actually uses the ship's facilities to cook extra for him, providing him with all sorts of traditional Chinese medicine. I shudder to think what she's been feeding him. Have you seen the outrageous things she's been doing? Burning incense at all hours of the night. Chanting to herself as she walks. There are rumours that she pokes him with needles. The other day, I actually saw her tossing live crabs and lobsters into the sea!"

Miss Marple raised her eyebrows. "Where did she get them from?"

Ellen shook her head. She seemed surprised by Miss Marple's matter-of-fact reaction. "The kitchen, I believe."

"That *is* a bit odd, but quite refreshing for the crabs and lobsters, I'd imagine."

Ellen lowered her voice, although the orchestra nearly drowned her words anyway. "She's a Chinese witch."

But instead of looking appropriately horrified, Miss Marple seemed quite fascinated. "I wonder if any of her techniques actually work."

"Of course not!" exclaimed Ellen. "Superstitious nonsense, not based on any type of science at all."

"Well, you would know better than I, I'm sure," said Miss Marple modestly. "I'm afraid I've led such a sheltered life."

Ellen gave a smug little smile that made it clear no one could expect such an elderly and provincial woman to have any grasp of logic anyway. "It will surely unsettle you, but I'm quite certain that witch only stays with the old man because of the treasure he's rumoured to possess."

It would astound *you*, thought Miss Marple, what shocking events one can experience in such a small village as St. Mary Mead, but, aloud, she merely said, "What sort of treasure?"

"A piece of extremely valuable jewellery."

Later that evening, Miss Marple lingered at Mr. Pang's door, which was only a few cabins down the corridor from her own. She really didn't want to intrude, and he clearly had the help of both his daughter and caregiver, the one Ellen had called a Chinese witch. Yet, she felt a vague sense of disquiet. Earlier on, Mr. Pang had seemed quite startled by something, despite his claims to the contrary.

As she was wondering if she should knock, the door opened. Miss Marple was startled by the surprised face of Mr. Pang's daughter, who appeared to be in her mid-twenties. She was tall, with broad shoulders and large hands, and wisps of black hair that were falling out of a messy bun.

"May I help you with something?" the daughter asked politely.

Miss Marple blushed a bit, feeling like a meddling old busybody. "I am sorry to bother you, but I danced with your father earlier and I was just wondering if he felt all right."

The daughter smiled, her expressive dark eyes lighting up her pleasant face. "I remember. My father was quite proud of his waltz with you. Miss Marple, yes? My name is Mudan and I'm grateful to you for caring about Pa's health." She frowned. "He did seem to have some trouble swallowing earlier, but I'm happy to say that he's asleep and resting now."

She opened the door further to show Miss Marple a darkened cabin, from which the faint sound of breathing emitted. There appeared to be the remnants of a meal on the sideboard: a bowl of rice and a plate of hard-boiled eggs next to a vase of flowers. On a little table near to the door, Miss Marple noticed a faded black-and-white photo of a woman holding a small child in her arms.

Mudan saw Miss Marple looking and picked it up to show her. "Pa mentioned he was telling you about my half-brother, Tao. The photo is of him as a toddler with his mother. This is the last time Pa saw him."

Mr. Pang's first wife had a serene, oval face that was visibly filled with love for the little boy in her arms, despite the dappled sunlight that cast shadows over them. One particularly dark patch obscured a part of the child's face and neck, which made it difficult to make out his expression, but Miss Marple noted his neatly pressed sailor's outfit and jaunty hat. He appeared well-cared-for. A beam of light cascaded off the sparkling brooch pinned to his mother's blouse.

Mudan's expression was sad as she gazed at the photo. "My father can't wait to see him again in Hong Kong. He's been talking about it for years."

Miss Marple understood. It was a little like the schoolteacher Mr. Murray back in St. Mary Mead, who pined after his long-lost love, a girl who had moved to London years earlier, while his wife languished from lack of attention. Miss Marple said gently, "It's hard to compete with a fantasy, isn't it?"

Mudan's fine eyes flew to Miss Marple's face, surprised. "How insightful of you, but, of course, the elderly are known for their wisdom."

Mudan gave Miss Marple a little bow, hands clasped together in a gesture of respect, then stepped out of the cabin, closing the door carefully behind her. After wishing Miss Marple a very fine evening, Mudan went into her own room across the hall from her father's.

Miss Marple was blushing. The reverence Asian cultures held for older generations was unexpected and very welcome.

The next morning there was a great deal of commotion in Miss Marple's corridor. She poked her head out into the hallway to see Dr. Grant, the ship's doctor, striding into Mr. Pang's room. Miss Marple had met the kindly and rotund medic once when her rheumatism was acting up. Even more alarmingly, Dr. Grant was quickly followed by Chief Webster, the ship's security officer, a tall and imposing figure.

Miss Marple got dressed quickly. She was coming out of her cabin just as one of the ship's stewards, a gentle young man, approached. Instead of his usual calm demeanour, he seemed agitated. His tanned face was white against his black hair, his lips pale as wax, and his dark brown eyes were wide with fear.

"What has happened?" Miss Marple asked. She had become quite friendly with this particular steward ever since she'd complimented him on the lovely shapes he created using the cloth napkins in her cabin: a crown, a double star, and, once, even a bird of paradise. Sometimes she came across him in other parts of the ship, serving cocktails on the top deck, for example, or handing out cards for bridge lessons.

The steward hesitated, then said, "I am so sorry to tell you unfortunate news, but the older gentleman down the corridor passed away in the night."

"Mr. Pang?" At the steward's nod, Miss Marple felt sad for her friend, who would now never see his son again, and for Mudan. "But he was *waltzing* just yesterday. He might not have been feeling entirely well, but not in a way where one would expect him to die."

The steward's hands were visibly shaking. He whispered, "There have been some strange goings-on in that cabin."

"Oh?"

"Very bad omens there."

"What in the world do you mean?"

The steward leaned in. "Terrible things. For a Chinese person, anyway. Other people wouldn't even realise anything was wrong. I once found a bowl of rice with a set of chopsticks stuck right in the middle, like we Chinese only use for burials. Duck eggs, which are very unlucky because they're associated with death. And pure white flowers, also a symbol of funerals. I've seen them in his cabin several times, including just yesterday. Each one of these items invites death into your house."

"Why would Mr. Pang have kept such unlucky things in his cabin?"

The steward shook his head. "That's just it. Mr. Pang was a very superstitious man. I'm sure he didn't bring those objects into his cabin. He was being terrorised."

When Miss Marple reached Mr. Pang's open door, she paused. Now that daylight was streaming into the room, she could see the sideboard clearly. It was empty. Had someone removed the ill-omened items? Miss Marple thought back to her last glimpse inside the cabin. There had definitely been rice, eggs and flowers, although they'd been hard to see clearly in the semi-darkness. Had some mysterious person been frightening Mr. Pang? For what possible reason? Had Mudan or Aunt Faith simply cleaned those things away?

As Miss Marple prepared to walk on before she was noticed hovering in the doorway, she realised something else: the photo of the first wife with the little boy was also missing.

Then the murmur of voices alerted her that the room was occupied. Miss Marple peered inside to find Mudan perched on the bed her father had died on, now stripped of its sheets and bedding, and Aunt Faith sitting in a chair. Chief Webster and Dr. Grant stood facing them. Mudan's eyes were red and puffy from weeping while Aunt Faith was white-faced and defiant, her hands clenched into fists. Miss Marple took a step back into the shadows of the hallway to avoid being noticed. She knew she should move on, but she couldn't help feeling that Mudan might need her help at some point. Fortunately, they were so intent upon their conversation that no one glanced in Miss Marple's direction.

"We just need to get a brief statement of what happened," Chief Webster said. "Can you tell us how you found your father?"

Mudan took in a gasping breath. "I—I went in—"

"It's all right," Aunt Faith said, patting Mudan on the arm. "You did nothing wrong."

"Of course not!" Mudan said, shocked. She inhaled and tried to calm herself. "I b-brought Pa his morning cup of tea b-but he didn't respond." She broke out in deep shuddering sobs again.

"I am truly sorry we need to do this," Dr. Grant said gently. "It's just that there are a few irregularities."

At this, Mudan's head reared up while Aunt Faith focused on him with her good eye. "Wh-what do you mean?" asked Mudan.

Chief Webster gave Dr. Grant a quelling look. Miss Marple understood no information was to be given to the witnesses or suspects before getting their statements. "Please know that the best way you could help your father now is to tell us everything you saw, in as much detail as possible. Did you notice anything unusual about Mr. Pang last night?"

This concept of being useful seemed to steady Mudan. "Pa wasn't feeling well last night, but I thought perhaps he'd eaten something that didn't agree with him. He had some difficulty swallowing and didn't speak much as the evening progressed, but finally he settled down and went to sleep."

Dr. Grant said, "*Did* he consume anything unusual last night?"

"Just his normal Chinese medicine," Aunt Faith said. Her glass eye glittered in the light.

"What would that consist of?" Dr. Grant asked in a mild voice.

"He has been very nervous these past weeks, so I have been giving him a strengthening brew to build up his courage: ginseng and ground cobra," Aunt Faith said calmly.

Chief Webster straightened abruptly. "You fed Mr. Pang cobra?"

"Surely, they removed the venom," Dr. Grant said.

"Oh no," Aunt Faith declared. "The venom is the best part! Fear is a poison and you must fight poison with poison."

Dr. Grant raised a bushy eyebrow. "Ah, similar to the concept of fighting fire with fire, I imagine. But don't you think that adding poison to poison could go terribly wrong?"

"Oh no," Mudan interrupted. "Aunt Faith is the best healer we know. She's famous within the Chinese community at home and has been with our family since before I was born. She only gave Pa a tiny bit of cobra each day, not enough to poison him. She would never make a mistake like that. Not enough to kill Pa."

At that, she broke down and buried her face in her hands. Aunt Faith crossed over to her and lay her hand on her shoulder while glaring at the two men.

Chief Webster cleared his throat. "That's enough for today."

A moment before the two women exited the room, Miss Marple stepped away from the doorway and busied herself with her purse, pretending she was looking for her cabin key. Mudan stiffened when she saw her, but then surprised Miss Marple by giving her a weak smile. Aunt Faith didn't even acknowledge her presence. After Mudan and Aunt Faith were out of sight, Miss Marple resumed her position by the cabin.

Chief Webster turned to the doctor. "What do you make of all that?"

Dr. Grant ran a hand down his face. "It would make sense. A small amount of snake venom can be ingested—not that I would ever recommend doing such a thing—but it would be broken down by stomach acids and digestive enzymes. However, higher amounts could make its way into the bloodstream, which could lead to an attack on the nervous system. Symptoms might include droopy eyelids and difficulty talking and swallowing, leading to the inability to breathe. As you know, I've already determined that the cause of death was suffocation."

Chief Webster said in his deep voice, "Manslaughter then, or murder."

"I'm surprised you didn't arrest her immediately."

"I want to go through Mr. Pang's possessions and papers first to try to determine if there might be a motive. After all, we're on a ship. There's nowhere for Aunt Faith to go."

Miss Marple pressed her lips together. First Mudan's father had passed away, then his companion was suspected of murder. What a terrible time this was for that gentle young woman.

Miss Marple did not see any sign of Mudan or Aunt Faith the rest of the day. The other passengers seemed unsettled by the sudden passing of Mr. Pang but not unduly worried. He had been quite advanced in years, after all, and there were rumours that he'd had some sort of nervous condition, which had surely led to his sudden expiration, as if all anxious elderly people were liable to drop dead at any moment, Miss Marple thought.

At dinnertime, Miss Marple stepped into the dining room, deep in thought. Mr. Pang and his stories . . . He'd spoken of his first wife and son. He loved peonies and delighted in them. Then he'd become quite agitated at the sight of either his daughter and caregiver, the so-called Chinese witch, or Victor and Ellen Richards. And there was what the steward had believed about someone trying to scare him on purpose. Miss Marple couldn't quite put her finger on something unusual about that moment on the dance floor. She was missing something. Furthermore, what could the connection be to the missing bad-luck items or photo? There was also that rumour about a fabulous piece of jewellery owned by Mr. Pang. Was that still in the cabin? And now he was dead. *She didn't like any of it, not one bit.*

There was still no sign of Mudan or her companion when the time came for the evening meal, but Victor and Ellen spotted Miss Marple and waved for her to join them.

As soon as Miss Marple sat down, Ellen said, "Have you heard the awful news about your friend?"

Miss Marple noted Mr. Pang's elevation in status from being her *dance partner* to *friend* in Ellen's depiction, but merely nodded. Many people found a vicarious thrill in being close to death. The closer the better, until death invariably came for them.

Victor added, with relish, "Well, clearly the cause of

his passing wasn't natural. They're planning to arrest that strange Chinese woman, Aunt Faith, tomorrow morning for poisoning Mr. Pang with ground cobra. She admitted to it herself."

"What?" said Miss Marple, feigning incredulity.

"Oh, the medical staff on board are very chummy with us," Ellen preened. "After all, we supply them. *They* believe she thought she was helping him . . . You must admit that she had some very suspicious practices."

When the waiter approached to take their order, Miss Marple was surprised to recognise her own steward. "I haven't seen you in the dining room before."

He gave her a little bow. "We have a small crew on this ship, so we all have various duties, and, tonight, they needed help here."

Miss Marple hesitated a moment, then pressed forward. "Would you mind explaining a few things to us?"

Victor and Ellen stared at her with alarmed expressions, apparently appalled that she was conversing with the Chinese waiter.

Victor exclaimed, "This is hardly proper—"

Miss Marple ignored him. "Can you tell us why a person might poke another with needles? Or toss live lobsters and crabs overboard? Or why they might consume ground cobra?"

The young steward flushed a bit but endeavoured to give Miss Marple her answers. "The use of needles is called acupuncture. It is an ancient Chinese treatment that alleviates pain and has been used effectively for thousands of years. Some believe in releasing animals like lobsters and crabs as an offering to the gods, a sort of cosmic gift to bring good fortune. And a small amount of medicine like cobra is given sometimes as a restorative, but the quantity has to be carefully controlled by the practitioner."

"Thank you for that enlightening explanation," Miss Marple said, smiling at the steward. "Do you know Aunt Faith at all?"

"Yes, somewhat. She often comes into the staff area. In fact, she was there earlier today because she needed some boiled water, but something seemed to startle her and she wound up spilling it all over the floor. The supervisor was quite cross."

Ellen then said, quite rudely, "Can we order now?"

As Miss Marple ate her dinner of succulent carp steamed in soy sauce, she felt disturbed. From her own knowledge of plants, she knew that a number of Chinese herbal treatments had merit. Despite the common mistrust of Aunt Faith on board, Miss Marple didn't believe Mudan would allow a charlatan to treat her beloved father. And none of this explained the missing items or photo.

She couldn't help but feel that there was more here than met the eye.

Miss Marple felt too agitated to go to the ballroom after dinner and so she headed back to her cabin. The peace and quiet might help her clear her mind and concentrate her thoughts about this suspicious death.

She had just made the turn on to her corridor when she heard a high-pitched scream.

Mudan came staggering out of one of the cabins, hugging herself with her hands. She was breathless and sobbing.

"What is it?" Miss Marple cried.

"A-Aunt Faith! Sh-she's dead!" Mudan swayed as if she might faint.

Miss Marple grasped her arm and then caught her breath as she saw the dark stains on Mudan's blouse and hands. Blood.

There was much gasping and talk around her as other inhabitants of the cabins opened their doors, drawn by the commotion. Someone ran off to fetch the doctor and security officer.

"You poor dear," Miss Marple said. "Come, you need to sit down."

Miss Marple led the young woman to Mudan's own cabin, where the door was ajar, and brought her to the bed. Mudan sat down heavily. She buried her face in her hands, not realising that she was smearing her cheeks with blood. Miss Marple poured her a glass of water and patted her on the back.

When Chief Webster and Dr. Grant came through the door several minutes later, Mudan's blood-streaked countenance was the first thing they saw.

"Goodness!" exclaimed Dr. Grant, stopping short.

"If you'll excuse us," Chief Webster said to Miss Marple, but Mudan clutched Miss Marple's hands.

"Please stay!" she begged. "I'm all alone now. P-please let this kind lady stay."

Dr. Grant and Chief Webster exchanged glances and, with a tiny nod, Chief Webster decided to allow Miss Marple to remain. "Can you tell us what happened?"

Mudan pressed her fingers against her closed eyelids as if she wanted to erase the images she'd seen. "Sh-she wasn't feeling well. She said she was seasick. I went to check on her and sh-she was covered in b-blood."

"Did you touch the body?" Chief Webster asked.

Miss Marple cast her eyes over Mudan's blood-soaked fingers and wanted to sigh. Of course she had.

"Y-yes," said Mudan. "I checked for a pulse. I-I was hoping—" She stared at the floor and said nothing more.

"How was Aunt Faith killed?" Miss Marple asked.

Dr. Grant said heavily, "A knife. The murder weapon is missing but she was stabbed quite recently, within the past hour, I'd say."

Here Chief Webster glowered again at the talkative doctor, but before he could say anything, Mudan wailed, "Papa! Aunt Faith!" She broke out in great, heaving sobs.

Miss Marple wrapped a bracing arm around Mudan's shoulders. "Gentlemen, are you finished? This poor young woman has been through a great deal."

"I'm afraid this matter is far from finished," Chief Webster said grimly. He stood up. "But we shall leave you for tonight."

After the men had left, Miss Marple helped Mudan clean herself up and get into bed. "Don't think too much. There's time enough for that tomorrow."

She stayed by the young woman's bedside holding her hand until Mudan drifted off into an exhausted sleep.

Although she had advised Mudan to rest, Miss Marple couldn't do so herself.

There was a murderer on board the *Jade Empress*.

"Why hasn't that daughter been arrested yet?" Victor hissed. "The safety of all of us is at stake! Is that her sitting by the window?"

Miss Marple took a bite of her pineapple bun, which, ironically, did not contain any pineapple. It was still sweet and delicious, however, and she took some comfort in it at breakfast after her restless night. "That's a different woman. I believe Mudan is taking her meals in her cabin. There's been no evidence found against her."

"Well, they all look alike anyway," Ellen said, taking a sip of her black coffee. "Of course it was her. Who else could it be? She found both bodies. I heard she was covered in blood. Everyone on board is riled up. And here we are, stuck at sea, with a murderer running loose. You can't trust those people."

Miss Marple looked up. "Which people?"

"Foreigners," Victor answered for his wife.

"In Hong Kong," Miss Marple said, "I believe we will be the foreigners."

When Miss Marple returned to her cabin after breakfast, she was surprised to find Mudan waiting by her door.

The young woman was pale and visibly shaking, but she managed to give a wan smile. "I wanted to thank you for your kindness last night."

"It was nothing. Are you all right?"

"No. I don't suppose I'll ever be all right again. Not in the same way, anyway." Mudan gave a little sniff.

"Why don't you come inside?" Miss Marple suggested, as she opened her door.

Mudan nodded and followed her into Miss Marple's tidy cabin. She sank into a chair by the table as if completely exhausted. Miss Marple took the seat next to her.

Miss Marple said, "The night your father passed away, did you notice anything strange in his cabin?" At Mudan's confused shake of her head, Miss Marple continued, "Food items, like rice or flowers?"

"Possibly? I was worried about Pa. I didn't really look around." She wrinkled her brow. "Although someone seems to have taken the photo of Pa's first wife and Tao."

"Yes, I had noticed that."

Mudan gave her a sharp look. "You are very observant."

There came a hard knock on the door. Miss Marple opened it to find Chief Webster, a number of security officers and her steward standing outside, the latter wringing his hands.

Chief Webster's face was hard and forbidding. "We thought we might find her here. Mudan Pang, you are under arrest."

"What? Why?" cried Mudan, leaping up from her chair.

The other security officers quickly entered the room and surrounded her, grabbing her arms on both sides.

"We found the murder weapon, a steak knife, hidden in a cloth napkin in your room, which had been folded into the shape of a tall, furled tower."

"But I didn't do anything. I would never, ever hurt—" wailed Mudan. She looked around wildly, settling on the steward. She pointed at him. "I saw him! He was leaving the hallway as I approached Aunt Faith's room. He must have done it just before I arrived and he hid the knife in the napkin in my room."

The steward's face turned ashen.

Chief Webster shook his head. "He's already been questioned. At the time of death, he was on duty in the dining room in front of many of the guests. And it seems quite suspicious that you didn't mention this before."

"I was distraught! Everything fled my mind. Please—"

"Why would she do such terrible things?" Miss Marple asked mildly.

"It appears her father had a large life insurance policy," Chief Webster said.

"She was the beneficiary?" Miss Marple asked.

"Yes, she and her half-brother. It appears upon closer investigation that she owns a bakery in Liverpool, and it hasn't been doing well."

"Business always goes up and down," Mudan said.

"We've asked around and it was no secret that the father greatly preferred the son. Perhaps it was envy as well."

Mudan staggered back as if he had struck her. She raised a trembling hand to her mouth.

"What would be her motive with regard to the second murder?" asked Miss Marple.

Chief Webster said, "That remains to be determined." He shrugged. "It is possible Aunt Faith found some proof of her wrong-doing."

Mudan moaned, "But I loved my father and Aunt Faith."

"You must believe me to be a silly old woman," Miss Marple said, "but my instincts tell me that she *did* care about them very much. Furthermore, my steward mentioned that a number of items had been put in Mr. Pang's cabin, possibly to terrorise him, such as white rice with chopsticks stuck straight up in it. There would have been no reason for Mudan to do such a thing since she had access to his food anyway."

The steward nodded.

A glimmer of respect entered the chief's eyes. "I have learned never to underestimate instinct. However, I cannot form a case based on that alone." He handed Miss Marple his business card. "If you should remember anything more concrete, day or night, please let me know. I will be returning to my position with the Hong Kong police after this cruise."

He turned to his officers and they marched a protesting Mudan out of the door. She gave Miss Marple one last pleading look as they took her into custody.

A few days later, Miss Marple was doing Tai Chi in the park in Hong Kong with a group of other elderly practitioners. She had had a troubled mind since disembarking from the cruise ship, puzzling over the details of what had happened on board. Raymond's house was lovely, but he did tend to sleep in, while Miss Marple preferred an early start. She had been delighted to find a group doing this gentle but invigorating exercise every morning.

Although she'd never done such a thing before, she found the simple exercises to be soothing. Together, they stretched their linked hands high in a movement she'd learned was called Lifting the Sky to get their energy flowing, then moved into the Crane, where Miss Marple held her arms out like an ascending bird, with her left knee raised. Her mind was free to fly while her body engaged in the meditative activity.

The murders on board the *Jade Empress* left her extremely unsettled. Had Mudan's innocence been an act, designed to beguile an elderly lady? Or could it have been the steward after all? It might have been possible for him to slip away during his dining room shift, although rather unlikely, Miss Marple had to admit, and it did not seem to be in character for him either. Perhaps even Victor or Ellen was involved. With their knowledge of and access to pharmaceuticals, it would have been very easy for them to poison Mr. Pang, and anyone could have obtained a steak knife. However, the bitter truth was that no one on board the cruise ship, except for Mudan, had a possible motive for those murders.

Miss Marple was paired up with another elderly lady for an exercise called push hands. As she mirrored her partner's movements, she noticed a large red birthmark on the side of the woman's face.

Suddenly, everything became clear.

"It is very good of you to join me on your day off," Miss Marple said. "These barbecue pork buns are excellent. May I tempt you with one?"

"Delicious," said Chief Webster. He surveyed their table, which was crowded with sweet lotus seed buns in bamboo steamer baskets, rice noodle rolls filled with beef on tiny plates, and small bowls of congee, a savoury rice porridge. Waiters and waitresses pushed carts filled with delicacies around the restaurant and the guests picked what they desired.

"I have recently learned that 'dim sum,' which I believe is what this style of food is called, means 'touch the heart,' " Miss Marple said. "That's lovely, isn't it?"

"Indeed," answered Chief Webster. His brows were furrowed, as if wondering why she had invited him to join her. She had worried that he might refuse to come, but she could tell from the way he now bit into a crystal prawn dumpling with relish that he clearly appreciated a good meal.

"Answers to such mysteries as murders are always linked to matters of the heart, aren't they?" she said.

Chief Webster stilled as he chewed, shifting his focus from his food to Miss Marple.

"There were at least two items missing from

Mr. Pang's cabin," she said. "A valuable brooch and a photo of his first wife and son."

"Such items were not found, but there is no proof they existed in the first place."

"That is the reason I did not mention this before," Miss Marple said. "However, I believe they are key to solving this mystery. On the evening before Mr. Pang died, I was waltzing with him and I noticed he became quite agitated when he saw something over my shoulder. I saw only Mudan, Aunt Faith, and Victor and Ellen Richards, but I was guilty of a fault that many of us share: *I didn't notice the staff.* They were invisible to me. The ballroom dance instructor was also dancing with a young man. It took me a long time to remember that there was something unusual about him, something quite obvious, because he kept looking down at his feet. At first, it appeared his neck was flushed with embarrassment, but it was more than that. He had a red birthmark on the side of his neck."

Chief Webster's eyes wandered back to the tender egg tart on his plate. He must have been wondering if there was a point to her story.

"I was reminded of an incident I had heard of," said Miss Marple, omitting the fact that she had in fact solved this particular mystery, "in which a woman disguised as a chambermaid had committed a murder, yet no one noticed her because all they saw was the uniform, rather than the person inside."

"I must admit I have no idea what you're trying to say," Chief Webster confessed.

"Why, it's all very simple," Miss Marple said. "You said yourself, there were two beneficiaries to the life insurance policy: Mudan and her half-brother, Tao. Tao is the young man with the birthmark on his neck. In the photo of Tao with his mother, his birthmark was visible but appeared as a dark spot due to the dappled sunlight. I suspect he came aboard the cruise ship as a passenger, then disguised himself as the steward. Since many people think all Asians—and servants—look alike, they didn't look to see that the steward going in and out of their cabin was not always the same person.

"Thus, our actual steward was innocent, but Tao pretended to be him at times. And while disguised as a steward, he had access to the keys. He placed frightening items in Mr. Pang's cabin to drive Aunt Faith to feeding him cobra, then ensured that Mr. Pang overdosed. His father must have recognised him during our waltz and so Tao had to strike that evening. That was relatively easy with his access to Mr. Pang's meals.

"I imagine he wanted Mudan to be accused, because that would invalidate her claim to the life insurance pay-out and he would be the sole beneficiary. Also, I was told that Aunt Faith was often in the staff area, and the *real* steward mentioned to me an incident in which she had been startled by something. I believe Aunt Faith recognised him because of the birthmark on his neck; she had been with the family for a long time. So that gave Tao a reason to get rid of her too. While the real steward was in the dining room, Tao stabbed Aunt Faith. Afterwards, he planted the knife in Mudan's room."

Chief Webster's mouth was hanging open. He closed it with a click. "What of the rumours about the priceless piece of jewellery in Mr. Pang's possession?"

"I believe that was the brooch. Tao's mother was wearing it in the photo. I think you'll find it when you search his home. He must be on your passenger list and the ballroom dance teacher will be able to help you identify him if he used a fake name."

"What sort of brooch should we search for?"

Miss Marple answered, "The image was unclear, but it was a flower. I suspect a peony, because Mr. Pang spoke of how much he delighted in seeing his peony every day. At first, I believed he had a plant in his room or perhaps some cuttings from Singapore, but then I remembered that it is impossible for a peony to bloom in the tropics. They need a hard winter. Therefore, he must have been referring to something else."

Chief Webster shook his head. "Why did you keep pursuing this matter when it appeared to be such a cut-and-dried case?"

Miss Marple took a sip of oolong tea, delighting in its smokey flavour. "It didn't make sense to me that Mudan would kill two people she clearly loved. As I said, murders are always linked to matters of the heart. Now, would you care for a wonton?"

Miss Marple had to blush when she read the newspaper. Chief Webster had given her full credit when the priceless peony brooch and the photo of his mother and himself were found in Tao's house. Tao made a full confession. It appeared that Tao had hated his father, because, contrary to Mr. Pang's assertions, he hadn't had a first and a second wife. Rather, Mr. Pang had been a bigamist. He left Tao and his mother in Hong Kong while he went to Liverpool and then married Mudan's mother. After his mother had died in poverty, Tao was deeply resentful of his father's second family, and especially of his half-sister. He wanted the full inheritance and the peony brooch for himself.

A Mr. and Mrs. Victor Richards from the cruise

line were quoted as being "absolutely astounded" that Miss Marple had solved this case, but her favourite part of the article was the end, when, upon being told that her father had spoken of his peony being the treasure of his heart, the newly-freed Mudan said, "That's my name. Mudan means peony."

A Deadly Wedding Day

Dreda Say Mitchell

One

Even murder wasn't enough to make Miss Marple interrupt a tender moment between a bride and groom, as she arrived—vexingly but unavoidably—late for the strangest wedding reception she had ever attended. Slipping quietly into the room where the wedding breakfast was to be held, she couldn't immediately put her finger on why it was so strange. There was nothing wrong with the venue, of course. A banqueting hall in a stately home was clearly a suitable place to celebrate the wedding of a baronet's son. The walls were lined with paintings of the groom's ancestors, and the furniture, fittings and dinner service had the heaviness of centuries' use. Everything brass and gilt sparkled. All was well with that.

Nor was there anything jarring about the guests, who were all respectable and well dressed. And the doting groom and his bride were playing their part as the happy couple on their wedding day too. Peter Apfel-Strand wore the traditional morning suit, while Marie Baptiste, his bride, looked a picture in a white chiffon gown. Though her dress was perhaps a touch too modish for Miss Marple's taste.

No, it was the collection of individuals seated at the top table that was baffling, resembling as they did a scene from one of those modern New Wave films that critics seemed to enjoy so much but which left their audiences thoroughly confused. The bride's end of the table was deserted, apart from Miss Marple's close friend, Miss Bella, the bride's aunt. Marie's family were from St. Honoré, a beautiful island in the Caribbean where Jane Marple had recently been on holiday. Maybe the distance between St. Honoré and England was the reason more of Marie's nearest and dearest couldn't attend? When Miss Marple had enquired after Miss Bella's niece's other relations, mildly surprised to merit an invitation, the answer had been the politely evasive "Families can be very complicated."

Indeed they can.

If the bride's side was almost empty, the groom's was crowded. There was Peter's father, Sir Herbert Apfel-Strand, his mother, Lady Margaret, and his maternal uncle, Bishop Ambrose, who had officiated at the ceremony. Other family members seemed to proliferate wherever one looked, and the groom's parents were wearing rictus grins as they greeted everyone, clearly determined to keep up appearances; like a family of vultures that had descended on a victim only to discover that the hyenas had got there first.

There was an unavoidable and unpleasant explanation for their obvious discomfort: while one might hope that, in the England of the 1960s, racial prejudice would be a thing of the past, sadly that was not the case. Was the fact that their son and heir was marrying a black woman from St. Honoré perhaps the reason for the Apfel-Strands' gloom? Miss Marple's lips compressed with disapproval.

"Jane! I'm so glad you could come." Miss Bella greeted Miss Marple with a warm hug, having temporarily excused herself from her place along from the happy couple.

"I'm sorry I'm late." Miss Marple had missed the wedding ceremony. "I'm afraid two trains from

St. Mary Mead were cancelled. That will be something to do with Lord Beeching and the axe he has taken to the railway service, no doubt."

Miss Bella's statuesque figure towered over her much smaller friend. She wore a no-frills mauve dress that offset the gloss of her brown skin, and a smart hat was perched atop her head. Miss Bella never left home without a hat. Although the women had last seen each other only recently, when Miss Marple had been holidaying on St. Honoré—a trip that had included the nasty business of the loss of a hotel guest—they had actually first become acquainted within the confines of an air-raid shelter during the Blitz. While bombs dropped on London, Miss Bella had whiled away the time explaining to Miss Marple, up for a brief visit to the metropolis, how she had not been allowed to serve in the Axillary Territorial Service, as the then young Princess Elizabeth had, but how she had recovered from that knock-back, and fought tooth and nail to be admitted to the Women's Auxiliary Air Force instead. The unit had contained other Caribbean women like her, who had answered the call to help the "Motherland," as they had been brought up to think of England. Miss Bella had then, post-war, stayed on and become a nurse in Britain's new National Health Service.

"Has Marie no friends she could invite?" Miss Marple asked.

"She keeps to herself. In fact, I don't know too much about her life in England at all. She only arrived from St. Honoré just over a year ago. I believe she has some type of office job."

"Do you know how she met the groom?"

"No. She is always vague about how it happened." Miss Bella added, "We don't know each other very well, what with my residing for so much of my adult life in England. I don't want her to think I'm sticking my nose into her business."

"Are you staying locally?" Miss Marple asked.

"I'm sharing a room with Marie at the Fruit Pickers Arms in the village. But I'm returning home tomorrow, while Marie and Peter are leaving on honeymoon this evening. At least I assume they are; Marie was rather fuzzy about that too."

Marie Baptiste appeared to be vague about many things.

Miss Marple's keen eye noticed someone else at the high table. "It appears your niece has a guest after all."

The newcomer was a woman in her early twenties, a few years younger than the bride, willowy tall, sporting a blonde Vidal Sassoon bobbed haircut and a tan, as if she had recently returned from warmer climes, and she was standing over Marie. She wore what was known in the more salacious newspapers as a "mini-skirt." It was immodestly short and certainly not the kind of attire you would expect a respectable young lady to wear to a wedding reception. Marie and her guest were exchanging what looked like terse words, and their exchange ended with a long pause and then Marie shrugging her shoulders. The woman then seated herself in the chair Miss Bella had vacated.

Miss Marple and Miss Bella weren't the only ones watching this curious exchange it seemed. Bishop Ambrose, the groom's venerable uncle, was carefully studying the woman's legs, and his expression suggested that he might well be considering a sermon railing against the sins of the flesh.

"Do you know that young lady?" Miss Marple asked Miss Bella.

Her friend shook her head. "I think I saw her briefly at the Fruit Pickers Arms at breakfast. Perhaps she's staying there too? Marie must know her well or she wouldn't be invited to sit at the top table. Oh, I see Sir Herbert is about to call everyone to their seats. I'd better go and find another for myself before he starts."

While Miss Marple wove through the mingling

guests and found her allocated table, the doughty peer of the realm got to his feet, a stiff grin still carved into his stony face. "My wife and I would like to welcome everyone to Strand Hall on the happy occasion of the wedding of our son, Peter. The wedding breakfast will be served now, before the speeches."

A chilled asparagus soup, followed by salmon and vegetables, and then a fruit salad for dessert, were complemented by an agreeable white wine, with champagne provided for the toasts. All good English fare, and, a little over an hour later, with everyone replete, Sir Herbert rose again and tapped his wine glass with a spoon. But before he could speak, there was a commotion on the bride's side of the table.

Marie's mysterious guest struggled to her feet, gulping for air. She clutched her chest in apparent agony, then her belly, before finally her hands desperately grabbed and clawed at her throat. Her chair tumbled backwards, crashing to the ground as she staggered past the horrified bride towards the father of the groom.

She rasped out: "Stra . . . Strand . . . B . . . B . . . Ap . . ."

Then she collapsed into the arms of the astonished baronet.

Instinctively, his arms cradled her twitching and

jerking body. Then she was still. Sir Herbert appeared on the verge of panic, until his wife stepped into the breach with phlegmatic upper-class sangfroid.

Lady Margaret addressed the guests. "Ah . . . this young lady seems to have fainted. It *is* dreadfully stuffy in here. Perhaps someone could open a few windows?" She turned to her husband, her voice tight, delivering her words through clenched teeth, "Let me help you escort our guest to the salon, where she can lie down and recover."

Quickly waving away the staff who had rushed forward to help, Lady Margaret took one of the woman's limp arms and draped it over her shoulder. The baronet and his wife then gamely half-carried, half-dragged the young woman through a door at the back of the banqueting hall.

Miss Marple and Miss Bella exchanged knowing glances. Miss Bella was a retired nurse, while Miss Marple, too, had seen much in her time.

Both women were certain that the unfortunate stranger was dead.

Two

"Did you establish that the young woman is indeed dead?" Miss Marple asked Miss Bella, as they both loitered by the door through which the baronet and his wife had disappeared.

Miss Bella had just that minute returned, after attempting to offer her services as a trained nurse. "I didn't get a chance. Sir Herbert and Lady Margaret wouldn't let me see her. They insist they don't need any help."

Just like Miss Marple, Miss Bella had something of a reputation as an amateur detective amongst London's Caribbean community. It was she and she alone, after all, who had deduced what had really happened in the infamous and so-called "Steel Pan Murders" in Notting Hill.

Miss Bella's expression was severe. "I don't know what they're playing at. . . Why don't you go and see for yourself?"

Miss Marple did exactly that. Through the door was a hallway with a number of closed doors. But there was no need to guess behind which of them the Apfel-Strands happened to be; their raised voices carried clearly along the corridor.

"I'm telling you, Herbert, for the final time, that we are *not* cancelling this reception. You know how much it cost." Lady Margaret sounded like a bulldog on the attack. "Don't you remember the grin on the face of that nasty little banker when we asked for an extension to our overdraft? With a stately home like this, there's no way we could have ducked out of providing the venue for the wedding. If we hadn't, everyone would've have guessed our situation. We can't afford to abandon this reception and then potentially have to pay for another one. It's not as if the bride's family are likely to come up to scratch, and appearances *must* be upheld."

Miss Marple stopped and listened.

"You're not seriously suggesting we leave this dead girl on a pile of orange boxes while we go and celebrate our son's wedding?" Sir Herbert rallied, "I'm calling the police and an ambulance. Right now."

"You'll do no such thing." His wife's response cracked in the air. "We'll wait until all the guests have departed and *then* we'll call them. We can easily explain the delay."

When Herbert Apfel-Strand spoke again, it was in a much softer, more wheedling tone. "Is it so bad that our son has married for love, Margaret? Marie is such a lovely girl."

"Marrying for love?" his wife sneered. "You sound like a chambermaid. We don't marry for love in this family, as well you know. If your son had done his duty and married a suitable *and monied* spouse, we wouldn't be in this mess. Or would you have preferred Peter to get hitched to a woman like this strumpet you invited to the wedding?"

The baronet remained silent, provoking her ladyship to even greater rage, "I see you don't even have the good manners to deny it."

Her voice then came to an abrupt halt, maybe sensing that someone was hovering outside of the door. Miss Marple thought it prudent to knock, and the door opened a few inches wide to reveal a sliver of Sir Herbert's deeply furrowed face. "Oh, Miss Marple, is it not? How may I help?"

"I was just wondering whether I could be of any assistance with the young lady who was taken ill. I'm an experienced first-aider, you know."

Apfel-Strand gave a light and not completely convincing laugh. "You'll be happy to hear the patient is upright and drinking a glass of water." He turned his head, calling out, "Isn't that right, Louise?" He turned back. "She's rather embarrassed, to be honest, and doesn't want any further fuss. We'll be back in our places shortly, so if you would be so kind as to return to the wedding party?"

The door closed firmly in her face. As it did so, Miss Marple heard a further snatch of their conversation.

Lady Margaret was saying bitterly, "Is that Jane Marple? My godmother lives in the same village as her, St. Mary Mead, and claims she's an interfering crackpot. Losing her marbles more likely, in her old age."

Miss Marple sighed. It wasn't the first and it wouldn't be the last time she was dismissed as a silly old woman with one foot in the grave, and, she reflected, it was in such strong contrast to the way Miss Bella was treated by her Caribbean community. Her friend was highly esteemed, and no one would ever dream of calling Bella Baptiste by her first name only. The honorific "Miss" was considered a mark of respect for her age and life experience.

Wandering back down the hallway, Miss Marple noticed that one of the other doors that led off it was ajar. Out of idle curiosity, she pushed at it and stepped inside. The room, which had clearly once been a rather grand drawing room, was now bare. In contrast to the opulence of the banqueting hall, the walls here showed marks where pictures had once hung. What appeared to be the last remaining contents of the room were now packed away in wooden boxes, stacked in haphazard piles on the now bare floorboards, seemingly awaiting collection. The Apfel-Strands had clearly fallen on hard times—what else might they be hiding?

Miss Marple and Miss Bella conferred together in a quiet corner. Miss Bella muttered to her friend, " 'Alligator lays eggs but it's no chicken,' as we say back home." For the avoidance of doubt, she elaborated further, "Things are not always as they seem, are they? Healthy young women don't drop dead at wedding receptions, and the family certainly don't then pretend a dead guest is alive. I don't need my years of nursing to know that her symptoms were those of someone who has been poisoned. Perhaps we should call the police ourselves?"

Miss Marple considered this but shook her head. "I fear the police would be sent away with a flea in their ear, should Sir Herbert and Lady Margaret want to deny there's a dead body on the premises. The provincial constabulary tend to be rather deferential where the gentry are concerned. I suggest we see if we can shed some light on the matter ourselves for the time being."

"The trouble is we don't even know who she is, much less who might have a motive for poisoning her, if that is what has happened. We need to speak to Marie and find out what she knows."

"We might already have a clue to her identity. Sir Herbert called her 'Louise.' He was too flustered by all that was going on to make that up, so that is quite probably her real name. And his wife as good as accused him of having an illicit liaison with 'this strumpet,' which I'm assuming is also a reference to the dead and, if we're correct, murdered young lady."

Miss Bella nodded in agreement. "To my ears, it sounded like she was trying to say his lordship's surname before collapsing into his arms. That looks *very* incriminating."

"Maybe not," Miss Marple countered, after a few seconds of silent thought. "In moments of medical distress, it is often natural to call out the name of the person in front of you for help."

"Except," her friend persisted, "Louise staggered past Marie to get to his lordship."

With so much unexplained, Miss Marple and Miss Bella proceeded to organise their plan of action with almost military precision. Miss Marple would use her eyes and ears, speaking to the bride for a start, and Miss Bella would attempt to track down the source of the poison.

After a short search, Miss Marple found Marie out on the lawn at the edge of the grand formal gardens. Several other guests were having a post-prandial stroll, but Marie was alone, and the newlywed woman's arms were wrapped tight around her middle. Miss Marple approached and said kindly, "I'm so sorry that your friend Louise was taken ill."

"I beg your pardon?" Marie's lashes fluttered wildly. "Who?"

"The young lady seated next to you? Who fainted. Louise?"

Marie looked off across the vast, manicured gardens. "She's not my friend. I've no idea who she is. Or what her name is. I didn't get much say in the guest list, I'm afraid."

"It still seems rather unusual to ask a stranger to sit next to you on your wedding day, dear."

"Oh, she told me she was a friend of Tante Bella's," Marie explained. She used the French for aunt, emphasising the long ee sound at the end. Though St. Honoré was English speaking, the odd French word remained. "Or maybe it was someone else in the family. I can't recall. She asked if she could join us, and I felt it would be rude to turn her away." She turned her face back to the older woman, her eyes wide, goosebumps rising on her bare arms in the cooling wind. "Is she all right?"

Miss Marple decided to play her cards close to her chest for now. "Your in-laws are taking care of her."

Quickly, she changed the subject. "How did you and your delightful new husband meet?"

Marie stammered, looking flustered, and replied with what seemed to be her habitual vagueness, "I can't remember."

Before Miss Marple could press her further, the groom appeared. He was attentive, sweetly grasping hold of his wife's hand. "Sorry to cut you both short, but I think my parents will be back shortly and the speeches will begin at last."

Miss Marple left them to have a quiet moment together and returned to the wedding reception. After all, she had another witness she particularly wanted to interview.

Taking advantage of the disruption to proceedings, she took the spare seat next to Bishop Ambrose at the top table. She didn't know him personally, of course, but was familiar with his voice and opinions. He was a regular guest on the wireless, particularly the BBC's Home Service, where he was known to hold forth on the evils of "the permissive society."

"Bishop Ambrose, please forgive the interruption, but I just thought I'd take this opportunity to say how much I enjoyed your talk warning good Christian folk about the dangers of listening to those young men from Liverpool—The Beatles, is it?"

Ambrose was flattered enough to forgive her mistake. "It was The Rolling Stones, madam, but thank you."

Miss Marple knew any attempt to interview the bishop would have to be brief, as the reception was about to resume with the return of the Apfel-Strands, so she proceeded with alacrity. "That young lady who was taken ill, do you know her, by chance?"

Ambrose pursed his lips with disapproval. "Regrettably, yes."

"Oh, is she not quite the thing?"

Bishop Ambrose confided, "I'm not one to cast the first stone, but my eyes know what they saw. I will merely say this. You can hardly expect the lower orders to behave properly when their social betters set such a bad example." With that, the bishop cast what might be considered an accusatory glare at his brother-in-law, Sir Herbert, who entered the room at that point. "A fish rots from the head."

Three

"Kitchen Personnel Only" warned the notice attached to the kitchen door below stairs. In normal circumstances, Miss Bella would have returned to the reception on sight of it; she was a stickler for the rules, especially where kitchens were concerned. However, a determination to get to the bottom of what had happened to that poor unfortunate girl drove her on. Inside there were plenty of staff rushing about, and orders being shouted every which way. No one noticed Miss Bella, but she spotted what looked like the staff cloakroom and ducked inside. There she found one of the grey smocks everyone seemed to be wearing and pulled it on, hoping that, as several of the catering team were also black, she would pass without comment. She replaced her hat with the white bonnet that came with the uniform and then headed off to the enormous butler's sink, where tray after tray of plates and bowls that had been cleared from the banqueting hall were stacked high. Her aim was to first examine the food for any evidence of anything unusual, anything that might suggest poison, and, if that yielded no results, to check the remnants of the drinks that had been served.

But there was only one way to examine the plates without drawing attention to herself, and that was to pretend to wash up. Miss Bella, ever indomitable, rolled up her sleeves, put in a plug, and began to fill the sink with soapy water. Putting on a good show of washing the dishes but never actually plunging them into the water, she carefully examined each plate for any sign or smell of foul play. She was focusing on the fish course to begin with, when one of the bowls of half-eaten fruit salad caught her eye.

"And *what* are you doing here?" a voice demanded.

Miss Bella turned to find a chef in his tall white hat looking at her with deep suspicion. His cheeks were ruddy, giving him the appearance of someone who maybe guzzled the cooking brandy on the quiet as he commanded the *batterie de cuisine*. Nevertheless, she couldn't fault his commitment to getting the food for the reception right, because she noticed he had the roughened hands of someone who worked hard for a living.

Quick off the mark, Miss Bella replied, "One of the waiters was asked what was in the fruit salad, and he asked me if I knew when he brought the dishes in. Delicious, apparently. I know how busy you chefs are, so I was checking myself."

With pride, the chef lengthened his neck, making his hat wobble. "My *salade de fruits*? A sprinkling of exotic spices and my special ingredient. You must tell them that it is a secret!"

He flounced off, and Miss Bella turned back to the fruit salad bowl that had caught her attention. Using a spoon, she pulled out a piece of the fruit and stared at it in horror.

What was it Marie Baptiste was hiding? Why was she pretending not to know Louise? And why did the bride become so ruffled and evasive when asked how she had met her groom? These questions plagued Miss Marple as she sat back at her table in the banqueting hall, waiting for the groom to commence giving his speech. Miss Marple's sharp mind ticked over, trying to think of a subtle way to somehow provoke Marie into talking about her relationship to the dead woman, as she was certain there was more to it than Marie had let on. Miss Marple smiled with satisfaction as she suddenly hit upon just the thing.

She turned to the other guests at her table, mildly observing: "I do so often think it's rather a pity that the bride doesn't get to have a speech at her own wedding, don't you? That it's just the groom and his best man and the rest of the men in this day and age?"

The ruddy-faced, balding man opposite her didn't agree. "Brides making speeches at weddings? What are you, a radical or something?"

Happily, however, his attractive and much younger wife was quick to pick up the baton. "Don't be rude, Giles. She's quite right. Why *doesn't* the bride get a chance to say a few words? Women do have tongues as well, you know."

Giles rolled his eyes, but he softened, demonstrating an indulgent affection for his wife. "I don't know, dear. I only deal with the law, I don't make it."

Their attention was then caught by the top table as the groom, Peter Apfel-Strand, rose to his feet and cleared his throat. He told several stories, but not the one Miss Marple had been hoping to hear: how he had met Marie. So, when he finished, she sighed to the attractive women at the table, "Oh, I would so like a few words from the bride about how they met. I am *such* a romantic."

On cue, the woman, who had maybe imbibed more of the wine than was wise, called out, "What about a bit from the bride about how you met!"

Some of the older guests looked a tad scandalised by her behaviour; shouting out at a high society wedding like a stallholder at Petticoat Lane Market just wasn't the done thing. However, a number of the younger women were firmly nodding in agreement. This was the 1960s; the world was swinging, and changing fast.

Gamely, Peter rose to the occasion. "We met in a solicitor's office—"

"No, we didn't," Marie interjected with a touch of

alarm, then, softening her voice, she continued, "It was at a party."

"Was it?" Peter appeared thoroughly confused by his bride's assertion, but whatever he read in her face made him swiftly change tack. "Of course . . . of course, it was a party! How could I forget?"

Miss Marple acknowledged wryly that her ploy had failed, and she was about to leave the table to go find Miss Bella and see how she'd been getting on when Giles, the red-faced husband of the vocal woman, suddenly spoke up. "I know how they met."

Miss Marple paused momentarily and then seized the moment. "Really? Do tell."

"I'm the family solicitor. Peter and his father were in my office one day discussing some financial business. My next two clients were seated outside and, out of the blue, started having a bit of ding-dong. Anyway, Peter, Sir Herbert and I broke up the dispute. One of the women was Marie. That was how Peter met her. He took her outside to calm things down and that was the start of their courtship. Meanwhile, Sir Herbert took the other young lady elsewhere to do the same." He coughed. "Calm her down, I mean." But he looked significantly at his wife and winked.

Miss Marple was all ears. "And who, may I ask, was this other young lady in the waiting room?"

He seemed rather surprised at the question. "Why, Louise McCracken. That woman who fainted at the top table."

Miss Marple hurried away, big with news, but stopped in her tracks as soon as she came across Miss Bella in the hallway and saw her stricken face. "What is it? What's happened?"

Bella opened up the folded napkin she held. Inside was what looked like half of a baby-sized green apple, but she batted Miss Marple away when she reached out for a closer look. "Don't touch it, Jane!"

"What on earth is it?"

Bella was terribly distressed. "It was in a bowl of fruit salad that must have been given to Louise—"

"McCracken. Louise McCracken."

Miss Bella continued. "They're called the Little Apples of Death. Highly poisonous. They can be deadly. There must have been more of them in her fruit salad, which she ate. They're said to have a very sweet, seductive taste."

Noticing her friend was deeply shaken, nearly in tears, Miss Marple said, "I don't fully understand. Why are you so upset?"

"Because they are the fruit of the Manchineel tree, which is native to the Caribbean. They grow in

St. Honoré, not here." She looked Miss Marple squarely in her eye. "There are only two people at this wedding who come from St. Honoré and would know about this tree. And *I* didn't put these apples of death in Louise McCracken's dessert."

That only left one other person. The bride.

Her beloved niece, Marie Baptiste.

Four

"Your niece is innocent, I'm sure if it, and we're going to prove it," Miss Marple asserted as they sat in the back of the taxi on their way to the Fruit Pickers Arms. "I'm sure, once we've had a good look in Miss McCracken's room, we'll get to the bottom of this. But we'll need to find the real killer as quickly as possible, or they will vanish like that golden eagle everyone made such a fuss over."

Miss Bella nodded at the reference to the now notorious Goldie, who had recently escaped from London Zoo and remained at large for thirteen days.

Miss Bella spoke with passion. "One of the reasons I fought long and hard, all those years ago, to gain admittance to the Women's Auxiliary Air Force was to pave the way for the next generation of black women, like my beloved niece, Marie, so that, when *her* time came, she could walk, head held high, right through the door." Bella Baptiste gave herself a shake and then straightened her shoulders with determination. "There is no way that my youngest sister's daughter could have taken another's life."

In that moment, Miss Marple understood. Their investigation was no longer just about who had killed Louise McCracken. For Miss Bella, this was about exonerating Marie, who she was certain could not be guilty of such a wicked crime. She was already facing deep-seated prejudice by marrying into the aristocracy, so the last thing she needed was any shadow attached to her name. But who could the guilty party be, and why did it seem that they were trying to frame the bride?

Sir Herbert was an obvious suspect. It was pretty clear he was involved in an illicit liaison with the unfortunate Louise. But it was surely highly unlikely he would have invited his paramour to his son's wedding. Of course, if it was indeed true that they were carrying on, then Lady Margaret would potentially have a motive. Or was Peter Apfel-Strand maybe exacting revenge against Louise for whatever she had done to his Marie, which was presumably the cause of the fracas at the solicitor's office? And what about Bishop Ambrose? Had his eyes lingered rather too long on the legs of the very tall and willowy Miss McCracken? Was he, secretly, a bit too fond of the sins of the flesh he so condemned? There was no greater hypocrite than one with a high moral tone, Miss Marple reflected.

"Tell me about the Manchineel tree, Bella."

"You probably saw them in St. Honoré on your recent holiday. The tree grows along the beach, a natural defence to keep the coastline safe from erosion. Unfortunately, everything about the tree is dangerous. It's not only the fruit of the tree that can be deadly, but so is the bark and leaves. The tree produces a milky sap that will burn skin and, if ingested, burn the throat and cause terrible stomach trouble. I have also heard that if the bark is lit, the fire produces poisonous fumes that can blind and kill. The authorities paint white crosses on them to warn people to stay clear. The toxin it produces is powerful and still very much a mystery."

She continued to speak looking down at her clenched hands. "Although most on St. Honoré know to stay away from this terrible tree, every now again there are deaths. Sadly, usually children. I remember one case where a child fell asleep under one of the trees on the beach. The sap from the bark and leaves dripped on their skin with the quiet of a silent killer. He was rushed to the local hospital, but there was nothing anyone could do." A wave of memory dulled the usual sparkle in her brown eyes. "The howl of grief from his mother will stay with me for all my days on this earth."

Frowning, Miss Marple racked her brains, trying to recall if she had ever heard of the Manchineel Tree or its poisonous fruit. As a keen gardener, she made it her business to increase her knowledge of the flora and fauna of the world, including the deadly varieties. And surely, if this tree was so harmful, there must be records of it causing deaths. Rightly guessing what her dear friend was thinking, Miss Bella raised her head, the tips of her mouth turning down. "The death of us native people on St. Honoré wasn't of much interest to the authorities, so why bother keeping records when one of them dies from an encounter with the malevolent Tree of Death?" Her brow pleated. "What is strange, though, is that Louise McCracken died so quickly."

"What do you mean?" Miss Marple pressed.

"All the cases I know of people sickening from eating the Manchineel's apple have either lingered long enough to receive treatment and have survived or died hours later because they had no access to medical intervention. There must be another explanation for why Marie's guest died so quickly."

The English countryside, so seemingly benevolent compared to such Caribbean dangers, flew by as the taxi carried them back to the local village, where the

Fruit Pickers Arms stood part way along a mediaeval high street. The inn itself was the picture-book image of an English country hostelry, half-timbered, but with some Georgian brickwork here and there, and luxuriant ivy insinuating itself where it was most needed to round off the overall effect. Dappled with early evening sunlight, the ancient sign swung in the breeze.

Miss Bella grimaced. "I should warn you now that the landlord isn't an overly sympathetic person. A perpetual grouch and growler. When Marie and I arrived, he reminded us that he didn't get many 'guests from the Commonwealth' staying at his establishment. He made that sound like a good thing."

"Did he indeed?" Miss Marple felt vexed that her wonderful friend and her beloved niece had had to deal with such blatant prejudice, especially compared to the warm welcome she herself had received in St. Honoré.

The whiskery old duffer behind the reception, whose clothes appeared to be wearing him, instead of the other way round, levelled them with a suspicious, bleary eye.

"Ladies. How may I help?"

Miss Bella stepped forward. "I'm afraid one of your guests has been taken ill and we're here to collect her belongings. Her name is Louise McCracken."

The landlord was very firm. "That's out of the question. In situations like that, we can only offer keys to the police or ambulance staff."

Miss Marple squeezed her friend's arm and stepped forward. "We quite understand. Normally we wouldn't dream of asking, but if you recall the young lady in question, you'll understand why her family wants to keep the authorities' involvement to a minimum. She will have left these premises in an ensemble some might conclude was more suitable for retiring at night rather than outdoor wear . . ."

The landlord sniffed. "You mean the young lady in room six?" He then took malicious pleasure in scoffing, "Come to some sort of sticky end, has she? I can't say I'm surprised, by the look of her. We get that kind of carry on even in a sleepy village like ours. Young men with long hair and females of questionable reputation driving around in open-top sports cars, blasting their horns at all hours of the night."

Miss Marple drew close. "Louise is from a very upright family, so, as you can imagine, they're anxious to avoid any scandal. If you could permit us to collect her things, they would be for ever grateful."

The landlord considered the situation for a few moments before his sympathy for the parents won out. As he handed over the key, he grumbled another complaint. "That Louise wouldn't stop chit-chatting with Elsie, my chambermaid, distracting the girl from her work. I'm not paying her to be idle and to cosy up to the clientele."

In room six there was very little sign that anyone had occupied the room at all. Some make-up sat on the dressing table along with an overnight bag that only contained a change of clothing.

Miss Marple sighed. "Disappointing."

But as they started to leave, Miss Bella retraced her steps and picked up what looked like a jewellery box. "This is a rather unusual item, don't you think? And it's got a crest engraved on it."

Miss Marple explained, "I think it's what the Scottish call a 'snuff mull,' which is a type of large snuff box." Her finger smoothed across the top. "Scottish snuff mulls were made of animal horn, like the top of this one, and very often they were left in the shape of the animal's horn. This is an antique and rather expensive item." A close inspection allowed Miss Marple to disentangle some of the details of the crest, which was expertly carved. "Cross of St. Andrew . . . a Stag . . . a mountain peak . . . definitely Scottish, if rather stereotypically so."

Miss Marple opened the box inside, which revealed

a few scratchy leaves and a small piece of wood, which was chipped, with shavings lying beside it. Urgently, Miss Bella snatched the box back.

"Don't touch them, Jane." She emptied the leaves and wood on to a piece of paper on the writing desk. She examined them under the desk lamp. "These are the leaves and bark of the Manchineel tree. They will be coated with the toxic, milky sap." Her gaze flicked to Miss Marple. "Did someone deliberately leave them in there, knowing she would place her hands in the box? Was this another way of trying to poison Louise McCracken?"

They left the room and locked the door. Miss Bella headed for the stairs, but her friend hesitated. "No, Bella, dear."

"Surely we're finished here?"

It had to be said. "We need to check Marie's possessions too. The police will be investigating shortly and it's better we get some answers before they do."

Once inside the room, Miss Marple conducted a thorough search of Marie's suitcase, where, in a side pocket, she found a slim, folded silver photograph frame. When it was opened, it displayed two black-and-white photos, one on each side. One was of a white naval officer with a black woman in a smart suit, her arm linked with his. In the background was a white clapboard church with a mountain in the background. When pulled from its frame, a pencil inscription on the back read "24th June 1940." The other picture was of the same woman, lovingly cradling a baby.

"Do you know who these people are, Bella?"

Her friend's hand shook as she took the photos. "The woman is my youngest sister, Colette, and the baby is her daughter, Marie. It must have been taken on St. Honoré, because that's the extinct volcano that dominates the island behind them."

She peered hard at the uniformed man. "I've never seen him before. There was a naval base on the island during the war, hunting U-Boats, that kind of thing. Perhaps he served on one, met my sister and, as these things happen, a baby was born. I was in London, but I am sure I heard she married. By the time I finally returned home after the war, there was the child, Marie, but no husband, and I asked no questions."

Without a word, Miss Bella took the twin photo frame and left the room. A few minutes later she returned with the snuff mull from Louise McCracken's room. She showed Miss Marple the crest on it and then the one, worn by time, on the silver photograph frame.

They were the same.

Downstairs, Miss Marple used the pay phone to

call her old friend, Sir Henry Clithering, a retired former commissioner of Scotland Yard. She spoke quietly and quickly to him. After she finished the call, she and Miss Bella partook of some refreshments while they waited for Sir Henry to call back, which he did in less than an hour. Furnished with the information he provided, Miss Marple and Miss Bella finally alighted on the truth of the murder committed earlier that day.

Miss Bella shared another of her shrewd Caribbean sayings: " 'Before a monkey buys trousers, he has to know where to put his tail.' " She explained, "This crime was carefully planned every step of the way."

Before they left, the landlord told them one thing more. "The girl in room six was a very busy bee yesterday." He squinted at Miss Bella. "In the morning I saw her talking to the young woman who travelled with you. And later that night I saw her deep in conversation with his Lordship, from up at the Hall."

Five

"Louise is dead?" Marie slumped back against the burgundy Chesterfield, tears springing to her eyes. Miss Marple noted she was no longer keeping up the falsehood of not knowing the other woman.

The reception was still in full swing in another part of the Hall. On their arrival back at Strand Hall and, after another visit to the kitchen, Miss Marple had discreetly gathered all the relevant parties, in a room she suspected Lady Margaret had chosen, because it was one with furniture still in it. It was here that Miss Marple revealed the tragic news of the unfortunate death at her wedding to the bride.

Peter protectively drew his wife close, snapping at Miss Marple, "What do you mean dead? She fainted, and I assumed by now she was on her way home."

Miss Marple's shrewd eyes rested on his parents. "She is lying dead in another room on the ground floor, isn't that correct, Sir Herbert?"

Herbert Apfel-Strand had the grace to look away, but his wife was another story; she mutinously compressed her lips. Then again, no answer was necessary; the silence of the truth was as loud as a scream.

Miss Marple began. "The young woman who died here today, as some of you will already know, was Louise McCracken. In her room at the Fruit Pickers Arms, we discovered an item that displayed the crest of a very wealthy Scottish family. Clyde McCracken, laird of Clan McCracken, recently passed away, which left his daughter, Louise, a very rich heiress.

"During the last war, however, Clyde McCracken

had been a naval officer stationed in the Caribbean, on St. Honoré, where he met and fell in love with a local woman—"

"My younger sister, Colette," interjected Miss Bella, the emotion in her shaking voice audible for all to hear.

"They had a daughter, who they named Marie," Miss Marple pressed on. "When Clyde came back to England, it was to find that his father had ploughed the family finances into some very unwise investment ventures. In the tradition of the upper classes, Clyde had to marry for money, which he did within the year. The heiress was from another landed Scottish family. And he worked hard to re-establish the family finances,"— Sir Henry had, in fact, estimated that he had tripled them—"as a tough businessman, on both sides of the border. But Clyde McCracken was hiding a secret.

"As a young naval officer, he had not only fathered a child with Colette Baptiste, but had also done the honourable thing and married her, in a ceremony at the local church in St. Honoré. This meant his marriage with Louise's mother was bigamous, and that Marie, his first and only legitimate born child, was his true heir, not Louise."

Peter looked down in astonishment at his new wife, "Darling, is this true?"

Marie gazed back up at him, clearly distraught. She

trembled slightly in his arms, and was about to speak, when his uncle's voice boomed out into the room.

"Eh?" Bishop Ambrose spluttered in clerical outrage. "Impossible! The church keeps meticulous records of all marriages. If he had tried to get married while he still had a wife, he would have been found out."

Miss Marple had already considered this. "The marriage records for Clyde and Colette were in the Caribbean, on the other side of the world; well out of the reach of anyone in England. This wouldn't be the first time such a thing has occurred. During and after the war, getting married twice was not unheard of, I'm sorry to say, whatever the Church might like to think."

Finally, Marie quietly spoke up. "I knew that Clyde McCracken was my father. But I didn't know that he was married to my mother until this nasty business with Louise started." Peter's embrace tightened. "Clyde bought a holiday home on St. Honoré, where he would bring his *wife* and Louise for the summer, while paying furtive visits to me and mummy on the other side of the island. He paid for me to have a good education and helped me get a good job when I came to England." Fire lit up her eyes. "But I was always a dirty little secret. I never asked for any of this. I did *not* murder my half-sister."

Miss Marple then settled her inquisitive gaze on Sir

Herbert and his wife. Lady Margaret scoffed, "You're not suggesting that *we* had anything to do with her death?"

Miss Marple focused on the baronet. "Were you having an illicit relationship with Louise McCracken?"

It was Miss Marple who answered, however, without waiting for Sir Herbert to speak, but with another question, this time directed at Marie, who remained notably silent, strain tightening her face. "But you know this not to be true, don't you, my dear? Your father-in-law wasn't having an affair with your half-sister. He was helping you."

"Marie is such a lovely girl." Miss Marple recalled Sir Herbert's words to his wife earlier. The words had been spoken with such tenderness that it was clear that he not only wholeheartedly approved of his son's choice of wife, but he also held a great personal affection for her. Enough to help her when she found herself in a troubling situation.

Her voice barely above a whisper, Marie said, "My father's solicitor summoned me to his office in London and this is where I met my half-sister for the first time. We were both informed of my parents' marriage and that I was the legal heir . . . We argued." Tenderly, she turned to her new husband. "And that's where I met Peter. He came to my rescue, but he didn't overhear the heated discussion I had with Louise, so was ignorant of the details. After that, Louise wouldn't leave me alone. She kept threatening me to stay quiet about my mother and father's marriage. And then Sir Herbert found me very distressed one day . . ."

"And decided to warn Louise off," Miss Marple finished. Her gaze turned to Marie's father-in-law. "You visited Louise at the Fruit Pickers Arms and confronted her. Unfortunately, your brother-in-law, Bishop Ambrose, saw you both outside. He reported back to Lady Margaret, his sister, that you were in the company of an attractive young woman, no doubt succumbing to the vices of sinners."

Looking sickly and stunned, Lady Margaret rounded on her husband, "Is this true? Why didn't you deny it earlier?"

"Marie told me what was going on in the strictest confidence. After the wedding, I was going to explain it all to you."

"But the girl collapsed into your arms and was trying to call out our family name, Apfel-Strand. *Your* name," his wife accused. The shape of her mouth turned ugly. "She was probably also trying to say 'Herbert,' but couldn't get it out."

"She was attempting to call out his Lordship's name,

but not for the reason you think," Miss Bella informed the group. "Miss McCracken died by poisoning. Someone placed a potentially fatal fruit in her dessert. Earlier, the chef told me that when he arrived in the kitchen, he found a bowl of fruit salad carefully covered on a counter. There was a handwritten note stating that it contained a certain delicacy from St. Honoré that Marie loved. The note was from Sir Herbert, and the special dessert a surprise for his new daughter-in-law."

Herbert Apfel-Strand was outraged. "That's preposterous. I requested no such thing."

"We know," Miss Marple affirmed. "In a box in Louise McCracken's room we found leaves and the bark of a very poisonous tree."

"The Manchineel tree from St. Honoré," Miss Bella explained. "It can be deadly."

Leaning forward, following all that was said avidly, Bishop Ambrose gasped. "Are you saying—?"

"Yes," Miss Marple confirmed. "It was Louise McCracken who placed the murder weapons, the poisonous fruit known on St. Honoré as the Little Apples of Death, into Marie's dessert. But that wasn't enough for her; she had to make sure that Marie died, and died quickly, so she also placed bark and leaves from the tree in the dish too. This would increase the potency of the poison in the fruit salad. She disguised the bark by chipping it to make it appear like a spice, something akin to ground cinnamon or grated nutmeg, along with leaves, which were shredded. You see, sometimes eating the apple is not enough. Marie's half-sister knew that she had to use other parts of the tree that had sap on them too to be sure."

Jane continued, "Marie has confirmed that Louise holidayed with her parents on St. Honoré as a child, so she will have known all about the Manchineel tree. And she appeared very tanned today, which suggests she had recently returned from somewhere with a very hot climate."

Hugging his bride even closer, a confused Peter said, "But Louise McCracken is the one who is dead and, thankfully, not my sweet Marie. I don't understand."

Miss Marple slotted the final piece of the puzzle into place. "Marie, your Tante Bella has told me that you don't like apples. I suspect that, when your dessert arrived, you swapped your bowl with Louise's because hers had no apples?"

Nodding, Marie shivered with the knowledge of how close she had come to her own death. On her very own wedding day.

Lady Margaret still wasn't convinced, "Surely this

McCracken woman would have recognised her own devious handiwork when the dessert was placed in front of her?"

Miss Bella held up a cautionary finger. "Marie's half-sister hadn't reckoned with the artistic eye of the chef. He did not like the overall presentation of the dish he found waiting with a note for him in the kitchen, so he cut up the apples and mixed the ingredients, inadvertently incorporating the bark and leaves deeper into the fruit salad. When I first saw him, his palms were deep pink in colour, which I assumed was a sign of work-worn hands, and his bloodshot eyes I mistook for an overindulgence of drink. I was wrong. Both his hands and eyes were irritated from touching the apples. Louise McCracken ate the fruit salad because she did not recognise it as the dish she had prepared."

"But how did she know what food was being served at our wedding breakfast?" It was Peter who asked this question.

"The landlord at the Fruit Picker's Arms was very displeased that Louise kept speaking to the young woman who cleaned the rooms," Miss Bella explained. "But Miss McCracken knew exactly what she was doing. She had discovered that Elsie, the chambermaid, was also one of a number of additional staff taken on to work in the kitchen during the wedding at Strand

Hall. It was through Elsie that Marie's half-sister found out what the menu would be. The fruit salad was the perfect dish to hide her lethal culinary cocktail."

Miss Marple picked up the tale again, "When Miss McCracken realised she had been poisoned, she staggered to her feet, her throat burning, her airways closing up. She stumbled, looking for help, but faced a dilemma. The nearest people to her were both her enemies, Marie on one side and Sir Herbert, who had confronted her at the inn, on the other. She chose the lesser enemy, the baronet. Miss McCracken was indeed calling out his Lordship's surname, Apfel-Strand, but not how you think. Apfel is the German for apple and strand is the old name for a beach, as in 'Apple-Beach.' The poisonous fruit of the Manchineel tree is not only called the little apple of death; it is also known as the beach apple. In her distressed state, Louise was trying to tell everyone that she'd eaten the beach apple, but she couldn't get the words out, so was also pointing to Sir Herbert, indicating his name. She even managed to say the word "strand.""

Miss Marple caught the eye of everyone in the room. "This is not a case of murder but that of the perpetrator and victim being one and the same, dying from the murderous malice of their own hand."

In a sorrowful voice, Marie murmured, "I told her

I would share all our father's wealth with her. That maybe we could get to know each other as sisters. But that wasn't good enough for her. She wanted it all for herself. And me dead."

Miss Marple looked kindly at Marie. "Your half-sister was a desperate, greedy person."

Miss Bella quietly added one of her sage Caribbean sayings. " 'Crave all, get none.' "

It wasn't until a week later that Miss Marple and Miss Bella, along with the Apfel-Strands, loudly cheered the happy couple off on their honeymoon. Their honeymoon had understandably been delayed due to the police investigation. But Sir Henry Clithering had assured the officer in charge that he could trust everything that Miss Marple told him, as she was a woman who conducted a meticulous investigation and understood the grave failings in human nature better than anyone else, in his experience.

Now, outside Strand Hall, Marie gave Miss Marple and Miss Bella an especially big kiss and hug. Wearing a huge grin, she joined her new husband in their super sleek E-Type Jag. The two women watched as it drove down the road, tin cans tied to the rear bumper and clanging after them, with a "Just Married" sign hanging from the boot.

Turning to her great friend, Miss Bella whispered with an amused twinkle, "It would seem that Sir Herbert and Lady Margaret's wish has come true. Their son has indeed married an heiress."

Miss Marple nodded, but added, with a returning twinkle, "More importantly, two young people have found each other and found love."

Murder at the Villa Rosa

Elly Griffiths

It's not necessary to travel to a beautiful place to commit murder, of course, but sometimes it does help. I thought this several times as I drove the hired car along the vertiginous Italian road, each corner revealing a scene of almost unbearable beauty and, at the same time, bringing me infinitely closer to my own demise. It was all too much: sea, cliffs, blue sky, white houses, the prospect of the afterlife. Now and then, with no warning, a tunnel would plunge me into darkness and, by the time I'd located the headlights, I was out in the blazing sun again, swerving to meet another hairpin bend. The worst moments were when I'd meet a car or a bus driving in the opposite direction. These vehicles showed no sign of slowing down and I soon learnt that the only option was to steer into the hedge and let them thunder past. Sweat poured from under the brow of my newly acquired Panama hat and my hands were rigid on the wheel.

I'd thought about killing Ricky for years. At first I loved him, of course I did. We've come a long way together and he's been a big part of my success. Everyone likes Ricky and I suppose that's part of the problem. I grew tired of him, every mannerism grated, every apparently spontaneous joke seemed signalled years ago, in the ice age of my memory. But still people laughed at those so-called witticisms and seemed never to tire of his company. The only answer, as I came to see it, was to kill him.

But how and where? It was too difficult to do it at home. My house in Battersea was large and comfortable. I had a book-lined study in the attic from which I could see the curve of the Thames. I also had a charming wife and two intermittently charming children. But the trouble was that No. 5 Waterway Drive was full of Ricky. I'd already had a few disconcerting experiences where I'd seen Ricky in places where he couldn't possibly have been; following me along the towpath to the pub or standing ruminatively on my balcony. No, I couldn't kill him there.

It was Paula, my wife, who first mentioned the Villa Rosa. She'd heard about it from Fran at one of Cassowary's cocktail parties. It was the perfect place, said Paula. It was on the Amalfi coast but not in a tourist trap like Sorrento or Positano. The photographs showed a dusky pink building, half hotel and half castle, on a rocky outcrop overlooking the Bay of Naples. "You can get away from it all," said Paula. "Do some work or just rest. Whatever you feel like." Paula knew that something was wrong. She just didn't know what. If she had known, she would have tried to stop me. And I didn't blame her at all.

I had the directions, typed by the travel agent, on the seat beside me. The trouble was, as the sun grew lower, I added blindness to my disadvantages as a driver. The sea sparkled on one side, the mountains loomed on the other, my hired Fiat ploughed into the hedge again and again to let the behemoths power past. It was lucky that I had memorised the instructions, partly because they sounded so picturesque. Past the shrine to the Madonna of the Rocks, past the umbrella pines, right at the ruined tower. These landmarks came in quick succession. I was now being followed by another monster bus, mooing impatiently, so I nearly missed the turning and only had time to wrench the car to the right, in the direction of the sea, and come to a shuddering halt under a canopy of vines.

Instantly the passenger door of my car was opened and a soothing voice said, "Good evening, Signor Jeffries. I am Bertrando. Welcome to the Villa Rosa."

I stepped out, swaying slightly after the long drive. It was blessedly cool in the portico and I listened to Bertrando telling me that "the boy" would collect my bags and park the car. As he spoke, he ushered me inside. I was aware of a dark hallway, hovering staff and the scent of lemons. Then Bertrando opened another set of doors and I blinked in wonder.

We were on a terrace, a square of tables and umbrellas. But, beyond the stone parapet, there was nothing. Only blue. The waters of the Mediterranean stretched to the horizon. On either side, in the distance, I could see the curve of the bay, the multi-coloured houses clinging to the wooded shore, a golden dome glittering in the evening sunlight.

"Welcome," said Bertrando again, "to the Villa Rosa."

My room was large and luxurious. The blinds were drawn but, opening them slightly, I saw that view again, almost sinister in its utter beauty.

"This is a wonderful location," I said.

"There was once a Roman villa on this site," said Bertrando. He spoke perfect English, his accent only noticeable on certain vowels. "In the Renaissance, it was rebuilt for an aristocratic family. They painted the frescos on the walls. Then it was a monastery, and a hospital during the war. So many stories. So many secrets. Now, I will leave you to relax."

I had my own bathroom (Bertrando had called it an "en-suite") tiled in blue and yellow. There was a bath, shower and, apparently, two lavatories. On inspection I discovered that one of them was the Continental contraption called a bidet. I showered and changed into fresh clothes. Bertrando had explained that it was the tradition of the hotel for guests to gather on the terrace for pre-dinner drinks at eight. As it was now half past, I smoothed down my hair with bay rum, tucked in my shirt and headed downstairs.

The enchanted space seemed very full of people. A grey-haired couple, a young woman with an older husband, a middle-aged man of military bearing and an elderly lady, who was incongruously wearing a tweed suit.

Bertrando was at my side, murmuring introductions, "Signor and Signora Martinelli, Lord and Lady Braithwaite, Colonel Peters, and Miss Marple."

"Felix Jeffries." I shook hands and bowed, as appropriate.

"The writer?" said Lady Braithwaite, the woman with the older husband. She had an American accent and was, I was realising slowly, quite staggeringly beautiful.

"Yes," I said, feeling embarrassed as I always do when admitting to spending my days in this way.

"We just love the Ricky Barber books. Don't we, darling?"

Lord Braithwaite, "darling," said, "Terrific stuff."

"Ricky Barber," said Signora Martinelli, the grey-haired lady. "I am a complete fan." Ricky is translated into thirty languages. He gets everywhere.

"It must be such an interesting thing, to be a novelist," said Miss Marple.

Something about the way she said it made me look at the last speaker more closely. She had an innocent pink-and-white face, untouched by the Italian sun, and white hair in a careful bun. Her eyes were pale blue and very bright. She looked at me for a second, an odd fluttery glance, and—maybe it was a trick of the light—it was as if she knew *just* how interesting I found my profession.

"I'm very lucky," I said, as I always do.

"Luck," said Colonel Peters, "is only another word for cunning."

Bertrando announced that dinner was served.

The food was absolutely sublime and seemed to go on for ever. Antipasti, pasta, chicken with green beans, fish in caper sauce, lemon sorbet, cheese, coffee in tiny brittle cups. By the end I was lolling in my chair, but Miss Marple, at the table next to me, was as upright as ever, still wearing her tweed jacket. After coffee, Bertrando offered us all a liqueur called limoncello, bright yellow liquid in miniature blue glasses. I accepted, feeling reckless, as did the Colonel and Signor Martinelli. The conversation became general and we discussed how we'd come to the Villa Rosa. I said that it had been recommended by my publisher. The Martinellis had stayed here the year before and "fallen in love with the place." Lord Braithwaite said that he'd had a special offer. He seemed pleased about this, which surprised me, because he was obviously a very rich man. He'd already mentioned racehorses and yachts. As for his beautiful wife, everything about her dripped luxury.

When second drinks were offered, the Braithwaites and Colonel Peters excused themselves.

Lady Braithwaite said that she was tired after a day in the sun. Colonel Peters announced his intention of retiring with a good book. Something in his tone suggested that this tome would not be penned by Felix Jeffries or one of his ilk.

By unspoken consent, the remaining diners drew together on one table. By now it was nearly midnight and the candles were burning low. Occasionally we would see the glow of a firefly or the lights of a late-night fishing boat, but otherwise the bay was in darkness. All around us, the crickets were singing.

We talked about home. The Martinellis were from Milan and Miss Marple from a village called St. Mary Mead. I spoke at length about the delights of Battersea.

"Of course," said Elisabetta Martinelli, "I lived in Sorrento once. When I was a nun."

I didn't at first take in her meaning. For this, the limoncello was partly to blame. But Miss Marple said, "The cloistered life must be fascinating."

"Yes," said Elisabetta. "Although I wasn't always cloistered. When the war came, we were part of a group—the Assisi network—trying to help Jewish Italians escape persecution. We hid men, women and children in our convent and eventually I was captured."

"What happened then?" I said. It was hard to reconcile this story with the grey-haired woman, elegant but unobtrusive in a green dress, who sat beside me. Luigi Martinelli was watching his wife, his gold-rimmed glasses glinting in the light from the candles, a gentle smile playing around his lips.

"I was taken to Naples and imprisoned there," said Elisabetta. "The fascists had recently arrested a young resistance fighter. They were going to shoot him. I stood in front of him and said, 'You will have to kill me first.' They were still too superstitious to murder a nun, so they reprieved the man."

"What happened to him?" I asked.

Elisabetta waved a hand towards her husband.

"I am that man," he told me gravely. "We met again after the war. I'd become a doctor and I met Elisabetta when she was nursing in Naples. I knew her immediately and we fell in love. Well, I had always been in love with her. Ever since she stood in front of a bullet for me."

"It was difficult," said Elisabetta, in her soft voice. "I had taken vows and I took those seriously. But love cannot be denied."

"We've been very happy," said Luigi. "We have four children and a rich life. Of course, I can never repay her."

"You repay me every day," said Elisabetta.

Once again, I blame the limoncello for the tears that came to my eyes.

"That's a beautiful story," I said.

"Just like a book," said Miss Marple.

The next morning, when we breakfasted on the terrace, it was hard to look at Luigi and Elisabetta in the same way. On the surface, they were the same contented couple enjoying a holiday in the sun. But to think that their past held so much danger and tragedy, so much *backstory*, made me almost shy of them. We greeted each other with "Buongiorno" and I sat down to eat melon and ham, an unusual but excellent start to the day. As I drank my coffee, I watched a lizard sunning itself on the white wall. I should go to my room and plan my murder, I thought. I'd requested a typewriter and it was now sitting accusingly on the desk in my bedroom, a brand new Olivetti. I'd told Fran that I would have a synopsis of the new book by the end of the week. Fran was my editor, one of the many young women at Cassowary who seemed to belong, not just to a different generation, but to a different world. She was in her late twenties or early thirties, unmarried, wore trousers and rode a small motorbike to work. A Vespa, I think it was called. My previous editor was a man called Martin, who took me for long lunches and spilled cigar ash on my manuscripts. I thought of Martin with nostalgia, even though he invariably called me Phil.

I should be writing. But suddenly I wanted to lie reptile-like on the sand.

A shadow fell over my *prima colazione*. It was Miss Marple, wearing a blue dress and a large straw hat.

"How do you plan to spend the day, Mr. Jeffries?" she asked.

"Felix, please. I should do some work."

"I thought I might explore the beach," she said. "Bertrando says the hotel has a private one. The steps are very steep but there's a sort of *ski lift*." She made these last words sound very exotic, almost dangerous.

When Miss Marple had twittered away, full of her funicular adventure, I thought of my room: bed, wardrobe, desk, typewriter. And I decided that I too would visit the beach.

The steps were cut into the rock and, like the road yesterday, took several twists and turns, offering snapshots of the glittering bay. When I reached the beach, I found Miss Marple already established on a deck chair, sipping a lime cordial. The beach was just a triangle of sand (which, extraordinarily to me, was black) surrounded by rocks. Lady Brathwaite was there too, stretched out on a sun lounger and wearing a two-piece costume that left very little to my imagination.

I remarked on the sand and Miss Marple told me that it was volcanic. "Of course," she said, "Vesuvius is not so very far away. I often think about those poor people in Pompeii. Such an *untidy* ending."

I had to stifle a smile at this. The residents of the Roman town had died in agony, buried under burning ash. Untidy was not the word I'd use. But I found Miss Marple's company soothing and, before long, I was telling her of my plans for Ricky.

"I've come to hate him," I said. "And I can never be free of him unless I kill him."

"It must be hard writing about a character you dislike," said Miss Marple.

"I don't mind writing baddies," I said. "After all, I'm a crime writer. Murder's my business. I love being inside the mind of someone truly evil. That's the trouble with Ricky. He's too nice. He was all right at first, when he'd just left the army and joined the police force. He was full of interesting angst. He had unhappy love affairs, he was estranged from his son, he had a health condition. But, as people came to like Ricky, I've been scared to make him suffer. He just drifts along, solving crimes that don't really affect him. He's reconciled with his son, and everyone—including my editor, Fran—has forgotten about his health problems."

"That reminds me of someone in my village," said Miss Marple, rather to my surprise. "Mrs. Randall disposed of her husband because every night, at ten o'clock precisely, he always said, 'I'm going up the wooden hill to Bedfordshire.'"

"I can see how that would get on your nerves," I said, "but divorce seems an extreme reaction."

"Oh, she didn't divorce him," said Miss Marple. "She killed him."

The sun was hot and, after a while, I ventured into the sea. The water was wonderfully cool and clear, very salty, with hardly any waves. I swam a long way out, until I could see the misty shape of Naples, with Vesuvius looming in the background. "Untidy ending," I said to myself, floating on my back and feeling the sun beating on my face. Endings are vital for a crime writer. You have to solve the crime, identify the culprit, dispense justice and tie up any loose ends, all in the last fifty pages. Any sooner and readers will complain it's too easy. Any later and they will feel shortchanged.

I swam back to shore and found that Louisa Braithwaite had joined Miss Marple, her ladyship now wearing a diaphanous pink-and-gold robe over her swimsuit. The hotel had constructed a small bar in the corner of the beach, with buckets of ice in which bobbed an assortment of bottles.

The young barman, who introduced himself as Carlo, said, "Would you like a drink, Signor Jeffries? Soda? Wine? Beer?"

I should have opted for a soda, but the thought of drinking a cold beer was suddenly too appealing. Carlo placed the sweating bottle on a rush table by my deck chair. Louisa was telling Miss Marple that she was Lord Braithwaite's third wife. Miss Marple didn't contribute much to the conversation beyond a few soothingly phatic murmurs, but, as had been the case earlier with me, she certainly seemed to inspire a confessional spirit in her companions.

"It's a lot to live up to," said Louisa. "Marcus is very particular. And, of course, he likes a particular sort of woman."

"What do you mean?" I said, entering the conversation rather abruptly. But I was intrigued.

In answer, Louisa delved into her expensive-looking handbag. To my surprise, she produced an envelope and drew out a newspaper cutting. Miss Marple and I leaned forward to examine it.

"Lord and Lady Braithwaite at Cannes," read the

caption. The picture showed the couple, dressed in pre-war fashions. This surprised me because Louisa didn't look older than thirty. Miss Marple said, "Quite a resemblance."

"Yes," said Louisa. "Number two looked like me too." And, from the same envelope, she drew a black-and-white photograph of a man and a woman standing next to a racehorse. The woman was also extraordinarily like Louisa, except maybe taller. Even allowing for her big hat, she was at eye level with her husband. I'd noticed last night that Louisa was a head shorter than Marcus.

"I mean, he has a type, right?" she said now. "I didn't realise it at first. I met Marcus in New York after the war. I was a dancer and he came to every show, sitting in the front row in his British pin-striped suit, staring straight at me all the time I was on stage. Someone told me that he was a lord but I didn't believe it. Eventually he asked me to go for a meal with him and we were married within the month. I didn't even know about the other wives until we were on honeymoon. It was at the Villa Rosa, as a matter of fact."

"Must be the perfect place for a honeymoon," I said.

"I suppose." Louisa looked out at the sea, glittering gold in the midday glare, but I got the impression that she was seeing something else. "I didn't mind that much about being wife number three. I mean, Marcus is older than me. You'd expect him to have some past. It was just, when I saw the photographs, I thought . . . what happens when I no longer look like this?" She tapped the Cannes picture, as if it really did display her likeness and not that of the first Lady Braithwaite.

"Lord Braithwaite reminds me of a dear friend in St. Mary Mead," said Miss Marple. "She's had three dogs since I've known her. All black-and-white cocker spaniels called George."

"Gee, thanks," said Louisa. "Cute analogy."

"You don't need to worry," I said, rather hurriedly. "Lord Braithwaite dotes on you. I noticed that immediately."

"He doted on the others too," said Louisa. "Until they died."

"They died?"

"Yeah," said Louisa. "Unlucky, right?" And she lay back in her sun-lounger and shut her eyes. I thought of what Colonel Peters had said last night.

Luck is only another word for cunning.

Carlo produced an extraordinary lunch from nowhere. I picked at salami and mozzarella. Miss Marple ate heartily, a napkin spread over her knees. Louisa did not open her eyes. Maybe it was the food, maybe it was the sun, maybe it was the beer (I had a second), but I started to feel very sleepy. I decided to go to my room for a siesta.

The stairs seemed incredibly steep going in this direction. When I reached the top, I swayed and almost fell.

"Signor?" came a woman's voice.

I opened my eyes. It was one of the maids. Simonetta, I think her name was.

"Are you all right?"

"Yes," I said. "It's just the stairs and the heat." And the beers, I added silently.

Simonetta seemed to be flickering in and out of focus like an old film. "Did Bertrando offer you his special limoncello last night?" she asked.

"Yes," I said.

"It can be very strong if you're not used to it," she said. "It can make you see things that aren't there."

When I opened my eyes again, she was gone.

I continued up to my room. The shutters were closed but I could see the typewriter shimmering in the gloom. I ignored it and lay down on the bed. A mosquito buzzed somewhere high in the rafters. *Zanzare* in Italian. A wonderfully onomatopoeic word. Suddenly I thought of Fran's motorbike. *Vespa.* A wasp. Another perfect name.

I thought I'd sleep immediately, but words and images whirred like insects around my head.

The cloistered life must be fascinating.

It must be hard writing about a character you dislike.

Vesuvius glimmering on the horizon.

Such an untidy ending.

Louisa proffering a photograph. He has a type, right?

Before I slept, I had one last, coherent thought: Simonetta looked very like Louisa Braithwaite.

At dinner, it transpired that Miss Marple's nephew had paid for her holiday. "He's very generous," she said.

"It is a wonderful thing to be an uncle or an aunt," said Bertrando. "My nephew Carlo works with me. I speak to my niece Francesca on the telephone every week."

"Can't stand my nephew," said Colonel Peters. "He killed my sister."

This remark was made to the company in general. Not surprisingly, a silence fell after these words. Elisabetta whispered something that sounded like a prayer.

"How did he kill your sister?" asked Miss Marple, looking up calmly from her risotto.

"He worried her to death," said the Colonel. We seemed to release our collective breath. "With his drinking and womanising and gambling. Well, I've had my revenge in my book."

Yes, the Colonel was another author. When he retired to bed with a good book, he meant his own. It turned out that he'd written two well-received military memoires but now he was embarking on a new venture. "It's a crime novel," he told us, becoming expansive over the limoncello. "Hope it's the start of a series. I'm putting all my enemies in it and killing them off one by one. Fancy that I've got a very good plot too. A killer hook, I think they call it." He leered around the terrace, showing yellowing teeth.

"A killer hook," repeated Elisabetta, rather nervously.

"Felix here could advise you," said Marcus Braithwaite.

"I don't need advice," said the Colonel. "In fact, I'm off to write another chapter." He marched, rather unsteadily, into the hotel.

Miss Marple and I found ourselves seated side-by-side on a wicker sofa, looking out over the blue-black sea.

Lord and Lady Braithwaite had gone for a stroll on the beach and the Martinellis were talking to Bertrando in Italian.

"It sometimes seems as if all the world is writing a book," I said.

"I always feel that it must be a very hard thing to do," said Miss Marple. "Much more difficult than it seems."

I warmed to my elderly companion. It's surprising how many people think that being an author is easy. "I've always wanted to write," they say, "if only I had the time." As if time is all it takes.

"Maybe it's easy if you have a killer hook," I said.

"I suspect there's no such thing," said Miss Marple. "Perhaps it's lots of little hooks, like crochet. When you put them together, it's a complete tapestry. I do like crochet. Knitting too. It's more of a winter pastime, though."

A woman passed from the light of the terrace into the dark of the hotel. A few minutes later, I saw her taking the stairs to the beach. She had long dark hair and, for a second, I thought she was Louisa Braithwaite.

"Simonetta looks very like Lady Braithwaite," I said to Miss Marple.

"Beautiful people do often look rather alike," she replied.

"That was quite a story she told us on the beach," I said. "About the three wives."

"Yes," said Miss Marple. "A modern-day Bluebeard." She laughed but the words made my skin contract, as if a mosquito had landed there. I thought of Lord Braithwaite. He seemed like a typical upper-class Englishman, rather reserved and aloof, perhaps not very bright. But who knows what lies beneath? Murderers aren't always evil geniuses like Moriarty. They are people you meet at parties, people with whom you share a meal, who you pass in the street or sit next to on a London omnibus. I thought of Bertrando saying, 'So many stories. So many secrets."

Then a scream cut through the night.

I sprang to my feet, but Bertrando was quicker. He hurtled down the steps. I followed as fast as I dared. I saw the black sea breaking in white waves on the black sand. I saw Lord Braithwaite, his face pale in the moonlight. And a woman lying at his feet, her hair as dark as death.

Then I saw no more.

When I came to, I was lying on a sofa in the hotel lobby. I could smell lemons and Italian cologne. Blearily I focused on a ceiling fan and the terracotta shades of a fresco. Then a man's face, eyes intent behind gold-rimmed glasses. Luigi Martinelli was bending over me.

"Just a slight concussion," I heard him say. I'd forgotten that he was a doctor.

"What happened?" I struggled to sit up. "Who died? Who was killed?"

"Nobody died." Bertrando's voice seemed to come from a long way off. "Simonetta saw a . . . what do you call it? . . . a jellyfish . . . on the beach. She screamed, ran for the steps and fell. She is very embarrassed."

That makes two of us, I thought.

"Why did I faint?" I said.

Dottore Martinelli put a glass of water in my hand.

"You fell down the steps. Easy to do in the dark. You hit your head on a rock."

"How did I get here?" I took a sip of the water. It tasted odd, sulphuric.

"Bertrando and Signor Braithwaite carried you. But you should be in your bed. Are you able to stand?"

I was, with help. Bertrando on one side, the doctor on the other. As we reached the stairs, I saw my fellow guests gathered in a concerned group by the French windows. Lord Braithwaite with his arm round his wife. Elisabetta comforting Simonetta. Miss Marple standing sightly apart, the electric light gleaming on her white hair.

Apart from a slight headache, I felt fine in the morning. Bertrando himself brought me breakfast in bed: small croissants that he called "cornetti," unsalted butter, jam, orange juice and coffee.

"Dottore Martinelli said to take it easy today," he said.

"Take it easy," I said. "How come you speak such good English?"

"I spent some time in London after the war," said Bertrando. "My brother lives there. It's where I learnt to be a hotelier."

"You're very good at it," I said. "How's Simonetta this morning?"

"She is well," said Bertrando. "Just embarrassed to have caused such . . . such commotion."

"Tell her not to worry," I said. "I blame it on the limoncello."

I thought that Bertrando looked slightly guilty as he bowed his way out.

After breakfast I showered, dressed and decided to walk into Priano, the nearest town. It wasn't far but the route took me along the coastal road, which felt almost as frightening on foot as it had behind the wheel of my hired Fiat. How long ago was it that I'd negotiated those hairpin bends? Was it really only two days past? And I'd got no further with killing Ricky. I thought of Colonel Peter's smug retort last night: "I don't need advice." I rather thought that *I* did.

The road led through one of the sudden tunnels cut into the cliffs. It felt very cold and dark after the heat of the day, but, as I progressed farther, I saw that it was lit with a faint phosphorescent glow. In the eerie light I made out a strange adornment. On a rough shelf cut into the stone wall was a model village: houses, domed church, ruined tower and a pink building that looked very like the Villa Rosa. There were lighted candles by the church and the tower, and it was these, reflected against the rocky roof, that gave out the ominous green light. I walked on quickly.

Priano was beautiful, all white-washed houses and winding steps. Apparently the church contained some important paintings, but I was happy just to sit outside a café with a *spremuta di limone* and a two-day-old copy of *The Times*. I asked the owner, who spoke English, about the model village in the tunnel and he said it was a *presepio*, a kind of Christmas nativity scene. It had been created by a local artist two years ago and no one had wanted to remove it. Instantly the candlelit houses seemed quaint rather than sinister. I had a sudden desire to write about it. Perhaps I should send Ricky to Italy, I thought, before remembering that Ricky was not going anywhere, except to his doom. I would make a start that evening.

The walk back was hard work, as the sun was at its hottest. The sky was a bright hard blue and the cicadas were like voices in my head. Maybe I had been too adventurous attempting such a trek. After all, the doctor had told me to take it easy. I remembered the day earlier, when I'd felt dizzy climbing the stairs from the beach. Maybe I was sickening for something? The tunnel was a relief and I stood for a moment, breathing in the clammy air. When I stepped out into the daylight, it was as if the sun were directing its rays directly on to my head. I wished I'd worn my Panama hat.

It was then that I saw a man walking in front of me. I thought it was odd that I hadn't seen him in the tunnel, but maybe he had joined the road from one of the coastal paths. He was tall, with greying dark hair, and he walked with a slightly uneven gait. I thought of Ricky, who used to limp in the early books, the result of a wartime injury, but now seemed to be as spry as an eighteen-year-old. I thought of the times I'd seen Ricky at my house in London. Maybe he had really been there all along? It suddenly seemed important to catch up with the Ricky walk-alike. I quickened my pace, although it made my heart beat faster and the sweat run into my brows.

At last, there was the Villa Rosa, its pink walls seeming almost red in the midday sun. I thought of the cool lobby, the jar of lemons that stood on the front desk, the fresco showing the judgement of Paris. I would sit in the dark and drink a glass of water before attempting the stairs to my room. Then I stopped. The limping man was also turning to go into the hotel. For some reason, I felt that I had to stop him. I ran forwards and lurched through the double doors.

Once inside, I was aware of several things simultaneously. The tiled floor was pulsating in an unpleasant way. The ceiling fan was circulating dust motes that looked to me like the keys of an Olivetti typewriter. I heard laughter. Then the voices of the cicadas formed a name.

Ricky Barber.

I saw a familiar face.

And I rushed forward, intent on murder.

This time, when I woke, I was lying on my bed. A woman's voice said, "How are you feeling?"

"Fran! What are you doing here?"

For a moment it seemed incredible that my editor should be sitting by my bedside in an Italian hotel. She belonged in London, part of another life. But, in another way, she looked oddly at home in this setting. She also reminded me of someone.

"I'm sorry," she was saying. "I just wanted to help."

I struggled to sit up. The shutters were closed and the fan was whirring in the ceiling.

"What happened?" I said. "Did I faint again? I thought I saw Ricky. He was walking just ahead of me."

"That was Salvatore," said Fran. "He works in the kitchens."

"I thought it was Ricky," I said, feeling very foolish. "I thought I had to stop him going into the hotel."

"You sort of lunged forward and fell to the floor," said Fran. "It was very dramatic. One of the guests is apparently a doctor and he said it was probably heatstroke."

"But I heard someone say 'Ricky Barber.'"

Fran looked perplexed for a moment and then she laughed, at the same time making a curious gesture of stroking her chin. "You heard me say *che barba*. It means "how boring." Literally, you could wait for a beard to grow." She made the gesture again. "Carlo must have been talking to me about football."

"You haven't said what you're doing here," I said. "Honestly, Fran. I think I'm going mad. This whole place is driving me insane. It's like something out of a book. You wouldn't believe the stories I've heard."

"I would," said Fran, "because I've been telling them to you."

"I don't understand."

"I was worried," said Fran. "I knew that you wanted to end the Ricky books. That's fine by me. It was just that you hadn't got an idea for a *new* book. Or a new series. I thought you'd fallen out of love with writing. With storytelling. I spoke to Paula about it."

"You spoke to Paula?"

"At the Cassowary author party. She was worried about you too. She asked if I could recommend a writers' retreat and I thought of this place. It's so beautiful here and there's so much history. I thought it might inspire you. Then, I thought, what if I filled the hotel with interesting characters? People who had stories to tell. My uncle suggested the Martinellis because they had stayed here before. He'd been very struck by them and by their history."

"Your uncle?" I said.

"Bertrando."

Then I remembered that Bertrando had once lived in London. Also that he had a niece called Francesca. That was the resemblance I had noticed earlier. They had the same dark eyes and high cheekbones.

"Lord and Lady Braithwaite had their honeymoon here," Fran continued. "Zio Bertrando remembered them well. He said that Lady Braithwaite had been rather disturbed to learn that her predecessors had looked rather like her. She even mentioned it to him. I thought, if she tells that story to the hotel manager, she'll tell it to anyone. I persuaded my uncle to give them a special offer. Rich people always like a bargain."

"And Colonel Peters?"

Fran laughed. "Terry is another one of my authors. There's nothing wrong with a bit of healthy competition. He's always going on about having a killer hook for his crime series. I thought that might spur you on."

I shut my eyes. I could hear the *zanzare* buzzing.

"So this whole thing was for my benefit? I'm not being poisoned by the limoncello?"

"Zio Bertrando's limoncello is rather lethal. But you're not being poisoned. I just think you had a touch too much sun today."

I thought of the tunnel with the candles burning, of the lights of the fireflies at night, of the ruins of Pompeii. Dust and ashes.

"Something's been happening to me," I said. "I'm not quite sure what."

"There's an old lady downstairs called Miss Marple,"

said Fran. "She's very keen to see you. Shall I send her up?"

"Yes, do." Suddenly I wanted to hear Miss Marple's gentle voice and see the world through her sharp blue gaze.

"Did you guess?" I said, as Miss Marple entered, neat and birdlike in a flowery dress.

"Not entirely," she said. "But that first night, Elisabetta's tale. You said yourself it was a beautiful story and I thought: just like a book. Then Louisa's performance on the beach. A fairy tale, a modern-day Bluebeard. I wondered if someone was collating these stories for you to find."

"But what about the husband and the two wives who died? That actually happened."

"Louisa made it sound very dramatic," said Miss Marple. "But I think that Marcus Braithwaite is just a man who likes a certain type of woman."

"What about Simonetta?" I said. "Was it a coincidence that she looked just like Louisa?"

"It's a vague resemblance," said Miss Marple. "That's all. As I said, beautiful people do tend to look rather alike. The three Lady Braithwaites are not really any more similar than my friend's three spaniels. It's just the name that makes them appear so."

"What about you?" I said. "Are you here for me too?"

"Oh no," said Miss Marple. "I'm just on holiday. Though I did meet Bertrando years ago in London. And my nephew did pay a very advantageous rate for my room."

"My editor is Bertrando's niece," I said. "She set up this whole thing to give me an idea for a new book."

"And have you got one?"

"Maybe," I said. "I'm thinking about what you said about lots of little hooks, like crochet or a tapestry."

"That's right," said Miss Marple. "I'm no author, but that's how I imagine you might put a story together. Especially a crime novel, where you need so many threads."

I looked towards the Olivetti on the desk. My fingers ached for the keys.

Miss Marple said, in a diffident voice, "If I might make a suggestion?"

"Please do."

"Don't kill Ricky. Do you remember what I said about Letty Randall and her husband?"

"Up the wooden hill to Bedfordshire?"

"That's the one. She was acquitted of his murder, but she was never free of him. Now, if she'd just left

Arthur, she would never have had to think of him again."

"You think I should divorce Ricky?"

"In my experience," said Miss Marple, "nothing puts a stop to curiosity quite like happiness. Could you give Ricky a happy ending?"

"I could certainly try," I said.

The Murdering Sort

Karen M. McManus

"Aunt Jane, this is *perfect*."

The words come out with a contented sigh as I fling myself on to what appears to be a plush velvet sofa across from my aunt's rocking chair. Appearances are deceiving, though, and I land uncomfortably on rock-hard cushions. "Well, nearly perfect," I amend, sitting up with the straightness the sofa demands. "How did Granddad manage to find a cottage that looks like something from the Home Counties in the middle of Cape Cod?"

"Raymond has always been so clever," Aunt Jane murmurs, eyes on the white fleecy wool that she's knitting into . . . something. A baby's blanket, probably. If you've met my great-great aunt even once, you can be certain of receiving a blanket in the post no more than two weeks after your baby is born. "And wonderfully generous too. Really, Nicola, I have never known why he should take so much trouble about his old aunt."

"Because he knew I'd like to see you," I say affectionately, although I'm sure that's only half the reason. St. Mary Mead can be cool and damp even during summer, and my grandfather is always on the lookout for drier climates to help with Aunt Jane's rheumatism. It's a bonus that I was already here, spending the summer with a school friend.

"And I you," Aunt Jane says, resting her knitting on her lap in order to give me her full attention. It's the first time we've seen one another since she arrived here in Chatham yesterday, and I'm suddenly aware that the patchwork shorts I borrowed from Diana don't blend particularly well with this time-warp room. "You look very. . ."

"American?" I break in. It's what my parents have been saying ever since I started hanging out with Diana. She was the talk of school when she showed up at the beginning of fifth form—the glamorous New York heiress whose English mother whisked her off to the countryside after an acrimonious divorce. I never expected her to notice me, but she'd tapped me on the shoulder her second day and said, "Nicola West, right? I'm Diana Westover. We have matching names, so we're destined to be the best of friends."

And then, like magic, we were. We became Di-and-Nic, together so much that our classmates called us by a single name. When school ended and I knew Diana would soon leave for her grandfather's beach-front estate in Cape Cod, the approaching summer felt endless and empty until she invited me to come along.

"I was going to say *grown-up*," Aunt Jane says diplomatically. "Though I still think seventeen is a bit young to spend the summer away from home. Of course, your father's generation has different ideas than mine. And David assures me the Westover family is *quite* above reproach."

"Quite," I echo. Then I clear my throat, a nervous childhood habit that even being one half of Di-and-Nic hasn't cured.

Aunt Jane looks up sharply. I don't know how old she is, exactly, but one thing's for sure: no matter her age, nothing gets past her. "Are they not?" she asks.

"Well—"

The doorbell rings before I can figure out how to

start. "Why don't I let Diana explain," I say, hurrying for the front door. When I pull it open, I find myself saying "Hello" to an enormous flowering plant.

"Nic, hi!" Diana calls happily, as though it's been half a year since she's seen me rather than half an hour. "Sorry I'm late, but I didn't want to arrive empty-handed."

"Mission accomplished," I say, stepping back so Diana can sweep inside. Somehow, she manages to make carrying an oversized plant look graceful, as though it's the latest must-have accessory. Her long dark hair is so perfectly straight and shiny that I wish I'd taken her advice and tried using her new Vidal Sassoon conditioner on my own unruly curls. Then I wrinkle my brow and add, "You changed?"

As soon as I say it, though, I realise that *of course* Diana wouldn't meet my aunt in shorts and a peasant blouse. She's a pro at matching her outfit to the occasion. Sure enough, even though Aunt Jane looks baffled by the plant, her expression softens into approval when Diana places it on the floor to reveal a sedate, perfectly tailored summer dress. "Hello, Miss Marple, I'm Diana Westover," Diana says warmly. "I brought a potted hydrangea for the yard."

"How kind," Aunt Jane says. She's far too polite to

mention any of the drawbacks to this gift, including the fact that the yard in question isn't hers. That's Diana for you, though; rich enough to assume that everyone owns multiple houses, and so passionate about the environment that she thinks the more usual gift of *cut* flowers to be an abomination.

"I'll just take this into the kitchen for now," I say.

By the time I've settled the pot beside the sink—Aunt Jane's companion, Cherry, will know what to do with it when she returns from the shops—Diana is perched on the edge of the sofa, talking animatedly. "And have you visited the seashore yet, Miss Marple?" she asks.

"We tried yesterday when we first arrived," Aunt Jane says. "But there were some rather large construction vehicles blocking the view."

Diana exhales in frustration. "Oh, it's awful, isn't it?" she asks. "They're putting in *condominiums*. Absolutely ruining the shoreline! It makes me miss being at school in Banbury, where everything was so wonderfully green. Nic says you live in quite a picture-perfect village, Miss Marple?"

"Not any more," Aunt Jane says with her own little sigh. "St. Mary's Mead also has a . . . Development." In response to Diana's raised eyebrows, she adds, "All sorts of new, modern homes. It's progress, of course, and young people must live *somewhere*. But I do miss the old days."

"Me too," Diana says fervently, earning a smile from my aunt.

"You're far too young to remember them, my dear."

Diana laughs. "I suppose you're right, but even ten years ago I could hear frogs singing from the pond across from Grandfather's house when I went to sleep, and now? I don't hear anything." She catches my eye and winks. "Other than Harry hacking away at that guitar. He's a charmer, my cousin, but a terrible musician."

I don't want my eagle-eyed aunt to notice that the name *Harry* makes me blush, so I quickly say, "Di has something she wanted to ask you, Aunt Jane. Because you're so, well, you know . . ." I clear my throat again. "Good at murders."

Aunt Jane blinks, startled enough to drop her knitting needles. "I beg your pardon?"

"Well, not at *doing* them, obviously. At solving them," I say.

It's an awkward start, so Diana tries to smooth things over. "Nic's been telling us that you're practically a one-woman Scotland Yard, Miss Marple," she says.

Aunt Jane's cheeks grow pink. "I assure you, I am not. I simply have a certain knowledge of human nature that has, on occasion, proved helpful to the police."

I poke Diana with my elbow. "Told you she'd say that."

I didn't think it was possible for Aunt Jane to sit up straighter, but she manages. "Why on earth are you girls discussing something so dreadful?" she asks.

Diana winds a strand of dark hair around one finger. It's not as obvious as my throat-clearing, but it's a signal that she's uncomfortable too. "Because of my grandfather," she says. "He's always been eccentric, but ever since the family arrived two weeks ago, he's been treating us like . . . well, like *criminals*." She flushes. "He's very rich, you know, and very old, and he's gotten it into his head that we want him gone so we can inherit his fortune."

"It's so unfair!" I break in, cheeks warming at the memory of Josiah Westover's bitter accusations. "Diana doesn't care about money at all! And even if she did, her father made an absolute fortune on Wall Street." Then I worry that was terribly crass—none of the Westovers except Josiah like to talk about money—but Diana flashes me a grateful smile.

"Thanks, Nic," she says. "But I don't take it personally."

"Oh dear," Aunt Jane murmurs. "Elderly gentlemen can be so difficult. It's hard to lose your health and your strength, and to feel that one is a burden on others."

"It's not that, so much," Diana says, tugging harder on her hair. "The problem, really, is that Grandfather is convinced that we're trying to murder him."

Aunt Jane's china-blue eyes widen. "Indeed? And is there . . ." She gets a little pink again. "Forgive the question, but is there evidence to support such an accusation?"

Diana and I exchange glances. Josiah Westover is one of the oddest, crankiest men I've ever met—but one thing he's *not* is paranoid. Two days after we arrived, the brakes on the car that only he drives failed, and could have caused a terrible accident if he hadn't noticed before leaving the driveway. A week later, the heavy vase on the shelf above his desk came crashing down beside his chair, missing his head by inches.

"There have been a couple of close calls," Diana says. "But all accidents!" she adds quickly, as Aunt Jane gives a sage nod. "You have to understand—my family is quirky, and, yes, some of them are a bit hard up, but they're not *killers*. It's been driving my father mad, and when he heard about you, he suggested we invite you to my great-aunt Edith's birthday celebration tomorrow night. Dad thought you might be able to reassure my grandfather. That you could tell him, perhaps . . ." Diana trails off, and I know she's worried that Josiah will be just as rude to Aunt Jane as he is to everyone else. "That we're not the murdering sort?"

"Ah, my dear," Aunt Jane smiles kindly, "the problem with that, you see, is that no one is ever the murdering sort until they are. The least likely people can shock you. Young mothers, elderly clergy, esteemed businessmen. You can't rule out anyone, I'm afraid." She picks up her knitting with a sideways glance toward me. "Even charming guitar players."

It's a little annoying, sometimes, how Aunt Jane never misses a thing.

When Josiah Westover throws a party—even a small one for his sister's birthday—he goes all out. The space that Diana calls "the great room"—something of a giant sitting room with sliding glass doors that open to a deck overlooking the ocean—is filled with flowers and candles. The doors are open, framing the deep blue of the evening sky and allowing a salt-scented breeze to pass through. A musician seated at a grand piano in the corner plays soft classical music, while white-coated servers pass trays of canapes and drinks.

All this, for ten people.

I fidget in my borrowed dress at the doorway, wishing I hadn't listened to Diana when she told me to head downstairs while she finished her hair. Most of her family intimidates me, except for—

"Drink, Nic?"

As if I'd summoned him, Harry Westover appears by my side, holding two champagne flutes. He's wearing the dark suit his grandfather insisted upon, but no tie, his white shirt unbuttoned at the top and more than a little wrinkled. "Go on," he adds with a dimpled grin when I hesitate. "No one cares that you're underage."

I accept the glass with murmured thanks. I don't particularly like champagne, but I do like Harry. Probably too much. When I first got to Westover House, Diana warned me that Harry is incapable of talking to any woman under fifty without flirting. *Don't take him seriously,* she said. So I try not to, but it's difficult with those bright blue eyes fixed on mine.

Diana was right; Harry's guitar playing isn't great. But he's been practicing "Fire and Rain" nonstop for the past two weeks, and you can almost recognise it now.

"I see you've gone full Diana tonight," Harry says.

I almost choke on my tentative sip of champagne. "Pardon?"

"*Pardon?*" Harry repeats, still grinning. "Everything sounds better with your accent." Then he gestures to my nearly straight hair, which Diana tamed into submission with lots of conditioner and a blowdryer. "What happened to the curls?"

"I'm trying something new," I say.

"You don't need to," Harry says, sounding unusually sincere.

That ties my tongue, but fortunately Diana enters the room then, grabbing a flute of champagne from a passing server. "We'll need this tonight," she says, clinking her glass against Harry's. "What do you suppose Grandfather is up to?"

"God knows," Harry says, then drops his voice into a raspy imitation of Josiah's peevish tone. "*I want to talk to each of you, alone.*" He gazes around the room at the rest of the guests—Diana's father, Michael, who's perfectly content to stand alone; Harry's father, Alan, deep in conversation with Josiah's assistant, Stephen Macfarlane; and Alan's second wife,

Lucretia, gesturing dramatically as she talks with Great-aunt Edith. Those last two make an odd pair; the glamorous Lucretia is what Harry uncharitably calls a failed actress, while Edith is no-nonsense and still wearing her gardening clothes. "Sounds different from the usual *you're all a deep disappointment* conversation."

Diana raises her eyebrows. "Even you? But you've fallen so beautifully into line. Heading to Harvard and majoring in economics like all the Westover men."

Harry scowls. "For now. I'll never last there, but Dad says we can't rock the boat. Not after his latest can't-fail business did, in fact, fail." Then he drains half his glass before turning to me. "What happened to that aunt of yours, Nic? Thought she was coming tonight?"

"She wanted to," I say. "But she gets so tired."

"Good idea avoiding Grandfather, then," Diana says, smoothing an invisible wrinkle from her dress. "He's exhausting."

"Speak of the devil," Harry says, as his grandfather enters the room.

Everyone quiets in Josiah Westover's commanding presence. He's small and wizened, his face a mass of wrinkles and his white hair nearly gone, but he has the energy and vitality of a man half his age. He's leaning on a gilt-topped black cane, head cocked to one side like a predatory bird as he surveys the room.

"Where's Sarah?" he demands.

"On her way," Alan Westover replies instantly. Sarah is his daughter, granted, but it doesn't matter what question Josiah asks; Harry's father is always the first to answer.

"With her mysterious fiancé, or without?" Harry murmurs. He's insisted to Diana and me that he overheard his older sister whispering about an engagement over the phone, but if she was referring to her own, no one else in the family has mentioned it.

Josiah's assistant, Stephen Macfarlane, steps forward. He's about thirty, and might be handsome if he ever dropped the eager expression. "Miss Sarah called before she left Boston and mentioned traffic might be difficult this time of day," he says. "Even so, she should arrive within half an hour."

"Well, I can't wait any longer," Josiah says, tapping his cane on the floor. He stares around the room until his eyes land on Lucretia. "You first."

Harry's stepmother puts a delicate hand to her throat. "First for *what*?" she asks.

"You'll see," Josiah says.

Out of the corner of my eye, I catch Diana's father heading our way. "Excuse me, I need the loo," I say, placing my champagne glass on an empty tray. I don't, really, but I can at least check how my hair is holding up—and maybe allow a few curls to spring back—while the Westovers discuss how to manage their patriarch.

I usually use the bathroom near my bedroom, but that's an entire floor and wing away, so I make my way down the hall and keep my eyes peeled for anything that resembles a powder room. I haven't spent much time in this part of the house, which is very much Josiah Westover's territory, and before I know it I've made a distinctly wrong turn. I'm in what looks like a small sitting room, and I can hear the sound of voices far too close. My heart starts beating uncomfortably fast; I don't want Diana's grandfather to accuse me of snooping. So I do what any normal, rational person would do and . . . dive for what looks like a cupboard door, shutting it quickly behind me.

Except it wasn't a cupboard door, after all.

I'm in an imposing room dominated by a mahogany desk positioned in front of the window. At least, I assume there's a window behind those richly patterned silk drapes. A leather sofa is on one side of the room, and two matching armchairs on the other. Three of the walls have floor-to-ceiling shelves, filled

with leather-bound books and the kind of model air-
planes Diana's grandfather likes to make. The plush
rug in the centre of the room features the Westover
family crest.

Oh no. I'm in Josiah Westover's *study*, aren't I?

The door opens, and before I can even think about
what I'm doing, I've ducked behind one of the armchairs. Then I peer around its corner to watch Stephen
Macfarlane stride across the room, reach out a hand to
part the drapes, and step behind them.

What on earth?

Maybe the drapes cover a door, not a window?
There's no sign of Stephen any more, and I'm about
to rise and flee when the sound of footsteps keeps
me in place. They grow nearer, and I watch in horror
from my hiding spot as Josiah and Lucretia enter the
room.

"Take a seat," he says, and if she chooses this armchair, I'm utterly doomed. How will I ever explain
myself? But she lowers herself on to the leather sofa,
and Josiah sits beside her.

"What's this about?" Lucretia asks.

"Just a little family business," Josiah says.

"I'm all ears." Lucretia's tone is neutral, but her
jaw is clenched. I wish, desperately, that I'd stayed put

with Diana and Harry instead of wandering in here, but it's too late now.

"Good," Josiah says, taking a prescription bottle from his pocket and settling it on the table in front of them, beside a glass of water. "You'll excuse me if I make sure my heart pills are handy. I've had palpitations lately, and you can't be too careful at my age."

"Naturally," Lucretia says.

"Here's the thing, Lucretia," Josiah says. "You've been a fine wife to Alan. I have nothing against you personally, but the fact is, Alan is never going to launch himself into the world when he knows he has my money to fall back on. So, tonight, I'm changing my will and leaving everything to charity. You and Alan get nothing, I'm afraid, except the model airplane of your choice." He sweeps a hand around the room. "You can pick one now, if you wish."

"I have no need for a model airplane," Lucretia says tightly.

"Wouldn't you like something to remember me by, though?" Josiah asks.

Lucinda's nostrils flare. "Have you told Alan about this?"

"No. I thought I'd tell you first."

"Why would you do that?"

"Because . . ." Josiah breaks off, inhaling sharply. "Excuse me. Had a bit of pain just then. What was I saying? Oh, Alan. The thing about Alan is—"

He stops again, clutching his chest. "Are you all right?" Lucretia asks, though she doesn't sound particularly concerned.

"Fine," Josiah says, but the word comes out like a gasp. "I'm fine." Then he slumps against the cushions, his face a mask of pain. "I think . . . I think I need my pills. Could you—"

"Of course," Lucretia says. My eyes zone in on Josiah's face, and despite the way it's twisted in agony, I don't think I'm wrong in thinking that he's watching her carefully.

He's testing her, I think. It seems supremely obvious to me; so obvious that I'm not surprised when Lucretia calmly extracts a pill from the bottle and hands it over, along with the glass of water. "Here you go," she says.

"Thank you," Josiah wheezes, gulping it down.

After Josiah "recovers," he rings a bell and the butler opens the door. "Roberts will take you to the east wing, where you'll be seated for dinner," Josiah says. "It will be served once I've had the opportunity to speak with the rest of the family."

"So I'll be separated from the others?" Lucretia

asks. "How interesting." She sounds frustrated, but leaves without further comment.

Once the door shuts behind her and Roberts, Josiah raps his cane on the floor and calls out, "Well? What did you think?"

My heart drops. *He knows I'm here.* But before I can nervously clear my throat and try to explain myself, Stephan Macfarlane steps out from behind the drapes.

"That needs a *lot* of work, Mr. Westover," he says.

One thing you can definitely say about Josiah Westover is that he's a quick study.

He spends nearly fifteen minutes with Harry, skilfully needling him about Harvard and his musical dreams, before he starts to exhibit much more subtle heart-attack symptoms. When he finally collapses, it's so convincing that I have to dig my nails into my palm to keep from crying out. I can't help but be relieved when Harry springs into action, even going so far as to put the pill—which, I've now learned from the back and forth between Josiah and Stephen Macfarlane, is made from sugar—into Josiah's mouth.

Harry's father Alan is a different story, though. When Josiah goes into what's now a very convincing portrayal of a heart attack, Alan does nothing except watch him gasp in pain. Eventually, Josiah slumps against the cushions, perfectly still. Minutes tick by with agonising slowness, until Alan tentatively says, "Father?" Then Josiah sits up so suddenly that Alan recoils and I nearly gasp out loud.

"False alarm," Josiah says, eyes narrowed at his son.

Alan's thin face turns tomato-red. "Oh, thank goodness!" he cries. "I . . . I was frozen with shock, and—"

"And you can go now," Josiah snaps, ringing for Roberts. "I have everything I need from you."

After Alan skulks away, Josiah confers briefly with Stephen, in such low tones that I can't hear them. Then Stephen heads back behind the curtains, and it's Diana's turn. "Well, here she is," Josiah says, when Diana takes a seat on the leather couch. "Our little English rose. Abandoning her family the first chance she gets."

Diana sighs. "You know I had no choice. My mother insisted."

"Nonsense. You're perfectly capable of getting your own way when it suits you," Josiah says. "And now that you're back, are you happy to see us? Hardly. All you do is complain about *frogs*. Ungrateful girl."

He's being so awful that I'm almost relieved when he falls into the now-familiar rhythm of his performance. Diana reacts just as quickly as Harry did, giving the cap of Josiah's medicine bottle such an energetic twist that she nearly stumbles, and I feel a burst of pride for my friend. Sarah, Harry's older sister, who has now arrived from Boston, takes longer to react, but ultimately helps out too.

Then Aunt Edith enters the room. I don't think she cares about Josiah's money any more than Diana does, and I can't help wondering what she'll do.

What Aunt Edith does, as it turns out, is burst into incredulous laughter once Josiah goes into his act. "Stop it, you ridiculous old crank," she snorts, as Josiah writhes in supposed pain. "Is that what you've been doing all this time? Happy birthday to me, eh?" Aunt Edith brushes at the knees of her practical trousers before adding, "You ought to be ashamed of yourself. Your family are *people*, not puppets you can yank back and forth."

"Edith, truly," Josiah moans with convincing agony. "Something's wrong."

"What's *wrong* is that you've let your fortune warp you," Edith says.

"Please," Josiah wheezes. "Call a doctor."

It's those words—*Call a doctor*—that make me act. "He's not pretending this time," I cry out, springing to my feet and wincing at the ache in my legs from squatting for so long in one place. "Something's wrong."

"Good lord!" Aunt Edith stares at me, open-mouthed. "Have you been there the entire time?" Then Stephen Macfarlane steps out from behind the curtains, and her jaw drops further. "Have *you*? What on earth are you two doing?"

Stephen ignores us both to bend over Josiah. "Mr. Westover?" he says, pressing his fingers against Josiah's neck. "Are you all right? Do you need your pills?" Aunt Edith grabs the bottle on the table and thrusts it toward him, but Stephen doesn't take it. Sweat beads on his forehead as he says, "Not those."

"What's happening?" Aunt Edith demands. "What kind of sick game is this?"

I swallow hard, unable to tear my eyes from Josiah's rigid, deathly pale face. "I don't think it's a game any more," I say.

"So what do you think? Who did it?"

I gaze between Aunt Jane and Detective Laura Wilcox from the Chatham Police Department, seated side by side in deck chairs behind Aunt Jane's cottage. After Detective Wilcox questioned me about Josiah Westover's death the week before, I told her that all she needed to do to solve the case was speak with my aunt. She brushed me off and drove me home—to Aunt Jane's, who insisted that I couldn't stay at Westover House with a murderer on the loose. Although part of me hated leaving Diana, the rest of me was relieved.

Then, right after Aunt Jane and I finished lunch this afternoon, Detective Wilcox stopped by. She told us, her tone deferential, that when she mentioned Aunt Jane to her chief, he recognised the name from a police convention in New York where my aunt's old friend, Inspector Dermot Craddock, had been a featured speaker. "I'm to provide you with whatever information you ask for, Miss Marple," Detective Wilcox said. Then she'd been treated to nearly fifteen minutes of St. Mary Mead gossip until I couldn't keep quiet for another second.

"Really, Nicola, I couldn't say," Aunt Jane says mildly, her knitting needles clacking.

If Detective Wilcox thinks I've oversold my aunt's crime-solving abilities after that lacklustre response, she doesn't show it. "It's tricky with these wealthy families," she says, taking a biscuit from the plate Cherry left for us. "They close ranks."

"But it was definitely poison that killed him?" Aunt Jane asks.

"Oh yes," Detective Wilcox says. "The autopsy

report was clear on that. Josiah had white baneberry in his system, which is highly toxic. It might not have killed a healthier man, but the plant's ability to sedate cardiac muscles is deadly for someone with a heart condition."

Aunt Jane tuts. "And you think this poison was administered through the pills that Josiah Westover had prepared for this little farce?"

"We believe so. It's possible more than one of the pills he took while speaking to his family were poisoned, but those remaining in the bottle were pure sugar."

"Dear me," Aunt Jane says. "Josiah was playing a dangerous game, wasn't he? And for what? To test his family?"

"That's what Stephen Macfarlane says," Detective Wilcox says. "Josiah had become paranoid after a few too many suspicious accidents. He wanted to know who would come to his aid when they thought he was having a heart attack, and who would let him die." She shakes her head. "Which is foolish, because the way people behave in a moment of crisis doesn't always reflect their intentions or character. But, apparently, he put an idea into someone's head."

"And yet, surely no one was meant to know about

this plan except for Stephen Macfarlane?" Aunt Jane says.

"Yes, but Macfarlane admits that he and Josiah worked through the logistics in Josiah's study, which has a window overlooking a large flower garden," Detective Wilcox says. "The window was open to take advantage of the good weather, so it's possible they were overheard. Other than Sarah, the entire family has been at the house for the past two weeks."

"Can anyone other than Stephen Macfarlane corroborate the open window?" Aunt Jane asks.

Detective Wilcox tilts her head. "I'm not sure. Why do you ask?"

"Well," Aunt Jane says gently, "it seems the sort of thing one might say to divert suspicion off oneself. I'm not saying that Stephen Macfarlane is guilty," she adds quickly. "But he is, of course, the only person that you know for certain was aware that Josiah Westover intended to ingest multiple sugar pills over the course of the afternoon. Being in that position is nerve-wracking for even an innocent person."

Detective Wilcox nods. "Very true. Macfarlane, though, is the only person in the house who doesn't benefit from Josiah's death. He received a generous salary, but there's no provision for him in Josiah's will. He was well aware of that."

"Was Josiah really going to change his will?" I ask. "Or was that a lie?"

"He'd already had his lawyer draw up a new version," Detective Wilcox says. "Left everything to charity. But here's the kicker—he hadn't yet signed it. His old will remains legally binding, and his family will inherit his assets."

"Who benefits most?" Aunt Jane asks.

"His sons, Michael and Alan. They split half the estate, and the other half will be divided between Edith, Sarah, Harry, and Diana."

"So, really, *Alan* benefits the most," I say. "He's practically destitute."

Aunt Jane frowns at a dropped stitch. "And yet, he seems the least likely culprit, doesn't he?" she asks. "One would imagine that, had he placed the poisoned pill in Josiah's bottle, he would have taken pains to appear as helpful and loving as possible during what he knew to be a false attack." She sets her knitting aside with a sigh and adds, "Although, if he were exceptionally devious, he might consider such inaction excellent cover."

"I don't think Alan Westover is that smart, Aunt Jane," I say.

"Well, I've never met him," Aunt Jane says placidly. "But perhaps, if he were the killer, he would *want* to give Josiah a pill. Since the more he took, the more likely he'd swallow a poisoned one." She turns toward Detective Wilcox. "How many pills were in the bottle?"

"According to Stephen Macfarlane, Josiah said that he prepared seven," Detective Wilcox replies. "One for each member of the family."

"Michael never made it into the study to speak with Josiah," Aunt Jane says. "And neither Alan nor Edith gave Josiah a pill. But Lucretia, Harry, Diana, and Sarah did. How many were left in the bottle after Josiah collapsed?"

"Well, it's interesting you should ask that, Miss Marple," Detective Wilcox says, shifting in her seat. "Four were left. Not three, which is what you'd expect when you're starting with seven pills. Stephen insists that Josiah was definite about the number, but perhaps he counted incorrectly."

"Perhaps," Aunt Jane says. Her voice turns musing. "Four left, all made of sugar. Potentially, Josiah could have missed the poisoned pill entirely. How odd that is. One would imagine that our murderer would not leave it to chance that the poison pill be the one ingested, and replace them all. Where was the bottle kept before Josiah brought it into the study?"

"Stephen Macfarlane says that the pills were on Josiah's person the entire time." Detective Wilcox shifts in her seat. "But, once again, we have only his word for that."

"He'd be your top suspect if he had a motive, wouldn't he?" I ask.

"It wouldn't look good," Detective Wilcox says wryly. "It's lucky for him, I suppose, that Josiah's death makes him poor and unemployed."

"Does it, though?" Aunt Jane murmurs, picking up her knitting once again. "I wonder about that. Yes, I wonder very much."

Later that evening, I'm helping Cherry clean up after dinner with Aunt Jane when the phone rings. "Could you get that, love?" she asks me.

"Of course," I say, plucking the receiver from its wall mount. "Hello?"

"Nic, you won't believe what happened!" Diana's voice is breathless. "You know my cousin Sarah's supposed secret fiancé?"

"Yes."

"Well, he's real. And you'll never guess who he is." She doesn't give me a chance to answer before adding, "Stephen Macfarlane!"

The telephone nearly slips from my hand. "Really? Are you sure?"

"Oh, yes," Diana says. "Somebody sent an anonymous note to the police, and Sarah broke down when she saw it. It's a proper scandal, let me tell you. Uncle Alan had no idea. Stephen and Sarah are both at the police station right now. I wouldn't be surprised if he's arrested before the night is over."

"Wow." It's an inadequate response, but I can't think of what else to say. I should be relieved, but there's something not quite right about this news. I can't put my finger on it, though. "That's unbelievable."

"You think so?" Diana asks. "I don't. Especially after how you said he acted in the study. He didn't even try to help Grandfather, did he? You had to step in."

"True," I say.

"It's always the outsider," Diana says. As if I'm not one too.

My aunt enters the kitchen as I hang up, an aspirin bottle in hand. "Nicola, could you open this for me, please? I have a bit of a headache, and my rheumatism makes it difficult to manage these childproof caps."

"Of course," I say, twisting it open. "Here you go. Aunt Jane, you won't believe what Diana just told me. It turns out that Stephen Macfarlane was secretly engaged to Sarah Westover, and now everyone thinks he's the one who killed Josiah."

"Ah." Aunt Jane looks troubled as she accepts a glass of water from Cherry and downs her aspirin. "I did wonder if Stephen might be the secret fiancé. It's not uncommon for ambitious young men and heiresses to find one another irresistible."

"You *knew*?" I gape at her. "Why didn't you say anything?"

"I didn't know," she corrects. "It was simply a guess. And I didn't say anything because I don't believe for a moment that Stephen Macfarlane killed Josiah Westover. If he wanted his employer dead, he could have devised a dozen easier ways of doing it—and none of those would have made him look suspicious."

"I suppose so." I put the cap back on the bottle, frowning as I think about Stephen slipping behind those drapes. Something is bothering me, tugging at the corners of my brain but refusing to show itself fully.

"I think we should arrange another conversation with Detective Wilcox tomorrow," Aunt Jane says. "In the meantime, Nicola, please keep your distance from Westover House. You were in the room with Josiah when he died, and saw things that nobody expected you to see. That's a dangerous position. So often, it's the tiniest observation coming to light that trips up a killer who thinks they're safe."

I take her hands in mine with a rush of affection. "You worry too much, Aunt Jane," I say. "I'll be fine. I promise, I'll stay right here."

A few hours later, though, I've gone back on my word.

Diana called again right before Aunt Jane went to bed, utterly distraught. "The police haven't charged Stephen. They just let him *leave*," she said tearfully. "He's gone to some hotel, apparently, but what if he doesn't stay there? What if he comes after us?"

"He'd be mad to do that," I said, Aunt Jane's words echoing through my mind. *If he wanted his boss dead, he could have devised a dozen easier ways of doing it.* "Please try not to worry, Di. The police must have let him go for a reason."

"Because they're incompetent!" she wailed, and then her voice dropped lower. "I'm scared, Nic. So horribly scared."

I did my best to reassure her. After we hung up, I tried to distract myself with a book, but I couldn't concentrate. Eventually, I gave up and decided to walk back to the Westover's. I'd surprise Diana, cheer her up, and maybe we could have a late-night snack like we used to when she stayed over at my house in Banbury.

Now, as I approach the driveway, lights are blazing from every window in Westover House, making it look deceptively cosy. My steps slow as I get closer, and I find myself reluctant to ring the doorbell. When it comes to murder, there's no one on earth smarter than my Aunt Jane. If she thinks it's unwise for me to return to the scene of the crime, then maybe I shouldn't.

What had she said? *So often, it's the tiniest observation coming to light that trips up a killer who thinks they're safe.*

I stop in my tracks then, as the memory that had been teasing me at Aunt Jane's cottage hits me with full force. Maybe it's nothing. But it could mean . . .

I bypass the front door and head towards the back of the house. There's something Diana calls a *bulkhead* leading into the basement that, she told me, is supposed to be locked but rarely is. Sure enough, it pulls open with a loud creak. I step into a dim, musty space that leaves me completely disoriented; I've never been in this part of the house before, and I'm not sure how to get to where I need to go—Josiah Davenport's bedroom.

Am I out of my mind, though? It's most likely locked, and even if it's not, what I'm looking for is probably with the police.

The police. *Right.* I feel around in my pocket for the card Detective Wilcox gave me right before she left. "Call any time if you remember something else you'd like to tell me," she said, writing her home number at the bottom.

I doubt there's a phone in the basement, but I know there's one in the upstairs hall. I inch my way through the darkened room, with only faint moonlight from a single window keeping me from bumping into walls and old pieces of furniture until I finally reach a staircase.

There's a sliver of light coming from beneath the door at the top, so I make my way up and grasp hold of the doorknob. Hinges squeak lightly as I push the door open and step into a hallway. I don't recognise where I am, but it's much less elegant and imposing than the rest of the house. More storage space, perhaps, or a place where the many employees who keep the house running spend their breaks? I don't know for sure, but it doesn't really matter. The most important thing, right now, is the phone on the wall.

I lift it and dial Detective Wilcox's home number. A woman picks up after the second ring. "Hello?"

"Detective Wilcox? It's Nicola West."

"Nicola, hi. Is everything all right?"

"Yes. I think so. But I have a question." I grip the phone tighter, ears straining against the quiet surrounding me. Did I hear a creak of some sort?

"What's that?" she asks.

"Josiah Westover's pill bottle. Did it have a child-proof cap, or the older kind—the ones that pop up?"

"It's the pop-up kind. Why?"

I close my eyes briefly and lean my head against the wall. Of course it is. I'd watched three Westovers open the bottle that way, without fully registering what they were doing. I probably wouldn't even have remembered if I hadn't opened Aunt Jane's aspirin bottle with a twist—the kind of motion you wouldn't need for Josiah's bottle.

But I'd seen one person make it.

"Nicola? Why are you asking?" Detective Wilcox asks.

I can't bring myself to answer her. "Are you absolutely sure there were four pills left in the bottle?" I ask. "Not three?"

"Yes, but—"

The creaking sound repeats, then morphs into footsteps. Someone's coming down the hall, and I need to get off the phone before they catch me talking to

Officer Wilcox. "Okay, Aunt Jane, I'll be right there," I say hastily before hanging up.

Diana comes around the corner, a mug in one hand. "Nicola!" she says, eyes widening in surprise. "I thought I heard your voice. What are you doing here?"

"Oh, I just—I was worried about you, so I wanted to check in." I attempt a smile, even though Diana is the last person I want to see right now.

Diana. Who twisted the bottle top. She made a great show of doing it, and yet—I don't remember seeing the cap come off. But Diana handed a pill to Josiah anyway.

"And you decided not to ring the doorbell?" Diana asks.

"It's late, I didn't want to wake anyone." My fake smile stretches to its breaking point. "But my aunt asked me to call when I got here, and she's so worried that I think I'd better go back. Sorry I disturbed you for no reason."

"Oh, it's no trouble. It was sweet of you to think of me. You don't have to walk, though. We can have a car take you. Here." She places the mug in my hands. "Have some of my tea while I arrange everything. You look cold."

"Okay, thank you." I clutch the mug, waiting for her to leave so I can take off.

She doesn't, though. "Go on, Nicola, take a sip."

I gaze down at the shimmering brown liquid. *What's in there?* "I'd better not," I say, backing up a few steps. "It keeps me up too late."

"You're such a little bit of a thing, Nic," Diana says, in her usual affectionate tone. "I think, you know, that if it comes to that—I could *make* you."

She reaches for me and I don't have time to think—I drop the mug with a loud clatter and run for the stairs behind me. Diana's on me in an instant, though, knocking me heavily to the ground. "I saw you," she hisses in my ear as I struggle. "Coming up the walk, and then sneaking around the back. I heard every word you said. You should have left well enough alone, Nicola." She has me on my back now, straddling me, one hand clamped over my mouth as I flail uselessly at her. "It's a shame you ruined my tea, but I have backup. One has to be prepared for anything."

I keep thrashing about, fighting to free myself so I can scream. Diana's twisting too, reaching for something, and then her hand lifts from my mouth. Before I can take a breath, she's pinching my cheeks to keep my mouth open, and attempting to shove something white past my lips. "Rat poison," she hisses. "Fitting, since you turned out to be such a rat of a friend." I manage to clamp my mouth closed and turn my head away, but Diana grabs hold of my nose, making it impossible to breathe. I'm going to run out of breath soon, and when I do . . .

"Stop!" calls a commanding voice. And then Diana's weight comes off me as she's yanked roughly to her feet by a man I've never seen before. "That's enough, Miss Westover," he says, pulling her backwards as I struggle into a sitting position. "More than enough."

I can barely catch my breath, but manage to ask, "Who are you?"

"Officer Peter Graves with the Chatham Police," he says. "Once your aunt heard that Stephen Macfarlane had been released, she made arrangements for me to be on site tonight. She thought Josiah's killer might turn desperate." He tightens his hold on Diana. "And I guess she did."

"But what was her motive?" I ask Detective Wilcox. We're back on Aunt Jane's deck, two days after the night Diana tried to poison me. "Did she need the money after all? Has her father gone bankrupt?"

"Why are you asking me?" Detective Wilcox asks with a smile. "Surely your aunt has figured it out by now."

"If she has, she hasn't told me," I say, unable to keep the annoyance out of my voice. "She keeps saying I need *rest*."

"Well, you do," Aunt Jane says calmly. "And of course, I don't know for sure, but I rather suspect that Diana and her grandfather clashed over a passion of hers. Perhaps . . ." She gazes at the hydrangea bush Diana gave her, which Cherry planted discreetly among several others in the yard. "Perhaps it had something to do with frogs."

"Frogs?" I echo. "I don't understand."

Aunt Jane inclines her head. "They don't sing any more, you see. Which is the sort of thing that happens when land is overdeveloped and species are displaced."

"Goodness, Miss Marple, you don't miss a trick, do you?" Detective Wilcox says admiringly. "That's exactly it. Diana was furious that Josiah planned to develop an enormous parcel of what she thought should be conservation land. She was eavesdropping at the window below his office, trying to understand the timing, when she heard about Josiah's plans with the sugar pills. She decided to make up her own pill, but couldn't figure out how to get it into the bottle—Stephen Macfarlane was right that it never left Josiah's possession—so she simply carried it with her. Pretended to open the bottle and handed over her pill instead. It was hastily done, and she was taking a risk that Josiah might have noticed. But, clearly, he didn't."

"What about the car, and the vase?" I ask. "Was that Diana too?"

"She says no," Detective Wilcox says. "But we certainly wonder."

"Why didn't Diana just slip poison into Josiah's tea, like she tried to do with me?" I ask.

Detective Wilcox's expression darkens. "We haven't gotten her to admit this yet, but I suspect she's the one who sent the anonymous note about Stephen Macfarlane and Sarah's engagement. She saw Josiah's plan as the perfect opportunity to frame Stephen, and she took it."

"How did she learn so much about white baneberry and . . . rat poison?" I ask with a shudder. *Fitting, since you turned out to be such a rat of a friend.* It's ridiculous, considering what Diana did, that her words have the power to sting. What hurts, I suppose, is that I never actually knew the girl I thought was my friend. Di-and-Nic wasn't real, and maybe I should've taken a clue from the fact that Diana's name came first. *Diana* always came first.

Today my hair is back to its usual curls, and I'm wearing my own clothes. But I can't shake the memory of how eager I was to be exactly like Diana.

"She's very knowledgeable when it comes to plants," Detective Wilcox says. "Especially ones that grow locally. She knew white baneberry would likely kill her grandfather, but not a healthy young person. As for the rat poison, that was initially intended for Harry."

"For *Harry*?" I ask, aghast.

"Oh dear," Aunt Jane murmurs. "A second victim."

"Exactly so, Miss Marple. Diana was frustrated that we hadn't arrested Stephen Macfarlane, and hoped we'd believe he wanted to increase Sarah's share of Josiah's fortune with another death. But when she saw Nicola heading for the house and overheard her conversation with me, plans changed."

My stomach rolls. "What will happen to her?"

"That's to be determined. She's still a minor. And her father has engaged the best lawyer possible for her," Detective Wilcox says. "But her actions have been quite cold-blooded. The Chatham Police would like her off the streets for a very long time."

"Good," Aunt Jane says crisply. "It's a shame, of course. She's a charming young woman in many respects, and almost as clever as she thinks. I could see she was reluctant to share her father's invitation to me, but I put that down to embarrassment. She played that part well. I thought we had some views in common, particularly when she spoke so glowingly of simpler times." She sighs. "I hadn't fully connected the dots, but thank goodness I listened to my instincts. It's a pleasure, Detective Wilcox, to work with someone who respects intuition."

"I'm grateful for your involvement," Detective Wilcox says. "When Nicola hung up so abruptly that night, I feared she was in immediate danger. If we'd waited until then to send someone, it might have been too late."

"So, essentially, Aunt Jane, you saved my life," I say. My spirits rise a little as I add, "Maybe Granddad will finally admit that you're the criminal mastermind of the century."

"Goodness, Nicola, the nonsense you talk," Aunt Jane says reprovingly. "I'm sure Raymond would think no such thing."

"You're right," I say. "But that's only because he's never understood you. Now, me, on the other hand—I want to learn your ways." I press my hands together in an act of mock supplication that's only half-joking. "Teach me, Aunt Jane, how to spot the murdering sort."

"Murderers are few and far between, thankfully. It's much more important to spot trouble of the *every-day* sort." She gives a prim little cough and adds, "In that vein, perhaps this would be a good time to tell us about the note you received from the Westover boy this morning?"

I drop my hands into my lap as Detective Wilcox blinks. "Note?" she asks.

"Aunt Jane, really, how could you know that?" I ask, flushing.

"It was a *most* high-quality envelope you opened, and you blushed quite a bit as you read it," Aunt Jane says serenely. "Just as you are doing now. I assumed the handsome young cousin had been in touch and, perhaps, extended an invitation of some kind?"

"You're not supposed to use your detecting skills on *me!*" I protest. Then honesty compels me to add, "All right, yes. It was Harry, apologising for what happened and asking if he could visit the cottage some day this week." I'd been desperate to say yes, and now that I know Harry was meant to be another one of Diana's victims, I'm even more so. But I don't trust my own judgement any more, after Diana fooled me so completely. "Should I tell him no?"

"A visit?" Aunt Jane asks. "I was concerned he might

want to whisk you off to some sort of *club,* but that sounds perfectly proper. I should be glad to meet him."

"Really?" I ask, smiling for what feels like the first time in days.

"Really," Aunt Jane confirms. "But do ask him to leave the guitar at home."

The Mystery
of the Acid Soil

Kate Mosse

One

There is nothing quite like being settled comfortably in a railway carriage in good time, one's luggage stowed, ten minutes before the train is due to depart.

Jane Marple was sitting in a first-class compartment of the Southern Railway service, or whatever it was called these days, the bustle of the concourse and the ticket office quite behind her. There had been no shortage of porters at Victoria Station, her suitcase was on the rack above her head, and the guard had let down the window to let in a little air. Her faded leather handbag and travelling gloves were on the seat beside her and there was a trail of grey wool in her lap, the beginnings of a pullover for a great-nephew.

It was a gentle afternoon in late August, that shimmering time of day when the air is heavy with heat. She had spent an enjoyable two days in London with her nephew, Raymond, and his wife Joan, a painter who was making quite a name for herself. Raymond had taken her to see the new comedy at the Vaudeville Theatre, they had dined at Simpson's and taken their boys to London Zoo to see the lions. She had stayed in a sister establishment to Bertram's Hotel, which, despite everything that London had put up with during the Blitz, seemed little altered: the same kind of people, the same steady pace, colonels and black-corseted widows and the memory of an older England, now swept away. Were it not for the shadows of bombed-out buildings, or notices in shop windows apologising for shortages, it might have been as if the past eight years had never happened.

Miss Marple had enjoyed herself, but she was rather tired. London was loud and noisy, so very many people rushing about. The air seemed all used up. A peaceful holiday in Sussex with her dear friend Emmeline Strickert would be most welcome. Her visit to Drovers had been originally planned for the autumn, but Emmeline had been operated on for a contracture in her right palm and so had invited her to come earlier to help her in what might be an uncomfortable convalescence. There were so few people who belonged to the old days, who knew the girl she had been. So, Miss Marple had had no hesitation in putting her maid on board wages, sending her plate and King Charles tankard to the bank for safe-keeping, and making arrangements to spend the last three weeks of August in the country. Her only concern was that her jasmine hedge might run riot while she was away.

The whistle blew.

Two

As they were pulling away, the door was flung open and a young man all but threw himself into the carriage. He sank into a seat opposite, his face red with exertion, the hem of his cassock rimmed with the dust of London streets.

"My apologies," said the curate, catching his breath. "I was anxious to not miss the train."

"I assumed as much," she replied, her faded blue eyes twinkling.

Miss Marple returned to her knitting; her travelling companion wiped his face with a handkerchief as the train jerked its way out of the terminus and stared out of the window. The sound of metal on the tracks, the hiss and steam of the engine. Over the Thames and past the grimy backs of the tenement buildings of Victoria and Battersea, into the leafy suburbs of Clapham and Streatham. Although he did not say anything, Miss Marple could not fail to be aware that the young man was in the grip of some strong emotion. He picked at a loose thread on his cassock until she thought the button would fall off, and bounced the toe of his shoe anxiously on the floor.

The suburbs gave way to countryside. Green fields and a heat haze over the river valleys. Lulled by the rhythm of the tracks, she found her hands growing heavy in her lap. In the distance, the South Downs came into view.

"But if only I knew for sure," he muttered.

Her eyes snapped open. "I beg your pardon?"

The curate flushed. "I'm sorry, I didn't realise—"

"It is so easy, if fancies oneself unobserved, to speak one's thoughts out loud."

"I suppose it is." He made an effort to pull himself together. "Are you travelling far?"

Miss Marple smiled. "To Fishbourne, beyond Chichester."

His face lit up. "That is my parish. It's my first post and where I . . ." He stopped.

She wondered what he had been about to say.

"I had an uncle who was a canon at Chichester Cathedral," she said. "My sister and I used to stay with him before the War—before the Great War, that is. It is a beautiful part of the world."

"It is, at least . . ." He broke off again, the frown back on his face.

Miss Marple waited, but he had once more retreated into his own thoughts.

"I am to stay with a friend from my school days," she offered. "We were together at a *pensionnat* in Florence when we were girls, so very many years ago now. We had so many ideals. I was going to nurse lepers and Emmeline was going to . . ." She shook her head. "Do you know, I can't remember."

The young man looked as if he was about to speak, but then he put his hands over his face.

"Forgive me," she said quietly, "but is something the matter, Mr. . . . ?"

"Kemp," he replied, looking at her with despairing eyes. "Ernest Kemp."

"I am Jane Marple. It is none of my business, of course," she said, "and perhaps I have misunderstood—I so often do—but you said you wished you could be sure. I wonder what you meant?"

For a moment, she feared she had presumed too much, but then she saw him straighten up. She resumed knitting and listened.

"There is a girl," he said. "I'm awfully fond of her and I thought she was of me, but . . ." He took a deep breath. "She has vanished."

Her eyes sharpened. "Vanished?"

"Her father—that's to say, her stepfather—says she simply upped and left. Gone to London to join a theatre company."

"Oh dear," Miss Marple murmured.

"I know what you're thinking," he said quickly, "but she's not that kind of girl. And when I went to the theatre near Waterloo today, they had never heard of her."

Many thoughts were going through Miss Marple's head, none of them, she thought, would be welcome.

"It's utterly out of character," he continued. "Elizabeth is unhappy at home, although she never complains. Her mother died two weeks ago, at the beginning of August—and she was devoted to her mother—but to leave without saying a word. Not even a letter."

Miss Marple was sadly aware of how often girls acted out of character. Or, rather, how young men could be rather innocent about those they admired.

"How long has it been since you saw her?" she asked kindly.

"Two days. Her mother's funeral was on Monday, and so we arranged to go for a walk yesterday. I thought she might need a shoulder to cry on. When she didn't arrive, I was worried, so I called on her at home. That's when her stepfather told me she had left that morning."

Two days did not seem a very long time and, although she felt sorry for the young man, she thought it was possible that Elizabeth simply did not want to see him, but lacked the courage to tell him to his face.

"No doubt there has been some misunderstanding. You say she has recently lost her mother. Is there anywhere she might have gone? To relatives, perhaps?"

"There is no one else. She's alone in the world."

"Except for her stepfather," Miss Marple said carefully.

"Him! Cooper doesn't care about anyone except himself!" he said fiercely, then was instantly embarrassed at his lack of Christian charity. "I apologise, I spoke out of turn. If only I could be sure she is all right."

She took pity on him. "If you are genuinely worried about your young lady, then why not speak to her neighbours. She might have said something to them. They have a daily, perhaps?"

Kemp shook his head. "Mrs. Hands was let go away after Mrs. Cooper died. It's rotten if he expects Elizabeth to wait on him."

The train began to slow. He looked out of the window, then made another effort to compose himself.

"We're coming in to Chichester, which is where I get off. Fishbourne is just a minute or two further on."

"Do you not live in Fishbourne, Mr. Kemp?"

"I do—I'm currently lodging at the rectory until I can find somewhere more permanent—but it's a shorter walk from Chichester than from Fishbourne station. Let me help you with your luggage."

Kemp pulled the suitcase down from the rack, bracing his feet against the rocking movement of the carriage. "You may need assistance when you get off, as it is quite heavy."

Miss Marple flushed. "It is rather. My friend is fond of both my damson gin and my cherry brandy. Of course it is so hard to get anything these days. Because I couldn't decide, I brought them both. I shall be there for three weeks, you see."

Kemp smiled as he set her suitcase on the floor beside the door. He pressed in the window latch and pulled down the glass as the brakes began to bind.

"You have been very kind, Miss Marple. Perhaps I am over-reacting. I might have misheard the name of the theatre, or . . . Well, as you say, there's bound to be an explanation. I do hope you enjoy your stay and I'll hope to see you on Sunday, perhaps."

"Yes, indeed," she smiled. "And I do hope your friend is in touch."

Kemp nodded, then stepped down on to the platform, closed the door and raised his hat. Miss Marple
watched the lovestruck curate grow smaller and smaller
as he walked away. But, as she packed away her knitting, she was frowning. One or two things the young
man had said had given her pause for thought.

There was no time to reflect further. Within minutes,
they were pulling into Fishbourne Halt, a tiny branch
station surrounded by fields and trees filled with nesting rooks. Miss Marple looked for the stationmaster, but
he was occupied with the railway crossing gates and the
signal. Before she could attract his attention, a big, florid
man in a rather loud checked suit was reaching into the
carriage and taking the case from her hands.

"Let's see if we can sort you out."

"Oh, do take care," she said, as he dropped it heavily on to the platform, fearing for her bottles and the jar
of night cream Joan had given her as a gift.

"There we go!"

Miss Marple was not, she hoped, an ungenerous
person. But although she was grateful, she did not like
to be addressed in so casual a manner.

"Thank you," she said, with studied politeness.

"Always happy to help a lady in distress," he said,
putting his finger to his temple by way of salute, then
climbed into the carriage.

"Jane! Jane!"

Miss Marple turned in the direction of the voice with relief and there was her old friend, looking exactly as she always did, standing at the end of the platform and ordering the stationmaster to hurry along with his trolley.

Three

Drovers was a pretty flint-faced cottage with trailing roses around the door, a white gate and a path lined with lavender. It stood in a generous plot of land on a quiet road that led down towards the Marshes, used only by farm vehicles and the occasional delivery van.

By six o'clock, the two ladies were happily settled in wicker chairs in Emmeline's back garden, surrounded by rhododendrons, azaleas, clematis crispa and other acid-loving plants. The afternoon sun filtered through the waxy, dark-green leaves, setting bands of light on the lawn. Jane Marple had changed from her travelling clothes and into her reliable summer dress. Emmy, meanwhile, was wearing a voluminous cotton frock of her own and an untidy wide-brimmed straw hat that looked as if it had seen better days. The cherry brandy had been put on a slate shelf in Emmeline's pantry; the damson gin was with them on a cane table on the lawn.

The two old friends each sipped at their respective tiny crystal glasses.

"It's my grandmother's recipe," Miss Marple said. "It is so pleasant, don't you think, to be taken back in time?"

"I do," said Emmeline, with a nostalgic smile.

"Of all our senses, it is smell and taste that seems to most capture—is that what I mean?—the past."

Her friend laughed.

Two spots of pink appeared on Miss Marple's cheeks. "Am I running on, Emmy? It's so easy to become rambling, isn't it, and one wanders from the point."

"Not at all. I was only thinking how you don't change a bit, Jane. Listening to you, we could be back in our *pensionnat* in Florence. Do you remember Fraulein Schweich?"

"I do. Those boots!"

"Do you ever hear from Ruth or Carrie Louise?"

The American sisters had seemed much more glamorous than the other girls at their finishing school, and Emmeline, who was forever being told to sit up straight and pull up her stockings, had been in awe of them.

"I haven't seen Carrie Louise for, oh, it must be twenty years. She took me to the opera at Covent Garden. I can't remember what we saw, only the red and gold of the magnificent curtains," Miss Marple replied. "But Ruth and I correspond from time to time. She's on her second, possibly even third marriage by now, all very successful."

The chair creaked as Emmy sat back. "I'll never forget Ruth saying how extraordinary it was that, despite your innocent appearance, you always believed the worst. And weren't you cross with her!"

"I don't think we spoke for a week," Miss Marple replied. "But, you see, the worst is so often true."

Emmy took another sip. "On which point, I'm not sure we should tell anyone that you have arrived to stay with two whole bottles of macerated spirits. It will give the village quite the wrong impression."

"I have never been an advocate of teetotalism," said Miss Marple, primly. "A little strong drink is always advisable on the premises in case there is a shock or an accident."

"Have we had a shock or an accident?"

"No," she twinkled, "but travel is wearying, is it not?"

From inside the house, the sound of the maid preparing the evening meal floated out into the still August air. They talked for a while of the problem of retaining servants and the continuing frustrations of rationing. Beyond the garden, Miss Marple could hear the sound of a tractor in the fields and the cry of gulls out at sea. It was all very soothing after the clamour of the city.

"I met a rather charming young man on the train," she said. "I believe he is your new curate, Ernest Kemp?"

"Oh, yes," said Emmeline, leaning over and pulling a tiny weed from the otherwise immaculate soil beneath the rhododendrons. "He's awfully young and rather athletic—he was in the Royal Sussex Regiment and fought at Arnhem—so he is already a firm favourite with the ladies who manage the flower rota!"

"That does not surprise me," Miss Marple said with a wry smile. "He told me a rather curious story."

After she'd finished recounting Mr. Kemp's tale, she looked fondly at her friend. Emmeline still had a wonderful mane of blonde hair, with perhaps only a little recourse to science, and her slightly bewildered expression was barely altered by the passage of the years. Emmy had always worn her heart on her sleeve, and did so now.

"Emmy?"

"Well, it is rather odd, now I come to think about it. Elizabeth going away like that without a word to anyone."

"Really?" She put her glass down on the table. "You interest me very much."

"Well, I'm not sure what to say. Or if I have anything to say. Only, that it *is* odd."

Miss Marple picked up her needles and started to knit. "Go on."

Emmy rubbed her nose, leaving a smudge of earth on her cheek. "It is rather as our curate said. She isn't that sort of a girl. She's awfully bookish, serious-minded. It's true she has a lovely voice—she sings in the church choir—but not at all the sort who'd to want to be an actress, I'd have thought."

"Where would she have met an acting company?"

Emmy waved her hand. "There was a repertory company, playing the south-coast tour earlier in the summer. You know, Gosport, Portsmouth, Bognor Regis, Worthing. She must have gone to one of their shows."

"Is she pretty?"

Emmeline looked doubtful. "Well, I'm not sure I would say that. Handsome, in an old-fashioned sense. She was very much devoted to her mother, even though Mrs. Cooper was rather a trying woman. Her only interests in life were her garden and her own ill health. Nothing was ever quite right." Emmy frowned. "Yes, it is peculiar Elizabeth should have gone off like that."

The sun suddenly went behind a wisp of cloud and

the garden, beneath its dark-green perimeter of waxy leaves, felt suddenly much colder.

"Mr. Kemp also said that the Coopers had let their daily go. Are they perhaps in straitened circumstances? So many are these days."

Emmy shook her head. "Far from it. Cooper is one of those men who was, as people put it, "rather useful" during the war and did well out of it. Very jolly, hail-fellow-well-met, you know the kind. Over familiar. He always seemed to be able to acquire things that were in short supply."

Miss Marple found it easy to imagine Fishbourne during the war. Coupons changing hands, meat and fish, black-market petrol, with Cooper at the heart of things. They had had a similar character in her own village of St. Mary Mead, but then that was hardly surprising. Human nature was much the same everywhere.

"You said his wife was in poor health. Do I take it her death was expected?"

"Not at all. Dr. Barden was of the opinion there was nothing actually wrong with her at all. No, she contracted tetanus."

"How terrible."

"Yes. You know how people put used razor blades

around the roots of plants like rhododendrons and the like to acidify the soil?"

"It's a very foolish habit."

"Poor Mrs. Cooper cut her finger on a rusting blade in her garden and died within days. Such a tragedy."

Miss Marple coughed gently. "The doctor was a local man, I assume? Was he satisfied?"

Emmeline nodded. "He was. I know, because there was talk and someone—I can't remember who— challenged him one evening in the public house. Accused him of not knowing what he was doing. Dr. Barden was *adamant* it was tetanus."

"I would like to know who challenged him," Miss Marple said lightly.

Emmeline glanced at her friend. "I will try to re- member, though I don't know why you should be in- terested."

Miss Marple was wondering. "And what do you think of Dr. Barden, Emmy?"

"He wasn't my doctor, I'm glad to say. He was set in his ways, terribly out of step with modern ideas. Very much opposed to the National Health Service."

She leant forward in her chair. "Was?"

Emmeline frowned. "He died just a few days after Mrs. Cooper."

"Good heavens, of what?"

Emmeline flushed. "I don't like to speak ill of the dead."

"It might be important, Emmy. I would not be asking if I didn't think it mattered."

Her friend sighed. "He had a weak heart and . . . He was found dead in his chair by Mrs. Hands—the same daily who did for the Coopers—with an empty bottle of whisky at his elbow. It was common knowledge he was much too fond of drink. What with that, and his heart . . ." Not wishing to be cast in the role of gossip, she started to get to her feet. "Shall we go in? It wouldn't do to catch a chill, Jane, when you've only just arrived."

Miss Marple didn't move. "Where does Mr. Cooper live?"

Reluctantly, Emmy sat down again. "In Salthill Road, very close to the railway station. In point of fact, he was on the platform yesterday when I was waiting for you."

"Ah, *that* was Mr. Cooper," she muttered, remembering the loud suit.

"What are you up to, Jane? Do you think there's something wrong?"

"Well," she replied carefully, "when three unusual events happen in close succession, one has to wonder. And the daily being let go, that is very suggestive."

"Of what?" asked Emmy, confusion on her placid face.

Miss Marple did not answer. "When a man is widowed, it is sometimes the case that his life goes on reasonably untroubled by grief. How did Mr. Cooper respond to the twin shocks of bereavement and now his stepdaughter's desertion?"

Emmeline considered. "I would say that the even tenor of his routine does not appear to have suffered so such much as a wrinkle."

Four

The next morning, Miss Marple rose at her usual time, having slept surprisingly well in an unfamiliar bed. She found Emmeline in the dining room, looking regretfully at a jar of shop-bought marmalade.

"Let me do that."

With deft practise, she twisted the reluctant lid, which popped open with a snap. "You should be resting your hand."

Her friend pulled a face. "I don't want to be a trouble."

Miss Marple smiled. "Don't be silly, Emmy. It's why I'm here."

The two ladies sat down to breakfast in companionable silence. The only sounds were the rattle of cutlery against china and tea being poured from the pot. French windows gave on to the back garden and a light breeze was blowing in from the Marshes. Jane Marple read the obituaries in *The Times* and Emmeline opened her post.

"We are invited to tea with the rector this afternoon," she said, brandishing a letter. "We don't have to go, of course."

Miss Marple thought of the young curate. "How very kind. I would be delighted."

Emmeline raised her eyebrows. "All right, I'll send a note. What would you like to do this morning?"

"Perhaps a walk before the sun becomes too hot? I'd like to get to know Fishbourne better."

"I've been very happy here at Drovers. Were it not for the road . . ." Emmeline began a long story about how the steady increase in through-traffic was changing the nature of the village for the worse. "But then things never seem to change for the better."

"Oh, I don't believe that's true," countered Miss Marple. "Think of the extraordinary advances in healthcare, many of them, so I am told, the result of research carried out during the two World Wars. There is always good in bad, as there must always be bad in good."

Looking unconvinced, Emmeline buttered a third piece of toast.

Jane chose an ash walking stick, Emmy stuck to her old faithful, and by nine-thirty they were setting out to explore the village.

The two ladies strolled gently along the main road, past the old bakery, the village school and the water treatment works. It was true that the traffic was depressing, the constant rumble setting up clouds of dust. Miss Marple thought of St. Mary Mead and how lucky it was that the lane outside her door wasn't a through road to anywhere.

They reached the old laundry and she saw they were at the junction with Salthill Road.

"Might we go this way for a while?"

"There's not much to see," Emmeline said, looking surprised. "Just the railway station."

Miss Marple was already walking north. They passed a lime pit and a row of modest new houses with long front gardens.

"Didn't you say that Mr. Cooper lived somewhere on Salthill Road?" she asked casually.

Emmeline peered at her from under the wide brim of her straw hat. "What are you up to, Jane?"

"Simply getting my bearings."

"Hmm. Well, in point of fact, that is Mr. Cooper's house opposite. Dr. Barden lived a few doors further down."

Miss Marple stared at the low brick wall topped with clay tiles, then crossed the road to take a closer look. The window frames needed attention, all the curtains were closed and there was moss in the gutters and growing thickly among the thatch. The garden was pretty, but it was unkempt. She fished her spectacles from her handbag and peered over the wall. "That's Lily of the Valley," she said, "quite lovely. And there is Phacelia, usually planted for its ability to improve the soil, but with beautiful mauve blooms if you let it. And those ornamental clovers beside the front door are a picture." She moved to the other side of the gate. "Ah," she said quietly, "I did wonder."

Emmeline looked rather fogged. "Wonder at what?"

"There's wild marjoram, very popular with butterflies, and Jacob's ladder with lovely blue flowers. And then the lawn, quite unusual and ragged, called, I believe, blue moor grass. They all go together."

"You *are* clever, Jane. The only plants I can recognise are the lavender along the path and honeysuckle."

"And what does that tell you?"

Emmeline shook her head. "I'm sure I don't know. That Mrs. Cooper had green fingers."

"Yes, indeed, but—"

Before she could explain, the front door opened and Cooper himself was striding down the front path towards them.

"Perhaps we should move on," Emmeline whispered. "We wouldn't want it to be thought we were snooping."

Miss Marple smiled. "There is nothing more commonplace than two elderly ladies admiring a neighbour's garden. It would be much odder if we did not."

Cooper was wearing a very white shirt with a red tie, and the same loud checked trousers she remembered from the day before. His eyes were slightly bloodshot. He did not, in her opinion, look like a grieving widower.

"Good morning, ladies. Miss Strickert, is it? Is there something I can do for you?"

His words were genial enough, but, instinctively, Miss Marple did not think he was a man to be trusted. He reminded her of a man she had met at a Hydro some years before the war. All bonhomie and nothing-too-much-trouble, but thoroughly wicked beneath the genial surface.

"My friend and I were admiring your garden," Emmeline said, in a fluster.

Jane Marple watched as Cooper rearranged his expression. "My wife was the gardener," he said, dropping his voice to a suitably sombre note. "Without her, I'm afraid it is running to seed."

"Please accept my condolences," Miss Marple said. "It must be so difficult. And, of course, for a daughter to lose her mother so unexpectedly."

Cooper's shrewd eyes narrowed. "It is," he said shortly. "Now, if there is nothing else, I'm sure you ladies have plenty you need to be doing."

Five

"Well!" Emmeline said, as soon as they were out of earshot. "What a disagreeable man."

Miss Marple was troubled. "Yes, indeed."

Her friend looked at her. "I'm not sure I like the way you say that, Jane."

She looked back at the Cooper house, then to the surgery three doors along, where a brass plaque glinted in the August sunshine: Dr. J Barden MD.

"I wonder, dear Emmy, if you are not too tired, might we find time to call upon Mrs. Hands before we return home? There are one or two questions I would very much like to put to her."

Mrs. Hands, who had previously done for both the Cooper household and for Dr. Barden, lived in a brick-built house beside The Bull's Head Public House, one of a narrow row designed to serve only the most basic needs of agricultural workers—a roof over their heads and a single cold-water tap at a large kitchen sink.

Miss Marple had to bow her head when they were invited in, but the inside of the premises was spotlessly clean and furnished with an eccentric, though well-tended, collection of unmatched bits and pieces.

"It must have been a terrible shock," she said, "finding Dr. Barden, as you did."

Mrs. Hands put her hand to her heart. "Oh, it was. And then, to receive a letter from the lawyer saying the doctor had left me fifty pounds and any pieces of furniture I might choose to have. Well, I came over all somehow."

She gestured round the room at a medical specimen cabinet, in which she kept her china ornaments, and a swivel desk-chair.

"And we are sitting on the chairs from the waiting room, I imagine?" said Miss Marple.

"That's correct. I prefer a straight."

"So do I," said Miss Marple, glancing at Emmeline, who looked like she didn't.

"Now then," said Mrs. Hands. "What did you want to know?"

"We were just passing," Emmeline said weakly.

"I mind there's more than that."

Miss Marple's blue eyes sparkled. "It seems you are a step ahead of us, Mrs. Hands. To be candid, we would like to know more about the circumstances of Dr. Barden's death."

The charwoman folded her arms. "It's about time someone took an interest, though I expected the police, not a couple of old maids."

"Mrs. Hands!" Emmeline protested weekly.

"I say it like it is. Now, I won't deny he had let himself go, because he had. His heart was ever so weak. And I won't say as he wasn't too fond of the bottle, because everyone knows he was. But he always knew when to stop."

"Do go on," said Miss Marple.

"Well, Dr. Barden and Cooper—I won't call him mister—they were friends, after a fashion."

"After the fashion of drinkers?" asked Miss Marple.

"Jane!" cried Emmeline, "how did you know?"

"A doctor's practice depends on his reputation, does

it not? Particularly before the advent of the National Health Service that Dr. Barden appears to have so resented."

"He hated it," exclaimed Mrs. Hands. "He said it 'broke the bond of trust that comes from the exchange of honest payment for services rendered.' I couldn't agree with that. What about them as couldn't afford the 'bond of trust'?"

"Quite so," said Miss Marple. "Now, may I make an appeal to your candour, Mrs. Hands? It will perhaps reassure you to know that I am lucky enough to count among my closest friends Sir Henry Clithering, formerly the Commissioner of Scotland Yard." Mrs. Hands looked suitably impressed. "Wouldn't you like to tell me what you know—or what you think you know?"

Mrs. Hands hesitated, then leant forward. "Well," she began, lowering her voice, "there were two glasses on the table."

Six

Three quarters of an hour later, Miss Marple and Emmeline were standing outside The Bull's Head on the main road. The early morning clouds had burnt off and the sun was now quite fierce in an intense blue sky. Miss Marple's face was sombre.

"Are we any further along, Jane?"

"Oh, I think so. After all, cases such as this are almost always the same. I know in books it is generally the most unlikely person, but I never find that rule applies in real life. Except . . ."

"Except?"

"It seems to me there is more to it." Miss Marple frowned. "It's the sequence of things all running together. There being two glasses, and Mrs. Hands being dismissed from Cooper's service."

Emmeline's eyes were bright. "And what do you think?"

"That Dr. Barden understood he had made a terrible mistake and regretted it, and Mr. Cooper realised."

"I can't begin to say I understand, but it really is most exciting."

Miss Marple's expression grew even more grave. "No, Emmy. Murder isn't a thing to be taken lightly."

"Murder!" Emmeline wailed. "Do you mean to say that Dr. Barden was murdered?"

"Oh, I think so."

Emmeline's eyes grew wide. "Shouldn't we tell someone?"

"Having a suspicion is not the same as proof." Miss Marple glanced at her wristwatch. "I wonder if the rector would forgive us for calling on him a little earlier than invited?"

Emmeline opened her mouth, then closed it again. "I will see if Williams might drive us—he's by way of being the informal village taxi service. It's quite a step from here to the rectory." She turned to knock on the door of a second cottage in the same row. "Oh, I've remembered! It was Williams who had the argument with Dr. Barden."

"So much the better," said Miss Marple, with a gleam in her sharp blue eyes.

Seven

Five minutes later they were heading east towards the rectory in Grove Park.

Pleading travel sickness, Miss Marple had contrived to sit up front with Williams, a lean country man who exuded a fragrance of bitter beer and pipe tobacco. It was the work of a moment to find out just why he and Barden had flung insults at one another in the saloon bar at the Bull's Head.

"He near as dammit—pardon me French—killed my little girl and I won't believe anyone who says the contrary. Impetigo, he said it was. Impetigo! I could see, and so could my wife, that it was the measles, and not the ordinary measles, it was the German measles, and nothing good's never come out of Germany that I can see."

"I trust your daughter recovered?"

"Yes, but no thanks to him. Turning up smelling of whisky and my little one almost gone because of it. Have you seen his garden?"

"I can't say I ever did," Emmeline said, startled.

"Weren't much of a garden, because every minute he spent in it was in his summer house." Williams snorted. "At least, he called it a summer house, though it was little better than a shed for tools he never found the inclination to use. You know what he used it for?"

"Somewhere to sit in private?" replied Miss Marple.

"Exactly. That's where he kept his supply, out of sight—but I knew." Williams put a leathery finger to his prominent nose and made a gruff noise in his throat, something between contempt and self-satisfaction. "Roof was leaking and he asked me to come round and replace a few shingles. Not much of a job but he paid me handsome. You know why?"

"Alcohol can loosen the tightest purse strings, I believe."

He graced Miss Marple with an admiring look.

"That's right. And I saw where he kept his tipple—in a tin chest brought back from the war, half buried in the dirt floor to keep it cool."

"And you confronted him about Mrs. Cooper in The Bull's Head?"

"Mrs. Cooper? Who told you that? No, I told him that he didn't know a rhododendron from a lilac, so he wasn't fooling anyone. I told him how the NHS spotted it was the rubella and fixed my girl up for free, so that if he was thinking of sending a bill, he could . . ."

"Quite," Miss Marple said hurriedly, seeing Emmeline's scandalised expression in the mirror. "So, who was it mentioned Mrs. Cooper?"

Williams put out his indicator and turned left into Grove Park. "You know, I believe it was him. And he had a funny look."

"Yes," murmured Miss Marple, "it is becoming clearer now."

"Is it?" said Emmeline.

"Might you wait?" Miss Marple asked, as Williams opened her door. "We might need your continuing services."

"Right you are, madam."

He helped Emmeline out of the back seat, then leaned against his bonnet and took out his pipe.

"I haven't the slightest idea of what is going on . . ."

hissed Emmeline as they hurried up the path to the rectory.

"In the course of his conversation with Williams," Miss Marple explained, "Dr. Barden realised he had taken too much on trust. Because Cooper and he had been friends, after a fashion."

"But what does any of that . . . ."

Miss Marple shook her head and pulled the bell.

Eight

The introductions dispensed with, Miss Marple and Emmeline Strickert were sitting in the rector's homely drawing room. If he was surprised the two ladies had arrived so very early, he had the good manners not to show it.

"Such a charming village," said Miss Marple, giving no indication of the troubling thoughts racing round her head. "But tragedy strikes even in the nicest of places. The death of Mr. Cooper's poor wife, for example."

"Indeed," murmured the rector, with an expression of professional sympathy.

"And then his stepdaughter leaving—like something out of a penny dreadful. I imagine you advised him?"

"Well . . ." said the rector doubtfully. He looked surprised that this pink-faced lady should eschew the usual old-maidish small-talk of knitwear and flower-arranging. "One does what one can."

"Mr. Cooper is an assiduous churchgoer?"

"No, I wouldn't say that. But Elizabeth is a most valued member of our choir."

"Does he perhaps attend the midweek evensong?"

"Things are not quite what they were, Miss Marple. Mr. Cooper has business interests that take him to Portsmouth in the afternoon, so—"

"Every day?" Miss Marple said quickly.

"I believe so."

"And what of Mrs. Cooper?"

The rector looked very uncomfortable. "She did occasionally attend Sunday services, but she was something of an invalid. Devoted to her garden."

"And she and Mr. Cooper made for a well-matched couple?"

The rector screwed up his eyes as the bright sunlight struck his glasses—or, perhaps, it was the incisiveness of Miss Marple's questioning. "I really couldn't say. *De mortuis nil nisi bonum.* I trust you will not oblige me to go further."

"Of course," Miss Marple said, but carried on regardless. "Might I ask if Elizabeth was a happy girl?"

The rector fidgeted on his chair. "I think things were

rather difficult at home. After the funeral, Elizabeth asked if she might speak to me, but then Mr. Cooper was in a hurry and he rushed her away. Grief affects people in different ways, Miss Marple, as I am sure you know." He sighed. "I regret that I did not insist."

Miss Marple had heard enough. And having lived all of her life in a small village, she had a certain knowledge of human nature. With impressive agility, she stood up, taking both the rector and Emmeline by surprise.

"I wonder if your curate is at home and might spare me a few minutes?"

Emmeline and the rector both watched, bewildered, as Miss Marple stood in the garden talking to Ernest Kemp. His expression altered from astonishment, to concentration, to urgency.

After a few minutes, she came back inside.

"Mr. Kemp has agreed to accompany us to Salthill Road," Miss Marple said, looking at her clock on the mantlepiece. She nodded to the rector. "Thank you for your hospitality, but I hope you will excuse us. We must hurry."

"Good heavens, Jane, why?"

"To prevent a third murder."

Emmeline opened her mouth but appeared to have nothing she thought adequate to say in reply.

Nine

Williams leapt to attention as the mismatched trio hurried down the path.

"To Drovers, Miss Strickert?" he asked.

It was Jane who answered. "To Salthill Road, if you please. Just past the lime pit. As fast as you can."

"Where are we going?" Emmeline asked, as they took the first corner at speed.

"To Cooper's house. The rector confirmed what Mrs. Hands said, namely that he goes every afternoon to Portsmouth. If we assume he takes the same train from which I disembarked yesterday, we can time our visit for when he is away from the house."

"But why—"

The car skidded to a halt.

"Force the door or break a window, if you have to, Mr. Kemp, but find Elizabeth," said Miss Marple.

Kemp ran up the path, his cassock flapping around his legs, with Williams following behind. The two ladies watched as Kemp knocked at the front door but received no answer. He bent down and called through the letter box, then stepped back and looked up at one of the curtained windows at the side of the house.

He called again and, this time, evidently had a response.

"She is here," Kemp shouted back to Miss Marple. "She's all right."

Jane Marple had not been aware she was holding her breath, but now she exhaled. "I am very glad to hear that."

Kemp disappeared from sight, appearing moments later with a ladder. With Williams steadying the base, the curate hitched up his cassock and began to climb.

"Jane!" Emmeline said, pulling at her sleeve.

"Don't worry, Emmy. Things are going to be all right."

"No," she said, panic in her voice. "Look."

Miss Marple turned. Cooper was storming down the road, his face red with fury.

"The Portsmouth train must have been cancelled," cried Emmeline. "Williams, do something."

But as Cooper pushed past them and thundered up the path, clearly intending to drag Ernest Kemp from the ladder, it was Miss Marple who thrust her ash walking stick between his legs and brought him crashing to the ground. Cooper roared and tried to throw a punch, but Kemp and Williams were on him in a moment. He was no match for the former soldier and the local man, and was quickly overcome. Williams removed his belt and tied Cooper's hands behind his back. Kemp went through his pockets until he found the latch key, and ran inside.

"Well, Emmy," said Miss Marple, "that was a close call, wasn't it?"

Ten

At the end of the long August day, the sun was sinking down to earth.

Miss Marple and Emmeline were back in the pleasant garden of Drovers, surrounded by acid-loving plants. Ernest Kemp and Elizabeth Cooper, none the worse for her ordeal, were sitting together on the bench. The rector sat in a wicker chair. The cherry brandy had been brought from the pantry and was on the table with three glasses. There was whisky and soda for the gentlemen.

"Now, Miss Marple, tell us everything," the rector said. "What made you suspect Mrs. Cooper's death was not what it seemed?"

Jane Marple put her head to one side. "There was never anything very clever. Complicated things only really happen in stories, not real life. This was a sadly commonplace story, driven by greed and the fact that Cooper clearly had had enough of his wife."

"So Dr. Barden was wrong?" Emmeline said. "She didn't die from tetanus?"

"No, she did have tetanus. It is only that the *reason* Cooper gave about how she had contracted it could not have been true."

Ernest Kemp leaned forward. "I'm afraid I don't follow, Miss Marple."

She smiled at the young curate. "I have a lovely jasmine hedge at home. I ask the maids to put tea leaves around the roots to acidify the soil. The idea of using razor blades is, I suppose, possible, and would achieve the same results, albeit with a degree of risk of injury when weeding and—"

"Yes, we know all that," said Emmeline.

"Cooper's garden was all alkali-loving plants. His cottage was next door to a lime pit, a source of alkali nutrients. Mrs. Cooper was a keen gardener and would never have mistaken acid soil for alkaline. She would have known it would never be possible to acidify the soil sufficiently to grow rhododendrons, and would never have put razor blades in their garden."

Emmeline sat back in her chair. "When you put it like that, it seems so obvious."

"So how did he do it?" Kemp asked.

"The rector, though of course discreet, intimated

that Mrs. Cooper was not an easy person to live with. Elizabeth says her mother cut her hand."

The girl nodded. "Quite badly."

"I assume Cooper found some way of infecting the wound when helping her to dress it. It is difficult to attend to an injury to one's own hand, is it not?"

Emmeline considered her own bandage and nodded.

"That is what made me worry," Elizabeth said. "My mother was concerned always about her health. He had grown impatient with her. They rowed a lot, so it seemed out of character that he should suddenly be so solicitous." She turned to the rector. "That is why I tried to speak privately to you after the funeral, but he must have realised I was suspicious and hurried me away." She took a deep breath. "When we got home, he forced me upstairs, closed all the curtains and locked me in my room."

"To think you were there," Kemp frowned, "and I didn't even know."

Elizabeth smiled at him. "But you went to London to try to find me."

Kemp turned red. "Well, I thought something was wrong. Why didn't you try to attract attention when he was out of the house?"

"I wanted to call out, but I was frightened. The

house is so far back from the main road, and my room is at the side, so no one can see it. I didn't know how long he was intending to keep me there. Or what he was going to do."

Miss Marple noticed Kemp reach out and take Elizabeth's hand, and she approved.

"I think Cooper would have waited until the fuss had died down and then I shudder to think. Wicked." She shook her head. "It is why he let Mrs. Hands go, of course, so there would be no witnesses."

"Why didn't you believe him when he said I had gone to London, Miss Marple? Everyone else did."

"Mr. Kemp didn't," she replied with an indulgent smile. "And it struck me as rather unlikely, as if he'd got the idea out of a book," she paused. "The writers of detective fiction have a great deal to answer for. Also, everyone said it was out of character."

"It sounds so obvious now you say," Emmeline said again.

"But why were you so sure Elizabeth was in the house?" Kemp asked.

Miss Marple inclined her head. "I wasn't. But Mr. Cooper was not a man to observe formalities. His attire, a matter of days after his wife's funeral, spoke to that. Such an inappropriate suit! That being the case, it seemed unlikely to me that he would observe the Victorian niceties of keeping all the curtains drawn after a funeral."

Emmeline waved her hat in front of her face. "Of course, that was odd too, especially in this heat."

"Then there was Dr. Barden," Miss Marple continued. "It was Williams who put me wise to that. When he confronted Dr. Barden in The Bull's Head, the doctor suddenly realised—as I did—that the explanation of how Mrs. Cooper had contracted tetanus could not have been right. And do you remember, Emmy, how Mrs. Hands said she found two glasses on the morning she discovered Dr. Barden?"

The rector looked appalled. "Are you saying that Cooper also murdered Dr. Barden?"

"A post-mortem will prove it one way or the other," Miss Marple answered solemnly, "but I fear so. I think Dr. Barden invited Cooper to his house to discuss things. It is so easy to make murder seem like an accident. It would have been a simple matter for Cooper to introduce something into his drink. He was gambling on the fact that everyone would assume Dr. Barden had, finally, drunk himself to death, so would not investigate properly."

Elizabeth shivered. "How awful."

"But, why?" Emmeline asked. "Why did Cooper do

it? If he had simply grown tired of his wife—forgive me, Elizabeth—divorce is not such a scandal as it used to be in our day."

The rector shook his head. "I fear that is true."

Miss Marple turned to Elizabeth. "Money, pure and simple," she said. "Am I right, my dear?"

"You *are* clever, Miss Marple," the girl replied. "He had been pressurising my mother to sign a new will in his favour for some months—he has some business interest in Portsmouth and he needed money to invest. I don't know what he said to bring her round, but, at the beginning of August, she gave in. My father left my mother quite well off, so it would have been a tidy sum."

Emmy finished her glass of cherry brandy. "Well, Jane, you've only been here for twenty-four hours and already you've discovered two murders that no one else even realised were murders. And in Fishbourne, of all places!"

"You have lived a sheltered life, Emmy. But there is wickedness everywhere."

Emmeline Strickert, who had driven an ambulance in France during the Great War, and tended to dying soldiers on the battlefield, wisely said nothing.

"And of course," Miss Marple added, "Mr. Cooper reminded me of a man called Sanders. I met him at Keston Spa Hydro, some years ago. He was a similar character, genial and ruddy, but with something un-comfortable underneath, if you see what I mean. The moment I set eyes on him, the Sanders man, I knew he intended to do away with his wife." For an instant, her blue eyes lost their sparkle. "On that occasion, I did not act quickly enough. I have always regretted it."

Emmeline shivered. The rector bowed his head. The curate squeezed Elizabeth's hand tighter, no longer minding if anyone saw. Beyond the garden, there was the sound of men coming home from the fields at dusk. A blackbird sang to her mate. The ordinary everyday world kept on turning.

"Well, we are very much in your debt, Miss Marple," Kemp said, raising his glass to her.

Miss Marple flushed with pleasure. "I am delighted to have been of service. Though, I do hope the remainder of my stay will be less eventful."

The Disappearance

Leigh Bardugo

Miss Marple gathered one of her many woolly scarves around her narrow shoulders and considered another cup of tea. Despite what should have been the pleasant warmth of a London summer, her nephew Raymond's fashionable flat was forever drafty, owing to the large windows that stretched from floor to ceiling. They offered little in the way of privacy, but Miss Marple had been told they were *essential* and very much sought after.

"Glorious light," Raymond's wife Joan had explained, as she bustled through on the way to her painting studio, but Miss Marple noted that she shivered.

"Glorious indeed," murmured Miss Marple, tucking her knitting into her lap. "But perhaps best enjoyed beside a fire."

From somewhere in the library, the phone began to ring, just as the doorbell buzzed merrily down the hall.

"Won't someone answer the phone?" Raymond shouted from the kitchen, where he was assembling a cold lunch.

"I've got to get the door!" Joan cried, already whirring away in a cloud of artistically arranged silks.

Someone was always coming or going at the flat—artists, writers, deliveries of champagne or flowers. Ordinarily Raymond and Joan would have decamped to the country or the south of France for the warmer months, but Joan was busily working on a gallery show and Raymond was determined to finish what he claimed was not a novel but "a collection of tone poems, quite revolutionary" in time for publication the following spring. It was all very lively, and Miss Marple was certainly grateful for the invitation to join them for the summer. Even so, she longed for the quiet of her cottage, the distant sound of Cherry humming in the kitchen, and the golden light that was perhaps not as emphatic as the determined sunbeams that pierced Raymond and Joan's fashionable windows, but that shone gently over her garden in the waning afternoon hours, so that each blossom glowed as if dipped in amber.

Raymond appeared in the doorway, breaking her

reverie. "Aunt Jane," he said, his tone accusatory. "It's for you."

"For me?" A faint alarm sounded in her head. Had something happened at the cottage? She'd been worried the pipes wouldn't make it through another winter, but perhaps they'd decided to give up early.

"It's Dolly Bantry," Raymond drawled, "and she sounds even more breathless than usual."

"What in the world could Dolly want?"

"I certainly don't know and I don't care to ask."

Miss Marple knew Dolly had been restless ever since she'd moved into the East Lodge, and it hadn't helped that her children and grandchildren had forgone their holiday visit this year. It was understandable, given how far away they lived, and Dolly had insisted she was relieved not to have to worry about meals and clean up for so many, but Jane suspected it had been a blow nonetheless.

Miss Marple bundled her knitting under her arm and joined Raymond in the library, where the telephone sat on a cluttered desk.

"Dolly?"

"Oh, Jane!" Dolly exclaimed. "You must come home at once. I need your marvellous brain."

"I'll be home at the end of August," Miss Marple

protested. "Raymond and his wife are taking me to a most intriguing play next week. Very controversial."

"Quite right," said Raymond, lighting a cigarette and leaning against the mantel. "The actors perform in nothing but red paint. Impossible to get tickets, even in summer."

Miss Marple suppressed a shudder. "What's wrong, Dolly?"

"I can't possibly explain it all."

"You must try."

Dolly took a deep breath. "You know the family who moved into Gossington Hall? The Barnsley-Davises? Their son has disappeared and you *must* come home and find him."

Miss Marple glanced at her nephew, who had crossed his arms and was looking at her with an air of bemused expectation.

"Disappeared?" she inquired.

"I knew it!" Raymond crowed. "I knew something horrid was taking place in that little village of yours."

"Yes, two days ago." Dolly's voice dropped. "Along with several pieces of jewellery from the Barnsley-Davises' guests, and my sapphire earrings."

"Your grandmother's earrings?"

"The very ones! Jane, you must come home and fix this immediately. He's to be married next week."

Raymond had sidled up to perch on the desk and eavesdrop. Now he laughed. "Doomed to matrimony next week? No wonder he's done a runner."

"I hardly see what I could do—" Miss Marple began.

"None of that, Jane. I'll expect you tomorrow."

"But what about the play?" sputtered Raymond.

"What about it?" his wife Joan asked, entering the library with a bottle of champagne in one hand and a jar full of dirty paint brushes in the other.

"Saturday at the latest," Dolly said. "Please, Jane. His fiancée is in a state and we can't afford another scandal at Gossington Hall."

Miss Marple considered. She knew Raymond and Joan would be disappointed, but she had to admit she wouldn't mind the chance to return home just a bit early.

"I'll see what I can do, Dolly," she said at last. "Now go fix yourself some tea with brandy in it . . . No, don't argue with me. Tea with brandy, and a good long rest. You'll feel much better."

She set down the receiver.

"You can't possibly go hieing back to that village just because something dreadful happened at Gossington," Raymond complained. "That happens practically every spring. What tragedy has befallen St. Mary Mead this time?"

"The son of the house has gone missing," Miss Marple said quietly.

Joan threw herself into an armchair. "Didn't the Barnsley-Davises move into Gossington?"

"You know them?" Raymond asked, with some surprise.

"We met Michael Barnsley-Davis last summer, didn't we? In cote de something or other?"

"Oh, yes, golden hair, white teeth, disgustingly charming."

Joan laughed. "Raymond's just peevish because he likes to be the centre of attention."

"I certainly do not. As a writer, it is essential I be free to observe and that is best done away from the spotlight."

"Michael truly was a delight, though," said Joan, "and completely smitten with his fiancée. You mean to say he's really gone missing?"

"This is hardly worthy of Aunt Jane's talents," said Raymond, searching for an ash tray, then settling for tapping his cigarette into a potted orchid on the mantel. "Charming youth hides dark secrets behind handsome face, vanishes rather than risk exposure. Mystery solved."

"Exposure for what?" cried Joan indignantly.

"Gambling debts, a secret wedding in some backwater, perhaps he was less smitten with his fiancée than we thought. She did seem dimmer than a dark theatre."

"Pure speculation. None of that sounds like the Michael we met. Surely he's just been called away somewhere suddenly."

Miss Marple cleared her throat. "There is the matter of some missing jewels."

"That might just be coincidence," Joan offered doubtfully.

Raymond cast her a wry glance. "There are no coincidences in St. Mary Mead."

"Dolly seemed genuinely upset," said Miss Marple slowly. "I don't think she'd make a fuss over nothing."

"You can't fool me, Aunt Jane," Joan said. "You've tired of our London clamour and you want to be back in your garden."

"I do find it harder to keep up these days," admitted Miss Marple. "And surely you'll want the guest room free for your dear friend, Juliette? The one married to the director?"

Joan blinked. "What does Juliette Henderson have to do with it?"

"She'll need somewhere to stay when she leaves her husband, of course."

Raymond nearly knocked the potted orchid from

the mantel. "When she does *what*? Why would she leave Ambrose?"

But Joan was staring at Miss Marple. "Aunt Jane, how could you possibly know? She hasn't said a word to anyone but me and I haven't told a soul."

"Well, my dear, if I'm not mistaken, you two made a little shopping trip to the jeweller—the same jeweller—this week and the last."

"So?" demanded Raymond. "Women like baubles. There's nothing sinister in that."

"Yes, but they didn't buy anything, did they? I imagine Juliette knows she will be in need of money soon and left her jewels to be appraised, then had to return to retrieve them."

"But . . ." Raymond sputtered. "They were here for dinner only last month. She's head over heels for him, I saw it myself!"

Miss Marple looked dubious. "No woman who has been married that long smiles at her husband so much. It isn't natural."

Joan barked a laugh. "And I thought Juliette did such a splendid job of covering it all up when she'd been crying only hours before."

"Poor Ambrose," said Raymond.

"I shouldn't worry too much about him," said Miss Marple. "I imagine he'll console himself with that actress, the one we saw in that most . . . interesting adaptation of Macbeth. He couldn't have cast her for her talent, so he must be very much in love with her indeed."

Raymond threw up his hands. "Send the witch back to her village. If she stays much longer, all of our secrets will be revealed."

Miss Marple smiled and returned to her knitting.

"Come straight to me," Dolly had insisted, when Miss Marple had called back to tell her she'd be arriving Saturday afternoon.

But Miss Marple was no longer of an age that accommodated such urgent demands. She wanted a chance to wash her face and perhaps eat a little something before she visited East Lodge.

At the first sight of her cottage and the heaps of purple clematis crowding the arbour, Miss Marple felt a sense of calm wash over her. Cherry waved at her from the doorway, her freshly platinumed hair swept up on her head and a tidy red apron tied around her waist.

"Did you take a cab, then? Terrible waste of money. I would have sent Jim to pick you up if I'd known you were coming," Cherry chided, hurrying down the walk to take Miss Marple's suitcase from her. "You got my letter, then? Or had you just had enough of . . . the city life?"

Miss Marple noted the pause. Cherry had never had much use for Raymond's snobbery or Joan's pretensions.

"I'm afraid I must have just missed your letter, Cherry."

Cherry waved away her concern and ushered Miss Marple into the cool entrance hall. "I'll catch you up on everything. I've got a nice little chop from last night's dinner I can heat up."

"I did tell Dolly I'd go to the lodge straightaway."

"Dolly Bantry can wait. Always so imperious, as if she was still the grand lady of the manor. I ran into her at the butcher's the other day and all she wanted to talk about was Michael Barnsley-Davis."

"Oh?" said Miss Marple, eager to hear what Cherry might offer by way of village gossip. If she was to put her mind to this problem, she needed information and she was at something of a disadvantage having been gone from St. Mary Mead for the better part of the summer. "What did you think of Michael?"

"Handsome as the devil, but only half as clever."

"I understand there's the matter of some missing jewels."

Cherry set down the little chop arranged with a small stack of carrots and new potatoes. "Now *that* I hadn't heard. Is that what you came back for? Missing jewels?"

"That isn't why you wrote?"

"Of course not! It's the poor girl, the student who went over the side of that bridge by the old mill. Police are saying she did herself in, just like they claimed with Rose Emmott, but . . ."

"But?"

"Well, there's been talk. She did quite a bit of work up at the Hall."

Miss Marple was not the least bit surprised. "Was she young? Pretty?"

"Young," said Cherry, considering. "But not pretty. You know the type. Couldn't be bothered with a scrap of powder or lipstick. Always mucking around the grounds in work boots and coveralls. Not the type to catch a man's eye. Here, I clipped the story out of the paper for you."

The article was brief: Miss Genevieve Andrews, nineteen years old, of Lyndhurst, Hampshire, a student of botany at nearby Moorlands College, was staying in St. Mary Mead for the summer to work on the grounds of a local estate. She had gone out for a walk on the evening of August 23rd and never returned to her rented lodgings. Her drowned body had been found the following day.

"So young," said Miss Marple, peering at the blurry photo of Genevieve Andrews. "She visited Gossington often?"

"Yes," said Cherry eagerly. "She was working on the grounds."

"And she took her own life. Was this before or after Michael left?"

Cherry leaned forward, nearly planting her elbow in the leftover carrots. "That was exactly my thought, Miss Marple. The Barnsley-Davis boy had something to do with that girl's death. He seduced her and she threatened to go to his fiancée or some such, he lost his temper, and pushed her right over."

"That's quite a lot of supposition. Did he seem the type?"

Now Cherry frowned. "I can't say that he did. He was always fussing over that fiancée of his, Lydia Adams. Truly devoted, not just for show. And Lydia may be the prettiest girl I've ever seen off the screen."

"It's a most dangerous bridge," Miss Marple observed, wondering why Dolly hadn't mentioned young Genevieve's death. She ate her lunch slowly, watching the clouds pass outside the window and listening to the clock tick.

"If you don't like it, I can fix you something else," Cherry offered.

"No, it's very good," Miss Marple assured her, but she was too distracted to do Cherry's fine cooking any justice.

"But what do you suppose happened?" Cherry demanded. "Did he push her most cruelly into the river? Did he drive her to take her own life and then run off in shame? Or is he just an innocent lad, himself the victim of foul play?"

"Cherry, you really must stop listening to those lurid radio dramas. Tell me, would you rather Michael was alive and well but a rogue? Or that he was blameless but met a bad end?"

Cherry paused, picking up Miss Marple's still half-full plate and setting it by the sink. "I suppose . . . Well, I suppose I'd want him to be innocent, even if that beautiful Miss Lydia had to lose him. Then she'd know he always loved her true." Cherry rested her hip against the counter and folded her arms. "But what do you think, Miss Marple?"

"I think Jim had better get the car out and drive me over to the Lodge."

———

"Jane!" Dolly exclaimed, throwing open the door to the East Lodge and hurrying down the path. "Where have you been?" She'd clearly been watching from the window, awaiting Miss Marple's arrival.

"I came as soon as I could, Dolly. I would have thought I'd find you working in the garden. Your borders are coming along so well."

"They are, aren't they?"

"Hollyhocks, delphinium, and are those asters?"

"I had to do something to fill all these empty hours this summer, with Bertram and Alice and the children off on their adventures. Now, let's go up to the house. I've secured us an invitation to tea."

"And how did you manage that, Dolly?"

"Rather shamelessly, I'm afraid. I may have mentioned that you were the person who solved the mystery of the body in Arthur's library."

"And did you perhaps suggest that two lonely old women had nothing better to do on a Sunday afternoon?"

"One does what one must."

"Too true, Dolly."

Dolly looped her arm through Miss Marple's as they headed up the slope. The day wasn't too hot, and despite the circumstances, Miss Marple couldn't help but rejoice in being away from London's smoke and bustle, strolling instead beneath a blue summer sky.

"Tell me about the family, Dolly, but don't do your usual job of it. I'll need details if I'm to see the situation clearly."

"Can't you just figure it all out yourself? You know I'm hopeless with this kind of thing."

"I know you can manage when you try."

Dolly heaved a great sigh. "Then try I shall. The mother is one of those hypochondriac women, always clucking over *dear Michael* and forever rambling on about her doctor's recommendations. I haven't seen much of the father. I think he made his money in spigots or widgets or something mechanical. I can't recall. Hard to say where the boy got his charm. Perhaps it skips a generation."

"And the fiancée?"

"Lydia? Poor thing. A darling girl. Beautiful and always game for a chat or a laugh."

"But not perhaps the brightest?"

"Now what makes you say that, Jane?"

"It was just the way you phrased that, Dolly. The way you described her sounded less like you than Arthur."

"Well," said Dolly, plucking the wilted head of a rose from a bush as they passed. "I suppose she is the kind of girl Arthur might have found distracting. But that doesn't mean her fiancé is a thief."

"Certainly not. And the other guests?"

"There's Vera Fowler. She's Lydia's best friend, down for the wedding. She's striking in her own way, and might be quite appealing if she didn't insist on drawling every word as if the mere act of speaking bored her. Then there's a professor and his nephew visiting, both archaeologists of some type. I can't remember if they dig up pots or people. I think they're hoping to get Mr. Barnsley-Davis to invest some of his widget money in their next excursion."

"Let's stop a moment, Dolly. I need to catch my breath."

Dolly paused beneath the leafy branches of a yew tree. "You're not unwell are you, Jane? London is no good for anyone's health, I always think."

"Just old, and I'm afraid we cannot blame London for *that* fact. What a view this is. I forget how lovely the village looks from here."

"If you squint and pretend you can't see the Development."

Miss Marple turned to gaze up at Gossington's impressive brick facade. "I see the new owners have made quite a few changes. It's almost as if . . ."

"I know. As if they've taken it back in time. When Marina Gregg bought the place, she made so many *improvements*. But I'm not sure they were entirely appreciated by the rest of the village."

"No, this feels much more like your Gossington now."

Dolly said nothing because of course it wasn't her Gossington any longer.

"I know you weren't sentimental about the place," Miss Marple added. "And the Lodge is so much more practical for heating and upkeep."

"Oh yes. Infinitely so."

"But perhaps not quite so convenient for larger gatherings?"

"No," mused Dolly, as they continued on. "I don't suppose it is. And people have so very many places to go these days."

"Why didn't you mention the poor girl who went over the side of the bridge?"

"Genevieve?" Dolly said, in surprise. "Very tragic, but I don't see what it has to do with anything."

"She and Michael Barnsley-Davis weren't close?"

"I never saw them together, but people were bound to talk with Michael disappearing so soon after her death. It's unspeakably cruel to put Lydia through it."

Dolly bent to yank a weed from one of the flowering pots. "Now Jane, do put your mind to the task at hand. Time is of the essence."

"So you keep saying. Is there anyone else in the party at the hall?"

"Only a rather weaselly American friend of Michael's. I believe they went to school together and he just turned up one afternoon. Very rich, very loud, only . . ."

"Go on."

Dolly rang the bell and lowered her voice. "I don't think he's quite so stupid and crass as he'd have everyone believe."

They gathered for afternoon tea in what had once been Dolly's shabby but comfortable drawing room. During Marina Gregg's tenure it had been transformed into a grand kind of salon peppered with modern art and bits of sculpture. But under the new owners' stewardship, it had reverted back to a traditional drawing room cast in dark wood, and matching sets of stately furniture, almost like a stage dressed for a play set in an English country house.

Tea itself was a generous if peculiar affair, served by a buck-toothed maid who set out dainty porcelain plates and cups. In place of scones or cake were biscuits made of shredded carrot, while the soft white bread that would usually be used for sandwiches and kept moist beneath a towel had instead been replaced by some kind of cracker composed of various nuts and seeds.

"My doctor," announced Mrs. Barnsley-Davis, clad in a lettuce-hued tunic and strings of coloured beads, "keeps me on a very strict diet of roots, seeds and assorted legumes. Dr. Martin Bickford, very sought after. Do you know him?"

"I can't say that I do," replied Miss Marple, discreetly hiding her uneaten carrot puck beneath her napkin. "But I am not well informed on medical developments."

"Are you well informed on quackery?" asked Reginald Marsh, slouched in his chair by the window. This was Dolly's weaselly American and the description did seem rather apt. He wore disreputable trousers and some kind of blue chambray shirt. The effect was both unsavoury and artistic—and exactly his aim, Miss Marple suspected.

But Marjorie Barnsley-Davis didn't seem at all offended; in fact, she looked at Reginald fondly. "Reggie has been such a comfort to me now that Michael has . . . well, with Michael not . . ." She took a handkerchief from her voluminous sleeve and wiped at her eyes. "With Michael *away* for a bit. But Reggie does love to provoke. Dr. Bickford says it's because he eats too many red foods. Bad for the spleen."

"Spleen?" demanded Mr. Barnsley-Davis, as he entered the room, rubbing his hands together, face red and moustache bristling. "Nothing wrong with his spleen. Just doesn't care for work at all."

"Don't be unpleasant, Lionel," chastised his wife.

"Yes, Lionel, don't be unpleasant," said Reginald Marsh. "That's my job."

"Your only job."

"Nonsense. I'm also pursuing a full regimen of lying about and being good for nothing."

Miss Marple was grateful for the opportunity to observe the house's occupants as tea was poured. Lydia Adams, Michael's fiancée, was just as beautiful as Dolly had said, her hair a warm honey-gold cloud that framed her cornflower-blue eyes, which would have been quite luminous had they not been red and swollen from crying. She sat with a plate on her knee, eating nothing, her gaze distant. Her friend Vera sprawled in a chair beside her, wearing a violently yellow frock, her head resting on her hand. Neither of them had said a word since they'd been introduced to Miss Marple.

Professor Helmut Roederer, Dolly's German archaeologist, rose awkwardly from the spot on the sofa he'd been occupying with his rather pallid nephew. "Lionel, I wonder if I might bend your ear—"

"Vile!" Lionel Barnsley-Davis roared, ignoring the professor and chewing vociferously on one of the seed crackers. "Can't one get a proper tea around this house?"

"Dr. Bickford—" began Mrs. Barnsley-Davis.

"Don't want to hear about that old fraud, Marjorie."

"Lionel—" Professor Roederer attempted again.

"Helmut!" Mr. Barnsley-Davis bellowed with such force that the professor toppled back on to the couch, as if blown over by a hard wind. The pallid nephew shrank into the cushions, blanching an even more milky hue. "My son's vanished into the godforsaken countryside and you have the bad taste to badger me for funds? I'm not giving you another dime until you prove you can find something more than heaps of dirt and some fragments of old custard cups!"

"I know the timing is not, perhaps, ideal," stammered the professor. "But the pottery we've found is vital to understanding Second Kingdom—"

"Vital? Where's the gold? The jewels?"

"Oh, Lionel," moaned Mrs. Barnsley-Davis, "*must* you be so vulgar?"

Reginald Marsh laughed and said, "Perhaps best not to mention jewels at this juncture."

A vein pulsed alarmingly on Lionel Barnsley-Davis's forehead. "You ungrateful little whelp. If you have the temerity to—"

At that moment, Lydia burst into tears and ran from the room, sobbing.

"Perhaps . . . perhaps we should go after her?" mumbled the pallid nephew, as her footsteps faded up the stairs. It was the first time he'd spoken.

"Won't do any good," said Marsh, real misery in his voice as he rose, and headed out the doors to the garden. "Nothing shall be right until the prodigal returns."

"Prodigal?" Miss Marple queried, as the Barnsley-Davises and their other guests made their exits, perhaps glad to put distance between themselves and the carrot biscuits. Only Vera Fowler remained, lounging in her chair, gazing disinterestedly at Dolly and Miss Marple, and the maid who had begun to clear the tea things.

"The Golden Boy," Vera drawled, lighting a cigarette in the silence that had followed the exodus. "Michael dearest."

"You didn't like him?" asked Miss Marple.

Vera raised a brow. "You don't stand on ceremony, do you?"

Miss Marple's cheeks pinked a little. "Oh, you must forgive me, dear. Old women have so little occupation.

We can't help but get wrapped up in the dramas and romances of the young."

Vera shrugged. "I couldn't find any fault with dear Michael, if that's what you mean. Rich, handsome, kind to orphans."

"Did he ever . . . well . . ."

"My, aren't you the old voyeur? No, he never made a pass at me, if that's what you're hinting at. More's the pity."

"Now, now," said Miss Marple gently. "You don't mean that. You aren't quite so callous as you pretend to be."

Vera took a long drag on her cigarette. "No. I suppose not. The truth is Michael seems to be a good egg and Lydia loves him dearly, and I don't understand what's happened at all."

"You think he's been hurt."

"I do. He didn't just run off with a wayward starlet or something. He's never put the make on me or any of our friends and he's certainly had the opportunity with every pretty girl from here to Devon."

A loud crash of dishes and silver sounded and Miss Marple turned to see the buck-toothed maid crouched on the floor, cleaning up broken porcelain and morsels of food with shaking hands. "Very sorry, miss. Very sorry, madam."

"Where do *you* think he went?" Dolly asked, leaning forward in her chair.

The girl stared out at the manicured grounds. "I've wondered about that. I think . . . for all his charm, I think Michael made someone angry or jealous and something awful happened."

Miss Marple studied Vera's profile, the dark slash of her brows. "When I asked if you liked him, you didn't really give me an answer."

"Didn't I? The truth is I had no reason *not* to like him."

"But you didn't."

"No. I don't know why. But I didn't trust him to be good to Lydia. And now . . ."

"And now you feel guilty because you think something terrible has befallen him."

"I do. I feel like the worst sort of person." She gave a brittle laugh. "Isn't that absurd? As if it changes anything."

"Dolly," said Miss Marple. "I think you and I should go speak to Lydia."

"She's who I really care about," said Vera, "and she wants him back desperately. Do you think there's hope?"

"Of course there is," Dolly replied. But Miss Marple said nothing.

———————

"Strange girl," whispered Dolly, as they left the drawing room.

"Perhaps," said Miss Marple. "But not a stupid one."

"Going hunting for poor Lydia?" inquired Reginald Marsh, slouching his way up from the garden through a side door. He'd found a tennis racket somewhere and was swinging it rather aggressively through the air. "No doubt you'll find her sobbing picturesquely in her boudoir. Not that dear Michael deserves such an outpouring of emotion."

"I thought you boys were friends at school?" Dolly asked.

"And we're still friends now."

"If that's the way you speak of your friends," said Dolly, "I'd rather not know how you hold forth on your enemies."

"Look," said Marsh, leaning against the wall and crossing his long legs in front of him, "Michael was good fun, always flush, always up for a lark, but not the man you'd want at your back when the wind got rough, understood?"

"I don't believe you were invited to the wedding," said Dolly coldly. "In fact, I don't think you were invited to the house at all. You just showed up on the doorstep."

"It's not your house any more, so what do you care?"

Dolly pressed her lips together.

Marsh swiped his tennis racket within inches of a nearby vase. "I happened to be visiting this area of the country and thought I'd call in. Maybe you Brits stand on ceremony, but Michael was perfectly happy to mooch off my family in the States, so I thought I'd return the favour."

"Michael Barnsley-Davis visited you in the United States?" Miss Marple asked.

"What about it? We have plenty of room."

"How fortunate to have a large family," Miss Marple twittered. "When one is alone in the world, it's a pleasure to hear of all these happy relations."

"Not so large as all that."

"But siblings certainly. A younger sister perhaps?"

Reginald Marsh pushed off from the wall. "Perhaps. Now where's Vera? I'm sure I can offend someone else before dusk falls."

"Such a rude, insufferable boy," Dolly said with a scowl, as they headed up the stairs. "Jane, what are you puzzling over with such fierce concentration?"

"Nothing really," said Miss Marple. "Only . . . did you see the way he was holding that racket, Dolly? His knuckles were positively white."

"I did wonder if he might take a swing at one of us. Wretched creature."

They found Lydia in her bedroom, curled into the window seat, surrounded by apricot cushions. She'd tucked her knees up and was resting her tear-stained face on her folded arms.

"Oh my dear," said Dolly, going to her. "You mustn't weep over him."

"I don't understand it," she said, fresh tears welling in her enormous blue eyes.

"How could you?" said Miss Marple, placing a clean handkerchief in her hands. "Such things aren't really understandable."

"He wouldn't just leave! He said he loved me. He told me he couldn't wait to be married to me."

"When did you last see him?" Miss Marple asked gently.

"The afternoon of the garden party. He stayed until the very last toast. He said I looked like a jonquil." She dabbed at her eyes and added, "I was wearing butter yellow."

"Ah," said Dolly.

"He had a train to catch to London."

"Did he take a car to the station?" asked Miss Marple. "Or drive himself?"

Lydia blew her nose. "Neither. He said he wanted to walk."

"Such a long way?" asked Dolly.

"He liked the exercise," Lydia replied defensively.

"I see," said Miss Marple.

"He has a flat in London," Lydia continued. "But the doorman never saw him that night and no one at the station could say for certain if he boarded the train."

Dolly patted the girl's hand. "The stations are very busy. He might easily have been missed."

"But no one misses Michael. He's . . . he's magnificent."

"You'll forgive me, my dear," Miss Marple ventured carefully. "But I must ask. Did he say or do anything out of the ordinary in the days before? Was there, perhaps, an argument or can you think of anyone who would want to do him harm?"

"No one!" cried Lydia. "Everyone loved Michael!"

"Everyone?"

"That professor whatshisname was always dunning him for money, telling him to pressure his father for funds. And perhaps not Mr. Marsh. But he doesn't like anyone."

"I suspect that's not strictly true."

Lydia burst into a fresh spate of tears. "What should I do? The wedding is a mere week away!"

"I think you should go home to London."

"But what if Michael comes back?"

Dolly gave her an encouraging pat on the knee.

"Then he shall call you on the telephone and you will make him apologise for behaving very badly and perhaps buy you something nice."

They fetched Lydia a damp washcloth to place on her eyes and left her tucked up in bed, already snoring softly.

"Poor girl," Dolly said in the hallway. "Do you really think Michael is just off clearing his head and will turn back up when he's ready?"

"I do not. But I think Lydia is a very pretty girl and will do much better for herself surrounded by eligible fellows in London rather than moping around here. And I suspect she'll have Reginald Marsh for company soon."

"Marsh?" Dolly asked incredulously, then seized Miss Marple's arm. "But if he'd fallen for his best friend's girl, then he'd have quite a motive to make Michael disappear."

"He would," agreed Miss Marple. "But I doubt very much that's what happened. Let's go back to the Lodge, Dolly, and we'll ring Jim to come get me. I need to put my feet up and have a think."

"We could ring from here, Jane."

"No," said Miss Marple firmly, watching Reginald Marsh and Vera Fowler walking along the terrace above the garden. "We've already stayed too long."

That night, Miss Marple had her supper on a tray in her room instead of in the kitchen with Jim and Cherry. Ordinarily she welcomed their company, but she craved quiet tonight, a chance to watch the fireflies gather in the twilight.

Cherry managed to hold her tongue until after she'd taken away the tray and brought Miss Marple a glass of warm milk.

"You've been deep in your thoughts," she noted.

"I have, Cherry. Getting old is a terrible thing."

"You're not so old as all that, Miss Marple, and sharper than most people half your age."

Maybe so, but tonight Miss Marple felt every year and every hour, heavy in her bones. Cherry bustled about the room, closing the curtains and straightening cushions, until at last Miss Marple smiled and said, "Cherry, you must stop fussing. Speak your mind."

Cherry planted her hands on her hips. "I'll stop fussing when you put me out of my misery! Did he do it or not? Did Michael Barnsley-Davis kill the gardener girl?"

"It's funny you should call her that. But, no, I don't think he did."

"Then why run off like that?"

"A very good question, Cherry."

"And are you going to tell me the answer?"

"You presume I have one."

"Because you always do!" cried Cherry in exasperation.

"What does Jim think?"

"Oh, you know how Jim is. He just laughs and says the butler did it and rolls over to go to sleep." Cherry sighed. "And I suppose I had better do the same."

"Will you open the window, Cherry?"

"It's cool tonight," Cherry said, as she obliged. "Make sure you don't catch a chill."

Miss Marple listened to the sounds of the garden, the summer insects buzzing, the soft rustle of something nesting in the hedgerow. She should shut the window. She should go to sleep. But she lay awake thinking just the same.

The next morning, Miss Marple rose and dressed, and ate a sparse breakfast of toast and tea. Then she asked Jim to take her to the Lodge.

"D'you want me to wait, Miss Marple?" Jim asked, when they arrived. "Or would you prefer to ring round?"

"Go on about your business, Jim. I'm sure you have plenty to do today without worrying about me."

"Mrs. Bantry's garden is looking fine. She's always

out there no matter the weather, looking like a flower herself in that big floppy hat."

But Dolly was inside today, so Miss Marple made her way slowly up the path, noting the new plantings.

"Jane!" Dolly exclaimed when she answered the door. "Have you solved it?"

"I fear I have," Miss Marple said, happy to step out of the sun and into the cool front rooms of the Lodge.

"Well?" said Dolly. "Is it the greedy archaeologist? The jealous American? The bitter best friend?"

"You could at least offer me a cup of tea, Dolly."

Dolly cast her eyes heavenward. "Very well," she said, as she strode into the kitchen. "But I expect a good story once the water boils."

"You got rid of your lovely brass kettle."

Dolly snorted. "Bertram and Alice gave me no end of ribbing over it during their last visit. They said it was an antique and probably poisoning me and any guests. The new electric kettle heats up much faster and is far more hygienic."

"Maybe so," said Miss Marple. "But we're not the type of people who cast off treasured things for the sake of fashion."

"Jane, you're getting sentimental in your old age."

Miss Marple smiled. "There's no doubt about that."

Once they were settled in the front room, Dolly in a comfortable armchair and Miss Marple on the sofa, Dolly could contain herself no longer.

"So which of them did it?" she demanded.

"None of them," said Miss Marple.

"Then he just ran off?"

"No, not precisely."

Dolly gave an unladylike grunt of frustration. "Then did he push that poor girl off the bridge?"

"He didn't do that either. I'm sorry to say poor Genevieve took her own life. She was so young, you see, and so afraid, and I don't think Michael Barnsley-Davis treated her very kindly, not when he found out she was . . . well, in a family way."

"But Vera said Michael wasn't that sort of man, that he'd never made a pass at her or—"

Miss Marple held up a finger. "He wasn't interested in pretty girls. He sought out the shy ones, the plain ones, the ones everyone else overlooked. Girls like Reginald Marsh's younger sister, I expect. He knew they were more vulnerable and less likely to be believed. Didn't you notice the way the maid reacted to what Vera said? I suspect Michael had made love to her too. And Genevieve wasn't a pretty girl, was she?"

"No," said Dolly quietly. "I don't suppose she was."

"But she had many other fine qualities, didn't she?"

"She had a real way with flowers. But that's not something men care about."

Miss Marple watched her friend's face, wistful and caught up in thought. "Did he threaten you, Dolly?"

Dolly looked up sharply. The clock on the mantel ticked and the shadows of the room seemed to deepen around them. She took a sip of her tea, then set her cup and saucer aside. "I guess I should have known you would see through me, Jane. You always do."

"I didn't at first," Miss Marple admitted. "I couldn't understand why you would call me back to St. Mary Mead if you'd done something wrong. But then Cherry mentioned she'd run into you at the butcher's. She told you that she was writing to me about Genevieve's death, didn't she?"

"Yes," said Dolly. "I thought if *I* was the one to demand you come home, you might not suspect me. Genevieve was a dear girl, a very dear girl, so young and full of ambition, and so devoted to the garden. We talked whenever she came to work. When Bertram and Alice didn't visit this year . . . Well, I suppose I was lonely and she was kind enough to indulge an old woman."

"And she killed herself because of Michael Barnsley-Davis. Because she was carrying his child."

Dolly's eyes flashed. "Do you think he cared? I saw him in the garden the day after they found her body, whistling, face turned to the sun as if he hadn't a care in the world."

"You confronted him."

"I did. In this very room. I saw him through the window, walking to the train station. I waved him over, offered him tea. He didn't know Genevieve had confided in me, that she'd sat on that sofa and wept over him." Dolly struck the arm of her chair with a small, clenched fist. "But he didn't care. Not a wit. He said Genevieve had made her own choices, that some people weren't strong enough for this world. And when I called him cruel . . . He laughed at me. He asked me what I was going to do about it. So I told him I would tell Lydia, his mother and father, anyone who would listen."

"That was very dangerous, Dolly. Men like that don't like to be told. Don't you remember the fishmonger's son, Ralph Wiles? All smiles and *good morning, ma'am* until someone questioned the receipts. Then he smashed clean through the display case and tried to pretend it was an accident."

"No," Dolly whispered. "Michael certainly didn't like it."

"You must tell me," Miss Marple said, her voice firm. "You must tell me all of it."

Dolly hesitated. Then, with the air of a woman leaping off a cliff, she spoke. "He changed . . . It was as if all his humour and handsomeness bled right out of him. I hadn't quite believed it when Genevieve said he'd threatened her. I thought he was just a rash young man, overcome by emotion. But now it was as if I was seeing him truly for the first time." She took a deep breath. "He said he could kill me right then and there, and that no one would ever suspect. They'd just think I'd taken a nasty fall, one more old bat whom no one would miss. He said . . . He said I could be dead for days and no one would know until I started to smell." When she looked up, her eyes were full of tears. "And do you know the worst part, Jane? He's right. Age is cruel, and crueller still to women. A woman becomes a ghost when she stops being worth looking at."

"A ghost can be quite frightening," murmured Miss Marple. "A ghost might get away with anything at all."

Dolly wiped her tears away brusquely. "He put his hands on my throat. He was smiling. I think . . . I think he was enjoying himself. I was so frightened; I picked up the kettle and . . . I struck him." She shuddered. "He didn't get up."

"It must have been quite difficult to move his body on your own."

Dolly gave a brief nod, eyes dry, back straight. This was the woman who had raised two children, who had managed a crowded household, and who had seen her husband through what was nearly a charge for murder. "I waited until dark and dragged him out to the garden. I'd been preparing one of the beds, but I hadn't decided what to plant yet. It took hours to dig the hole deep enough, working in the dark. And then I just . . . rolled him into it."

"And you planted the bed with asters from up at the hall."

"The gardener had bought far too many. No one would notice."

"That's what made me wonder, Dolly. You've never liked asters. I knew you would only choose them if you needed to fill a space in a hurry. You hid the jewels too, didn't you? Your earrings and a few little items from up at the hall, to create a kind of motive?"

"My grandmother's sapphires. I loved those earrings."

"I suppose they're all buried with him in the garden."

Dolly nodded. "Was it really just the asters that gave me away?"

"Not just that," said Miss Marple. "You'll pardon me for saying so, but Lydia isn't the kind of girl to elicit such compassion from you. And, of course, I noticed the kettle missing when I insisted on ringing Jim from the Lodge yesterday."

"That's the problem with you, Jane. You always seem to *know*."

"I wasn't certain," Miss Marple said. "Not until we sat down in the parlour. You took the chair facing away from the window. I've never seen you do that, Dolly. You always take such pleasure in your garden."

Dolly glanced toward the window, her eyes sad. "It's rather ruined now. But I don't suppose it matters. You'll have to tell the authorities, the poor Barnsley-Davises."

Miss Marple was quiet for a long time, watching the flowers bordering the garden path bob their heads as if to say "good morning."

"It's unfortunate," she said at last. "That men hold so much power in this world. But you know, Dolly, it's not really strength that's necessary to survive. It's cleverness."

Mrs. Bantry held herself very still. "Is it?"

"My nephew Raymond has invited me to winter in the Canary Islands. Such a generous offer. I hadn't planned to accept, but now I'm of a mind to spend some time in warmer climes. We might go together."

Dolly's brows rose. "Might we?"

"Yes. Who knows whom we may encounter in a

crowded marketplace, maybe even a magnificent, golden-haired young man, seen at a distance. Nothing that can be confirmed, of course."

"But nothing that can be denied either?"

"Precisely. Shall we go for a walk in the garden before it gets too warm?"

"I'd like that very much," said Dolly.

Arm in arm, the two friends strolled out of the lodge to let the late summer sun warm their old bones and to listen to the bees hum. They kept their backs to the new beds, brimming with red asters, their green stalks bending gently in the summer breeze, their red petals the colour of blood.

About the Authors

Naomi Alderman's most recent novel, *The Power*, was the winner of the 2017 Baileys' Women's Prize for Fiction, topped Barack Obama's book list from 2017, and has been translated into more than thirty languages. Her first novel, *Disobedience*, was published in ten languages and was recently adapted into a feature-length film by Oscar-winning director Sebastián Lelio, starring Rachel Weisz and Rachel McAdams. Alderman has been mentored by Margaret Atwood and, in April 2013, she was named one of Granta's Best British Novelists. She is Professor of Creative Writing at Bath Spa University, is a Fellow of the Royal Society of Literature, and is currently executive producer for the forthcoming television adaptation of *The Power* for Amazon.

Leigh Bardugo is the *New York Times* bestselling author of *Ninth House* and the creator of the Grishaverse, which spans the Shadow and Bone trilogy (now a Netflix original series), the Six of Crows duology, the King of Scars duology, *The Language of Thorns*, and *The Lives of Saints*—with more to come. Her short stories can be found in multiple anthologies, including *The Best American Science Fiction and Fantasy*. She lives in Los Angeles.

Alyssa Cole is a *New York Times* and *USA Today* bestselling author of romance, thrillers, and graphic novels. Her Civil War–set espionage romance *An Extraordinary Union* was the American Library Association's RUSA Best Romance for 2018; her contemporary rom-com *A Princess in Theory* was one of the *New York Times*' 100 Notable Books of 2018; and her debut thriller, *When No One Is Watching,* won the 2021 Edgar Award for Best Paperback Original. Her books have received critical acclaim from the *Washington Post, Library Journal, Kirkus, BuzzFeed, Book Riot, Entertainment Weekly,* and various other outlets. When she's not working, she can usually be found watching anime or wrangling her menagerie of animals.

Lucy Foley is a number-one *Sunday Times* and *New York Times* bestselling author with over two and a half million copies sold worldwide. Her contemporary murder mystery thrillers, *The Hunting Party* and *The Guest List*, were shortlisted for the Crime & Thriller Book of the Year Award at the British Book Awards and were selected as one of *The Times* and *Sunday Times Crime Books of the Year*, and *The Guest List* was selected as a Reese's Book Club choice. Foley's most recent thriller, *The Paris Apartment*, was an instant *Sunday Times* bestseller and a number-one *New York Times* bestseller. She lives in Brussels with her husband and baby son.

Elly Griffiths is the author of the bestselling Dr. Ruth Galloway books. Her first standalone, *The Stranger Diaries*, won the 2020 Edgar Award for Best Crime Novel. The second, *The Postscript Murders*, was shortlisted for the CWA Gold Dagger. In 2016 Elly was awarded the CWA Dagger in the Library for her body of work. She also writes the historical Brighton Mysteries and A Girl Called Justice, a series for children. *The Locked Room* (Ruth 15) came out in February 2022 and was a *Sunday Times* number-one bestseller.

Natalie Haynes is a writer and broadcaster, and tours the world speaking on the modern relevance of the classical world, so far on three continents. Her retellings of Greek myth, *A Thousand Ships* and *The Children of Jocasta*, bring women's perspectives to the fore, and *A Thousand Ships* was shortlisted for the 2020 Women's Prize for Fiction. Her non-fiction book on women in Greek myth, *Pandora's Jar*, featured on the *New York Times* bestseller list in 2022.

Jean Kwok is the internationally bestselling author of *Girl in Translation*, *Mambo in Chinatown*, and *Searching for Sylvie Lee*, which was an instant *New York Times* bestseller. Her work has been published in twenty countries and is taught in schools across the world. She immigrated from Hong Kong to Brooklyn when she was five and worked in a Chinatown clothing factory for much of her childhood. Kwok received her bachelor's degree from Harvard University and earned an MFA from Columbia University. She currently lives in the Netherlands.

Val McDermid is a number-one internationally bestselling author whose books have been translated into more than forty languages. Her multi-award-winning series and standalone novels have been adapted for TV and radio, most notably the Wire in the Blood series featuring clinical psychologist Dr. Tony Hill and DCI Carol Jordan. She is the recipient of six honorary doctorates and is an Honorary Fellow of St. Hilda's College, Oxford. Among her many awards are the CWA Diamond Dagger recognising lifetime achievement and the Theakstons Old Peculier award for Outstanding Contribution to Crime Writing. Val is also an experienced broadcaster and much-sought-after columnist and commentator across print media.

Karen M. McManus is a number-one *New York Times*, *USA Today*, and internationally bestselling author of young adult thrillers. Her work includes the *One of Us Is Lying* series, which has been turned into a television show on Peacock and Netflix, as well as the standalone novels *Two Can Keep a Secret*, *The Cousins*, *You'll Be the Death of Me*, and *Nothing More to Tell*. Karen's critically acclaimed, award-winning books have been translated into more than forty languages.

Dreda Say Mitchell is a bestselling and award-winning author who was appointed an MBE by Her Majesty Queen Elizabeth II for services to literature and education work in prisons. She scooped the Crime

Writers' Association's John Creasey Memorial Dagger in 2004, the first time a Black British author has received this honour, and is a cultural and social commentator, broadcaster, and journalist, who has written for the *Guardian*, presented BBC Radio 4's flagship arts programme, *Open Book*, and appeared on BBC Television's *Newsnight*, *Question Time*, and *The Late Review*. She is a trustee of the Royal Literary Fund and an ambassador for the Reading Agency. Her family are from the beautiful Caribbean island of Grenada and her name is Irish and pronounced with a long ee sound in the middle.

Kate Mosse is the multi-million bestselling author of ten novels and short story collections, four works of non-fiction and four plays, including the Languedoc Trilogy (*Labyrinth*, *Sepulchre* and *Citadel*), *The Burning Chambers*, *The City of Tears*, and Gothic fiction *The Winter Ghosts* and *The Taxidermist's Daughter*. Non-fiction includes *An Extra Pair of Hands* and *Warrior Queens & Quiet Revolutionaries: How Women (Also) Built the World*, publishing in October 2022 and based on her global #womaninhistory campaign. The Founder Director of the Women's Prize for Fiction, she is a Fellow of the Royal Society of Literature, Patron of the Chichester Festival of Music, Dance and Speech, and a Visiting Professor in Creative Writing & Contemporary Fiction at the University of Chichester.

Ruth Ware is a number-one international bestseller. Her thrillers *In a Dark, Dark Wood*; *The Woman in Cabin 10*; *The Lying Game*; *The Death of Mrs. Westaway*; *The Turn of the Key*; and *One by One* have appeared on bestseller lists around the world, including the *Sunday Times* and *New York Times*. Her books have been optioned for both film and TV, and she is published in more than forty languages. Ruth lives near Brighton with her family.

HARPER
LARGE PRINT

We hope you enjoyed reading
our new, comfortable print size and found it
an experience you would like to repeat.

Well – you're in luck!

Harper Large Print offers the finest in
fiction and nonfiction books in this same larger
print size and paperback format. Light and easy to read,
Harper Large Print paperbacks are for the book lovers
who want to see what they are reading without strain.

For a full listing of titles and
new releases to come, please visit our website:
www.hc.com

HARPER LARGE PRINT

SEEING IS BELIEVING!